HAUNTED REELS II

MORE STORIES FROM THE MINDS OF PROFESSIONAL FILMMAKERS

Curated by David Lawson Jr.
Copy Edited by Rob Carroll
Book Design and Layout by Rob Carroll
Cover Art by Olly Jeavons
Cover Design by Rob Carroll

Library of Congress Control Number: 2025944207

ISBN 978-1-958598-53-5 (paperback)
ISBN 978-1-958598-89-4 (eBook)

darkmatter-ink.com

HAUNTED REELS II

MORE STORIES FROM THE MINDS OF PROFESSIONAL FILMMAKERS

CURATED BY DAVID LAWSON JR.

CONTENTS

INTRODUCTION

David Lawson Jr.

TODAY IS MY birthday. I'm forty-four years old, I've just enjoyed four of the best frozen margaritas from the iconic Chili's on 45th and Lamar, and *Haunted Reels, Volume 2* is just about wrapped up, two years after the release of *Volume 1*. I remember wanting to subtitle it *Volume 1* because I wanted to do this over and over again, but if I'm being one hundred percent honest, at the time, I wasn't sure I'd still be doing film by the time these books released. Our industry was in the midst of two strikes, and even with the moderate success that I had been having, it felt like there were always far more failures. The hill felt ever-growing.

I was having conversation after conversation that year with close friends about how I was feeling and how insurmountable the odds constantly felt. It was my friends that helped push me through those dark times. Their help was always reminding me of a quote from the film *Finding Forrester* (a brilliant film starring Sean Connery, if you haven't seen it).

> *"Losing family obliges us to find our family. Not always the family that is our blood, but the family that can become our blood. And should we have the wisdom to open our door to this new family, we will find that the wishes we once had for the father, who once guided us, for the brother, who once inspired us, those wishes..."*

That quote has always stuck with me. I've moved around a ton in my life. I did four years in the military, dropped out of two different colleges, moved all the way across the country, and then halfway back. I've been blessed with so many friendships along the way, every one of which I hold so close to me. A lot of those friends have stories in this volume. I made films with two of the writers included in these pages: Addison Heimann and Peter Cilella. Their films *Touch Me* and *Descendent*, respectively, both premiered at prestigious festivals this year and are now getting ready for distribution.

I say all of this to remind you—and probably myself—of the value of friends. Without them, I wouldn't be half the man I am today. I certainly wouldn't be fortunate enough to produce films for a living, and you probably wouldn't be reading this collection of stories.

It's my sincere hope that if you haven't already, you find your collection of weirdos. I know I've found mine, I hope you enjoy reading their stories herein.

—Dave

SUNDAY DINNER

April Wolfe

MONDAY

YOU'RE COMING. YOU'LL show yourself to me soon. You've been watching for so long now I forget how me became we. Was it at the junior high basketball game, the flutter of my spirit fingers conjuring you from the stands? Or maybe at my sister's wedding, our toes dug into the sand, feeling the same ancient vibrations, you hovering behind a rock carved by the sharp talons of endless time. Or maybe it was you in the grocery store when I tried so very hard to stay calm—it wasn't the cashier's fault she didn't know how to work the register, they should have trained her properly—but I had just spilled coffee on my favorite shirt, and I screamed and yelled and the glass shattered, her blood dripping on the tan flecked tile. Were you behind me in line? Did you hang onto my skirt hem as I fled and drove a hundred-and-three miles north to a lake where the ice froze in the motion of the wind, and I wept in the backseat until a man rapped on my window and asked if he might take me home… home… home… Of course he could take me home. You would be hungry soon, wouldn't you?

No, no, none of that's true. Because the first moment I knew— really accepted—you were there was when I was ten, at the foot of my grandfather's deathbed, his face already waxen white, eyes slumping to the right, fixed on a phantom I could not see. I felt you take my hand and gently run your finger inside my palm until my fist bloomed open in an instant and felt naked in your absence. Did they feel it, too? Your little finger licking their palms like a cat's tongue. No, they said, what on *Earth* was I going on about at a time like this. No, I was special, and you chose me, though I wonder why as I tug off my cuticles one by one, opening the wounds again and again—they always grow back. What a fun thing for you to witness, these little indignities I inflict upon myself, the late bourbon nights, the Bloody Mary mornings, the ways in which I poison my cells, hoping the stink finally repels you, wondering when you might show yourself to me.

I buy flowers. I cut the stems diagonal to let the water in. You tickle my ear with handy tips, like, *Maybe this will work for you. Have you tried it? Cut, cut, cut, and let the water in.*

TUESDAY

I WONDER WHERE the word "unbridled" comes from. From the German, *bridel*: to rein in or bring under one's control. I find a horse. Any horse. But I try for one marbled like rye with chaotic legs and mount him. I pull my kegels tight and feel what the horse girls have been feeling for years—uncrushable muscle, a body to absorb my violence, my heavy pants, my edged knees, my needy palms, my needling guilt, my glassy breath, my… My, my manners. I thank the horse—always thank the horse—and crunch my teeth into an apple just out of his reach. I watch him flay round in his stall and know that I can't talk to him when he's like this.

Why am I like this? Did you make me this way? Inject me with your cruelty back when I was still taking cootie shots. I always knew I was different. The teachers would whisper to themselves, casting suspicious glances so my neck itched with anxiety, wondering what they knew that I did not. I felt you guiding me even then, an external force floating above me like a weather balloon, and always the weather said "storms ahead," like when I pushed that boy, and his chin skidded across the pavement, plunking teeth asunder like hail. Was that you? Were you proud? I felt your applause in a crack of lightning, the satisfied prick of excitement down my vertebrae when I sat in the wet grass still smelling of the mower, scratching my inflamed legs, wishing this one act of violence would keep you at bay. But it wouldn't, would it? You're insatiable.

If I squint, I can see you through the crack in the door, crouching in my childhood closet, and I ask in exasperation what in the hell you want me to do, but you don't answer. You wait. You let the shapes take form in my head, like the therapist who couldn't tell me how I should or shouldn't act but could illuminate the possibilities. They never *had* to die; it was just one possibility.

WEDNESDAY

HUMP DAY. I part the gauzy curtains in the front window and peer into the darkness. I've been waiting all day. On the glass, my breath etches messages from deep in my gut. This is Morse code for romantics. Do I see someone out there? Maybe. I wonder how it's possible to mistake anything for a human form. Like food molded into other food, people are reshaped as well.

I invite them all here. They want to know what it's like to still live in my childhood home. Is it a kink for me? Can I call them daddy? Will I wear pigtails? I smile and comply, because what's one last dying request, even if they don't know it's their last? It's *polite*. They nose around the room, touching the silk ribbons and bulletin boards filled with dusty homework assignment reminders, the Mickey Mouse nightlight in the socket, and I can see it in their eyes, the sense that this isn't as arousing as they'd thought it would be, a grown woman living in a time capsule of her own making. It's weird. It's shameful, but not enough that they leave. I don't hear you, but I know you're in there, because you are everywhere I am, the air I breathe.

They don't even suspect they are the food. There's no equation that makes this possible in their heads, where x and y add up to *feed*, and frankly it's all a little confusing to me, too, but isn't that love? I know you're coming for me soon. I've done my part, served myself to you on hand and foot, and I'm not afraid. I'm just so happy it's an ending to something.

THURSDAY

THIS DAY IS my jaws of life, my salvation from the car crash and stink of singed hair caught in the heating grate of my dashboard. Thursday peels my puzzle-pieced skull from the web in my windshield and glues me up right, dribbles of gray matter seeping from the sutures. But it's okay. There was too much in my head anyway. At least that's what you always said.

What if I just stopped feeding you? What if I joined an intramural sports team and went out for drinks and pizza after games, and we all sang karaoke and talked about Carol the boss's assistant, and how Rod and Kate are probably having an affair—Katie, that *slut*—and then went to sleep early, full of friendship and food, the television marking time in half hours and infomercials for male virility? A pottery class maybe. Or yoga and hiking. You wouldn't like any of that. You'd punish me like the time I stayed late at work—just a couple hours, because my boss said I was distracted and wouldn't I want to put in the effort to show I was dedicated to my work?

You'd feasted without me. I'd told you they were off limits. They of the entire world that you could not have, and you took them anyway. There is no room for family with you. You are the atomic blast vacuuming up all the oxygen. You should have taken me a long time ago. I'm almost giddy with the thought that you will. I count down the days. Maybe then you will finally be full.

In the meantime, I nibble the edges of a Saltine that crumbles in my lap as the smell of fermented apples creeps into the room again. This is your scent, something old and sour and timeless.

FRIDAY

I HOLD GOOD thoughts in my head and grind my teeth into them. I apologize to the child who wants to play in my front yard, because it's not that I'm one of those people who cares about a lawn or anything, it's just that I worry that I can't trust you around new young things anymore, not after the last time. I clutch my mother's locket in my hands and feel the object, not its past. All that matters is this week.

How do you chew them? Do you have teeth, or acid for spit? Or maybe it's your mere presence that deflates them to the withered skins I find waiting around the house for me every morning. Sometimes I can see you've toyed with them, because they are wet purses, a bone or a blood vessel still clinging to the subcutaneous. It's the leftovers that really get to me, the sense that you could take it all any time but don't, like the IRS or mother nature. Your wastefulness irks me when there are other nether evils out there starving in the world.

I open the door and take in the bedroom where my parents once slept and quarreled and fucked to make me, but in it now are burial mounds of shirts and ties and dress shoes worn specially for business trips or first dates. Sometimes I dive into them and inhale the scent of competing colognes and sweat, each one more pathetic than the last. I know I shouldn't save them, but I can't help myself. I abhor wastefulness. Sometimes I dress in them and pretend to be my victims, reason out how they could possibly fall for this again and again, ignoring every instinct, and the answer is they trust me. They have no reason not to. I am small with a voice like sweet tea, and that's why you chose me, isn't it? You've dripped honey on the floor, and the ants are marching to their demise in a single-file line.

SATURDAY

I NEED MORE flowers; these ones are already dead.

I run down to the corner store with the woman with the glass eye, get the first green thing in dirt I see and bring it home. The leaves close up when it feels my touch, like hugging or begging for its life, which are the same thing to me now. You leave me these skins, which are tanned to perfection and which glide through the dulled needles of my sewing machine. Each life added to the quilt is precious and forever now. It's folded up like a lonely parachute in the hall closet. Just show yourself already. I'm fucking tired. Someday someone will find it, tug it down from a shelf, and feel the weight of what's happened here in good old American pounds.

What do you plan to do with me tomorrow? Will you leave me dangling on the banister like that repairman from Kenosha, or draped across the toilet like the flasher on the bus who shook with tremors the whole way home, filled with excitement that his predilection had for once brought him closer to intimacy with another? Throughout the day, I whisper where I would like to be lain, hoping you grant me this last request—*fling me out the window and let me dry to dust in the backyard.* Or better yet, *take all of me as though I had never walked the earth at all.* Yes.

That's it. Make me disappear with no scraps. It's the thought that I may be half-devoured that pricks at my temples. I beg you, leave no trace.

I pick at my cuticles, imagining I can peel myself entirely away. I know it will hurt, but the closer I grow to the prospect of pain, the realer it feels. I wish I knew. I wish you had told me how you chew, but I am left to wonder and fill in the shapes in my head. I consider something drastic, and I think you know exactly what it is, because your scratchy finger tongues my palm again. Your voice comes to me in the scissor-swish of my satin pants, like the sharpening of knives. You say, *You'll spoil it this way, you can't take what I said seriously,* but I am already thinking and dreaming it. I think of Saint Bartholomew. I am a bride on the eve of her wedding.

SUNDAY

I BRING OUT the heavy shears, taken to the cutler in the van at the farmers' market so many times the blade tips are thinner than an onion peel. *Are you a cook?* he'd asked me, and I nodded, because there was a sort of truth to it. A cook prepares meals.

The church bells from down the street ring out their racket until everything is quiet again. I hear you prattling in my ears, but I refuse to listen now. Out the window, I can see the children playing safely in the street, riding bikes in lazy circles, wobbling then righting the ship, then wobbling again, testing the strength of their tender ankles on the asphalt. I was like them once. Or maybe not exactly like them, but the shape of them, the form of them, a younger machine. I have to look away, because the urge to feast on their innocence is inside me now. Was I always this way? I undress in my parents' room, adding my worn cigarette pants and checked blouse to the pool of orphaned clothes, mingling my smell with theirs, like I am sending them off to school. Farewell.

I sit in the kitchen. A lone dish in my mother's pattern, clotted with breadcrumbs, loiters on the counter. Who knows for how long it will be there? I imagine a realtor itching with suspicion of an abandoned property, climbing in the back window, and finding it here like this, untouched for days, months, years, however long it takes for anyone to notice I've gone. Maybe never. I make the first cut, an incision from the kneecap down the tibialis anterior, then back up again. There are fewer nerve endings here. I peel this strip of skin away one inch at a time, allowing the blade to shave through the connective tissues and separate it from the underlying muscle. I've shorn skin before but never my own. I thought there would be more pain, but maybe I am already numb. Maybe I always have been. I am not, perhaps, human.

The skin drops on my plate like a noodle. This is what I imagine it is as I cut it into bite-sized pieces. I want to savor this, but I worry about the time I have left, if it will be enough. *It's never enough.* That's what my grandfather shouted at us before he went pale and waxen, and you tickled my palm. Was he speaking of you? Or were you speaking through him? I cut more. I ribbon my skin. If I had been born many hundreds of years ago, they would worship me.

I eat. I consecrate the marriage of my skin to my stomach. The acid roils, the blood seeps, but I can't stop now. I hear your voice now in the clattering of my fork on the plate. *Look what you're doing to yourself, you always take things too far, that imagination of yours.* I want to tell you to shut up, but my mouth is full. You're always doing that, playing tricks, shredding my nerves, making me believe you're not there, but then I pull out the patchwork quilt from the closet and remember. It's not me. It's we.

Wind blows the chimes my mother hung one summer. Birds visit the window and peck at the frame. I eat. I laugh a little, my teeth chattering now as I unwind the ribbon from the sole of my foot, this part stubbornly clinging to the tissue. Finally, it eases, and I eat this, too. I chuckle, how funny it would be to watch this now. How funny it would be to be you watching me, I thought you would be so happy, but you're sullen and tugging at the tendon on my heel, reduced to the size of a little puppy. Why *do* you leave the skins for me? Why *do* you ask so much of me? We are an old married couple reviewing the terms of their divorce. We are a million things that are all the same thing, the we of it all.

I've waited so long for this, the blood is draining from my face onto the floor, and yet I only have a little more to go. *It won't be as fun,* you coo to me. You're such a child. The light dims, flashes, there's a knocking upstairs on the ceiling above me, a loose screw in my chair—did you see that? The scurrying, the furtive feet scrambling across the linoleum, into the wall, swollen with bad things. I laugh and laugh, teeth crack into one another, the guests all gone. The skin stripped. I watch the faucet drip. I laugh and laugh and laugh, because I have thought of the funniest thing, my last thought perhaps.

I think how funny it would be if you were never really there. But then I hear the small holler of the closet door, your footsteps like an echo of something long ago whispered, and of course you are here. You are coming down to dinner.

EAT THE RICH

C. Robert Cargill

I AIN'T A psychopath or nothin', but you don't understand power—real power—until you've heard the pop of an axe being pried out of a well-cleft skull. Sure, feeling the knees buckle and the legs turn to jelly before the body slumps to the ground like a sack of soggy, rotten potatoes is a thrill all its own. And that weak little *urk* as the axe goes in gives you a hell of a bump of dopamine. You ever get a murder boner? Yeah, nothing will give you a murder boner like that sound. The *pop*. That's my favorite part. That's the part that makes the mess of it all worthwhile.

The other really rewarding bits are a tad rarer. Like one time, I cracked this rich bastard upside the head with a baseball bat. Not the wooden professional kind; the aluminum softball kind that makes a nice *bong* sound that rattles your hands when you connect with a good clean hit. His eyes went blank like all the lights were turned out at once, and a thin trickle of blood immediately streamed down from his well-coifed, $300-a-cut, head of perfect gray hair. But it was the sound of the splatter, the way he shit his shorts the moment I snuffed him, that was just so gnarly. *Whoosh. Bong. Splat. Slump.* You could smell it right away. That was the smell of well-fed shit. That motherfucker never went a day in his life without a vegetable, and you could fucking tell.

There's just something about truly humiliating a rich old bastard like that—taking an evil fucking leech of a man, who looks down his nose at us every fucking minute of his miserable spoiled fucking life, and not just putting him in the ground but reducing him to a pathetic pile of blood and piss and shit, and just leaving him to rot like that until the pigs find him beneath the stench of his own fetid demise. Him and his bitch. Him and his bitch and his rotten-ass rich-kid spawn. Yeah. Sometimes we leave them where they lie. Other times, we play dress up with 'em. Leave a message. Put them around the dinner table or set them up on the couch watching Fox News like nothing has changed.

"Hello, Louis," the chatbot says as I walk into the Whataburger. "Welcome back. Would you like your usual?"

The black, glassy, dome-shaped eye of the camera reads not only my face, but my expressions, my body language. It's been trained to both identify my mood in hopes of milking every nickel out of me possible while also making sure not to alienate me, leaving me making a cheaper choice. It's a delicate dance of well-programmed AI. The large, brightly lit LED screen in front of me has my usual order displayed—with a number of alternatives, all based on my purchase history. It will offer me breakfast when I usually eat breakfast, dinner when I normally order dinner. And it's Tuesday. I sometimes order a deep-fried handheld peach pie on Tuesdays. So that's definitely coming.

This is an old school, retro Whataburger, designed to look like they did in the twentieth century: yellow tables, orange stripes, white everywhere. Uncomfortable bench seating. I love this fucking place. I often sit here with my burger and wonder what it was like to bring a date here in the old days. Just ride up with your best girl in your pickup truck, pocket full of cash from your job, tunes piped in from the local radio station, listening to whatever they decided they wanted to play that day, DJ rattling on about some local concert they're sponsoring for the band they won't stop playing every hour on the hour. It must have been fucking heaven.

I always get myself a Whataburger before a mission. It centers me. The family that owned the chain sold it off to private equity long ago. Quality is now outsourced to the lowest bidder. Every time I take a bite of their burgers, I don't know exactly what I'm eating. Is it really, as they advertise, one hundred percent beef?

Or is it like some of the other chains, mixed with filler, like bone meal or starch, to stretch the meat out? Or is it, like internet rumors claim, made partially with human remains? Am I sitting down to enjoy a nice, juicy patty of human flesh between two perfectly buttered pieces of Texas toast, with three pickles, a spray of diced onion, a slice of American cheese, and jalapenos?

Was my burger's name Jason, Madison, Tucker, or Lucas? Aiden? Jayden? Braydon? Or maybe a mix of all of them—a mélange of poor bastards who gave their bodies to science only to be ground up and sold off as food once their organs had been properly harvested for other uses.

I don't know.

All I know is that it's fucking delicious.

Every juicy, fatty, unctuous-fucking-bite tastes like goddamn heaven, and it's worth the day's fucking rations just to get one with a side of crispy shoestring fries and a thick banana pudding milkshake. Fuck three hots for the day; this is my pre-reward for a job well done—or maybe the perfect last meal for a soon-to-be-condemned man.

"Yes," I tell Whatabuddy, the Whataburger chatbot.

"Would you like to add a fried peach pie, today? You've enjoyed them in the past."

There it is. "Not today, Whatabuddy."

"Alright, Louis. We've deducted the total from your savings. Would you like us to email you a receipt?"

"No thanks, Whatabuddy."

"Your meal will be ready in two minutes and forty-eight seconds. Your order number is fifty-two. Please take your table tent and have a seat."

I look back at the box behind the counter that's making my dinner, and it makes me think of the old science fiction novels that imagined some robot in back, doing the exact same jobs humans once did, working the grill, flipping burgers, deep frying french fries between flips, maybe doing a little dance and cracking jokes to amuse the customers. The future sucks. Like, it really sucks. It's a boring-ass box. No shucking-and-jiving robot line-jockey. Just a boring chrome box with a slot for spitting out my food.

There's a vat of oil in there that my fries are shot into while my burger is being double-griddled on the other side of a dividing wall—two metal plates press the patty to the perfect size every time, applying the same heat to both sides, getting the same Maillard every time. Meanwhile, a shake machine is drooling my banana pudding shake into a wax paper cup right next to it.

I know, I know. I'm making it sound mechanical and gross. But it's not. It really is fucking delicious. I'm just doing what you don't: thinking about how my food is made. I mean, really. How often have you fucking thought about it? Have you ever wondered what name the rancher gave the cow you fucking ate in your triple meat, triple cheese, bacon and jalapeno Whataburger?

I know, I know.

It's better if you don't.

This isn't some vegetarian/vegan guilt-trip nonsense, I promise. This will be important later. I just want you thinking about it. You know, before it's important.

One of the things I love about Whataburger is its branding. It's one of the chains that really embraced the nostalgia of the twentieth century. Like all the other burger joints in town, there's only one person on duty: *the manager.* These days, "manager" is mostly just a fancy title for the repair guy on duty who serves as quality control, fixes the machines when they futz up, and cleans the equipment.But the manager at Whataburger also wraps your order by hand and delivers it to you at the table. It's one of the few times in any given week that I deal with a real human employee, doing an old-school job. And that's how they sell it. Even their slogan leans in hard: *Whataburger. It's the humans that make our burgers.* I think that's where the internet rumors started. I'm pretty sure they farmed out their marketing to AI, too.

Three and a half minutes later, the manager walks out with my tray. Burger. Fries. Shake. And for the next fifteen minutes, I take my time, savoring every bite. Maybe I'll grab something from a fridge later on. Otherwise, this is today's meal. I only get this once a week, and I gotta make it last. Don't want to get overzealous again, like I have in the past, and end up scrounging from friends and even trash cans until the next payday.

That's the problem with fixed incomes. Lobby Congress all you want to raise Universal Basic Income, but as long as capitalism still exists, even in its diminished form, the prices rise to meet everyone's new wages. They'll price-cap milk, bread, and eggs, but they won't touch the chains or restaurants. *We live under socialism, not communism*, they say. *And because of that, the American Dream still persists*. Even if most of us never sleep enough to witness it.

Yes, before you ask, I've tried to get a job. Even jumped through all the hoops. But a community college degree isn't worth the paper it's printed on, and I wasn't born to parents with jobs able to afford a real college. I did a stint on an oil rig once for a rocket fuel company. Watched three of my crew get incinerated in an accident before I noped out of that. A main blew and caught a spark, and I watched as the skin charred and blistered off their muscle before even that began to melt into puddles under their blackened bones. The money was good for a while, though. And if you're wondering why they still have humans do that shit, it's because the payouts to the families of the deceased cost less than buying new robots.

Some families call it the lottery. You can stretch a death payment out and live high on the hog for years on the oil company's dime. But my parents never gave me nothin', so why the fuck would I ever think about giving back to them? Especially like that. No, I blew my money on booze and escorts, the way most of us riggers did, and that was that. My taste of the good life. Deep-fried friends and all.

Miss you guys.

I take the last bite of my burger and savor the fatty burnt edge between the final corner of my Texas toast. It even has the last bit of tangy mustard. Perfect. Just perfect. If this were, in fact, my last meal, I'd have no complaints.

I walk out the front door and throw a wave to the manager. He smiles and hits me with a "Y'all come back real soon." I fucking love this place.

As I open the door, Whatabuddy chimes in. "Have a great day, Louis."

"Thanks, Whatabuddy."

I turn down the sidewalk and make my way down the street toward a cluster park—a series of the same businesses you see outside of every apartment block, or on the edges of suburban sprawls. Low end groceries. Liquor. Cannabis and hallucinogens. Vape shop. And a drip joint—a sit-down coffee shop full of couches, chairs, and tables. Some charge you by the hour, some by the cup. Others, especially in denser neighborhoods without many of the employed, charge you to rent a mug by the day—one price for all the coffee you can sip.

Not everyone is content to sit in their spartan apartment, take an edible every few hours and drift off to whatever nonsense is streaming on the freebie channels. That's actually why I gotta watch my food cost. I splurge. I'm a movie nut. Love old films and fucking hate commercials—especially for things I'll never in my life be able to afford. So, I pay for a couple of streams and try to keep the edibles to one or two a day—usually late at night to help me sleep. America may not grant access to the American Dream that it used to, but these days it affords us a lot of weed naps.

I get to a dead spot on the street, a blind spot where all the cameras are just out of sight and there are multiple directions to walk. That's when I flip on my scrambler—a UV projector that displays someone else's features on my face. Not visible to the naked eye, but the cameras see it bright as day. As far as AI is concerned, I'm now Miles Johnson, mild mannered citizen who clearly just stepped out from visiting a friend at their apartment building. It's illegal for AI to track someone without a warrant, so unless someone looks at the camera footage from one camera to the next, no one will ever know I vanished right before Miles was conjured out of thin air. And why would someone look? I'm nowhere near my mission objective yet. In order for someone to retrace my movements, they'd have to sit down and go through the video footage, camera to camera, of everyone in the city just to find out I vanished for a few blocks only to take a leak or something behind a coffee shop.

I walk past Drip Time, this neighborhood's drip joint and make a beeline to the back of the building. That's where I find it: a rusty old pipe covered in insulation, near the dumpsters. Written on it are two things: an address and a code (#8c1e80). The address is a cypher. If you took it literally, you'd end up blocks away from the objective. You gotta take the day of the week and count the days from Sunday—that'll give you the key. Shift every digit up by the number you get and count the number of streets north (in a month with thirty-one days) or south (in a month without). That's the real address. The code is even simpler. It's the color of spray paint we're using. Purple. It's a nice one, too. I'm fond of it.

Every gang has its look, its signature. Ours is that we all wear black balaclavas and spray paint an X over the front. We're very careful. We don't know each other's names. We don't know what each other looks like. Fuck, we don't even know what each other sounds like. No, I won't tell you how we met, but I will tell you that the quickest way to get an axe in the skull and your body set on fire as a message is to show up at the mark's house with the wrong color spray paint on your hood. It's how we make sure no one who is followed is ever followed again.

So far, no one has cocked up. But it only takes one, right?

I open my bag and rifle through the eight spray cans I have in there. If I'm stopped by police, I'm just a cheap vandal graffiti artist without any paint on his hands. *Move along, buddy. We've got real criminals to worry about.* I pull out a balaclava and the purple spray can and quickly paint an X over it. Then I put everything away and I'm off.

I find another blind spot and switch Miles off, moving on to Brian Merryweather. I have no idea who either of these guys are—just profiles I downloaded from the dark web—but I doubt they'll ever know they were seen walking down a dark street at 8:30 at night on a Tuesday, nowhere near the scene of a crime. I won't use them at the house. I just need to juggle enough identities through half a dozen blind spots and a pair of crowded areas to absolutely flummox any AI that tries to piece footage together after the fact. After tonight, there will be a number of warrants that all lead to dead ends. If all goes to plan, I'll blind-spot my way back with half a dozen other identities until I walk out as myself from that initial blind spot by an alley up the road from the Whatabuger. It will appear like I'd just slept off an edible in the alley, like any other loser UBID.

Universal. Basic. Income. Deadhead.

The only good part of being one of the unwashed masses is how invisible you become to everything but AI. And like I said before, you don't even exist to street tracking until there's a warrant. Only businesses can make you consent to tracking as a condition for entering.

Last blind spot before the house. I click on my voice vocoder and set it to randomize and set my UV Projector to scramble. Now any video of me is gonna show nothing but static. I tug on my balaclava and turn the corner.

And there it is, the house. Black tinted glass the whole way around. You know, for privacy. No one needs to see how rich you really are these days. Also, pretty great when you're playing hide and seek with a mark and they bang on the window, screaming at the top of their lungs, forgetting that while they can plainly see their neighbors drive by, all their neighbors can see is their own reflection. And they all love that new soundproof glass that keeps your house quiet like you live in the country instead of walking distance from rows of UBID tract housing.

Yeah. Those wealthy fucks don't think much through at all.

Within thirty seconds, the gang's all here. Five of us. All in nondescript clothing. All with purple Xs. Good sign. I check my watch. You don't bring phones on a mission—rule number-fucking-one. I'm not being tracked. We've got seventeen seconds until go-time. If nothing happens, we bolt. They call us "The Blackouts." And you're about to see why.

Boom.

You can hear the whole neighborhood POP and wind down as our sixth man has blown a nearby transformer, plunging several blocks into darkness. Every light is out. Every AC unit CACHUNKS and powers down. And most importantly, every AI security system is on localized backup power.

X Prime—he calls the shots—looks at us and says, "Five family members. Mom, dad. Three kids. Two young ones are in bed—first door on the left. Teen is playing video games upstairs— first door on the right." He looks at one of us, a smallish woman and says, "The box is by the pool equipment." She runs off. He looks at two others. Both medium-sized men. "He has a gun in his nightstand. Up the stairs. Two doors to the left. And a shotgun. In a gun rack in the den. Basement. North wall." Those two run for the front door.

Then he looks at me. "Tools are in the garage. There's a door to it in the backyard. Kid has a baseball bat in his bedroom. I'm getting that."

"Copy," I say. And we're off.

We've been doing this a while. We're a fucking campfire story. No one knows how many groups like us there are, but there are several. Numerous gangs, numerous cities. Different names. Different methodologies. But ours is fucking signature. These days, when the lights go out anywhere in America, people freak the fuck out. Because when the power is out, The Blackouts might be there.

We've been seen. Caught on camera. Different night, different Xs. So, they know us.

And when the lights go out, the paranoid go for their guns.

The small woman I like to call Whistler is already in back, cutting the localized battery power to the AI security system before flipping the switch that reverses the lockdown for when the power goes out. Simple enough to do if you know your security boxes. And she does.

We hear a whistle to know it's done. The house is pitch black and wide open. The whistle is barely out of Whistler's mouth when the two medium men I call Brick and Brack burst through the front door, running for the guns. X Prime walks briskly through the open door, pulling a 3D-printed pistol from beneath his shirt. He's only had to use it a few times, and he tries hard not to kill anyone with it. Those things are shit in a real gunfight but make a fine point.

Me, I dart inside the back door of the garage like a shot, slipping on my Nightshades—kind of like reverse sunglasses. Not as bright, showy, or as far-reaching as night vision goggles, but really good at seeing in the dark at medium ranges. And man alive, does this rich fuck like his tools. And by the looks of the blades and handles, there isn't a callous on his gentle little hands. They're barely, if ever, used. Just some good old fashioned conspicuous consumption.

Can you believe it? He's got a machete. A fucking machete. Motherfucker lives on a nice suburban street, in a major metropolitan area, and he owns a machete, like he's chopping through the jungles of deepest Malaysia in his spare time.

A sledgehammer? For fucking real? This guy has a sledgehammer? It's like I'm in a candy store at Christmas, and I'm a fucking Make-a-Wish kid.

Ho. Ly. Shit.

Cordless. Power. Saw.

I've always wanted to play around with one of these. X Prime picked a really rich pack of bastards today. I grab the sledgehammer, the machete, and the power saw before slipping quietly into the house. This is the scariest part—the part where my heart races and I can hear the blood thundering in my ears.

We've lost people before. Things do not always go to plan— chiefly because the plan is as scantily detailed as you've seen. Someone who knows security does the recon, maps out the who, what, and where by tapping into the security feed. But the one thing we can never know is how prepared a family will be when the lights go out. Do they have a plan? And if they do, have we planned properly to foil it?

I've walked in on a dead Blackout more than once. A homeowner even took a shot at me one time before X Prime batted the gun from their hand.

The door from the garage silently swings open into the kitchen. It's pitch-black, but I see just fine. The kitchen is a lot like the garage, loaded top to bottom with kitchen gadgets, all shiny and new like they don't see much use. Rich fucks probably order out on the regular, and mom or dad cooks as a hobby. You know— they watch all the YouTube cooking shows and buy the gadgets all the chefs use, promising to make that classic Michelin-star recipe they drooled over one day.

There's a waffle iron and a tortilla press. A mandolin for slicing vegetables, an ice cream machine, and a bread mixer with a meat grinding attachment. Air fryer. They have a convection oven! Why would you have an air fryer when you already have—

No, focus. Eyes on the prize. There'll be time to question the lunacy of their consumption when all is said and done.

I see dad first. He's running into the kitchen with fear in his eyes, terrified, running straight for the butcher block.

But X Prime got there first. Ain't a knife left in the block. There's only the faintest light coming in through the window, so dad doesn't know how fucked he is until his hand gets there. I see his face go white with panic before he turns and sees the faint outline of my shape in the darkness.

I don't think he even sees the sledgehammer.

The crack of the skull as it swings down is so fucking satisfying. It's both a crunch and a sploosh at the same time. Blood and bone and brain erupting from his head as the blunt end of it buries deep inside that rotten fucking cabbage of his. He stands there, stunned. Maybe dead already. Maybe in the last fleeting seconds of consciousness.

So, when X Prime walks into the room and dad's still standing. X rushes over and perforates the man with a big, razor-sharp chef's knife. I love the absolute ASMR of the knife going in and out of the body before it topples to the ground, leaving a growing pool of blood.

Then I hear mom. She's running through the house scream-ing as Brick and Brack torment her. They're not going to kill her. They only do that if something goes to shit. No. They're cattle-driving her to me. The butchery is my job. Prime likes to get his licks in, but I'm the wetwork guy. I do the messy stuff. Mostly because I like it and people decide to stay out of my way. Is it because they don't really have the stomach for it, or because they're worried one day they'll get between me and the business end of a power tool? Who's to say?

I walk into the dining room as mom runs in, almost slamming into me. By the time she stops and begins to realize exactly who or what is standing in front of her, I've spun up the power saw. She loses her left hand before she can turn around, and her left foot the second she does. She hits the ground absolutely bellowing, her dark, silky hair in her face, tears streaming down her cheeks, cementing it there. I stand over her a second before taking her right hand and then her remaining foot.

She. Fucking. Howls.

"Why??? WHY???" she screams.

"It's not personal," I say softly. "It's political. Did you know it's cheaper to feed America than it is to police it? Did you know that? Your security system is pretty expensive. A lot of money just to keep out the poor."

But she just caterwauls *why, why, why.* She's not listening.

Prime and I watch as she turtle crawls on her severed limbs, blood spraying across the immaculate white walls. We keep pace behind her, watching, drinking in her last moments before she passes out and everything just goes limp all at once.

Then there's the first two kids. No, no, no. You don't want to hear about that, and I get it. So, we're there, it happens. Moving on.

But the third kid. He's eight. This is a fuckup.

We don't kill anyone under ten. The recon is usually pretty good about this. By ten, the brain is corrupted. You're deep in it. You've grown up rich and you'll always be rich, and more importantly, you'll always *think* rich. So, what the fuck do we do now?

Prime looks at me as Brick and Brack bring me the kid. Little squirt. Dark black hair, eyes red from crying. He absolutely loses his fucking shit when he sees his mom splayed out on the floor like a dead bird.

"What do you wanna do?" Prime asks me.

I think for a minute. I don't fucking know. I don't want to do an innocent kid like that, but he knows enough of our methodology that he could give some clues to the cops. Kill a UBID in the blocks downtown, they ain't gonna find shit. Kill a rich white family in the 'burbs? That's who they fucking work for.

Then it hits me. I watch YouTube cooking shows, too.

And it all comes back to Whataburger.

Mom and dad grind surprisingly well in the grinder attachment. I'm fucking jealous. If I were an absolute idiot, I'd take this home with me and make my own burgers and buns for a fraction of the price of takeout. But trophies are how you get caught. *Where'd you get a bread mixer with attachments that costs a week's UBI, Louis?* No. This is my one chance with this bad boy and boy howdy does it grind like a master.

Mom and dad sizzle on the gas griddle just right. I'm no robot, so the Maillard ain't the same, but it's got a good crust. They've got some brioche buns in the pantry and fresh tomatoes—FRESH!

The burger I set down in front of the kid is as close to a culinary fucking masterpiece as I am ever likely to achieve. And he knows where it comes from.

"Do you wanna die with your mom and dad, kid? Or do you wanna eat every bite of this hamburger?"

The kid looks at me with hateful, cold steel eyes, and without muttering a word, wipes the tears from his cheek and picks up the burger. That kid eats every. Last. God. Damned. Bite. All without blinking or taking his eyes off me. He just stares me down and eats his mom and dad, griddled to juicy, unctuous perfection. What were their names? Jason? Madison? Where they the Smiths? I don't know. We never know. But for the first time in his life, this kid knows exactly who and what he is eating.

Whistler can't watch. She leaves to go be sick. Brack checks on her, and Brick excuses himself for some air. Only Prime and I stay to watch. And as the kid finishes, Prime looks at me and says, "What now?"

"You see that?" I ask.

"Yeah."

"Kid's already got it. Rich disease. He'll do whatever it takes to survive and doesn't care who or what gets in his way."

Prime nods and swallows hard.

"You don't have to watch," I say. "I'll do it quick."

OUR HOUSE IN THE WOODS

Gustavo Cooper & Ben Powell

IT WAS TIME. Maria and I had to get out of the city—the noise and the madness, the endless struggle just to hang on. We yearned for a change, a place where we could escape the chaos and embrace a simpler, quieter life. The opportunity arose to purchase a charming house where Maria had grown up—Rockport, Maine, I wouldn't talk her out of it even if I could. There was still life in her, and she was ready to get back home. Maria was terminally ill. We went so many rounds with this thing, and she was tired of the fight. The doctors said she had about six months to a year. She was so brave through the whole thing. I'd never met someone so strong. It was like she had a piece of her left in that old house that she needed.

So, we packed our stuff and bid farewell to the pollution and piss smell of the city streets. Driving down the small, two-lane road, I thought to myself, *This is peaceful?* The idea haunted me. I am a recovering alcoholic and knew that going down this road without the city distractions could be a slippery slope. Being without my program, my meetings, my support system was scary, but I knew I didn't have to do it alone. I looked at Maria as the wind hit her hair. A gold cross glistened on her neck. She had recently found God. I was glad she found comfort in it, but I couldn't believe in a deity that would take such a beautiful creature from this planet. Theodore, our big, dumb Golden Retriever who thinks he's a lap dog, pushed his nose between the seats and rested it on Maria's shoulder. My wife looked at me like she knew that I was panicking inside. She put her hand on mine and turned the radio up. "She Sells Sanctuary" by the

Cult became the soundtrack for the moment. I haven't been able to get through that song since.

We entered the small town and felt its embrace. The quaint working harbor and its little main street, a block of elevated sidewalk tilting down toward the aging river bridge. It was a place where time seemed to move at a slower pace, where the scent of blooming flowers mixes with the salty tang of the ocean. I buzzed the car window down and inhaled, understanding how a place like this could maintain its hold on my wife even after all these years.

A few miles outside of town, we pulled onto a dirt road cloaked by trees that led us to the house. It looked like shit. It was missing a few of its weather-beached shingles, giving it a strange, toothless look. The moss-grown roof seemed to sag under its own weight. The house looked like I felt: tired and ready to give up. This was the plan. To share as much time as I could with Maria while we clean up and rehabilitate this house. This is what she wanted. Teamwork. A project. Something to leave me? Something we could focus on besides the monster chewing her up from the inside out?

We knew little about its history or who lived here before. The house had been owned by an older couple who had died years ago, and it sat vacant for a long while despite the ravenous real estate market of Mid Coast Maine.

As we stepped inside, the echoes of our footsteps resonated through the empty rooms. I looked at Maria, and I could see her brain turning. Each room was a blank canvas waiting to be filled with her dreams. The wooden floors creaked beneath our feet, the sun's rays highlighting the dust particles as if the house itself was waking up from a long sleep.

Maria looked at me and smiled. There was a light in her eyes that hadn't been there for a long time. She brought me into every room as we explored, envisioning the possibilities that lay within those walls. It was hard not to see a hospital bed in one of them one day. I basked in the glow of her happiness, but my heart was cold. This was the place my wife was going to die.

Over the next couple days we cleaned, unpacked, and set up our home. Boxes everywhere! I've never seen a house come together faster! I could feel every little bit of Maria's hard work. That night, I cooked my world-famous baked ziti. It's just extra hamburger, sauce from a can, and about two pounds of cheese, but alongside garlic bread and a decent red wine I picked out for her, I pulled it off gracefully. She barely drank half a glass of the wine. Later, doing the dishes, the smell coming out of that glass hit me like a trip in a time machine. It was the first night in the new house. I deserved to be celebrating, too. I let myself have a taste. Just a little one. I didn't even like it that much.

Stress is cumulative. Maria's sickness. The move. It was all adding up. I should have tried to find a meeting that night, to build the network of church basements and empty classrooms that would have helped me hold onto my sobriety. The episode with the wine should have scared me more. I let it go. Every minute with Maria was precious, but there was a jangly feeling in me that had been quiet for a long time. It was like the seed of an idea finding a fertile spot in the back of my mind where it could get lost in the noise and grow with no one noticing.

That night, as the moon cast its light through the bedroom window, a deep thud that echoed through the house jolted me awake. Theodore wasn't at his normal place by our feet. My heart pounded in my chest. I couldn't ignore the sound. It didn't sound like one of those old-house noises, and so I got up to check it out.

With a flashlight gripped in my trembling hand, its beam cutting through the darkness like a sword, I stepped into the shadowy hallway. CREAK! The old wooden floors moved beneath my feet, the sound echoing through the empty halls. I could feel each hair stand on my neck with every step, sending shivers down my spine. It felt as if the house itself held its breath, too. Just then, I heard Theodore growl. This was not a sound I'd ever heard him make.

With each step I took, the anticipation grew. "Hello," I said with little confidence. I grabbed the hammer from the toolbox. I realized how I just sounded and said it again with bass, "HELLO! If someone is in our house, you need to get the fuck out now!" No one answered. Theodore was growling and barking at whatever or whomever was down there. The flashlight's glow illuminated the hidden corners and empty rooms, casting strange and unsettling shadows along the walls. My breath shortened. Theodore's barks became louder and louder. Then a high, frightened yelp ended in a sudden and instant silence.

As I reached the bottom of the stairs, the silence was deafening. The air was heavy with a presence, and a cloak of darkness draped over the house. A loud thud broke the silence, followed by a faint shuffle of feet. My heart skipped a beat, and I directed the beam of light toward the sound.

There, lying on the cold, hard floor, was our beloved Theodore, lifeless and ripped apart. His once playful and lively body now resembled a macabre offering. Something had torn it apart with an animalistic intent. The flashlight's beam revealed the gruesome aftermath, and I felt a mixture of fear, confusion, and a growing sense of dread. I vomited.

In a state of shock, I noticed that the front door was wide open. Who or what was in our home? I shouted for Maria to stay upstairs. I stepped outside. The surrounding forest was draped in darkness. I could hear my racing heartbeat in my ears. I took the flashlight and scanned the darkness, hoping to catch a glimpse of whatever had done this.

I saw something rush across the beam of light and disappear into the darkness. It was roughly a hundred feet away, so it was hard to make out what it was, but it looked like something on all fours. I wanted to chase it. I really did, but when you see *something* in the dark going the other way, it's harder than you think to make your feet move. Then I remembered… Maria! That's when she started screaming.

I turned around to see Maria standing over Theodore's lifeless body. The screams had faded to a ragged gasping. She teetered. I rushed to her side to catch her before she fell. I led her to the stairs and held her while she cried herself to exhaustion. I carried her up the stairs. How many more times would I have to do this? How many more times would I *get* to do this. She felt so small. I tucked her into the bed and then slipped down the stairs to double-check the locks and put in a call to the police. My mouth was dry as I explained the details. Two glasses of water didn't help.

Later, the local police came to the house. I learned that, for all the wilderness in Maine, there haven't been wolves or mountain lions in the state for most of a century. Coyotes and bobcats abound, though, and there's a weasel-type critter called a fisher cat that could have made short work of our beloved dog. After the police left, I did some googling and tried to put together a match with the fleeing shape I saw in the woods. Nothing looked close, but for the sake of my mental well-being, I told myself that a flashlight in the dark can do funny things to a distant shape. I checked the locks again and climbed the stairs to bed.

The next morning was sunny and beautiful—a picturesque landscape, with blooming flowers and buzzing bees. The events of last night seemed impossible in the bright New England sunshine until I tiptoed down the stairs and saw the bloodstains in the foyer. I scrubbed at the old hardwood and put away Theodore's things—his bowls, and bed, and the battered remnants of his old tennis balls. I didn't want those reminders around when Maria woke up, but once they were gone, I knew I'd made a mistake. Sanitizing the house just made Theodore's absence more obvious.

I didn't notice Maria entering the kitchen until she gently wrapped her arms around me from behind, her touch offering some comfort. She rested her chin on my shoulder, her eyes meeting mine in the reflection in the window.

"Did you get any sleep?" she whispered. Her voice was heavy with grief.

We buried Theodore in the backyard. I brought a chair out for Maria to sit in while I dug the little grave. She said some prayers. I tried to focus, but my gaze kept veering to the spot where my flashlight beam chased the strange animal shape into the forest. We shared some memories of Theodore and let the tears flow one more time before we let him go. I wanted to go back inside. I couldn't shake the feeling that something was watching us from the woods. Maria called from the house, asking what happened to the rest of the bottle of wine. I told her I poured it out when I did the dishes.

There's a little hardware store on the town line. The kind that smells of sawdust and machine oil. The sort of place that sells a little of everything you might need, where a bell over the door gives a friendly welcome when you walk in. Maria was tired. She waited in the car. I wanted some new locks and security cameras, and I wasn't about to wait even the two days it was going to take for Amazon to get them to me. Security cameras weren't going to happen, but the hardware store had a pretty solid selection of deer cameras. I dreaded the thought of the woods behind my house turning into a shooting range in the fall. I was working my way through the features of the various models when a man in his late forties appeared next to me. He was wearing a clergy collar and had a warm, welcoming smile.

His name was Pastor Davis. He wasn't much of a hunter, either, but he had set up a few of these units for wildlife pictures. The pastor helped me make my choice. While we shopped, I asked him if he'd ever gotten pictures of anything capable of taking down a fat old Golden Retriever. He said he'd seen coyotes for sure but that he'd heard that even a raccoon, particularly a rabid one, could do a number on an innocent house pet. I eventually chose a pair of camouflage units with little solar chargers to keep them going.

"Just make sure you don't point these at my place," he said with a laugh. Taking in my confused expression, he laughed again. "I thought you knew, we're neighbors," he said.

I didn't realize that we even had neighbors, but Pastor Davis assured me that when the leaves came down in fall, I'd be able to see his house in the distance. That morbid little voice that lived in the back of my mind wondered if Maria would make it until then.

I followed the pastor to the front of the store and watched him checkout. The little bell over the door rang its pleasant goodbye. There was something about the way the woman behind the counter watched him go that told me there was a story there. I pressed her. I didn't have to press hard, and Ruby—that was her name—gave up the goods.

Pastor Davis' story was a small-town tragedy. A decade or so back, his wife and child were killed in a hit-and-run. The driver fled the scene. Pastor Davis was never the same (bless his heart).

The tragedy hardened him, but it also brought him closer to God. The pastor believed, and most of the town believed right with him, that losing his family was a test from the Almighty, a trial that shaped Pastor Davis into the man he is today.

The story sounded a little hollow to me. Treacly small-town melodrama. But I knew Maria would love it. A tragic story like that would hit her right in the middle of her newfound faith. I was hoping she wouldn't get a chance to meet the pastor. A little shiver ran down my spine when I saw him in the parking lot, leaned in through the car window, talking to her.

I spent half the day installing dead bolts on the doors, and the rest of the day installing the cameras, fine-tuning them to catch as many angles as they could. Sure enough, once I looked, I saw the Pastor's neat little house through the trees. After it got dark, my anxieties flared up. I was keyed up. I should have found a meeting, but it was another day that just seemed too busy. Worry about a repeat of last night's traumatic events kept me glued to my phone, watching the feeds from cameras. Nothing happened. I drifted off around two and slept until Maria's coughing woke me up.

It kept on like that for days. Nothing strange. Nothing out of the ordinary. We worked around the house. Peeling old wallpaper and pulling up old carpets. I developed quite a knack for pulling up the devious little tack strips around the edges of the rooms, but not before turning the knuckles of both hands to hamburger. We were nesting. Settling in with each other and enjoying the space, just like we'd hoped and imagined. The voice nagging me about sobriety and meetings and all that garbage quieted. I'd tasted that wine, and it hadn't killed me. Hell, I finished the bottle that night to help me sleep. I was fine. Maria was fine. Maybe it didn't matter. Maria and I were here together. That's what mattered. I offered to make pasta again. Maria's stomach wasn't up to it. That's how it went with her. Good days and bad.

Our property is mostly wooded. There's a little strip of grass that fades back to a sort of hedge and rolling woodlot. Our place backed up on something the locals called The Bog, hundreds of acres of swampy lowland and mosquito breeding grounds. I looked it up on Google maps, and the local cops can say what they want, but there's room for a *pack* of wolves back there. Two packs, a catamount, and a family of Sasquatches.

I was in the backyard one day with some hedge clippers, trying to forge some kind of line between wilderness and civilization, when I noticed something that stopped me cold. There was a path through the woods. It was overgrown and covered with years and years of decaying leaves, but if you held your head just right, it was there. I kicked more and more of the leaves back, and the path became clearer, running from somewhere in the woods right to the back of my house!

Determined to find out where it led, I followed the path, winding my way into the forest. As I worked my way through the dense thicket, the foliage revealed a hidden path winding its way through the woods.

With every step, the leaves beneath my feet crackled. Someone or something had made these steps. I got that scared warm feeling, the same one I got the other night. I took another step. A sudden snap echoed through the woods. I looked down, my eyes fixated on a twig that had broken under my weight.

Attached to it, a long piece of thick hair dangled—thick and matted. It looked like it was from a dog. My eyes fixated on the discovery. Could this be from the creature that had killed Theodore? The woods went silent, amplifying the feeling that the beast might be watching.

Then, a sharp break in the stillness—

"Paul!" Maria's voice sliced through the quiet, snapping me out of the trance induced by the find. "Paul!" Her urgent cries echoed through the woods, breaking the eerie calm.

"Coming," I called back, tearing my gaze away from the hair. With a crackling step and a long glance at the hair, I retraced my steps, making my way back toward the house. I'd revisit this trail another day.

The smell of bacon from Maria's red beans and rice filled the air. We sat at the table. Something was coming. Sailors learn to read the wind and the sea to divine the coming weather because their lives and livelihoods depend on it. I could read my wife the same way. This meal was a favorite of mine, and she knew it. She was making a moment of normalcy before whatever she was about to hit me with. The look on her face carried a weight.

"Paul," she began, her voice carrying a mix of vulnerability and importance, "we need to talk about what's coming."

I kept my eyes on my plate. It was childish, and I knew it, but I figured that if I kept my mouth full, maybe I could avoid *the talk.*

She reached across the table, her hand covering mine. "Paul, I know it's hard, but we have to face it. This was the plan. To be with you, at home, surrounded by the things we love, not stuck in a sterile hospital room. If this is going to work, I think it's time to move me downstairs."

The vulnerability in Maria's eyes chipped away at my shitty defensiveness. I nodded. "Okay, Maria. We'll talk about it. But let's take it one step at a time, all right?"

"That's the point, Paul. It's sixteen steps each way up and down those stairs and… Paul, I'm struggling."

My throat was too thick to swallow the meal, but I forced it down and met her eyes. I agreed. We'd start the transformation tomorrow. The happy home we'd spent barely two weeks building for ourselves was about to change.

Paul," she added, her voice softening, "there's something else. Can you come to church with me tomorrow? It would mean a lot."

A thousand excuses ran through my mind. All the work we had to do. My *complicated* relationship with religion. My honest hostility toward God. None of it mattered. She wanted to go, and for whatever time we had left, I wanted to be next to her. "I'll go," I said.

A small, relieved smile played on her lips. "Thank you, Paul. I love you so much."

I cleared the dinner table while Maria stayed seated. Between preparing the meal and the emotional heft of the conversation, she was drained. I made a mental note: Maria's time in the kitchen was over. That was the last time she was ever going to cook for me. From here on out, every time we did anything, it might be the last time we did it. Last meal. Last dance. Last kiss. Last laugh. I dropped a plate in the sink. It didn't break.

My hands were shaking. How the fuck was I supposed to go to God's house when I hated him as much as I did right then?

There was a 24-hour gas station about six miles from the house. I drove there as the sun started to paint the eastern sky. The overbright fluorescent lighting felt like a time machine to my worst days, the days before Maria, before I felt like there could be anything good in my life. The people of Maine drink a horrible brew called Allen's Coffee Brandy. It's just what you think it is, but I hoped that the coffee part would mask the other part. It comes in little shot bottles, so you don't have to keep an open container in the car. Those little bottles line the edges of Maine's most picturesque little roads. Maria wouldn't notice. It wouldn't get bad. I just needed to even out, to calm my nerves. I bought six little bottles and drank two on my way home. I hid the rest around the house like ugly thoughts.

I paced the downstairs of the house for a few hours. I didn't want to wake Maria up. I kept finding myself at the window, staring into the shadows. I couldn't let go of that clump of hair on the branch. There was something out there in the dark, and I needed to know what it was. This was our house. It was supposed to be a place of safety, but it wouldn't be with that thing out there. Maria didn't have much time left, and I promised her that night that I'd make sure our home was safe and secure, no matter the cost.

I woke up with a headache and an acid burn in my stomach. Church didn't help. The small sanctuary smelled like cheap perfume and Pine Sol. Sunlight filtered through stained glass windows, casting colorful patterns on the wooden pews. Pastor Davis welcomed us warmly. He sermonized on pain, loss, and the power of forgiveness. His words seemed custom-made for Maria and I, but I could see that he inspired the whole congregation. Everyone there felt seen in their unique struggles. I can admit it, he was good at his job. After the service, Pastor Davis approached us with a smile.

"Paul, Maria, it's good to see you here. I hope you found some comfort in the service."

I nodded, feeling like I had to do something. Then I felt the conversation shift.

"I know you're going through a tough time. Grief can make us question many things and feel lost."

This conversation was not what I signed up for, especially after the previous night with Maria. "Pastor, I appreciate it," I said just to end the conversation as quickly as I could.

I think he saw right through it. "Maria shared her concerns about your well-being, Paul, and what happened with Theodore. She cares for you, and so do I. If you ever need someone to talk to, I'm here."

I shifted uncomfortably, I'm also not into discussing my personal struggles, especially with someone who believes that a floating man in the sky is calling all the shots. I told him I wasn't much of a believer and that I was only there for Maria. He smiled bigger and clapped a friendly hand on my shoulder.

"No offense taken, Paul. I'm here for anyone who needs support, regardless of their beliefs. Sometimes, just talking can be a step toward healing. If it helps, you can think of me as a neighbor instead of a priest."

I caught something on his breath then, under the aftershave and breath mints, the vague burn of alcohol. Was it a little something to level the padre's nerves before he got out in front of the congregation? It was enough for the drunk in me to throw up every kind of wall and barricade imaginable against this guy. I didn't want another thing to do with the padre, and I think my sullen voice and body language sent the message plain and clear. I expected Maria to give it to me with both barrels once we got to the car, but she didn't say a word. She just took my hand and asked if I wanted to go for a drive. No time for fights now. Only good stuff for the two of us.

We spent the day out, cruising up and down the Maine coast, taking in the sights and picking up groceries. After we got home, I got busy screwing up a box of mac and cheese, and by the time I was done, it was too late to explore that trail again. I looked at it through the window over the kitchen sink. It would still be there tomorrow. No problem.

I laid down with Maria even though I wasn't tired and counted freckles until…

BOOM…. BOOM… BOOM…

I jolted out of bed. The deafening onslaught continued, each pound echoed through the walls as I looked around the pitch-black room. Maria was immune to the pounding, thanks to the pain meds. Adrenaline surged through me as I stumbled toward the security cameras to see if I could make out what was happening. Nothing. Something was hiding in the blind spot of the two cameras. I grabbed a flashlight and charged down the stairs. The pounding persisted. First it was at the front door. The new lock held its own. Silence as the pounding stopped. I froze, staring at the front door.

BOOM…. BOOM… BOOM…

I spun around. It was coming from the back door now, its intensity growing with each moment. Whatever it was was trying to get in. The door flexed as the pounding persisted. Then silence.

BOOM… BOOOM… BOOM… It moved to the wall. Newly hung photos shook, dancing and spilling onto the ground, adding the crash of glass to the noise.

"Stop it! I'm calling the police!" I called out. My voice sounded weak and hollow in the dark. I aimed the flashlight around, turning a slow circle, looking for the source of the sound. Was it within the walls? Or outside? Or in my head? Was some force playing tricks on my sanity?

BOOM… BOOM… BOOM…

A picture of our wedding day crashed onto the floor, joining the others.

My palms were sweaty, and my heart pounded, as I walked closer to the wall, a visceral reaction to whatever was going on.

BOOM… BOOM… BOOOOOOOOM…

"STOOOOP!" I screamed at the top of my lungs.

It stopped.

The abrupt silence hung in the air.

I stood alone in the dark living room, my breaths shallow, the flashlight still clutched tight in my hand. Maria was still asleep. There was glass everywhere.

A rustle came from the bushes in the backyard. I raced toward the kitchen, thinking about the window over the sink. If it was going where I thought, I'd be able to—CRUNCH. My foot came down on a ragged shard of glass. Pain shot up my leg, and I sagged into the doorframe. I could see the window. A flash of movement in the dark. I staggered forward. Blood slicked the floor under me as I went.

I aimed my flashlight through the glass, but it only made the surface more reflective. Damn it! I lurched to the back door and fumbled the locks open. I staggered out into the night. This was the second attack on my home. I'd been scared, but now I was hurt, and I was mad as I limped down the stairs on my bare and bleeding foot. I thrust the beam of the flashlight ahead of me, eyes peeled for movement. The trunks of the trees were ghostly pillars in the dark. No movement. Nothing.

I froze. Twin reflective discs—a pair of eyes—shone at me in the distance. Something was looking back at me from deep in the woods.

"I see you!" I called.

The eyes blinked once, flashing to black and then returning. Unmoving. Unwavering.

I took a few more steps, but my old friend Anger was abating, leaving me in my time of need. Another step. Two more. The pain in my foot throbbed through the ebbing adrenaline. The eyes kept watching me, and my guts turned to water. I stopped moving. Suddenly, I was struggling to even hold my ground. Blink. The eyes. I retreated a step. Then another. You're not supposed to run from a wild animal. You're supposed to make yourself big and slowly back away. I knew that. Everybody knows that by now. Nobody tells you how fucking hard that is. I backed away ten steps, then I broke and ran. I don't have real memories of the headlong sprint back to my house. Just a raw, shapeless fear of the thing behind me until I felt myself inside, gasping, with my back to the locked door.

I pulled the memory cards from the game cameras and plugged them straight into my laptop. There had to be something there. Proof! There was triumph on my face as I scrolled through the shots. I pictured showing Maria the thing in the woods, demonstrating once and for all that there was something out there. In the end, there wasn't much—just a couple of pictures of blackness. The last shot was me standing in the yard, barefoot, looking like a Wildman. I stared at it for a long time. There was something there! Glinting eyes in the woods, watching me. But I knew that the only thing Maria would see in that picture was the little bottle in my hand, so I deleted it. That wasn't the proof I was looking for.

I didn't sleep. I bandaged my foot, then swept up the glass. I couldn't even lay down. My body was a coiled spring. I needed to act. I wanted to scream in frustration at the whole thing, but with my poor, dying Maria clinging to her few hours of precious sleep, I had to keep it all inside, where it just boiled. She wanted to move downstairs tomorrow. How could we do that with something out there assaulting the house in the dead of night? Could I even tell her what I'd seen? I would have done anything to keep Maria comfortable. The house was impossibly quiet, and I was amped. The seed that had been growing in my head since the day we got here blossomed.

Once Maria was situated for the morning, I slipped off to a nearby town to pick up some paint for the walls, and some other supplies to get me through my late-night vigils. I explained the missing pictures as a sudden urge to make progress on the painting. I returned home to find an unwelcome visitor in my home. Pastor Davis was in the living room with Maria. There were tear tracks on her cheeks, and he had her hand cupped in both of his. He was fellowshipping or pastoring or whatever these kooks call their Biblicisms. I didn't like it. I know that it's crazy, but somehow, I felt just a little bit cheated on. They welcomed me back but then put their heads close and talked low while I puttered around the house, pretending to get ready to paint. After a few minutes of this, Pastor Davis caught up to me and invited me to walk him home.

"She's worried about you, Paul," he confided as we crunched up the gravel road toward his house. I said nothing and kept my eyes on my toes. "Maria's making peace with moving on. She knows she's going to a better place, but she's afraid of leaving you behind. She said she smelled alcohol on your breath this morning." My teeth ground together. "I can tell you're angry, and I'm sorry. I know how that feels. After the accident, I felt the same way. I was angry at everything. Of course, I was enraged at the man who did it, that unknown person who took everything from me. But as time went on, that anger grew. I hated the police for their impotent failure to even try to investigate. My anger spread to the people of the community. My congregation. Their sorrow. Their attempts to help me, to console me. It only made the pain inside me burn brighter. I hated myself for not being in the car. I hated God for forsaking me."

Somewhere along the way, we'd stopped walking. He was describing everything I was going through, and I hated that, too.

"Something killed my dog," I blurted. I just wanted him to shut the hell up. To stop seeing me. To stop trying to help. I didn't want to help. I just wanted time with my wife, and it was all being ruined by him. Being ruined by whatever was in the woods… And by my inability to live in the moment.

Pastor Davis was looking at me hard in the eyes. I kept going. "Something big came right into my house and ripped my dog to pieces. It's been back. Banging on the walls. Making noise in the night. Have you seen anything like that? Heard anything?"

"No."

"Okay then." I said. "Thanks for trying, Father, but I'd better get back to Maria." His house was in sight, a few hundred feet farther up the road. My duty as an unwilling host was done.

"Paul, wait."

I stopped.

"There is something. I've never seen it, but people have been talking about the *Wahant* for many years," he said.

"What is that?"

"'Wahant' is an old Passamaquoddy word for devil or demon. What it really is, I don't know." Davis shrugged. "Maybe it's an old black bear or an extra-large coyote. Maybe there's a wolf or a mountain lion hiding up there. I know the ATV kids and the mountain bikers find a deer or two every season that's pretty torn up. It doesn't eat its prey like the other animals around, it just rips them up and spreads them around in some kind of gruesome display or warning. Not too many locals will spend the night in these woods. Sometimes during hunting season, when it starts to get dark, you'll see some tough old boys hoofing it out of these woods like their tails are on fire. It's a folktale, but people around here treat it like gospel. It's never bothered me, but I'm inside by dark all year round. I reckon maybe there was some kind of territorial confusion when you first moved in, but Paul… I think that confusion's over. If you respect the woods, I don't think you're going to have any more trouble."

"Unacceptable," I said.

Davis's eyes snapped up to meet mine. I was on fire. I could feel the heat of anger in my face, but I knew I was right. That fire, that certainty. Feeling right no matter what. That's what drinking does to me. It wasn't the two little bottles that were in me, it was the other four hidden back at the house. Pushing. Making chaos. Making me need them.

"Whatever that was, was in my house. It killed my dog. I need to *know* it's not coming back. I need to do something."

Pastor Davis dipped into his jacket pocket and came up with a little stainless steel flask. He unscrewed the top and treated himself to a little pull. He met my eyes. I can't tell you it wasn't intense. The look was soft and peaceful. Was what you think of when you think of a priest. Absolution. I was forgiven. He offered the flask, and I took it. It was bourbon. Good bourbon. Every cell in my body woke up when that burn hit. I handed it back, like we were sharing a secret.

"Paul," he said quietly. "You need to focus on Maria right now. She needs you. There's not much time left, and you can't afford to waste a minute of it. All these other feelings that you're going through right now, that's you trying to avoid the pain that's coming. I understand. She understands, but you have to give this time to her. She's all that matters. Let the rest of it go."

My anger rushed back in, setting the alcohol in my system alight. Who the fuck was he to tell me this? Who the fuck was he to be right about my wife, my marriage, her death? I felt my fists clenched up at my sides. I was ready to pop him one, glaring white fury. He held my eyes fast. I think he would have taken the shot to make his point. We spent a long moment like that, two men on a dirt road sizing each other up. I barely noticed my phone buzzing away in my pocket.

It was Maria. Caller ID told me that. There was no voice on the other end of the line, just a choking, strangulated breath. I shouted her name and ran. I'd think about what the pastor said later, but not for a while. Maria had taken a turn for the worse. She rode an ambulance to Pen Bay Medical Center that night. I followed in the car, steering wildly with my shaking hands.

Maria spent the night in Intensive Care, and then a week on the cancer ward. It was some kind of secondary infection she was too weak to fight off. I never left the hospital. I slept when I could in a chair by her bed, holding her hand. A terrible thing about hospitals, they tell you again and again how important it is to rest but they never turn the lights all the way off, and they come in every few minutes to bother you. On the third day, in spite of it all, Maria started to get better. When they told me she'd be able to come home one more time, my vision misted with tears until I couldn't even see her face.

I went home to get the place ready. I finished my painting project and aired the fumes out of the house. I drank the rest of the coffee brandy, rehung the paintings, and started putting the hospital bed together in the living room. Somewhere along the way, I lost it. The walls started closing in. I thought about the weeks I might have left with Maria. I thought about how little of her was left. How she used to be, how we used to be, laughing and running around in the sun. All that was already gone. This was what remained, sadness and memories in a smaller and smaller corner of this rickety old house, three thousand miles from home, and... My hand slipped. I bashed my knuckles into the stainless steel railing of the hospital bed. Hard. I lost it. Next thing I knew, I was screaming my head off and punching a hole in the wall.

I ran outside, clattering through the kitchen to the back door, and threw up in the grass. I stood up, wiping my mouth with the back of a hand and looked into the woods. The path was so visible now, like a highway into oblivion.

"Fuck you!" I shouted at the unseen Wahant. "FUCK YOU!!!"

I turned back to the house and froze in my tracks. The back door was scarred with huge, deep claw marks. Something had ripped at the old wood with everything it had. There was blood, too, like it had torn is paws, claws, or whatever down to the bone while trying to get into my house. My house. Maria's house. The fire in my blood turned to ice. I felt this amazing stillness come over my body. A sense of peace and purpose that I hadn't felt since we got here. I knew what I was doing. I had a job to do. A purpose. I was going to kill this thing. I was going to make the house safe for my wife. And I was going to do it tonight.

I went back to the hospital. I was supposed to bring Maria home. She looked almost like herself, nestled in all those pillows and smiling to see me. She wanted to go right away, but I begged off. I pleaded for one more night to be sure, and so I could get the house perfect for her to come back. Everything I said made perfect sense. I just needed a little time. I wanted it to be perfect for her.

She didn't buy any of it. She looked so sad. My explanations and excuses dried up. I ran out of words. She knew everything. She always had.

"I'm okay here," she said. "I can stay."

I shook my head. I didn't understand.

"I don't want you to come back. Not like this. I want to come home with you but only if you're really going to be there. No more secrets. No more lies. No more staying up all night and… You don't have to come back. I won't be mad. I understand."

She was right. I'd been half-there for weeks. Raving about monsters. Drinking all night. Wasting so much time. I wanted to scream. I held it all in. I kissed her cheek.

"I'll be here first thing in the morning," I said.

I stopped at the gas station on the way home and bought a pint bottle of that toxic coffee brandy.

An hour later found me standing in the dark over the kitchen sink, gripping my trusty flashlight in one hand and a kitchen knife in the other. Waiting, watching, keeping my eyes on that little ghost of a trail behind the house. The drip of the sink got hypnotic. I pulled a chair over and sat down. I took a tug off the brandy bottle and did the math. I could drink for another hour and still be sober by morning. Maria wouldn't have to find out, and I'd start clean tomorrow. Be there for her. Start fresh. The sink kept dripping. Somewhere along the way, the drip merged with a dream, driving down the highway in the dark, yellow lines flashing in the headlights. Drip… Drip…

BANG! Something hit the back door again. The entire house rattled. A horrible, moaning scream cut the night. I jumped up. Knife and flashlight clattered to the floor. I scrambled to pick them up. It hit the house again, another horrible crash. It didn't feel like the door could hold much longer. I scrambled on hands and knees in the dark, looking for my weapons. I found the knife blade first and nicked my finger a pretty good one before I got hold of it. The flashlight had rolled under the table. The Wahant hit the back door three more apocalyptic blows before I found it. By then I was ready. My blood sang with anger and adrenaline.

I crossed to the door in three steps and flipped the lock open. I screamed as I opened the door and blasted the light into its face, a primal roar that sucked the air out of me and felt like it was tearing meat and blood from my vocal cords.

The light hit the Wahant straight in the face as my scream washed over it. I saw it, full in the light, inches from my face. It was a man. Or at least it had once been a man. It was skeletal and weak and small. It looked malnourished. The skull stood out under a roadmap of scars and gashes. It half-turned away, throwing up a hand to ward off the beam of my light. The Wahant's hand was a ruin: two fingers, two stumps, no thumb. It ran.

I chased it. It was fast. It knew the forest, every twist and turn of the trail. I couldn't keep the light on it while I ran. The beam jerked among the trees as I sprinted. I fought to keep enough of the beam on it to direct me in the dark. It was fast. I was faster. But the trail was slippery under its coating of old, dry vegetation. I slipped and went down. It's a miracle I didn't put that knife into my guts. I got back up and paused. I heard the scrambling sounds of the Wahant and found it with my light. It was far ahead and still moving fast. I could have stopped. It would have ended there, I have no doubt. I'd put the fear into that thing, staked my claim on the house and the yard. It wouldn't come back again.

I liked the power. I liked that it was afraid of me. I liked that I was in charge for the first time since the doctor sat us down and gave us the diagnosis. I was ready to take something from the world that had been taking from me for almost a year.

And then it was gone.

I slowed and then stopped, panning the light around the empty forest. There were lights in the distance, the golden glow of house windows. Where had the damned thing gone? It couldn't just disappear, could it? I slowed down further. Caught my breath. I tried to think, to turn the raging noise in my head down enough to figure out where this monster could be.

It took a moment, but I found it, a narrow strip of darkness among the torn-up root ball of a fallen tree. A cave? A tunnel. I approached it carefully. The hole was tiny, a slit in the earth. It seemed impossible that even as wraithlike a figure like the Wahant could have fit through there, but it had. A clawed handprint in the dirt showed his path. I took a deep breath. This was where it came from. So close to my house.

I couldn't live with that. I got down on all fours and shone my light into the creature's den. I saw a narrow tunnel through the earth as tight as a coffin. No sign of the thing. It was in there somewhere. Had to be. I don't know when I decided to follow it, but before I had time to think, I was pushing my head and shoulders into the darkness.

The tunnel was just wide enough for me to get my shoulders through. I hoped it would widen out, but for a dozen claustrophobic feet, I had to worm through the dark earth with my arms stretched over my head. At one point, the space became so narrow that I had to push all the air out of my lungs to forge ahead. But if the creature had done it, then I knew I could, too.

The light was intermittent. I plunged into darkness more than once as the lens ended up facing the dirt all around me. I twisted, turning my shoulders like a key to keep pushing through the narrow space. My heart was pounding in my chest. The sound of rushing blood filled my ears. My back fetched up on the top of the tunnel, and for a moment, I was stuck fast. I couldn't move at all. You think that the sound of terror is a scream, but I learned that night that, for me, it's a low, dumb moan in the dark.

Panic flared. I twisted and writhed but only got stuck worse in the hole. I dropped the light and the knife and clawed at the dirt all around me. I want to say that I thought about Maria, and that her light was the anchor that got me through it, but I didn't. I couldn't think at all. My sadness, my rage, my disappointment at the hand life had dealt us were all gone. There was nothing in me but white noise and terror.

Something grabbed my hand. It pulled. Hard. The joint stretched and popped. I found my voice in a wail of agony, but I was moving. My hips and back broke free, sending me sliding through the dark.

I fell out of the tunnel onto a hard, stone floor. The flashlight was nearby, pointing off into nothing but giving me enough spilled light to see by. I was in a low, stone-walled room. It had the musty smell of a basement mixed with the thick reek of animal. I rolled over on my side, trying to take some pressure off my dislocated shoulder, and saw it standing over me. The Wahant.

What had once been a man was worn away now, abraded and emaciated down to a skeleton wrapped in wiry muscle and scar tissue. Thin hair slumped from one side of its head, and the other side had a lumpen, caved-in appearance. Its breath whistled through the crushed ruin of a boxer's oft-shattered nose. One eye was gray and dead, the other glared at me with malignant light. For a long moment, the two of us stayed like that, staring at each other across the semi-dark. Its few fingers flexed, long and nail-less, strangler's hands. I tensed, despite the agony in my shoulder. This was the fight I'd been looking for. I didn't want it anymore, but it was coming for me.

Then I thought of Maria. In the hospital alone. Waiting for me. Her face when I didn't show up. The questions. The confusion. Maria, facing the last battle with her cancer alone. I dragged myself up to my knees and got ready to fight.

THUMP... THUMP... THUMP... The unmistakable sound of feet on stairs. Close and coming closer. The change in the room was instantaneous. The Wahant turned and ran. It crouched in the corner and whimpered as the footsteps came closer.

"Go upstairs, now!" a man's voice grated as he stepped from the darkness. He was holding a fireplace poker in both hands, cocked over his shoulder like a bat.

I ran. In my wake, I heard the awful banging sounds of iron on flesh and bone, and the high, whimpering cry of a man in pain. I found the stairs. Light flowed down from above, and I staggered toward it as the screaming below fell to silence.

I ended my run in a cozy, New England kitchen. There was a bottle of bourbon on the table and a single glass, half drunk. I slumped into the chair at the table and tried to find a way to sit that didn't hurt. The bottle grew in my mind while I sat there. I could feel its shadow falling over me. I wanted it, but I kept my hands in my lap and counted the keys hanging on hooks by the door. After a long time, I heard him come up the stairs.

"Go ahead, have a drink," said Pastor Davis. He poured me off a generous three fingers in a plastic tumbler and slid it across the table. "We have a lot to talk about."

My mouth was dry. The sweet smell of the liquor wafted from the cup. The offer was clear. The preacher wanted me to drink. It was okay. It was encouraged. There was a deal implied. This thing for that thing downstairs. Suddenly, I didn't want it. I didn't want the fog, the soft edge on the world. I didn't want the lack of control. It's always a deal, and it never works. After a lifetime of struggling with this thing, I finally understood that everything that liquor offered was a lie. I could have thrown the bourbon in Pastor Davis's face or dumped it on the floor, but I didn't need to. A gesture like that gives a thing power, and the preacher's booze had none left for me.

"I'm sorry you had to see that," he said. "It seems my guest has been sneaking out at night for some time. I guess he was trying to get back into his parents' house. I didn't realize it, but rest assured, you and Maria won't be bothered again."

Naturally, I had questions, starting with: What the fuck?! But the pastor didn't give me a chance to ask.

"You have to understand," he began. "I'm doing God's work. After my Lorraine and Joey died, I lost my way. I was like you, in a pit of anger and despair. I didn't trust God. How could He have taken them from me? How could He have given me this pain, these feelings…this rage. And then, God gave me the answer."

"I was drunk and alone, sitting in the dark when I saw a car pull up to my neighbors' house—your house. It was their son, James. I hadn't seen him in a long time. Years. He was an addict. A loser. From fifteen years old, a disappointment and a heartbreak to his parents. I could hear them fighting from here. I got my jacket and went outside to listen."

"He wanted to come home. He'd lost everything, again. He'd been living in his car and had finally returned to the only place he thought might take him. But they wouldn't. Not after what he'd done. Not after last time. His mother gave him money—not much, but it's what she had—and told him to get out of town before the sun rose. I knew what they were talking about. I knew what it was. It was my family. He'd been the one!"

"I thought I might pass out, standing there in the dark listening as the pieces fell into place. He'd been back before, just like this in the night. Only last time, he'd had an accident. He'd hit someone. He'd hit someone and fled the scene. No one knew he was in town. No one knew he left. That's why nobody had been able to find him, why there weren't clues, why there was no sign of a damaged car on the road after that night. It all made so much sense."

"He cried as he begged his parents for another chance. I felt God harden my heart against that boy, just like He did to Pharaoh when Moses came knocking."

"He was about to drive away again, to live his life like he hadn't destroyed mine, but I ran back here and got my car and followed him. I thought I lost him, but no… I caught up with him on the way out of town and stayed with him until he stopped. It took me three days of watching him, tailing, before I made my move. I was more careful than I had to be. Nobody was looking for that man. Nobody ever is. Even his parents assumed he met his end somewhere lonely and sad at the far end of his addiction. But he's clean and sober now. Ten long years."

Pastor Davis chose that moment to reach for his glass. He never took his eyes off me, though. I got the feeling he was sizing me up, deciding if I could be trusted with his secret, or if he'd have to do something about me.

"You're torturing him," I said.

"I'm punishing him," Davis responded. "There's no satisfaction in what I do. I'm doing it for the Lord."

I didn't buy it. Davis could tell.

He tried again to explain it. "I'm doing that man a service. I'm freeing him of his guilt. I'm purging his flesh so that his spirit will be free. I'm giving him the chance to pay now for what he did and earn his place in heaven when it's all over."

"At first, it was blind rage. You, of all people, understand that. I know what you're going through. Losing your wife. Watching her suffer. Knowing that there's nothing you can do. Imagine that there *was* something you could do? Imagine that cancer right in front of you, where you could put your hands on it."

I tried. The feeling burned a little, but I liked it.

"I admit it. It started off as revenge," Davis said. "He hurt me, and I wanted to hurt him back. I thought I was going to kill him. If you'd asked me the plan back then, that was it. I brought him to my basement, and I chained him up. I beat him. Badly. I broke his skull with a bat and took two fingers and three toes. I was sick. Disgusted with myself. I thought about turning myself in. Ending my life. I tried to help him. I tended his wounds. I nursed him back to health. And then, one day, I caught that look in his eye again. He felt sorry for himself. He was a victim. But he wasn't sorry. Not really. He still didn't see what he'd done. I pushed his face into the hot soup. He screamed for mercy, but I heard God, and that's when I understood. This wasn't about making me feel better, this was about the Lord's justice. I prayed over him that night, and I felt my faith return. I went back to the church to minister the people of this town, and they welcomed me home."

"How much is enough?" I asked. My throat was tight with horror and disgust. Partly at what this man had done—was doing—and partly because I understood it.

Davis shrugged and drained his glass. "I'm waiting for God to tell me," he said.

So, there it was. The full story laid out for me. I was disgusted. Horrified. Years of brutality. Torture. How could a person do that? On some level, I knew. Deep down, I got it. Someday soon, my Maria would be gone, but the man who took one precious day with her away... That's when it hit me.

"I want to see him again," I said.

Pastor Davis couldn't hide the look of surprise on his face. His mouth twitched a little. He looked from the still-full cup in front of me to my face. This wasn't how he pictured it going. He wanted to say something, to explain himself again, but he could see that there was nothing left to say. He silently slid his chair back and rose to his feet.

The dark, reeking basement closed in around us. I looked around at that world of suffering and pain. I saw the Wahant cowering in the corner. A thick link of new chain hung around his neck, mounted to a staple in the wall. The padlock glinted dimly in the gloom. I could see the fear in its eye as it looked at me. I could smell the acid reek of its terror. There was nothing left of the man here, nothing capable of giving Pastor Davis what he needed.

"You have to let him go," I said.

"Not yet," said Davis. "God hasn't given me the sign."

I turned away from the monster on the floor, shaking my head. "You're making a terrible mistake," I said.

"That's for God—"

CLICK.

The sound was unmistakable. A lock snapping open. When I first got into the pastor's kitchen, I'd noticed a row of keys hanging on hooks from the wall near the door. Spare house keys, car keys, church keys... Whatever they might have been. Out of those eleven keys, one was new. Shiny. I'd snatched one on the way by, and as I knelt, I pressed it into the Wahant's mutilated hand. It turned out, I'd picked the right one. The Wahant rose up in the dark and something else gleamed in his hand. My knife.

The monster shoved me aside and lunged for Pastor Davis. I didn't stay to watch but headed for the stairs. This was between them. It always had been. Maybe they'd been even once. Maybe there's no such thing. Maybe it's just "rage begets violence begets vengeance," like a chapter from Davis's good book.

I could still hear the screams as I walked away from that house, but my part in that story was over. There was only one story that mattered to me now, making the most of my final chapter with Maria.

The death of Pastor Davis was a local sensation. The police figured it was thieves. My report about a suspected break-in from a few weeks earlier was added to the evidence list, even though they'd been dismissively certain it was raccoons at the time. As far as his "guest" goes, nobody found much of anything. It seemed he slipped away into the night. Rumors of the Wahant persist. The kids on the trails and in the party spots around the bog still find torn-up deer and other things, and there have been a few break-ins in the area lately. I like to think that it's the thing from Davis's basement living out whatever time it has left in the best way it knows how.

In the end, I really did see something of myself in Pastor Davis. We shared the same anger and rage at what God or fate or whatever you want to call it had given us. But I also saw how that anger keeps the wound open. Davis didn't just lose his family in the accident, he lost them again when he decided to replace grieving with revenge. You could see it in his eyes and hear it in his voice when he spoke. His wife and child weren't people to him anymore, they were things that had been taken from him. Their memories were replaced by the monster he kept in his basement, hurting it again and again in failed attempts to bring back some of what he'd lost. But in reality, he was only pushing his loved ones further away.

I didn't find God after that. My revelation was simpler and more personal. I didn't need to drink. I didn't want to drink. Maybe it won't last, but since that night, the desire is burned clean out of me. I went back to the hospital and looked at my wife. She was small and sick in that bed, but she was there. For whatever time we had left, she was mine, and I wasn't going to spend another minute dwelling on what I was losing. In the end, it was just under six weeks, but we packed a lifetime into every single day of it.

DO YOU BELIEVE IN GHOSTS?

Mali Elfman

"DO YOU BELIEVE in ghosts?"

Every three and a half minutes my grandmother asks me this question. That's how long the Alzheimer's takes to reset.

Today, we're in the middle of a debate. She's deciding if she wants to be religious or not at the end of her life. She wants to know what happens next. She wants to know if there's heaven or hell, if there's an "other side," or if she's going to float around for eternity, tormented.

There's an intensity to these debates because we both know we're racing against her mind's clock.

She looks at me and stiffens. Has she reset? Is this a dramatic pause? Her eyes search for something, and finally she leans in and says, "You like scary things."

"I do."

"So… Do you believe in ghosts?" she asks me again.

"What *is* a ghost?" I say.

This was evidently not the answer she wanted. "Come on. You believe in all this stuff!"

"I *believe* that I understand very little and want to know more."

"And you like all that horror stuff."

"I think it likes me, Grandma." She smiles when I say this, but then regains her seriousness.

"Do you think I'll become a ghost and haunt you?" she asks.

"I would love it if you would."

"Ah! Mali, you're avoiding the question."

I think for a moment before answering. "A ghost is that thing that—try as we might—we cannot seem to explain. It's the unknown. It's the thing hiding in the shadows of our minds that we can't quite grasp but we want to be true."

"So, what is going to happen to me?" she asks.

"Well, I don't think you'll wander around with a sheet over your head and say 'boo', and I don't believe that you'll waste your time here much longer. You have shit to do."

I can see that our once playful banter means something different to her now. There's a desperation to her tone. I watch her milky eyes probe the material world for answers. Our time is almost up. I hurry.

"I believe we make them real," I say. "I believe they are real, because…as this world slips away, you don't go 'nowhere.'"

I point to a dark corner of the room that the sunlight never touches. "Look over there, to that corner that's always dark. What do you see?"

Frustrated, she does what I say. "I don't see anything."

"Right, it's too dark. But then what if I shine a light there?" I take a lamp and twist it sideways to shine a light in the corner. "What do you see now?"

She looks even harder, but to no avail. "Nothing is there! I don't understand!"

"But now if I turn off the light, that "nothing" becomes… something. It becomes darkness."

Grandma looks deeply into the dark now. Wonder takes over as she sees something she hasn't seen before inside of it.

"A ghost is just a shadow in a corner that you can't shine a light on. It doesn't mean anything is there. But… I also think that it doesn't mean anything isn't. And what if we are brave enough to let the darkness exist, just let it be real. To—"

I pause to realize that her eyes are not on mine, but fixed on something in the darkness. Her hand glides up her arm, then stops, as if she's met someone else's hand there. She startles, then blushes, caressing the hand on her. She giggles to herself.

"Grandma? What is it?"

Just then, she effortlessly rises from her chair. I lunge forward to help her but…she's steady. It's almost as if someone or some-*thing* is already holding her.

Her eyes don't break from the darkness. A tear falls down her cheek.

"Grandma? What do you see?" I look into the darkness. It's now my pleading eyes that look to her for answers.

She goes to speak, but not to me, and right as she does—

Her eyes drop. Her hand drops. She slumps backward into the chair.

I run to her, catching her fall. I settle her into the chair and crouch in front of her. I search her eyes, eager to know more, but—

Her mind has reset.

The moment is lost.

She smiles at me in the familiar way she always does. It's the look that says she wants to ask me something.

"Mali, dear, do you believe in ghosts?" she says.

"I want to."

IT'S MIDNIGHT, AND I find myself at her door. I've brought a candle. It smells of macarons, one of her favorite scents.

I've gone back to her house many times to see her, but I still don't know what happened that day.

I'll never know because she passed away two months ago. My family put her house on the market and tomorrow it will no longer be hers.

I find the hide-away key and let myself in. The lights aren't working, and there's just the moonlight shining through the windows, revealing her empty house. It's so lonely without her things here.

I sit on the floor exactly where she sat that day and I look into the corner.

I light my candle, and as it begins to glow, the darkness around me starts to dance.

I think about what she was looking at that day. *Was it a ghost? A trick of her mind? Her medication? My wishful thinking?*

The more I look, the darker it gets. The darkness seems to shift as I do.

Just then, I feel the hairs prickle on my arm. Someone leans toward me and—

The candle blows out.

I jump to my feet and run for the door but before I make it outside I—

Stop.

Is this not the darkness I longed for? The one that made her blush?

I have to know. I turn around, and that's when I see…the candle in the living room. It's lit. *Still? Again?*

The candle flickers, beckoning me over.

I walk back. The space no longer feels lonely but full. Elements unseen all around.

I hear creaks, groans, and every whisper of wind moving through the house. *Do I hear her?*

Despite my heightened senses, I sit back down.

I take a deep breath, slowing my heartbeat. I settle my nerves.

Once again, I look into the darkness. It sways. Oscillating in the wavering candlelight. And then… Someone leans in next to me. I push against my instinct to run and focus on the dark. I welcome it.

And that's when I feel it—not hear it—it's more like a fizz on the back of my skull, and it asks, "Do you believe in ghosts?"

A tear rolls down my cheek as I exhale.

I smile and blow out the candle.

I do.

JINNEH

Babou Ceesay

The following is a true account. The subject is a family member who lived into the 1970s, near Kaur, The Gambia, West Africa. The narrator is still alive today and told me this story.

I NEVER UNDERSTOOD why my father suddenly stopped speaking. At first, I put it down to illness, but he was still as powerful as an ox. His actions were clear and, in many ways, more focused. I later reasoned that he stopped talking because there were so many of us. He decided the best policy was to stop connecting. Three wives and seventeen children were a lot to ask of any man. I have more questions today than I ever did answers.

My father was a living legend. Over the years, I'd heard many stories about him, but chose to not believe a single one. I took that lack of belief with me to the capital when I went to study and kept it when I stayed there to work and raise a family of my own. I was determined to not be sucked into superstition and madness.

It's true, I couldn't deny that I always felt there was something different about him. But the day it all changed for me was the day we laid my father to rest. I remember that entire day, every second of it, as if I am re-living it. And I am not alone in that. Many others report the same experience. The day itself was unremarkable. There was the story of what happened at Death House that could not be explained. But it was the events that occurred at his grave that have left an everlasting impression on me. Whether you choose to believe it or not, I can assure you with certainty that there is more to this world—*much more*—than meets the eye. Up until that day, I had been a devout skeptic myself.

The story was that my father had the ability to affect outcomes. How he did it was the subject of great debate. The closest I ever came to experiencing his so-called power was when I had trouble at work.

It was the sixties, and we were on the cusp of independence from the British empire. It was a frantic time, as preparations were being made for the handover. My area was finance, and I was one of the shining lights at the central bank. Many expected that I would be invited to fill one of the managerial positions. I had an eye on the financial controller position. Unfortunately, a new Director General had been brought in and took an instant and profound disliking for me. I knew that over time, most people found my pride and lack of flexibility difficult. My wife, who I know loves me very much, sometimes has to remind me to let up. The day I met this man, I was on my best behavior, and yet, within a few seconds, it was clear that my days at the bank were numbered. I spoke to my mum that evening. At the very end of the call, almost as an afterthought, I mentioned that I may be needing a new job soon and joked about why. She went silent for a while and then asked me to come up to the village to see my father. She had never asked before, so I assumed the old man was dying.

In the few days before I was granted compassionate leave, I was called by head office and was asked unfounded questions about missing funds. This man did not simply seek to remove me but to destroy me.

It didn't take long after I arrived to learn that my father was in excellent health. My mother took me round the entire village to greet all the elders and their families. They made a show of being happy to see me, but they knew I was the son that didn't believe. She then took me to our compound. In those days we lived in large compounds, and ours was one of the largest. My father lived in the main building and each wife had a building of their own to house them and their children. There were a couple of other structures. A small mosque and a building that was off limits.

It was not her day to be in the main house, so we stood outside until my father's third wife came out to fetch us. As a child I never understood why my mother hated this woman, but as a grown man it was plain to see. This woman, now old, was the young bride that usurped her marital bed. She paid almost no mind to the fact that she had done the same thing to my father's first wife.

We were welcomed into the house and asked to wait. Once we were alone, my mother told me that when I was with my father, I should tell him everything I could about the man at work. And further, that I should tell him what it is I wished for. I almost kissed my teeth at her but knew better. My mother did not yet understand that I was a grown man and would have happily cuffed the back of my head. She told me to look deep in my soul and think of what it is I want, and then to tell the old man to pray for it. She said if what I asked for was for the greater good, I would see it come true. I could tell that this trip had been a complete waste of time and would actually make matters worse for me at work. When I return and tell them the old man is in fact very much alive, I will not only be seen as a thief, I would also be seen as a liar. Soon after, the third wife came to fetch me.

My father greeted me with a huge smile and a warm embrace. To my shock, I welled up. His scent, the comfort of that loving embrace. I composed myself as he guided me to a chair and fetched me a glass of water from his calabash. As I watched him through my stifled tears, I resolved to get a borehole for the village. It was time they evolved from this ancient technique of filtering water. But as the liquid hit my lips, that thought instantly dissipated. The water tasted of home.

I couldn't maintain eye contact with him. He remained open and warm. I realized that the feeling I had was shame. I had avoided my father when he stopped speaking, and I had distanced myself as his legend grew. People traveled from as far as Kenya to be granted audience with him. Men and women of influence would sit at his feet as he prayed for them. He never spoke and yet they always came.

Finally, I took my mother's advice. I looked at the floor as I spoke. He did the same. The few times I glanced at him I could see that he stared at the same spot I was staring at, a hole in his sheepskin carpet. It was worn and old, but I could still smell the animal. I let my father know about the investigation that was pending and the efforts that were being made to destroy me. I let him know what a hard and honest worker I was. That I was in charge of the vault and would sometimes wake up in a sweat, convinced I had left it open. I would go back to the bank in the middle of the night to double-check. I was now being accused of using that opportunity to steal. I reassured him that I had never forgotten what he had said to us as children: "If you didn't bring it, don't take it. If you didn't earn it, it is not yours." I told him I was afraid. I told him I had hoped to be promoted into a managerial position. That I wanted my share of the responsibility. This country would need people like me to see it through. I spoke my truth, and he listened.

When I stopped, after I was spent and had nothing else to add, we sat in silence. It was strangely comforting, and every time I looked over at him, I noticed that his eyes were closed. It was almost as if he was replaying the conversation to himself. Finally, he opened his eyes, leaned forward, and reached for my hand. He simply drew a line across my palm with his finger. Then he blew on my hand and rose. I instinctively rose with him. He embraced me and looked into my eyes. I could see reassurance. He then smiled and guided me out. He did not stop at his door but walked me through the house, right up to the threshold. Several people had arrived at the house and now filled the front room. Everyone that was present there, and outside in the compound, rose to their feet. He only focused on me. That was the last time I saw him alive, although it would be many years before he died.

When I returned to the capital, nothing changed, not at first. The odds were still firmly stacked against me. Then gradually the pendulum swung. Looking back, I was impatient to be out of the woods. However, the slow unraveling of the conspiracy against me, and the many sleepless nights it brought with it, were formative. I learnt many things about human nature that has held true to this day. In the end, I was made the first financial controller of the bank and the Director General was found to be involved in a plot to overthrow our early government. He would live in exile for twenty years. I see him at the mosque these days. Occasionally we acknowledge each other.

As for my father, I never gave another thought to our final meeting. That is until the day of his burial. What happened at the grave was the culmination of years of rumor and intrigue. Questions that date back thirty years. Back to the time he fell silent.

The rules of a funeral are simple. A person dies and is taken to Death House. Our village had grown into a thriving town in the years since my childhood and had its own Death House. There, experienced religious figures bathe the body, ensuring that all the last rites are performed. The cleansing bath and ablutions prepare the person for the day they meet Allah and answer for their life. After Death House, the body is brought to the mosque, where the community pays its last respects. Then the body is brought to the compound where everyone, particularly the women, lament. They are afforded this because no women are allowed at the burial. I found this archaic, but the day of my father's funeral was not the time to start my campaign against it.

The first incident that arose that day was at Death House. The men all claimed that they arrived and found my father had been washed, wrapped in a shroud, and that incense had been lit in the room. They all had wild tales of how they had lost their way to Death House when they all vied for the honor of giving the great man his last rites. The wildest of all being the story of the man who lived right next door. He claims to have stepped out of his house and directly into the middle of a field. He thankfully recognized the field and made his way back but arrived to find his fellow bathers standing agog, staring at my father as he lay cleansed and shrouded on the slab.

The mosque and compound went without incident. It was at the burial that matters took a turn. The cemetery is located by the forest. In the old days, people were buried closer to the town. Over the years, as the land was filled with the dead, we had arrived at the tree line. My father would be buried at what felt like a boundary between nature and humanity. And like everything in his life, that fact eventually became part of his legend.

There is no great ceremony at a burial. The body is brought in an open wooden coffin, often made of plywood. It is removed from the coffin and buried in its shroud. Before soil is thrown on the body, we say a final prayer. No speeches are made, and very few people cry.

Everything went smoothly until he was lowered into the ground. The moment he was laid on the soil, a group of men and women, all dressed in simple white robes, their heads covered so we could barely make out their faces, appeared at the tree line. We were all stunned at their sudden appearance. Nothing had given them away, not even the twigs and leaf litter that carpeted the forest floor. They were completely silent, and try as we might, none of them made any eye contact. They simply walked up to my father's grave and stood amongst us.

The arrival of women would have usually caused a commotion. And the men present were not reasonable men. They owned land and had influence. Any one of them could have quoted the hadith that advised against the presence of women at a burial and asked for them to leave. But not a single person protested or said a single word, for that matter. The group started praying for my father. Some of us were able to join them in prayer, but most stood mute. The prayers were heartfelt and deeply moving. They prayed and then helped us bury his body. During all this, none of us communicated with them. I had an overwhelming desire to speak, and yet I was completely unable to. Once they were done, they turned and left, disappearing amongst the trees. It was only then that any of us could speak. I knew this because I could feel it, and yet not one of us still found the need to utter a single word.

Later, I sat in the family compound, full of questions. I was not alone. The whole town was there, as well as many from much farther afield. The women asked questions of those at the burial, and many made attempts to recount the events that took place. Nothing any of them said, or that I say to you today, could do it justice. One thing I did notice, however, was that my mother—all of my father's wives, in fact—didn't ask a single question. That intrigued me.

That night, sleep evaded me. After many hours tossing and turning, I decided I'd give up the ghost. I found my mother in the living room. She looked at me as if she were seeing me for the first time. We sat and talked for a while. We even managed to laugh at a few stories from my childhood. Seeing as she was in such a great mood, I took a risk and asked her why she didn't ask any questions about the events at the burial. She grew distant and thoughtful. After a while, she rose and asked me to follow her.

She took me to my father's house and told me to wait. A few moments later, she returned with the other wives, and we sat in the front room. It was clear none of them had been asleep.

As I sat there, my mother convinced the other wives that it was time for the children to know my father's secret. And since I was the one that refused to believe, it was me that should be entrusted with it, to do with as I pleased. I was intrigued, but my overriding feeling was trepidation. There was something altogether too harmonious between these three rivals. A common ground that I had never known they had. The women agreed, and my mother spoke.

She started by asking me if I had ever wondered who or what was in that building on the compound. The building that was off limits and had been throughout my father's life.

I thought about it. Indeed, it was strange that up to this point I had simply taken that building at face value. It had been in the compound long before I was born and was still there today, and yet I had never questioned the fact that it was off limits. It just simply was.

My mother went on to add that my father stayed in that chamber every Thursday night and had done so for as long as any of them had known him. She added that after many years, they all wanted to know what was in that room and what my father did there on a Thursday night.

Their desire to know was sparked when the third wife had noticed my father leave the room one Thursday night with a bucket. Innocently, she had asked him what he was doing. He told her that he was fetching water from the well. Even I was shocked to hear that. My father never ever fetched water. With so many women and children in his care, why would he carry out a menial task like that? She said she had offered to fetch the water for him, and he had refused. As he left the compound, to her shock, she had noticed that the door to the secret room was open. Unable to resist, and knowing he would be away for a while, she sneaked in.

According to her, there was a woman in there, sitting on a bed with her exposed back to the door. Instinctively she retreated, aware that she had seen something she was not supposed to see. But a few steps from the door, she thought better of her retreat and decided to go back to ask this woman, who's back was exposed, what in the name of all marital promises she was doing in that room. But by the time she turned to the door, it was closed. She felt a deep unease but decided that it was best to tell the wives of my father's infidelity and discuss a way forward. They all agreed that my father would have to answer some questions.

The significance of the fact that he had repeated this behavior every Thursday was not lost on any of them. Thursday was the only night my father did not spend with one of them. My mother was his second wife, and her days were Tuesday and Wednesday. The third wife was on Friday and Saturday, and the eldest, and first wife, had Sunday and Monday. Those were the days that they would each get their turn to be with my father. They would be responsible for my father's care and would spend the night in his chambers. That the third wife had seen a woman in there meant that this woman was being afforded a wife's privilege—and from what they could see, none of the many burdens. It seemed she was so special that he was willing to fetch water for her.

They had initially confronted my father by asking him to reveal what he did in that room. He had simply stated that no one must ever go there. Ever. Usually, my father's words were final. But the three women would not be deterred. They each used their own personal brand of influence to test his resolve. The eldest wife knew he respected her the most, so she appealed to his honor as a family man and warned against the dangers of secrets in a large family. The third wife rested on his passion for her and burdened him with declarations of love and the threat of broken trust on that love. But my mother, always the most direct one, simply said that she suspected he was hiding a woman in there. They said my father fell silent, and they waited. Eventually he made a deal with them. They were to choose a single item, something that in some way belonged to all three of them, and they would place that item in the room on a Thursday night. He would not sleep in the room that night. In the morning, he would lead all three of them into the room and let them look. They agreed.

That Thursday night, the three wives had decided that the Baku, a large mortar and pestle, was the one thing that they felt belonged to all three of them. It had been carved out of a single piece of solid wood. It was heavy, indestructible, and was used by all three women to pound millet. It was the perfect thing. My father had led all three of them into the room, which to their surprise was completely empty. Not a stick of furniture. Not even a floor mat. They had placed the Baku in the middle of the room and then left. My father locked the door, and they all went to bed. In the middle of the night, they heard a single sound ring out. At this point in their story, they looked visibly shaken. The memory of that sound affected them. The first wife remarked that the one extraordinary thing about the sound was its hollowness. It was unbelievably loud and yet had the distinct timbre of a silent thud. It was simple and direct. I noticed in that moment that I was barely breathing as I listened.

At dawn my father opened the door and took them inside. To their horror, the Baku had been smashed into a thousand pieces. My mother described a dark halo right at the center, where the

Baku had stood. Around it, in perfect concentric circles, were the many tiny shards of wood. Even the pestle was gone. They said their minds raced as they tried to comprehend how a single blow could create what they witnessed. More than that, they could feel the rage in the room. They weren't the only ones. My mother said that as my father stood there, he closed his eyes and lowered his head. He stood in that silence for a long time, long enough that they left him in there. When he finally emerged, he looked troubled. My father had turned to the third wife and asked her directly if she had entered the room when he went to fetch water. The third wife said she opened her mouth, fully intending to lie, but the truth came out instead. My father had fallen silent. They were not sure if it was shame or choler. Eventually he told them the truth. The chamber did in fact belong to someone. And that she was his true first wife. But he added that she was no woman. She was a jinneh.

The word sent a chill down my spine. In religious folklore, the belief is that every living human is a twin. For every one of us born, a djinn—jinneh in the local language—is born behind the veil of this existence. Some djinns are interested in the lives of their human counterpart and will exert an influence on it. In extreme cases, your djinn may develop an infatuation for you and destroy any romantic relationships you form. At the other extreme, a djinn may have little to no interest in your life and will part ways with you at birth. I had heard many stories about the djinn and always subconsciously dismissed them as nonsense. And yet, the events at the burial that day left me wondering. The truth is that those visitors were not human. I knew it, and so did everyone there. They had a power that we could not comprehend, and as I sit here today, I can still feel that power at the mere memory. They were jinneh. Djinn. And they respected and loved my father enough to be at his funeral. Here, on our plane of existence.

Since then, I have had many theories about how my father got into his dealings with the djinn. The truth is that I will never know. I did, however, hear a theory on why he stopped speaking, one that fits with what I knew of him.

It was my mother's theory. When she finally reached her deathbed, she unburdened herself from years of thought. She told me that she could only speculate, but she believed that my father had stopped speaking to protect his family. After the incident in the secret room, he seemed troubled. He avoided the building for months and kept to himself. She believed that the djinns were unhappy with him. He didn't seem cowed but was deep in thought wherever she encountered him. Eventually he stopped talking altogether, and soon after was back to his full power. She had asked him countless questions, which he responded to with silence. But one thing she asked him garnered a look of mutual understanding. She had asked him if the djinn had threatened to take one of the children. The look he gave her confirmed her worst fears. Djinn were known to take children as atonement for the sins committed against them. She believed that my father had sinned against his djinn wife when he shared their secret. The only way to control a djinn is by words, but you are at their mercy should you make the wrong utterance. She believed with clarity, right at the end, that he had forgone all words so that he never mistakenly uttered anything that would risk the lives of one of his children.

I don't know why, but that theory has the ring of truth to me.

LITTLE ROOM, RED BUTTON

Nicholas Tecosky

Adapted from a screenplay by David Bruckner & Nicholas Tecosky

HE WAS TAKING a shower.

He was not prepared for the ground beneath him to disappear, for the world to go white and then black and then again the brightest white, so blinding that he could not see the ground as it rose violently to meet his face and naked form. The slick clap of his wet skin on the hard floor and the deafening crack inside his skull from his nose breaking and the vile nausea that accompanied caused his consciousness to waver, to wink, but his brain fought hard against it, and after a long moment, it stabilized.

He lay there, blind, taking stock of his body. He was shivering from the shock. He must have slipped. He slipped in the shower and fell and broke his nose, and now he was lying in his tub in agonizing pain. Where does it hurt? The face. Jesus, his face. He tried to exhale through his nose, and the air escaped in a pathetic whine through one nostril. He slowly raised his hand to it, expecting perhaps to find it caved in, mangled, perhaps flattened entirely. He was relieved at least to recognize it as a nose—pitched sharply left, gushing blood, but still more or less as he'd left it.

He opened his eyes. Nothing he saw was particularly comforting, none of it familiar. None of it even seemed to follow the basic rules of reality.

He was not in his tub. He didn't seem to be in his bathroom at *all,* in fact. And though the realization caused a wave of panic to pulsate outward from his stomach and into his chest and extremities, tingling his scalp, he told himself to be calm, and he almost was.

He blinked, tried to focus. The room was a slate-gray blur.

It was stark. Rectangular. Maybe twenty by thirty? The size of his classroom, but empty. In the walls were rows of inset bulbs, together casting a uniform white light. Each corner had a thin vent that ran from the floor up to the ceiling, which was fifteen or so feet high, covered in uniform square tiles. But no door, no windows. No egress at all, in fact.

He looked up. Nothing screamed trapdoor at him, though he supposed any one of the ceiling tiles could open. They provided more than enough space for a full-sized man to fall through. But...*why?*

And then his eyes landed on the pedestal in the center of the room. It was the same dull gray as the rest of the room. From his vantage point, he couldn't tell if there was anything on the top of it (a note, maybe), and so for the first time, he attempted to move. Groaning, he slowly sat up, his broken nose throbbing, dripping blood down his bare chest. He took a moment to breathe through the pain before slowly standing.

Atop the podium was a small red light—a button, which stared at him, unblinking. His fingers twitched. Itching to touch. Wondering how hard the button would have to be pressed, how it would feel. Would it be light, a click? Like the little remote that controlled slides in his lectures. Or perhaps like pressing hard on a brake, a resistance that would cause the muscles in his arm to flex as he compressed? His hand moved toward it as if some outside force drew it in. But he stopped short, thinking better of it.

It felt somehow *malevolent.* This glowing red button, on this pedestal in this room that he should not be in, wet and bloody and naked. Of all of the things wrong in this moment, the button disturbed him the most. Panic threatened again, so he breathed deeply. He needed to think clearly, to allow his brain to collect enough puzzle pieces to make a picture of his situation. *Think, dummy.* He wiped his wet hair out of his face, clipping his nose with the gesture, sending a fresh shock of pain through his body. It was finally enough to make him call out. He shouted a few meek "Hellos" at the ceiling, then paced around the room, inspecting the walls for some chink or hidden door. The ceiling tiles were uniformly blank and revealed nothing.

He stopped at a corner vent and pressed his ear against it. A very slight hum, a gentle breath of continuous air that caused his damp skin to contract, gooseflesh raising the ample hair on his arms, legs, chest. His scrotum tightened unpleasantly. Something about that finally caused him to scream.

The sound echoed around the room and was met with silence. He called out again, this time at the top of his lungs, directly into the vent. Maybe there was someone out there? Someone who could help? He listened for a reply, for anything, a rattle or footsteps through the ducts, but nothing came. Had he expected differently? He hadn't stumbled into this room by accident, he'd been *brought* here. By *someone*. Someone, he could only assume, with a plan. There was a reason he was here. They clearly wanted him trapped. They weren't answering or giving him any clues on *purpose*.

Unless...

He eyeballed the button again. It seemed to be his only option. He edged closer to the pedestal. Would pressing the button answer any of his questions?

Fuck it, he thought, and pushed the button.

Of course, he immediately regretted it.

THERESA SCREAMED AT the dry cleaner, the pathetic little lump of a man, the *worm*. *How the fuck do these people stay in business, treating regulars this way?* She hated the way he looked at her like a dumb fucking animal, dull eyes like a goddamn cow, not blinking, not giving any answers, just taking her in, her rage, this injustice, her loss. How could they lose a fucking blouse? It shouldn't have left the building unless Theresa was the one to take it away. Did he rip it? Stain it? Did *he* take it home? Was he covering for his simpering wife, that bitch? She always looked at Theresa like she was some loud fucking idiot. Of course she would destroy her favorite blouse out of spite. These people, these fucking people. So petty, so *jealous*. She pounded the counter again, demanding her blouse, demanding that someone be called to answer, her fist slamming the wood laminate over and over, and her voice rising to a scream. Rising as the counter, the racks, the stench of the fluids, those empty fucking eyes, all disappeared.

She was falling now, somersaulting, weightless, through the dark and into the light, unable to comprehend the ground as it came up to meet her, her knees buckling as her feet hit the floor, and the impact knocked the wind out of her, the scream dying in her throat. *That shit!* That little *shit* must've hit her, knocked her over. But how? He was clearly a brittle little fucker. How dare he? How *dare* he?

He grabbed her arm, tried to turn her over to face him.

Big mistake, she thought.

But when she rolled over, eyes blazing, she was shocked to see the man naked and bloodied. She gagged at the sight of his disgusting, shrunken member, hiding in a thicket of black pubic hair. She swore she could *smell* the animal musk of it, and this made her gag again. With all of the force she could muster, she struck out at the member, a meaty fist making hard contact with it, as she let loose a banshee shriek. The man collapsed backward onto the floor in a heap, and she took the opportunity to stand and make her escape. Her eyes darted around the alien space, uncomprehending. No door. Where's the goddamn door? Lighting on the pedestal. What is it? She moved toward it, the red button. What is this? This has to have the answer. This has to call someone—someone who can take care of this pervert. Without another thought, she mashed the button two, three times, before he stopped her.

AVI THOUGHT HE'D slipped in the kitchen and was too busy trying to keep the dish bin from hitting the floor to realize how long the fall actually was.

HARRY WAS SITTING, and then he wasn't. And then he was sitting again, in pain.

HANNAH WOKE FROM a dream of falling, and landed. People were screaming. She sat up painfully and turned to find a young man in a stained white shirt sprawled on the floor, covered in glass and food, looking at her, confounded. And then there was the woman—a large, frenetic woman, descending on him, screaming that the naked man had kidnapped her, that he was trying to kill her. *"Please help, please."* The bloody, naked man in question was hunched over another older man, who groaned and cursed on the ground. A plate was spinning next to him, and it seemed to be the only thing his mind could handle. He placed his hand on it gently, stopping it.

"Hey," Hannah said to the din. "Hey, listen." But the panic in the room was too intense, so she pulled herself up and took stock of the room. Gray walls, no door. A pedestal in the center of the room, a glowing red button atop it. She walked over to inspect the button, and the naked man took note immediately.

"Don't touch it!" he said urgently. Hannah turned to find him standing beside her, one hand held out to her, one covering his nakedness. "Please," he said. "Don't touch it. Every time you touch it, the tiles in the ceiling open up and someone gets dropped in."

The larger woman let out a barking laugh. A great, bitter laugh. Hannah turned to her. She stood next to the busboy—a beanpole, barely out of school, eyes wide as he took in the scene, fingers thoughtlessly picking glass off of his shirt. "*He* brought us here," the woman said. "This is some sick game. Look at him! He knew what he was doing when he brought me here. He's sick!"

"Lady," the naked man said, "I was in the goddamn shower, and then I was here. I don't know what this place is any more than you do."

But the woman laughed again, that pointed, joyless laugh. "Sure," she said. "Sure."

"Who are you people?" the busboy asked. "I have to get back to work." He bent down and began to pick up the shattered glass and broken stoneware around him, without any sort of urgency, shaking his head.

The naked man looked back down at the old man beneath him. "Are you hurt badly?" he asked.

"My ankle is broken," the old man said weakly. "I broke it before. It's broken now."

"I'm sorry," the naked man said. "I wish I could make you more comfortable."

"I'll be comfortable when I figure out what the hell it is I'm doing here," the old man said, and the naked guy laughed. Finally, there was a moment of calm.

"I'm Philip," the naked man said.

THE OLD MAN, whose name was Harry, was resting as comfortably as one could on the floor. They'd debated the floor over this last hour—the composition, how it may have been set or forged or carved. They'd debated the dimensions of the room, the purpose, the builders. The most heated debate was in regard to why they were there, but no one had a theory good enough to convince the others. They'd compared notes on their own lives—age, career, geography. Avi, the busboy, had a neon-pink paint marker on him. He would use it to write menu specials on sandwich boards—at his job but now he used it to take fastidious notes on everything the imprisoned group discussed. The notes soon covered the slate wall with facts and conjectures, with Harry once or twice remarking how good the young man's handwriting was. "Most kids," he noted, "don't write legibly anymore, which only goes to show the sorry state of education these days."

The whole time, Philip paced. Avi had given the man his apron to tie around his waist and cover his nakedness, but Hannah felt this made Philip's nakedness somehow more obscene. She was disgusted by the way his bare chest and ass hung out, blood streaking his body like some crazed butcher as he gesticulated and told Avi what to write.

And all the while, the other woman, Theresa, grew quiet. At first, she had argued. "*Somebody* brought us here. We just need to speak to whoever is in charge and tell them to fucking let us *go*. Just push the button, push the button. *Someone* will come. If not the people in charge, maybe someone who can come and *take* charge."

"That's what *we're* doing," Philip said as if speaking to a fussy child.

"What you're doing is *talking*," Theresa said. "Any fucking idiot can *talk*. We need *action*." She looked around at the others, at Hannah, and receiving nothing, crossed her arms tightly. "*Somebody* needs to take charge." After receiving no reply, she begrudgingly shut her mouth, merely grunting in disapproval as the conversation progressed without her. Eventually, she watched Philip in silence, her eyes two slivers of distrust, fists quietly opening and closing on her lap.

Hannah knew this type of silence. Her mother became this kind of quiet whenever she drank. There was no peace in this kind of quiet. It was a simmering, seething sort of silence, and one that would not last. There was order in the room for the moment, but there could be no lasting peace so long as Theresa seethed. It was only a matter of time until the fragile dam that was her patience broke and flooded the room once with her rage.

Without a sound, Theresa sprang from the floor and bolted toward the pedestal, hitting the button four more times before Philip tackled her to the ground.

LEIGH WAS CARRYING her groceries home, cursing the city for letting these sidewalks get so goddamned janky, when she tripped and fell…and fell…and fell.

LIU JING WAS writing an email to her father to ask about her mother's health, when she was pitched backward and thrown into bright light, somersaulting backward and landing painfully on her ass, knocking the wind out of her.

Dennis was watching *Jeopardy* and had been chuckling at how hapless the contestants seemed in the face of these simple questions about Shakespeare's plays, and he was shouting out "MacDuff! MacDuff, you idiot!" when the world began to spin.

OFFICER MICHAEL SHOUP was patrolling the subway. *Too many cops around,* he thought. *No one would dare jump a turnstile, let alone commit a crime.* So instead of policing, he was playing games on his phone, flinging little cartoon birds at little green pigs, when he was attacked. *Why wasn't I paying attention?* he thought as he toppled. As the light changed and the screams began in earnest around him. As he hit the ground and bounced, his hand found his sidearm and fumbled with the holster's snap. As the attacker was on him, over him, while he shouted for backup. As he pulled his gun from the holster and in a clean motion, practiced over years at the range, aimed it at his assailant and squeezed the trigger three times.

I WAS ONLY *trying to help,* Avi thought as the barrel of the gun swung up toward his face. And then he thought no more.

HANNAH WATCHED, FROZEN in shock, as Avi's skull opened, and a fine red mist exploded backward, out across the floor and against the wall with all of the neon-pink conjecture, which suddenly seemed ridiculous now that human brains had been splattered across it so haphazardly.

The cop was up now, wild-eyed, his gun sweeping the room. "Everyone get down!" he barked. "Get the fuck down! Hands where I can see them!" He used his radio to call for backup, but after getting no response, he barked more orders, though the others had already cowered, their hands up. They whimpered quietly, but showed no more resistance than a flower shows the wind. "Who fucking knocked me down? Who did it?" he shouted, but no one answered.

Theresa, under the weight of Philip, was the only other voice in the room, and she was screaming for help; and the cop, finding a way to be useful, moved toward them, yelling at Philip to get off of her; and Philip, clocking the precarious situation he was in, rolled off the woman and onto the floor on his back next to her, his hands up.

In this way, order was restored.

THERE WERE NINE now. Eight living, one dead. Poor Avi's corpse had been dragged to the corner, and his dish tray had been placed atop his head to cover his broken skull. Hannah had placed it there herself. In the privacy of her mind, she'd given him a short eulogy. *I only knew you a little,* she thought, *but you seemed like a nice kid, like you probably had a bunch of people who would mourn you properly. A mom who would weep, and a dad who would hold her. Friends who would get drunk after the funeral and end up on the swings at the playground, where you'd all smoke pot in high school—one of those rites of passage in suburbia. They'd cry about you that night, tell your favorite jokes to each other, tell silly Avi-stories, talk about what good a listener you were, and they'd carry your memory forward into their lives and think about you from time to time, what you'd be doing with your life, and the ache of your loss would never quite leave them. You'd be missed forever and ever, world without end, Amen, Amen. But here you were in this room, with these other people who did not know you, who were more concerned about their own sorry situation to think much of you at all. So it goes.*

Officer Shoup had been filled-in by this point, had secured the room and called for backup over and over, had tried his cell phone, had instructed the others to call out for help until they were hoarse, had ended up zip-tying Theresa in the corner when she tried to make another run at the button in the middle of the room. "No use causing more mayhem until we figure out our situation," he'd said. "Better to be safe than sorry."

Theresa, of course, had screamed herself hoarse in rage.

A woman—Leigh—had come through the hatch with groceries: eggs, which had broken, and milk and vegetables and apples and bread, and peanut butter for her kids, who were with her mom, thank God, while she had been at work. And so they had divvied up bread and apples and peanut butter, which they'd spread with a butter knife from poor Avi's bin. They ate joylessly, the peanut butter sticking to their dry mouths, little nibbles of apple the only thing allowing it to go down at all. They were no closer to a solution to their problem, though an intense series of arguments had rendered all further conversations stilted and awkward.

"We just need the right person to figure out the clue!"

"*What* clues?"

"I don't know, man. Maybe an architect or engineer could figure it out."

"The only way to figure out a pattern is to push the button a bunch of times. And that means more people."

"Maybe we'll get someone who understands?"

"Are *you* happy to be here? Aren't you pissed that someone pushed the button to get you here?"

The cop said "I know *I'm* not happy to be here." He eyeballed Theresa, who glared back, unfazed.

Harry finally verbalized it: "We have a moral obligation to not spread this further. We're all adults here. We know what this thing does. It doesn't solve our problems. It only makes them other peoples' problems, as well."

"The button is not the answer," Philip agreed.

Hannah glanced around the room at the captives, bruised and anxious and suspicious of one another. One woman couldn't speak English and was perhaps the most anxious of all, and anytime anyone addressed her, she nodded and smiled invitingly, but her eyes were desperate for understanding, and no one had any to spare. So she sat, as taut as a bear trap, ready to spring as soon as someone uttered the right syllables in her direction.

Philip paced compulsively in front of their neon-pink notes on the wall. He clutched Avi's marker and peppered the others with fresh questions, scribbling in great sweeping letters, and then pausing to consider them seriously. "THE BUTTON IS NOT THE ANSWER," he'd written in the center of it all, and had underlined it three times. A bloody, naked Sherlock, so sure that there was a solution to their predicament. He invited the others to brainstorm with him, occasionally having to point back to his central rule to remind them.

The others were game for a while. Look at the patterns of the tiles. It's a clock! What time was it when everyone fell in?"

"It's a puzzle box. Maybe we're pieces that need to be moved in certain ways?"

"Maybe the tiles have a pattern?"

"This is a waiting room."

"It's Hell."

With every theory was the belief that there was some concrete way out of all this if only they could just figure it out. With every silence, the counter argument sat there, waiting, atop the pedestal.

"How do we test these theories?"

"Well," Philip said, staring at the notes, "we've inspected every corner of the room. If the walls move, we're not strong enough to move them. But if it's a *clock*…the one thing we have plenty of at the moment is time."

"So, what? We wait?"

"What else is there to do?"

"I hate waiting," Leigh said. "It's torture."

"Maybe it *was* the CIA," said Shoup. No one knew if he was joking, so no one laughed.

IT WAS JING Siu who broke the hours-long silence by whispering quietly in Mandarin.

"What's she doing?" asked Leigh. The others turned to inspect.

"She's praying," said Harry. "I guess it can't hurt."

"This doesn't seem like a thing God would be much interested in," said Leigh.

"I don't know," said Officer Shoup. "Maybe this is *exactly* the sort of thing the Lord would be interested in. Think of Jesus in the desert."

"Job losing everything," Harry added.

"Maybe we're being tested," Shoup said. "Maybe we've been put here to see what we're made of. To see how we react."

"You really think praying is going to get us out of here?" Philip asked.

Shoup turned to him, fixing him in a hard stare. "Oh, I'm sorry, professor. I'd forgotten that you had this all figured out, and we were all on our fuckin' way out the door."

"Easy," said Philip. "You're right. We may as well consider it all."

With his eyes focused on Philip, Shoup said, "Let us pray." Philip did not argue.

When Shoup bowed his head, they all did the same. Hannah closed her eyes and listened. Shoup spoke the Lord's Prayer once, eyes tight, hands pressed together in a knot. It was a humble prayer, gentle. *Almost peaceful,* Hannah thought. When Shoup was done, he paused, then began the prayer again. A little more pointed the second time. He repeated the prayer a third time, then a fourth. Philip and Harry no longer kept their heads bowed, choosing instead to watch Shoup as his prayers became more fervent, more desperate. Jing Liu had paused, as well. And Leigh, who had lifted Theresa up from the floor so that she too could pray, cleared her throat, hoping perhaps to gently break the officer from his cycle before he spun himself out in frustration. But it did no good. Shoup began again, his teeth clenched, brows knit, his knuckles white. He was close to shouting now, shouting at God, terrified and angry. The others looked around at each other, wondering how to defuse the man.

It was Theresa who got him to stop.

"You're doing it wrong," she said plainly.

Shoup stopped mid-prayer, cut his eyes to her. There was a warning in them, but Theresa was not the type to heed warnings.

"The Lord helps those who help themselves," she said, freeing her hands. In one hand, she held a steak knife from Avi's bin. She dropped it on the floor and held her hands up.

"Don't listen to her," Philip said, but Shoup shushed him, and he listened.

"Well, go on," Shoup said to Theresa.

"God put a giant red button right there in the middle of the room, and you whiny assholes are sitting around and talking about what it all *means*. But it's right there, the answer. It's glowing, for Christ's sake. Like a beacon."

"Or a warning," Hannah said. "Flashing red lights usually mean danger."

Theresa chuckled. Her laugher dripped with contempt. "You're scared," she said. "You're all scared. And stupid. *Waiting* to be saved when you can just save *yourselves*." She turned to Officer Shoup. "You're a goddamned cop. Do you sit around and wait for a sign when shit goes down? Or do you take action?"

Finally, Shoup smiled. "You're right," he said and walked toward the button.

"Wait!" Hannah said, and Philip lunged forward to stop him.

Shoup paused just long enough to slap Philip's hand off his arm and clench him by the throat. "The next time you touch me or anyone else, I will fucking smash your face in. You hear me?" He pushed Philip away, and the naked man crumpled to the floor. He would be of no further use to anyone.

JOHN TURNER HAD been mowing the lawn.

ADEBAYO CLUTCHED THE cleaver tightly, hoping not to cut himself too deeply in the fall.

SARAH WAS JOGGING.

JERRY AND RICHARD and Madeline and June and Rose and Gabby and Marshall and Adil and Jorge and Fraser and Billy and Gordon and Malachi and Jade and Syed and David and Nicholas and Daniel and Zoe and Gareth and Elliot And Sahar and Leonard and Tim and Shelby and Mack and Heidi and Jon and Dani and Elliot and James and Rowan and Amanda and Annie and Vera and Walter and Holly and Aisha and Kelly and Lewis and Gus and Sumaiya and Madison and Colin and Isaac and Zane and Robert and Tara and Michael and Brent and Alexis and Judith and Milton and Marcus and Aaron and Nori and Ailis and Jonathon and Ashley and Jeremy and Samanth and Thomas and Jasper and…

HANNAH CLOSED HER eyes and breathed deep, centering herself. Meditation helped her feel alone in the crowded room, helped lower the noise to a quiet hum. The faint breath of air from the nearest vent tickled her neck, causing the small hairs there to raise gently, almost pleasantly. When she opened her eyes, she saw that the button still watched her intently from atop the pedestal. She smiled at it, knowingly, and turned away from it to sit on the floor. She would wait, she thought. She would sit quietly, all alone, and wait. And if she starved, and if she grew weak and ill with dehydration, if she ended up a wasted corpse on the floor, if she were never found, at least she would be able to say it was on her terms.

Perhaps that was the lesson, if a lesson was to be gleaned. She didn't know who had built this room. If they wanted her to know, they would have made themselves known, she reasoned. But she would have quiet before she went.

She would wait, she thought, and was still.

People were asphyxiating, legs and rib cages and skulls crushed under the increasing pressure, blood pouring forth from the eyes and noses and mouths, from punctured lungs and other injuries, and soon there would not be enough space in the room for a scream to escape. The sound was like the great dying breath of the earth itself.

As more people fell, and as the button was pressed and pressed again under the growing weight of these helpless bodies, Hannah watched. She watched as faceless strangers pulled other faceless strangers down into a world they did not ask for and of which they would never know.

CHERRY LANE

Nonie Shiverick

FROM HER VANTAGE point by the dock, Ruth watched as the battered Toyota nearly missed the driveway for a fourth time. The driver jerked the steering wheel, swerved, and almost bottomed out the car's undercarriage on a lurking boulder. There were six cabins on the compound, all for rent, and Ruth's favorite game was to take bets with herself on which guest was renting which cabin, judging solely by their cars. The big minivan full of screaming children? For sure headed up the main driveway to #5 Cherry Lane, the big cabin with the screened-in porch. The Volkswagen with the elderly couple and all the cameras and no less than four telescopic lenses were obviously headed to #2, the cabin on the water—lots of birds to see there.

But those guests didn't interest Ruth. In fact, she actively avoided them. She was only interested in the Toyota. She watched keenly as it stopped in front of #4, the miniscule cabin at the far end of the compound. It barely qualified as a shack and was Ruth's favorite. This was the only cabin that Tom, the landlord, hadn't bothered to outfit with modern trimmings yet. It was rustic, bordering on primitive, and extremely cheap to rent. Because of this, it attracted exactly the kind of guests that Ruth loved: lonely, broken people who carried more trauma and emotional baggage than actual luggage. They were the most fun to watch.

Her stomach growled loudly. She had dawdled too long watching the driveway and missed lunchtime. She hissed in annoyance, then focused her attention on the anxious-looking woman in the Toyota. The woman stared out the window in her direction, and Ruth slunk down to hide. The woman would never notice her if she kept still, but she didn't like to take chances, especially when a guest had just arrived. Ruth's stomach growled again, and she slipped away unseen.

FOR THE UMPTEENTH time that day, Melissa found herself wondering what the hell she was doing. She could write an entire novel on the events of the last forty-eight hours—a solace, perhaps—but solace did nothing to quiet the hissing snakes of dread that coiled inside her guts.

Congratulations, the snakes told her, *now you officially have no one.*

She cut the Toyota's engine, and the hardy little car answered with a concerning, rattling whine, courtesy of its ordeal with the driveway moments ago.

"You'll get over it," she said to the car, patting the steering wheel. Suddenly, a cramp in her lower abdomen wrenched, and sent her scrambling to the car's center console for Advil. She quickly located the bottle and popped four pills, disregarding the recommended dosage. She washed them down with warm gas station iced tea. "You will too," she said, patting her stomach. The snakes hissed mockingly at the pathetic attempt to soothe herself.

That's when she caught her reflection in the rear-view mirror. Her close-shorn hair—the result of a tequila-fueled evening spent binge-watching TikTok videos that proclaimed *"radical change starts with radical action"*—was greasy and sticking up at odd ends. Her oversized sunglasses hadn't been fashionable since at least 2007. Melissa had never been beautiful. Her mother had once gone so far as to call her homely, but now she looked… *like absolute ass.* She shrugged. *Oh well.*

Her phone blinked with a new notification: a news alert. Melissa stared straight ahead at the cabin, then out at the lake, then down at her clenched fists. The stupid phone kept blinking. Cell service had been spotty ever since she'd passed through the town, so the likelihood of the article even loading was slim, but still she found herself fighting the urge to look—willed herself not to.

What good will it do?

But her right hand ignored her, and, acting of its own treacherous volition, snatched the phone from the passenger seat and opened the news article.

"DETROIT WOMAN STILL MISSING."

Beneath the headline, an accompanying video showed a man, *the loving husband of the missing person*, giving an interview to the press, his mouth curling into the smile he used only in public. The video cut out just as he looked into the camera… at *her*. Melissa's shoulders tightened.

A knock at the window ripped her back to reality.

"Hellooooooo!" said a man's voice.

"Jesus, FUCK!" Melissa shouted, flailing in surprise, the phone flying from her hand and careening under the passenger seat.

"Sorry! Didn't mean to scare ya!"

Melissa turned to see a man's face hovering inches from her window, his smile disconcertingly genuine. He was portly and sported a big, bushy beard. "Glad ya found the place!" He nodded at her and retreated from the car, waiting.

She stared back at him, blankly. Her brain had flatlined at some point during the last five minutes, and the entire English language had drifted away somewhere unreachable.

"Tom?" she managed.

The man smiled again. "In the flesh."

After an embarrassing amount of time, it dawned on her that she was meant to get out of the car… if she could remember how that worked. *Unbuckle seat belt. Left hand opens door. One foot out, then the other.*

After she exited the car, Tom presented her with a rusted key that looked better suited for an abandoned toolshed than a residence. He caught sight of the bruises on her forearms and stared.

Melissa took the key and angrily yanked her bunched-up shirt sleeves back down to her wrists so as to shield her bruises from the man's curious looks.

He yammered incessantly as he led her to the cabin, chirping about "trails this" and "fishing that," as she attempted to coax her brain back online. He was halfway through a detailed explanation of something involving mousetraps in the kitchen, when she finally found the words to speak.

"I think I need to lie down."

He laughed, unoffended. "Of course. You're tired. One final thing before I leave ya: Don't go in the lake. It's just—" He paused to gaze out at the water, waiting, as if it might explain itself for him. "Boats are fine. Just don't go in to swim, ya know?" He nodded a goodbye and marched back across the compound.

Melissa regarded her new home. She'd paid for it months ago with the cash she'd been hoarding in an old dog food tin she'd buried behind the tomato plant in her backyard. Her *former* backyard. *Poor plant's probably dead by now*, she thought, before another violent cramp came over her. This one was accompanied by a disconcerting gushing feeling between her legs and the dark certainty that the absorbent underwear she was wearing—helpfully provided by the clinic staff that morning—was about to give up the ghost. She raced into the house.

AFTER CHANGING CLOTHES, Melissa stuffed a pad the size of Alaska into her underwear, microwaved some food she'd bought at the local gas station, and went outside to get some fresh air. She took a seat on the single plastic lawn chair that Tom had placed in the driveway as a sort of patio, and picked through the microwaved abomination from the gas station, the flavor of which could roughly be described as vaguely spiced canned dog food.

At least it's food. Sort of.

All things considered, the house wasn't so bad. Yes, she found mouse droppings in the cutlery drawer, and the oven was being used to store towels and other random shit, but all the other appliances seemed to function and the hot water in the bathroom and the kitchen worked. And if you opened enough windows, you could almost ignore the mold.

She shifted uncomfortably in the chair, the pad riding up her ass.

I'm also alone. So fucking alone.

"FUUUUUUUCK!" she shouted. Her voice echoed across the compound, causing birds to leave their trees and branches and take flight in the opposite direction. It was incredibly cathartic. She took a deep breath to do it again but remembered that there were other people around who would probably call the cops if she kept screaming "fuck" like an insane person.

One look at my ID and they'll take me back to—

She cut herself off before the panic could set in.

She looked out at the lake, the water there reflecting reds and oranges beneath the setting sun. A cold breeze blew off of it and caused her skin to prickle. The wind felt as though it were wrapping itself around her, breathing on her face and down her neck… But then it retreated to its former place.

"I'm alone, but I'm also alive," she told herself and the lake.

SNAP!

The sound had come from inside the cabin. There was silence, then a pained squeak. One of Tom's mousetraps had evidently deployed.

"Can't say the same for that guy," Melissa informed the lake, and headed inside to survey the damage.

THE METAL BAR of the trap had clamped firmly down on the mouse's back, but it failed to kill it. Instead, it had only done half its job, leaving Melissa to finish the rest. The mouse squirmed and squeaked in pain. She searched the drawers for a hammer, and after finding one, primed herself to deliver the killing blow. Her hand quaked. She'd never taken a life before—not until recently, at least—but that one was different. Her mother would have disagreed, and her father would have been horrified, and Lord help her if her husband found out, but Melissa hadn't asked them, didn't need their approval. Just like she didn't need the approval of the crowd outside the clinic, despite their loud protests telling her exactly how they felt about her..

Murdering whore!

She looked down at the mouse. *There is kindness in death,* she told herself, repeating the mantra in her mind.

"I'm sorry, little buddy," she said out loud, and brought the hammer down with a sickening *CRACK.* Corpse in one hand and hammer still in the other, she was out the door and almost to the dumpster before she had fully processed what she had done. It was the dumpster that brought her back to her senses. Not the awful smell, but the long, animal-like scratches down one side. Five scratches, all in a row, cut deep into the rusting metal. Melissa was familiar with the local wildlife. This area was not known to have bears or any other large predators capable of leaving marks like that. Her stomach churned, the snakes returning as she crouched down to study the damage.

There it was again: that feeling of breath on her neck; of something, someone, watching her.

If it's him—

She spun around, hammer raised. But there was no one, just empty woods and the lake, shining silver in the growing dark, pulling at her, drawing her in. She was about twenty feet down the path when she saw them: two lights, glowing green, hovering above the surface of the water. They reminded her of cats' eyes reflecting the dim light of a basement. The lights blinked, then vanished with a *SPLASH.*

The sun had set during her time with the mouse, and now in the darkness, she could barely make out the shapes in front of her, but still, something on the shoreline caught her attention. It was hard to make out from this distance, but it appeared to be lumpy. Gripping the hammer tighter, she crept down the path to investigate. Upon approach, she could see now that the lumpy mass was the body of a dead buck. The antlers were what first gave it away since there wasn't much else left. The body lay half in the water, ribcage exposed, butchered by something massive, fueled by savagery and rage. She could feel eyes on her again, but she was not brave enough to look around. Instead, she shot back up the path, threw the mouse at the dumpster, and ran inside the cabin, making sure to lock and bolt the door behind her.

IN HER DREAMS, Melissa ran. And his voice followed her.

I'll find you; I'll find you, it said.

After running for what felt like forever, she woke with a start, rolled over, and pled with herself to stay awake until dawn. But in defiance, her subconscious dropped her into a new nightmare. *Running. Hiding. Escaping. Through a city, the woods, a cornfield, around her house.* It always ended the same way: with him finding her. He'd yank open the closet door where she was cowering, or pull her out from her hiding spot beneath the bed, or bust through her car window while she was locked alone inside.

I told you I'd find you, he'd whisper.

And in reply, she'd sob helplessly.

THE DAYS THAT followed bled into one another. She couldn't bring herself to go into town—not yet. She wasn't ready to reconnect with the outside world, hear what they had to say. So instead, she stayed locked away in her cabin, seized by a constant state of hypervigilance. Anxiety-naps served to break the monotony but also gave rise to more nightmares. She was lying on the couch one afternoon, staring at nothing in particular, when she was forced to admit to herself that she would need to find a way to move forward, or everything she had done for herself would be for nothing.

You can't go on like this, she told herself. *This is not living.*

She kicked her feet up into the air in frustration and let them flop lazily back onto the couch.

Go do a normal-person activity, she told herself firmly. *You might start to feel like a normal person.*

It had been days since she'd showered, so she opted to try that first. The water was blissfully hot, but the opaque shower curtain blocked her view of the door, and every noise sounded like *him.* After ripping the shower curtain open at every little noise, she was left drained and exhausted. Eventually, a panic attack had her sobbing on her knees. Wet, naked, and exhausted, she crawled from the shower to the bed and burrowed beneath the covers. She told herself that she'd do better tomorrow.

THE NEXT MORNING, she found inspiration in Tom's self-published guide to the region's hiking options. Fresh air would make her feel better, as would wearing something besides pajamas and granny panties. She opted for a trail that ended at the water. The guide promised winding, shaded paths, and after a short hike through some switchbacks, a panoramic view of the lake. The air was clean and cold and full of pine. Medicinal, almost. The lake was flat enough to reflect the surrounding trees and hills so perfectly, it was almost impossible to tell which way was up and which was down. A few boats dotted the lake, rendering the scene like something out of one of those paintings in a fancy art gallery.

There was a curious disturbance in the water near the shoreline where she walked, and while she had initially chalked it up to a fish or amphibian of some sort, she later realized that the disturbance was far too large for such things. As the path wound back toward the water once more, she found that the disturbance was back, this time right in front of her.

Melissa thought back to the buck, to the unknown *thing* that had obviously pulled it into the water and dispatched it so brutally. She almost turned back, but something within her—some dormant desire for danger—stopped her.

No, the voice inside her said. *You're done with fear.*

She stepped off the trail, then clamored over the brush and rocks on her way down to the water's edge. The water was as clear as glass in the shallows, and she could see right down to the bottom until about ten feet out, where the shallows dropped sharply into the deep. A few feet in front of her, a large boulder jutted out of the water, making for a good place to stand. She could make it with a good jump. She wondered briefly if this was technically against Tom's rule of getting in the water, but if people were allowed on boats, she should be allowed out on a rock, she reasoned. She jumped, landed, windmilled her arms frantically to not lose her balance and fall in, then steadied herself. With hands triumphantly on hips, she surveyed the lake from her new perch, the water's surface mere inches from her feet. From atop the rock, she could better see where the lake's floor dropped from the shallows into nothingness, like a black hole had taken residence there. She crouched down and leaned out over the water, staring into the abyss, hair rising on the back of her neck. The feeling of being watched returned. Something down in the depths was looking up at her, she was sure of it. She could see a shadow shifting, sunlight reflecting off something beneath the surface, something big with iridescent scales that was moving at great speed toward her. Its eyes were black and its teeth sharp and serrated.

Startled, Melissa slipped on the rock and tumbled into the water. She tried to scream, but the icy water choked her, turning her screams into gasping croaks. After flailing for a bit, her muscles went limp, and she sank like a stone. Her final thought as the darkness took her was, *Oh my God, I'm going to die down here with that thing—*

That's when someone grabbed her around the waist and pulled, raking her through the shallows. Her rescuer, whoever they were, then deposited her roughly onto the shore and pounded her between the shoulder blades with incredible force. Water shot out of her lungs, and she gasped and hacked, her air returning painfully.

After regaining her faculties, she looked up at her savior. She expected to see a monster looming over her, preparing to devour her, or more likely, Tom. But instead, she found herself staring at an older woman. Perplexed, she rolled over to get a better view. The woman was tall and slender, and her long gray hair was pulled back tightly into a ponytail. She was soaked head to toe and held a walking stick. Melissa gaped at her, and the woman scowled menacingly in reply.

"Uh, hello." Melissa said to her.

"You wanna get hypothermia? Cuz that's how ya get hypo-thermia!" The woman gesticulated at the lake to emphasize her point.

Melissa stared dumbly out at the water, gears slowly clicking into place. "So, that's why he said not to go in." Suddenly, she felt incredibly stupid. "I sort of assumed there was sewage or something." Her teeth were chattering so badly, she sounded intoxicated.

The woman jabbed a finger at a passing fishing boat. "Would folks be fishing if that were the case?"

Melissa shrugged. The hell did she know about fishing? "Or I guess I thought, maybe, there were… things… living in it. *Dangerous* things." The second it left her mouth, she regretted it. *Clown shoes, Mel. Way to go.* "Forget I said that. Just me being paranoid."

The woman threw her head back and laughed. She wiped water off her face and regarded Melissa with amusement. "Yeah, we got ourselves a regular Nessie. Get in the water, and she'll chomp your toes."

Melissa looked away, embarrassed.

"You staying in one of them cabins up there?"

She nodded.

"Tom the one who told you not to go in the lake?"

"Yes. He was kind of vague—"

"Ha! Well, that's Tom for ya. Always looking out." The woman extended her hand down to help Melissa up. As she did, she glanced at Melissa's arm, where the sleeve had rolled up. The bruises had faded to green. Melissa yanked the sleeve down.

"Thanks for saving me." Melissa cut in before the woman could say anything. "Anyways, I'm fine now." A breeze carrying the chill of autumn blew past them, and Melissa violently shivered, her legs threatening to quit. The woman grabbed her shoulder, steadying her in an iron grip. She didn't seem to register the cold. *They really make these local women different.* "Suppose I'll go take a hot shower—"

"That's a good idea."

"See you around." Melissa fled up the path.

"Hey!"

Melissa turned, praying she wouldn't have to field any personal questions.

"I'm Ruth. In case you want to give me a holler before jumping in next time."

"Melissa. Nice to meet you."

Ruth turned and headed the other way up the path, rounding the corner out of sight before Melissa could say anything else. She was remarkably quick for her age.

WITH THE CURTAIN held open and towels on the floor to soak up the water, the shower was a considerably less traumatizing ordeal. Melissa's mind kept wandering back to the thing she saw in the water, with its scales and dark eyes and clawed hand reaching toward her. No. There was no monster in the water. "Monsters don't exist," she said out loud. Still, in some dark crevice at the back of her mind, a voice whispered to her the truth: She saw what she saw.

As she mulled this over, she scrubbed at the marks on her arms and back. She resented her vulnerable nature, her ability to feel pain. She imagined how different her life would be if she hadn't been burdened by such weakness. She dug her fingernails into her bruised flesh and clawed it from bone. Beneath the flesh were shining scales like armor that couldn't even feel cold, let alone pain. Her fingernails extended into long claws that could rip the fake smile off someone's face. Her legs fused into a powerful tail. Her lips bared a snarl, revealing the sharpest of teeth. She was strong, magnificent, *terrifying*. She hissed menacingly. Then she laughed. It was a very silly fantasy, of course, ridiculous and impossible. But then, she had already done something impossible, hadn't she? She raised her pretend claws again and hissed at herself in the mirror, before descending into giggles. She would go into town today. She was ready.

SHE HAD COAXED the Toyota back to life and was nearly in town when her phone started dinging and beeping and buzzing and making every kind of racket a phone could make. She wanted to ignore it, and she really tried. But the notifications crawled under her skin and festered there until finally, she wrenched the long-suffering car onto the shoulder and opened the needy device.

To her horror, her story had made national news. Beneath the headlines, breaking stories reported on where her cell phone had last pinged. A photo of her with hair long and no black eye accompanied the reports. She was relieved in this moment to have purchased a burner phone back in Indiana. There were endless social media threads and comment sections debating whether or not she was alive and what she was doing. Everyone had opinions, and Melissa hated most of them. After several minutes of scrolling, she came across a comment far worse than some dipshit's ignorant feelings about her.

"Cops taking too long. I'll find her myself."

It was the last post from an account belonging to…*her husband. Jeff.*

"Fuck." Melissa swung her car into a U-turn and raced back to the cabin at twice the legal speed limit. When she got there, she backed into the driveway and left the car running.

THE FRONT DOOR was open, but while standing on the front steps, every instinct told Melissa to flee, to run to the car and find some other hole to hide in, somewhere even farther away. But a place deep inside of her—maybe the same part that told her the creature in the water was real—told her that running would not end things. *He'll find you there too*, it said, and she knew that it was right. She crept inside.

"There you are," Jeff said from his seat upon the couch. "Browser history, Mel."

She stood in the doorway, unable to speak, silently cursing her error.

"What the fuck were you thinking?"

She searched herself but found no words, no course of action. She thought bitterly of her imagined claws and scales, lamented their absence. Tears welled in her eyes. She knew she couldn't fight him without help. She also knew that her silence was annoying him, but she couldn't speak, or move, or do anything. Like a frightened, useless little animal, she froze. She stood still as he stormed across the room, cringed when he grabbed her arm so tight she was certain he was going to rip it off. She winced and apologized while he screamed into her face. If Melissa had believed God cared about her, she supposed she might have prayed in that moment, but when Jeff's fist crashed into her face with such force she saw stars, she merely hoped it would be over quickly. Submission would save her, just like it had in the past. This, she knew. But once again, her right hand had its own ideas. Without Melissa's consent, it grabbed a cutting board off the counter and brought it down over her husband's head with alarming force. He staggered backwards, tripped, and fell with a *CRASH*. She stood over him in shock.

"You BITCH!" He groaned and rolled over, pulling his hands underneath him. He was getting ready to stand back up, and she knew it would be bad for her when he did.

She looked down at her right hand, but when it did not explain itself or offer further support, she fled the cabin.

THERE IS KINDNESS in death. But kindness to whom?

Melissa ran down the path toward the lake. She could hear Jeff on the path behind her, cursing her existence and screaming that he would end her life. Her legs and lungs ached, and her head was still fuzzy after the blow to her face, but she pushed herself to go faster.

There is kindness in death, she thought, and she wondered if the universe was feeling particularly kind tonight.

She had nearly reached the dock when he slammed into her from behind, snapping her collarbone with a nauseating *CRACK* that echoed across the lake. The pain made breathing nearly impossible, but she kicked away from him and wormed her way toward the water, the steady decline of the shore aiding her. The icy water sent needles into her skin, but she pushed farther in. He crawled after her, snarling at what a useless little bitch she was, but she ignored him. It didn't matter anymore. He grabbed her by the throat and slammed her head back into the rocks, forcing her to look up and meet his eyes, to see his face twisted by hate and rage.

"They're not going to miss you," he promised and leaned his full weight onto her throat.

Until recently, Melissa had never stood up for herself, fought back, or broken a rule. She'd never fought for anything. Until recently, it never would have occurred to her to buy a burner cell, or to climb out of a back window at 3:00 a.m., so the neighbor's dog wouldn't bark. She would never have made it past the gauntlet outside the clinic, and she definitely wouldn't have made it here. Melissa wasn't certain of the person she was now, but as she looked up at her husband, she knew she didn't want to die. Not like this.

So she fought. And when he tightened his hands around her throat, she brought her knee up into his nuts and spat in his face. When he shoved her head down into the icy lake so that water filled her lungs when she screamed, she raked her nails across his eyes. She thrashed her legs, snapped her teeth, dug her fingernails in. And when her vision exploded with the light of a billion stars, she fought so desperately that she didn't even notice when he was no longer above her. She could hear him, *somewhere*, thrashing violently, his screams turning into animal wailing and then silence, but she let the sounds wash over her—they were as unimportant as distant horns on the highway. While fighting to keep her head above water, every breath felt like a renewal, a rebirth. Old Melissa allowed herself to die. New Melissa would not.

RUTH WATCHED THE rescue team pull what was left of the body from the water. It was barely recognizable as human. Of course, they had fancy technology now, so he would be identified eventually. The police would come and question everyone in the surrounding area. Most knew nothing, and those that did would never say. The matter would forever remain a mystery.

Had Ruth been in a chaotic mood that morning, she may have waved to the officers on duty. But instead, she turned away to better admire how the rising sun colored the stones on the lake's floor dazzling golds and greens. She moved slowly now. She would have to skip breakfast. Last night's dinner had been much too indulgent for someone her age.

THE COURIER

Peter Cilella

THE JOB WAS simple enough: Pick people up in the middle of nowhere and bring them back to a rendezvous point.

Deb could handle that. She had returned from two tours in Afghanistan with all her limbs intact and could still hear out of one ear. Her nightmares were now once a month instead of every night. She felt more hope now that she had an envelope filled with a thousand dollars sitting on the passenger seat of her black Ford Ranger and didn't have to scrub toilets in the evening at a shitty roadside motel.

She didn't know who these people were or where she was taking them, but she didn't care. She figured it was a military operation. *Don't ask questions,* they told her. *Just pick them up. Drop them off. All cash. No taxes.* It was the least they could do. They wouldn't cover her therapy bills after returning because some number-crunching bureaucratic asshat in Washington determined no definitive link between her very combat-specific suicide bomber nightmares and her PTSD.

Fuck them. I'll take all their goddamn money.

She turned up the volume and drove faster. The factory speakers rattled outlaw country. Redneck poetry—a song about cocaine and dry humping. It sounded like a fine symphony to her one good ear.

The road was empty. It felt like the entire county was asleep. No moonlight. No artificial light. The stretch between Columbia and Myrtle Beach was ninety percent forest. Nights as dark as squid ink made her job easier. Usually, a bright light flashed briefly in the area where she would find her passenger. She had questions.

Just pick them up. Drop them off. Don't ask questions.

"OR ELSE, WHAT?" she had asked the man in the khaki pants and the bad government haircut, his features shadowed by a single overhead fluorescent light.

She did not like the cut of his jib. She had been introduced to him by a Marine pal who helped vets like Deb get work after they served, gigs that paid better than scrubbing toilets.

"Let's not let it get to that." He let that hang in the air for a long, uncomfortable moment and stared at her as if trying to read her mind. It was invasive, and Deb didn't care for it, but she wasn't easily flustered.

"What if—"

The man in the khaki pants slid an envelope across the table to her. He waited and watched her. Long, uncomfortable moments were his favorite kind of moments—the sort of fella who thrives in awkward space.

She fidgeted with the car keys in her pocket. "Do you want me to say something? I feel like you want me to say something."

"Are you in?"

SHE CHECKED THE nav on her phone—not far from the pin drop. A private number would text her a location pin in the morning, and before she could even have her first sip of coffee and a bowel movement, there'd be an envelope with ten one-hundred-dollar bills in her mailbox. The bills were so crisp you'd think they were fake. Michael sure thought they were, but what the hell did he know?

He was sweet and kinda slow. Just like Deb, he grew up on the outskirts of Bishopville, and just like Deb, he enlisted right out of high school.

She had known Michael since he was a baby. His dad and Deb's dad had been fishing buddies since they were old enough to ride bikes to the river. Michael was seven years younger than Deb, and she was his go-to babysitter by the time she was twelve. Deb had no siblings, and Michael was the sweet yet oft-directionless little brother she never had.

When he came back from Afghanistan, Deb resumed the role of babysitter. Sure, he lived on his own. Sure, he was a grown-ass man. But he seemed, in some ways, less capable than the boy she once knew. She checked in on him. Brought him homemade fried chicken just like he liked it: twenty-four-hour buttermilk brine. Drove him to doctor appointments whenever she could convince him to go. He never talked about his service. The things he saw. The things he did. But he was different. Vacant. There were stretches of time when he would stare off into the distance like he was looking for something.

And then, about five months ago, he vanished.

DEB TURNED ONTO a dirt road and slowed to a stop. She lowered the volume on the radio and then reached over and opened the glove box. She stretched for a Ruger ES9s in a holster and swapped it out with the cash envelope. She liked the Ruger.

It was light and compact, and the edges never snagged on the holster. Deb had completed dozens of pickups in the year since meeting the man in the khakis with the bad government haircut, and she never needed to use it, but she knew that the day she didn't have it would be the day she needed it.

Every passenger was heavily sedated, nonsensical. If they could talk, they mostly drooled when they opened their mouths, and generally, they were too debilitated to pose a threat. They were always thirsty. She had so many questions.

Just pick them up. Drop them off. Don't ask questions.

A bright light flashed in the woods ahead. It was time. She slipped on her holster and walked. She liked this part. It reminded her of early morning hunts as a kid with her dad. He would slip into her room at four a.m. on a Sunday and gently squeeze her shoulder. She hated it at first—no twelve-year-old wants to wake up that early on a Sunday—but the smell of bacon and coffee wafting from the kitchen made that first step out from beneath the warmth of her blanket palatable. It beat the hell out of sitting in a church pew for an hour, wondering if she would spend eternity in the good place or the bad place. She certainly didn't want to end up in the bad place, but the idea of forever anywhere, no matter how good, made her physically uncomfortable. Maybe you just die and that's it. Blackness. That scared the shit out of her, too.

She didn't want to think about any of that, and she didn't have to in the woods. This was her church.

She looked down at her phone. She was almost at the pin when she heard it. A low moan. She quickened her pace. On the off-chance there was a camper or a grifter in the area, she needed to be the one to make first contact.

She could still see a faint glow as she approached a clearing. Her phone told her she was close. The glow vanished like a snuffed candle. She reached for her flashlight and turned it on. It was the only light for miles. She heard the sound again. It was different this time. The pitch of the moan was higher, almost like a low sob. Deb stopped to listen. Silence. She scanned the woods with her flashlight. A raccoon sprinted by. She jumped.

"Shit," she muttered to herself. She wasn't the jumpy type. She took a breath and continued. Her heart thumped hard in her chest. She hated herself for that. These pickups were unsettling, but she was never flustered. She was unflappable.

Not tonight.

She walked farther, flashlight continuously scanning the dense woods. More sounds: heavy wheezing… scratching… flesh scraping against the bark of a tree… a loud groan.

She tilted her light up a tree, and there he was, ten feet off the ground.

Michael.

He looked older now, as if five months had been twenty years, but in the bright beam of Deb's flashlight, she still saw that seven-year-old boy perched in a tree, blood and tree bark stuck to his shoulder. A scared little boy trapped in the body of a withered man.

In his hand was a bloody piece of metal. He opened his fingers and let it drop. She watched it fall to the ground.

"Michael?" Her voice sounded familiar to him, but he couldn't place it. She turned the light on her own face. He exhaled for what felt like the first time in hours.

"Help me. Please," Michael begged.

DEB DROVE. THE morning orange sky emerged behind them. No music on the radio this time. Michael was in and out of consciousness, his head bobbing against the passenger-side window. Her phone buzzed—a private caller. She looked at Michael and then back at her phone. It buzzed and buzzed and buzzed again.

She rolled down the window and tossed it onto the road.

She accelerated and turned the volume up on the radio. Outlaw country pumping from factory speakers sounded like a fine symphony to her one good ear.

Deb wanted answers.

THE METHOD

Alex Chew

EVERYTHING INSIDE ME screamed TURN AROUND, but I was used to ignoring my body. Last year, I braved the 20/4 diet. Twenty hours of fasting, four hours of shoving Cool Ranch Doritos and Ale 8 One soda down my throat. Out of everyone in my acting class encouraged to slim down, I was the only one who surpassed my goal weight. My rotting teeth and newfound rib cage even led to me being cast as Enslaved Woman #4 in a failed production of *Roots: The Musical!* Then there was that time in LA when I auditioned for a fast-rising screenwriter in his bathroom because he liked to consume actors the way he consumed all media: sitting on his porcelain throne, crouched over a tablet, squeezing out a fart. I didn't get the part, but I proved to myself how dedicated I was to my career. So when I heard that Broadway's most reclusive and exclusive financier—Pony Goldwyn—frequented a certain upscale Midtown bar with the intent of casting The Pony Goldwyn Theater Company's next rising star, I considered it my job to make an appearance.

Every Thursday after dark, I perched my bony ass on a chic wool stool at The Grand Parlor bar and waited. It's forty-two dollars plus tax and tip for a Wagyu burger salad, but I heard Tennessee Williams threw up here once, so I knew this joint was classy. The bartender and I used to study at the Bronx Experimental Puppet Studio together, so he was kind enough to serve me complimentary lemon water in a martini glass. I dined on free pistachios and pretended to annotate a collection of August Wilson essays while surveying the ballroom across from me. It was the land of pink ivory columns, Art Deco wallpaper, and vape pens encased in gold. Every dining table boasted either an artist with a dream or an investor with a kink. They nibbled on tortured goose livers and live baby octopi, all while a pianist tinkled in swing time like the Gilded Age never ended.

An old scene partner who has a cousin who dated a very high-profile agent told me that Pony Goldwyn despises traditional casting calls. He prefers to discover talent and personally invite fresh finds to audition at a secret stage. This felt like the place. I could feel someone's eyes searing into the open back of my secondhand Dur Doux dress and fought the urge to turn around and declare, "I'm poor. I'm Black. I used to be ugly. But dear God I'm here!" when—

"KA-KAA!" a screaming cardinal swooped down from the gaslit chandelier over my head, its feathers nicking my nose on its way past the bar. The last remaining starlets—my competition—scattered like insects. Cowards. Everyone's eyes swung to the back of my gold gown. Finally, I had an audience. The bird was watching too. My heart fluttered with every maniacal squawk and flap of the red beast's wings, but as the sole girl from a brood of six brothers growing up in the limestone hills of Central Kentucky, I was used to showing no fear. The only terror that persisted deep in my stomach was that attic scene from Hitchcock's starkest nightmare, *The Birds*. No clue why, but I hated my state bird more than most and had not seen one since buying a one-way ticket to 42nd Street. Maybe it was stalking me. Yet even while my knees knocked under the bar counter, my upper half stayed in character. After years of being unchosen and unlucky, I could finally feel fate approaching.

Custom-tailored Oxfords tapped on the vinyl floor toward me with a slow, confident stride. "I was looking for a woman who doesn't scare easy." His voice sounded expensive.

I grinned with both dimples as his snakeskin suit coiled up next to my seat. His slanted cobalt eyes danced to the pulse of a jazz quartet firing up behind us. White hair. Whiter skin. Pony Goldwyn had not one wrinkle in sight. If it even was him. No one knew what the benefactors of Broadway looked like until they rescued you from obscurity.

"Three questions." His eyes skimmed over my décolletage. I folded my arms over my cleavage as politely as possible. For once, my Foxy Brown breasts were both a curse and blessing.

"Go ahead." I glanced up at the chandelier, which was empty.

"Are you an actress?" That was usually men's way of declaring me beautiful, so I played my part and pretended to be offended. "I don't mean it in a bad way. We're not in LA for Christ's sake. You have the glow of a stage." His hand playfully stroked my arm, grazing the side of my chest on its way back to his lap. Something inside shrieked: TURN AROUND. TURN AROUND AND GO HOME! Apt advice. Except my studio apartment was a storage closet with no heat.

"Yes, I'm an actress. My name's Ketty Kay King."

Pony grabbed someone else's French 75 off a passing server's tray. "Ketty, are you familiar with…Hamlet and Ophelia?"

That crazy bitch who couldn't bear being dumped by the Prince of Denmark? "Ophelia's the soul of the show," I replied.

His ocean blue eyes sparkled as he sipped someone else's champagne. "You're gooood. So… Care to learn the divine secrets of The Method actor?"

Lord William Shakespeare. Sir William Smith. Queen Viola Davis. These were the masters of thespianship I could get behind. Method actors, on the other hand, were a pill I'd never prescribe. Tormenting your fellow artists, only answering to "Ophelia," and trying to access adolescent *trauma* in order to produce a few tears sounded even more pretentious than my shoes, which were a dead ringer for Louboutins after I painted the red bottoms myself. I could already cry on command, dance like a Rockette, and sing like a Dreamgirl. I had zero desire to engage in improv therapy. However, I had never seen my name at the top of a Pony Goldwyn playbill.

And I had bills to pay.

"Absolutely I want to learn," was the only answer. "In that case, I'm Pony Goldwyn. Follow me."

PONY STOOD FIVE feet tall, neatly placed my hand inside of his arm, and escorted me away from the bar. As we glided through the million-dollar dining hall, heads turned. Impressed murmurs mixed with the music. Medium rare steaks and caviar were abundant here, but formerly blue-collar broads like me—we were extra bloody rare.

My new companion led me out of the warm pendant lights into a dark cool corridor with scarlet walls. In the hallway that never seemed to end, we connected.

"Before we dig into *the secret*, tell me about Ketty Kay King. I've never met a Black woman from Kentucky with those initials!" He giggled like a rattlesnake poking out the tip of his tongue, spitting out a lispy *sssssss*.

"Sorry, I don't remember saying I was from Kentucky."

"I have an ear for accents." He winked.

Dammit. Miss Kimmel, my favorite drama teacher who first instructed me in iambic pentameter, was a hillbilly from East Appalachia. Imagine repeating *"Suuuch stuffs es drayyyms err made ohhhn"* ten thousand times. Some tragedies can't be undone.

"You're good," I affirmed Pony. "Yes, my Christian name was Kathy, but my dad was a tobacco farmer who hollered 'Keeeetttty!' whenever he called on me for help with women's work inside the house. I realized seeing KKK on a marquee might entice the wrong crowd, but the joke would be on them. Because I don't accept refunds."

"You're bad!" Pony chuckled, clutching my arm tighter.

This hall must have been off limits even to staff, because not another soul passed us on the way to our final destination. As one passageway twisted and turned into another, we shared childhood memories and first loves. Pony's first was a boy named Andre, a magazine editor who introduced him to silk floral capes and Studio 54. Mine was a neighborhood pack leader we called Lefty Lee.

"You could say Lefty Lee was the Hamlet-type. The, uhh, Crown Prince of Mount Silver. Yes, all my brothers wanted to be like Lefty. And all the girls wanted their first kiss to be with Lefty. He had these Barbie-pink lips and light green cat eyes. Along with a birthmark shaped like a tiger tail on his left cheek. 'Course Lefty barely made eye contact with me by the time we got to high school. He ended up as Prom King, and I…was there too."

As we mazed into a dead end, I clocked the giant wall ahead of us but kept showing off my bleached teeth. No fear.

"You are just an all-American girl! Tell me: What's the worst thing that ever happened to you?"

TURN AROUND. DON'T DROWN. TURN AROUND. RIGHT NOW!

"I…was raised not to complain. And we were so blessed. Really."

Pony feigned half a smile and slowed to a halt. We gaped up at a tan textured wall as tall as New York City, splashed with cave-like paintings that seemed to have existed before Manhattan was an island, before America was even an idea. My shoulders tensed at the sight.

"Is that….me?

She sure looked like me. A primitive sketch of preteen Ketty Kay King stuck inside of a black triangle, holding her knees up to her chest and staring up to heaven only to find, instead of God and sky, legions of crudely drawn hands without arms. Were they clapping or praying?

"Oh no, honey. That's a Basquiat," he assured me. "Beautiful, isn't it?"

It was. Except for the red river swimming beneath the poor girl. I prayed it wasn't blood. My fingers reached out to inspect, but Pony's smooth, manicured hands landed first. With one swift push, the cave wall gave. Ahead of us was pitch black. Pony waited for me to enter the void first.

As I contemplated running, the band played "Someone to Watch Over Me," and I knew that I was the little lamb they were singing about. Perhaps Pony would be my shepherd.

"Come on down, Ketty." Pony's voice drifted from inside the infinite pit of darkness, though I hadn't seen him move past me.

"*I shall obey, my Lord!*" Ophelia's words leapt out from me before I could stop them.

Pony's footsteps proceeded down a staircase too dark to discern, but I couldn't stand being left behind. My brothers were always doing that. Riding their bikes faster. Walking ahead of me at school. One spring, they let me chase them into the deep end of Elkhorn Creek even though they knew I couldn't swim yet. I sank to the stone-cold bottom before someone else's brother rescued me. Everyone in town whispered about my five minutes of heart failure. The worst part about dying was Lefty scoffing every time the story was told. Like I made it all up.

As soon as I stepped inside the secret gateway, it creaked behind me, winding slowly before sealing me in with an earth-quaking BOOM. Rushing to catch Pony's tail, a single bulb swung above us, illuminating him in hasty flashes. When he whipped back with a bent smile, I noticed angry creases carved into his face for the first time. He was older than I thought.

"Shhhhh. Quiet steps!"

God, I hated being shushed. Spiraling endlessly down with no floor in sight, every step pounding louder than my chest, I couldn't help but hearken back to the parable of the Good Baptist Gone Bad. You know the girl who took a bus to Hollywood and soon found herself in a pornographic torture shed? Miss Stars-In-Her-Eyes finally got her big close-up, but the camera was focused on the wrong set of lips. My Sunday School teachers recounted this to us the week after my first Christmas play, after I confessed during Bible study that I wanted to be a thespian instead of a missionary. In retrospect, they may have thought I said lesbian. Anyway, the tale ends with the whore's church family welcoming her back with open arms after she returns home to The Bluegrass covered in tattoos and semen. So the moral was that it was best to never leave in the first place.

Maybe the Baptists were right.

"Almost there!" Pony's voice echoed. I couldn't hear the music upstairs anymore, but I could feel the bottom rising up to meet us when suddenly—

Pony lunged back, stopping me on the final steps. "Ketty Kay King. Are you ready to learn the divine secret of The Method actor... which includes a *sacrifice*?"

Rent was over three thousand dollars a month, and the cement walls hugging our shoulders were closing in. "Yes."

"Good. The Company has a new take on Hamlet." As if Mel Gibson hadn't done enough. "We're restructuring the show from Ophelia's point of view, and we need an actress who can access her *trauma*. The trauma of being seduced and used, betrayed and thrown away, before Ophelia goes mad. We believe the role demands The Method, which is not to be confused with the generic method acting of amateurs. This is a ritual as old as the first play, known only to a select few."

He waited for me to sound awed. "Awesome," I said in my quiet voice.

"Before you go in, dig a fingernail into the pink side of your thumb. Silently read your lines. Then before you bleed, close your eyes and repeat the word, KA!"

"Okay… And then…?"

Pony pursed his cracked pale lips into a circle and SUUUCKED the air. "You sip!"

More than two decades of research, night classes, vocal frys, no fries, insomnia, colon cleanses, going home alone, going home with the casting director's assistant, grief and rejection boiled down to one ridiculous question: *To drink my own blood, or to pretend to drink my own blood?*

"Sorry. What happens…when I *sip* my blood?" Or pretend to.

"What happens is you will stop being an actor and start becoming the character for the first time in your life. Or you can do things your way and *perform*. Your choice." With a smug grin, Pony stepped into an unlit foyer. *Tap. Tap.* His heels clicked on the concrete floor. Then mine. At the staircase's conclusion, we stood in front of a diminutive door. Before Pony could grab the handle, the knob shook—

BANG! The door swung open. Out of the black box room, The Attendant greeted us dressed in the stiff uniform of a eighteenth-century redcoat oddly complemented by his twentieth-century bowl cut.

"When you're ready, join us." Pony disappeared while the door shut in my face.

Staring down at the unbroken skin on my thumb, I thought about my first play. It didn't require magic or even Jesus to bring down God's house on Christmas Eve. I became Mother Mary because of my gift for playing the room. No magic method. No bodily fluids.

I've done everything my craft ever demanded. I trained. I studied. I sacrificed carbs. I shouldn't have to bleed too. Instead of sacrificing my finger, I tried summoning as many lines from the Ethan Hawke adaptation of *Hamlet* as possible, breathed deeply, and raised my hand to knock when—

The door burst open. The Attendant with a child's haircut ushered me in with a bow and—

Snatched my lambskin clutch! I wanted to cling to my last vestige of safety (my cell phone) but I froze!

Did anyone else hear wings flapping?

Catching my breath, I took in the space. The Grand Basement was an arena stage with no seats and, as far as I could tell, no birds. It was a black floor with four black walls.

Ahead of us, studio lights shone over three regal chairs. No, not chairs…thrones.

The Playwright sat far-left, wearing mismatched clothes, metal braces over her nicotine-stained teeth, and a scowl. She wrote something down about my appearance, letting her cheap tortoise shell glasses slide down her snooty nose.

Smoothing back my pinned updo, I smiled at The Director on my far right. In Hollywood, they were the Senior Pastor. On Broadway, they were just a deacon. But something about the way this one kept crossing and recrossing his legs made me wonder if he had a hard on. I kept a slotted screwdriver in my Kate Spade knockoff for such an occasion. Of course, my purse had just been kidnapped.

"Glad you could make it, Ketty!" The Director shifted in his chair.

Seated on the center throne, Pony moved so little it was hard to tell if he was breathing. But he was certainly not my giggly champion from upstairs. He was a statue. And he was in charge.

"Whenever you're ready," The Playwright mumbled without looking up. The sound of her pencil attacking paper injected spates of panic up my spine. What the hell was she writing? I didn't even have a—

The Attendant handed me a script before jogging back to his place by the door, which he promptly locked and deadbolted.

Now there was nowhere to run. No one to run to. Skimming over the dialogue, I prepared in silence. Aristotle. Chekhov. Adler. Ball. Kimmel. Smith. Weston. Davis. I was ready.

"*O, what a noble mind is here o'erthrown! The courtier—*"

"A few questions actually," Pony interrupted. My concentration was definitely *o'erthrown*. Maybe he really could tell I was *acting* instead of *becoming*. "Have you ever been in love?"

"What? Sorry, I mean… Lefty? The childhood crush I was telling you about? That was so long ago I don't even remember. It's stupid really. Just forget I said anything. Umm…no. I've never been in love." I could hear the blood in my body washing up like waves in a hurricane as they stared through me with pity. "Some ladies wait for Godot. I'm waiting for Michael B. Jordan."

No one laughed. Rude.

"What is your greatest fear?" The Playwright snapped.

"I—No big ones." Just birds. And confined spaces. And drowning. And volcanoes right before the lava erupts. Also caves and darkness. Were those studio lights dimming? I really, *really* hate the dark.

"I'd like to hear about the closet?" The Director didn't really seem to be asking.

Pony glared unblinking, and The Playwright scribbled into her notebook even louder.

"I…don't know what you're talking about." For once I wasn't lying.

"We think you do, ssssweetheart." Pony hissed.

The baby hairs on the back of my neck electrified, and my toes began to curl. But then Pony pushed a fingernail into his thumb. His azure eyes assured mine, and somehow I knew what to do. I read over Ophelia's soliloquies, her ditsy songs and feelings of betrayal and shame and mania. Plunging my acrylic nail into my thumb, my skin crawled with goosebumps, everything inside of me roiling when—

All of the plasma in my body exploded like a waterfall at the tip of my finger. I spun around, stuck the thumb in my mouth and inhaled!

Miss Kimmel taught me that artists were made of two parts: The Soul that bared itself onstage, and The Source of the actor's buried pain.

As hot sticky blood oozed over my tongue and down my throat, I knew the conscious part of me was flying toward pain. Weightless, My Source soared over the secret stage. Out of The Grand Parlor basement. Out of the greatest metropolis on earth. Into…

A CLOSET. I turned back around, but instead of three royal assholes, I stared through the ashen slats of a closet door.

Shifting my focus down, I saw my chubby body draped in mud-stained OshKosh B'gosh shorteralls. The pair I used to wear every other day that year my chest filled in. Slowly, I came to realize when and where I stood.

I was nine years old in my family's moldy basement closet! The Method must have placed me in a hypnotic trance. Whether I had been transported through space and time was dubious, but the moment itself felt tangible. Especially when—

"Can we let her out now?" The child's voice was familiar. One of my brothers.

Around town, my six siblings and our best friend Lefty Lee were known as the "King Brothers." I watched twelve of their brown eyes step into a beam of sunlight that shone through a singular window. Only one pair of eyes missing.

Suddenly, Lefty's glowing green orbs leapt out of the dark next to my cage. I cowered back, my knees knocking. Itchy and achy, I rubbed the goosebumps on my arms raw and covered my chest but couldn't recall why or what might happen next.

"Let her stay in dere a lil longer," Lefty ordered. "'Less she scurrrrred."

I searched my brothers' eyes for compassion but found compliance. My hands reached for a pull, but the doorknob was missing! I tried to enunciate, and only a hoarse whisper escaped.

Was it possible that somewhere My Soul was still on stage reciting Shakespeare with the terror and confusion Ophelia felt when Hamlet cornered her? I hoped so.

"Ketty? If ya wanna come out just say yer scurrrred!" Lefty taunted.

The nine-year-old me wouldn't have answered even if she could. Fear of the dark, the birds, the closet—none of it compared to the horror of remaining in the shadows of the King Brothers.

Billy was the quarterback star, Brad the best point guard, Barry the future war hero, Buddy everyone's best bud, then Ben with the brains, and Byron with the jokes. At nine, I wasn't known for anything. Not one single attribute. So in the closet I stayed. It was a silly dare, but in the face of being nothing, I had to at least be brave.

"BOYSSSS!" Dad called from upstairs.

"Come on, let's go." Lefty turned and everyone followed the leader, leaving me behind in a closet with no way out.

The empty basement was all silver concrete, cobwebs, and cardboard boxes labeled "books" and "tools." I laid down on a pile of lint and crumbs. The sun sank lower. Wind howled louder. Eventually, fuchsia showered my cement prison with twilight. My eyelids put on considerable weight, and I grew eager to welcome oblivion when… I heard wings.

Rising sharply, I watched through the horizontal bars as cherry red wings flapped up a storm.

Rubbery talons poked out from the black corner across from me.

The cardinal stalked forward, its nails scraping against the floor, making the basement echo with rasps.

As it creeped into the shrinking pink light between us, I squeezed my eyes, sheltered my ears, and thought of music.

I feel pretty and witty and bright!

And I pity

Any girl who isn't me tonight…

The sunset between us died, and the bird's sage eyes glimmered in the dark gray of nighttime.

Upstairs, Mom's *West Side Story* ballads spun on a turntable. I could hear my family's dinner plates scratched clean. Hamburger casserole with green beans and Derby pie flooded my nostrils, making my nose itch and gut starve.

Somehow in my quest to be remembered, it dawned on me that I had been forgotten.

Creeeeeeeak. The basement door at the top of the staircase winded shut. CLICK. A deadbolt.

Someone's shadow wandered toward me, thumping against a box on their way to my closet.

I pulled my knees up to my chest and squeezed, shut my eyes and tried to swallow spit in a mouth full of cotton.

The lock on the other side of my door unhooked and squealed open. Lefty stepped inside, towering over my shrunken body. My eyes shot open as his glared down. He reached for my hand, and I let him raise me. Even in the blinding darkness, I could feel where his gaze roamed. Past my innocent brown eyes and over the braless knolls growing on top of my fourth-grade chest. I hadn't noticed those hills before that moment. But Lefty did.

"Shhh." Lefty held a finger to his Barbie-pink lips.

His hands tugged me close enough to feel the glass soda bottle of Ale 8 One in his front pocket. Gradually, those hands slithered from my waist into my shorteralls. The straps unlatched, and he cradled my chest before grazing his fingers across my landscape, further and deeper than I knew they could go, into the cave between my legs, until something pinched.

"Ow!" I found my voice again.

His hand vanished into his gym shorts as he shifted this way and that. His face contorted. The closet shook. I froze, thinking only of the cardinal in my corner, unwilling to abandon me. My sole companion.

"Sorry, sweetheart." Calm again, Lefty wiped the snot off his fingertips onto his leg. Grinning and giddy, he dove straight into my chapped elementary school lips. His breath was more rotten than Denmark. His tongue rough and slimy. But the worst part came next when Lefty squinted through me, the real me, the confused dreamy kid who hated every inch of her body and he… He… HE SCOFFED!

Dismissing my first kiss with a cruel smirk, Lefty turned and left. Stomping up the splintered steps, he let the door *whiiiiine* to a close, trapping me back inside. I crumbled, unable to fall asleep. Unable to feel anything at all.

The bird and I spent the next day together listening to the King Brothers play above us, Dad yelling for them to stop running in the house. Lefty rang the doorbell and was invited to stay the night if he pleased.

There was only one thing that reanimated my spirit: singing along to Mom's favorite show tunes while she fixed a fried bologna lunch. Mr. Cardinal stood by as my audience.

It's alarming how charming I feel…

"Where's Ketty?" Mom finally asked.
"Still at mah sister's slumber party, ma'am," Lefty lied.
"It's all weekend," one of the King Brothers added.

I'm so pretty…

That I hardly can believe I'm real!

Something deep inside me growled, and I grabbed my stomach. My shirt was wet with humidity. Most full-grown adults can only go two days without water. But my thirst wasn't as powerful as the isolation. By the time my family licked their dessert plates clean, hunger was overpowering me. Desperately, I drank my own spit, and it nourished me. As did memories of my church's Christmas pageant. And Bluegrass Regional Theater's rendition of *The Piano Lesson*. And *Hamlet for Kids* in the park. I recited all the words, and that allowed me to walk free of my closet, in my imagination.

KA! KA! Mr. Cardinal woke me up to my second pitch-black night. With a CLAP of his wings, he sprung from the floor onto one of Dad's boxes marked "tools." He captured my stare and held me there for a beat when…

His pointy beak plunged into the cardboard! Again and again, as if possessed, Mr. Cardinal bore a hole straight through. Rummaging inside like a feral fiend, my confidant suddenly launched out of the box and headed straight at my closet, barging into the door like an earthquake!

BANG! BANG! BANG! BANG! Until… It opened.

Mr. Cardinal flew onto my hand and burrowed his nails into my skin, begging for me to act. Without thinking, I *riiiiiiipppped* off his talon! A burst of ruby-red sprinkled onto my jeans as his wings clipped my nose, and he retreated out a window.

Gripping his hook in my fist, I knew exactly what to do.

Every step up the staircase pounded louder than a rumbling thunder. I opened the basement door to find the kitchen dim, steady rain patting the roof. There was a slumber party in my living room. Most of my brothers claimed the floor while Lefty's stupid camo sleeping bag lay comfortably on our sofa. The floor beneath my bare feet was firm, freshly vacuumed carpet. My pupils stretched wide, welcoming the lightening that flashed through oversized bay windows.

TURN AROUND! TURN AROUND! I DARE YOU TO TURN AROUND AND SEE ME NOW!

Lefty obeyed. His shoulders yawned and eyes shot wide as I slashed my talon across his left cheek in one blur of motion. I watched the beautiful red shape of a tiger tail bleed through his skin. Only then did I recognize one of Dad's slotted screwdrivers in my hand. But I wasn't thinking about how it got there. For the first time, I thought to myself:

I feel fucking pretty.

Gawking at the warm blood coating my fingers like chocolate syrup, the hunger inside of me cried out. For once I listened. I stuck my fingers into my mouth and feasted. Lefty's blood tasted like salty pennies.

Just then the storm cleared for a full blue moon, radiating brighter by the second until my eyes were forced shut.

WHEN I BLINKED again, the moon had transformed into a spotlight and I was on stage as Ophelia. No longer in the Grand Parlor Basement, but on Broadway. I drowned happily in the lights of the Pony Goldwyn Theater.

> *"Like sweet bells jangled, out of tune and harsh;*
>
> *That unmatch'd form and feature of blown youth*
>
> *Blasted with ecstasy: O, woe is me,*
>
> *To have seen what I have seen, see what I see!"*

Blood trickled down from my thumb as I took a bow. Pony Goldwyn was first to applaud. The packed audience followed in a grand ovation that included Mom, Dad, Miss Kimmel, The Grand Parlor Bartender, The Director, and The Playwright.

Ophelia was sold out for the entire spring season. Reviews certified Kathy Kay King as "transcendent in her madness" and "dangerously talented."

Pony next cast me in The Company's hot new take on *West Side Story*. In this revival, Maria would be a single, Black fashion designer from the Bronx who commits suicide in the East River. Her biggest moment would be dying on stage, which would require a fresh sacrifice. An even greater one.

Once Broadway fell dark after rehearsal, I was chauffeured to my Soho townhouse. In the back seat, I slid on Prada gloves to hide the thousands of tiny cuts covering my fingertips. Nothing a little plastic surgery wouldn't fix if Hollywood should ever call for a close up.

At home, I ignored never-ending calls of congratulations, shed my couture attire, and retired to the bedroom. Opening a slatted closet door, I climbed inside and embraced the black void. And starved. And thirsted. And bled.

When I woke up, I was underwater, plummeting to the stone-cold bottom of Elkhorn Creek.

MAKING *PRIVATE HELLS*

Andrew Adams

SOME SAY THAT The Living Haite's "Dead To Me" reunion tour was named in bad taste, given the ultimate fate of Alden Haite. "But if we cared what you thought, then it wouldn't be rock n' roll," says Sierra Taylor, de facto band leader in Mr. Haite's absence.

The band has just finished a nationwide tour, and it's the first time they've ever played much of their most famous music live. We're talking, of course, about the songs that make up *Private Hells*, one of the most revered rock albums of all time. Famous not just for its eleven perfect tracks, but because many believe that the album is cursed, that the trauma of its creation is baked into the fiber of its being. And that listening to it even once means you are complicit in the death at its center.

Now, twenty years after the album's original release, we caught up with the three remaining members of The Living Haite, as well as former band manager Colm McCarthy and producer Moses Kaluuya, for an expansive oral history… inside *Private Hells*.

I. UNDER THE RADAR

The Living Haite first formed in 2003, during NYC's garage rock revival.

Edgar Humboldt (Bassist): We weren't The Strokes, but we wanted to be.

DaShawn Jones (Drummer): We always kind of sucked until Sierra came along.

Colm McCarthy (Manager): The three boys kept bumping into each other at shows. White Stripes at the Bowery, Yeah Yeah Yeahs at Mercury Lounge, TV On the Radio at the Stinger. And a thousand other venues you've never heard of with a thousand bands you've since forgotten.

Edgar Humboldt: Alden was on X a lot.

DaShawn Jones: He was a true rock star. Had the swagger, the skill, the ego. Skinny jeans and leather jackets and grease in his hair. He knew how to rage. Back before folk destroyed the scene, Alden and I had a reputation for, uh… Being the life of the party. We got black-out drunk at one of [James] Murphy's throwdowns and woke up in a bathroom, curled around the same toilet bowl. That's when I was invited into the band.

Edgar Humboldt: Alden needed a wingman.

DaShawn Jones: He wouldn't let me say 'no.'

Colm McCarthy: They had a new name at every show. The Lost Souls. The Manic Racket. Panic Eaters. But Alden Haite's stage presence was the draw. So, I made them lean in. Called them The Living Haite.

Edgar Humboldt: It wasn't even his real last name.

Sierra Taylor (Additional Vocals, Guitar, Keyboard, Orchestral Arrangements): I despised the band name. From the get-go. Alden already let every damn thing go to his head.

DaShawn Jones: Sierra caused problems right from the start.

Colm McCarthy: There were creative differences, yeah. But look at Fleetwood Mac, Lennon and McCartney, Liam and Noel. Great art comes from the flame.

Sierra Taylor: I was in a shitty band called The Golden Fleece. We met doing avant-garde theater at KGB Bar. I wanted to top Karen O, as insane as it sounds. I went to art school, studied performance, did a few semesters of music theory in grad school. I thought if I went "in character" as a rock star, then I could lose myself and put on a show.

DaShawn Jones: She lit up the stage. Every time.

Colm McCarthy: I wanted a band that would make the room horny. I knew we'd be big if every person who came to our shows got laid. And when Sierra and Alden took the stage together... They made you wanna fuck.

Edgar Humboldt: She elevated everything. She actually liked music.

DaShawn Jones: The whole damn history of The Living Haite was all about the push and the pull, you know? The search for balance. You've got Edgar and Sierra on one side, obsessing over craft. Then you've got me and Alden on the other, doing our damnedest to embody rock. And Colm was there to fuse us all together. That's what made us so good. Push and pull.

Colm McCarthy: The debut album came together fast. The boys had a bunch of scraps that weren't working, but Sierra added a magic touch. She could see the big picture in ways they couldn't and worked those songs into something special. Something memorable.

Edgar Humboldt: She's the one who titled it *Under the Radar*. Betting it'd be ironic.

DaShawn Jones: "Astrostatic" made us huge.

Colm McCarthy: The blues stomp got everybody amped in the verse, then the chorus took it home. Sierra was listening to a lot of post-rock and made the hook anthemic. Like blasting into space. "Astrostatic" topped *Billboard* and crossed the pond.

Sierra Taylor: The rest of the album sucked. Those songs were catchy, but they didn't mean much.

DaShawn Jones: That's when we got groupies. We were being booked at small clubs but selling out every show. Breaking every fire code we could. Alden started bringing up audience members if they were willing to have sex on stage.

Edgar Humboldt: *New York Times* said Alden performed "like a man possessed." If only they knew.

II. SOULLESS CITY

Without a follow-up single, The Living Haite rushed to record their sophomore effort.

DaShawn Jones: Oh, we embraced the rumors. For sure. People were saying that Alden was the son of a blues man who'd sold his soul. Meaning Alden only had half of his own. That's where we got the title for our second album.

Colm McCarthy: I have no idea how those stories started, but they were a godsend. In terms of press.

Edgar Humboldt: God had nothing to do with it. It was Colm.

DaShawn Jones: There wasn't a damn thing Alden and I couldn't do back then. We were coked-up every night, hungover every morning, and girls would do whatever we wanted.

Sierra Taylor: All the warning signs were there. In retrospect. Eddie and I stayed away from all that, spent most nights hanging out in hotel rooms.

Colm McCarthy: I thought they were an item.

Edgar Humboldt: I wasn't out yet.

Sierra Taylor: But DaShawn and Alden stoked something in one another. Like they were constantly trying to see who could live most dangerously.

Colm McCarthy: Sierra hasn't said a single nice thing about Alden in fifteen years. She forgets they used to be friends. Real tight, like. They made one another laugh, they improved each other's music. Alden had popular taste, the ear for the riff. Sierra made it art.

Sierra Taylor: We were aware of the narrative, that Alden had half a soul. So, we thought it was fun to weave misinformation into the lyrics. Like how The Beatles deliberately made people think McCartney was dead.

DaShawn Jones: You look at the big singles, like the title track or "Blissed Out Blues" and "Drilling In," and they come from the album's first half. The part that tells you how much fun drugs and sex can be. That's what got us on the radio, sold out stadiums, let us headline festivals. People are primal, man. You can't deny 'em their instincts.

Sierra Taylor: But Side B endeared us to critics. I had noticed the toll fame took on Alden. He was hollowing out. So, I wrote about it. "Great Comeuppance," "Halfway Home," and "Damned If You Do" were all inspired by those times when Alden looked…off.

Colm McCarthy: You put Sierra and Alden's halves side-by-side, and it turns into a concept album about the corrosive effects of fame.

Edgar Humboldt: An Icarus arc.

Sierra Taylor: That tour was huge. Twelve people jammed on a bus. You'd drift off to sleep in Georgia and wake up in Arizona, guess where you were by the shape of the trees. We sold out stadiums. I never thought I'd look into a crowd and see forty thousand people shouting lyrics I wrote.

Colm McCarthy: We made so much money.

Sierra Taylor: But I worried about Alden and DaShawn. They ran off together at the end of every show, out doing… Well… Out being rock stars, I guess.

DaShawn Jones: I was alone those nights. Getting hooked on H and trying to score. I had no idea what Alden was up to.

Edgar Humboldt: We learned soon enough.

III. WILLOWDOWN HALL

After the Soulless City Tour, the band reconvened at a derelict plantation house in Louisiana to record their third and final LP (Private Hells).

Colm McCarthy: Sierra pitched the idea of Willowdown Hall.

DaShawn Jones: Pulled us aside one by one. Said Alden's lifestyle was undermining the music. That he came to rehearsals high or got distracted by groupies. Which was true. She said we needed a private place to record. "For Alden's sake."

Sierra Taylor: I found it in a book of historical lodgings. The bayou just seemed like the sort of space that might…inspire. I even found a producer.

Moses Kaluuya (Producer/Engineer): I thought *Soulless City* was a perfect album, so I was happy to hop on board. I actually turned down Interpol for it. And Willowdown seemed perfect. We all agreed that recording on location gives an album specificity. That it lets a musician pour their soul into a project. If they have one.

Edgar Humboldt: There were no roads in or out.

Moses Kaluuya: We arrived on an airboat. Captained by a Cajun man with four teeth.

DaShawn Jones: The locals sucked. I mean, they dangled raw chicken off trees to feed wild gators. They practiced Voodoo. What were we doing there?! I'm from New Jersey!

Sierra Taylor: The housekeeper was there to greet us at the dock, Miss LaFonte. Pale and gaunt, underfed, long black hair and bangs. In other words: Alden's type. She lived in a little cabin tucked in the trees. It's famous now.

Moses Kaluuya: Alden hit on her straight away. She was not charmed.

Colm McCarthy: The LaFonte lady led us through the weeping willows to a sugar plantation built on the banks of Bayou Teche in the early 1800s.

Sierra Taylor: Two-and-a-half stories. Sixteen rooms. Everything falling apart. The floors were covered in ancient furs, like bears from the seventeenth century that had been turned into rugs. Teeth still on 'em. I remember antique furniture and bad lighting and floral wallpaper that peeled at the edges. And, of course, the axe on the wall.

DaShawn Jones: Just being there made me sick.

Edgar Humboldt: It's called withdrawal.

Colm McCarthy: I tagged along to manage personalities and to make sure that the work got done. But no one could ever really manage Alden Haite.

IV. RECORDING PRIVATE HELLS

A track-by-track look.

1. "FRENZY (INTRO)"

Moses Kaluuya: We retrofitted the dining hall into a recording studio. The acoustics were great. All the dead animals on the walls dampened any echo.

Colm McCarthy: Everybody was in a good mood that night.

Edgar Humboldt: We didn't know what was coming.

Sierra Taylor: I'm the one who suggested that we start with a jam session. A chance to explore, to find new noises, to sync up with one another after that exhausting tour. Alden was into it because it didn't require prep.

DaShawn Jones: There were drugs. There was liquor. We loosened up fast.

Sierra Taylor: Only DaShawn was high.

Moses Kaluuya: DaShawn locked in on a Dilla-style groove, pulled straight from the ether, and the rest of the band began to build on it bit by bit. Eddie added that dark, fuzzed-out jazz bass, Sierra used her guitar to create an uneasy drone that built 'til it broke, and then, out of nowhere… Alden began to weep.

Edgar Humboldt: Crying straight into the mic.

Sierra Taylor: We all stopped playing one by one as we noticed something wrong. Like the music was crumbling. Alden's whimpers bounced around the room. And I asked, "Are you okay?"

Moses Kaluuya: That two-minute jam became the intro. Eventually.

DaShawn Jones: I thought it was a messed-up thing to put on the LP.

Moses Kaluuya: I've seen people on forums note how the audio cracks just a few seconds before Alden breaks down. I maintain that Sierra's guitar got too loud and the mic peaked, but some people believe that the audio distortion was…otherworldly.

Sierra Taylor: Alden was not okay.

2. "DEN OF INIQUITY"

Sierra Taylor: "Den of Iniquity" was Alden's brainchild. One of the only tracks written in advance. The original version was very much something of the *Soulless City* era. Another track celebrating excess and all the trouble it brings.

DaShawn Jones: We'd played that song a thousand times live. We perfected it live.

Moses Kaluuya: I've seen early recordings. The first version was a rock 'n' roll anthem. DaShawn pushed the drums to their limit, and Alden practically screamed the lyrics. The crowd would pulse to the beat. It was the heaviest, catchiest song that The Living Haite had ever written.

Edgar Humboldt: But something happened that first night.

DaShawn Jones: The house had a mind of its own, man.

Sierra Taylor: We heard voices.

Moses Kaluuya: Colm and I were on cots downstairs, while the band took bedrooms up top. I remember hearing footsteps all night. Pacing, back and forth. Creaking and keeping me up.

Colm McCarthy: Old houses make noise.

Edgar Humboldt: We heard it, too.

Sierra Taylor: I was always cold all night, no matter how many blankets I used. And I remember sobbing coming from Alden's room.

DaShawn Jones: I knocked at one point, but the man clammed up. Never came to the door. Just got quiet, then got back to crying after I was gone.

Edgar Humboldt: We were choking on the atmosphere.

Moses Kaluuya: When we assembled the next morning, Alden was in a strange state. All that rock star swagger? Gone.

Sierra Taylor: He didn't look well.

DaShawn Jones: He said he was fine.

Moses Kaluuya: We did one take of "Den of Iniquity," and it was like he couldn't even complete it. Got to the chorus, sang those words: "Welcome, girl, to my den of sin / It's not nice, but that's the bed we're in." Then he gave up.

DaShawn Jones: He turned and said, "Why don't we try it half-speed?"

Sierra Taylor: It all clicked. This song that I had secretly hated suddenly felt like a funeral dirge. It went from celebratory to self-loathing, and that inflection gave the whole track a greater depth of meaning. It probably tanked its chances as a single, but it made the album cohesive.

Colm McCarthy: That song peaked at number six. But it could have been number one for months if they hadn't changed it. Thank Christ they kept the chorus loud, or we wouldn't have charted at all.

DaShawn Jones: That was the last time things were good.

3. "PALE CREATURE"

Moses Kaluuya: We didn't record again all week.

Sierra Taylor: It was an exploratory time. We were writing a lot. Trying to figure out what the album could be. I had the idea of a dark mirror. Something where Side A and Side B would reflect one another, so that every track would have a sister song on the opposite side, with repeating themes and styles. Alden's voice would define the first half, and I would respond in the second. A lot of the music came together then. We just needed lyrics.

Edgar Humboldt: Then I saw the woman.

DaShawn Jones: She walked the halls at night. If you got up for a drink, or to check on Alden's sobbing—*again*—then you would see her at the end of the hall. She was naked and hard to ignore.

Edgar Humboldt: Her flesh wasn't colored right. You could see her veins.

Colm McCarthy: Alden knew a lot of drug addicts.

DaShawn Jones: Gangly limbs, a body rail thin. I remember big buck teeth and dark bags under the eyes, sunken cheeks. Flat-chested, and you could see all her ribs. I'm telling you. The girl looked dead, and she made croaking sounds.

Sierra Taylor: Like someone had crushed her windpipe.

Colm McCarthy: There's all this talk of ghosts but it's bullshit. Do you really think a man like Alden Haite wouldn't be sneaking in girls after dark? He was into the junkie aesthetic.

Edgar Humboldt: Where would they come from?

Sierra Taylor: I saw her once. For a second. Stepping into his room. I asked Alden about it, but he said I was crazy. Said to leave him alone.

Edgar Humboldt: Solitude is an elemental part of the creative process.

DaShawn Jones: He stopped eating. He stopped laughing. And I tried to level, one on one. We were best friends at the time, but he wouldn't tell me shit.

Sierra Taylor: I assumed he was fucking the housekeeper. Miss LaFonte. He was always staring at her too long. So yeah, it startled me to see a naked woman in the halls, but honestly… It happened all the time. That was most nights on tour. [Alden] came down at the end of the week with the lyrics to "Pale Creature" fully formed, so something was working.

Colm McCarthy: We all know the chorus by now. "Cover your eyes if you don't want to see / Riding pale creatures all night / I'll cover your eyes if you look at me / Scream my sorrow when I meet the light."

Moses Kaluuya: It sounded like a sex song to me. 'Riding all night.'

DaShawn Jones: That woman's skin… It was lifeless.

Edgar Humboldt: I thought the creature was a horse. Death rides a Pale Horse.

Sierra Taylor: Which is how I got the idea for a "musical stampede." I thought we needed a kinetic onslaught of emotion after those first two tracks. Like "Immigrant Song."

DaShawn Jones: It's kinda twisted that it hit number one.

Colm McCarthy: People don't pay attention to lyrics. "Semi-Charmed Life" is about meth and it's still huge. So, I wasn't surprised when Alden's song about killing became such a sensation.

Sierra Taylor: Then I got busted.

4. "CLOAK AND DAGGER"

DaShawn Jones: She knew the whole time.

Colm McCarthy: It was a solid publicity stunt.

Sierra Taylor: I thought if the "man with half a soul" recorded in a haunted house, we could go platinum. So, I looked up the most haunted places in America. A lot of people had died at Willowdown Hall. Legend held that the barriers between dimensions were exceptionally thin there, that it was a hub for ghostly encounters. The label doubled our budget.

DaShawn Jones: "For Alden's sake." That's what she said.

Colm McCarthy: I didn't see the harm. Ghosts aren't real.

Edgar Humboldt: Of course I believe in them now.

Moses Kaluuya: Edgar and DaShawn felt betrayed but kept their cool. Alden did not. I remember yelling and screaming. Plates got smashed. Dude had anger issues. Obviously.

Sierra Taylor: Alden wanted to kill me. I could see blood vessels pop in his eyes. Veins bulging from his neck. He flipped a table and stormed out of the house. Colm chased after.

DaShawn Jones: "The cloak and the dagger / that goes in your back." I came up with that line. I was pissed. And yeah, a lot of those feelings found their way into the music, like they always do. The whole song's about hiding secrets, and there's a lot of stabbing imagery. But we were talking about Sierra. Believe it or not.

Sierra Taylor: We were all hiding something.

5. "PRIVATE HELLS"

Moses Kaluuya: Things began to deteriorate unnaturally fast.

DaShawn Jones: My stash was gone and it's not like I had a way to get more.

Edgar Humboldt: I was miserable. I was seeing this guy Paul, but he stopped speaking to me before we arrived. I was being ghosted in more ways than one.

Sierra Taylor: The boys had written a song about how much I sucked. So, I spent a lot of time wandering the willows, letting myself spiral into fits of shame and self-loathing. I was out there later that day, hating myself, when I noticed Alden. In a daze. I told him how I felt, and he seemed to understand. We co-wrote the lyrics out there on the swamp banks, about the pain of keeping secrets. I never asked what his secret was.

Moses Kaluuya: Around dinner time, I noticed Colm was missing.

Sierra Taylor: We searched every room. Wandered the willows, shouting his name. Called his phone a thousand times. There was no sign of him.

Edgar Humboldt: Alden told us to focus on the music. Diverted our attention.

6. "IN SPECTER (INTERLUDE)"

Moses Kaluuya: That was one long, improvised take. The next night. Even though it seems like the centerpiece of the album, with all its swirling drones and the two lead guitars locked together like lattice, we were just killing time with another jam. It was almost an instrumental, until Sierra mimicked the ghost. With her high-pitched falsetto.

That's the last thing I recorded before I fell down the stairs.

DaShawn Jones: Nobody saw it happen.

Moses Kaluuya: It was late. Everybody else was asleep. Colm was still gone, and we were getting worried. But I had to use the bathroom. So, I started up the steps…and I saw her at the top. The pale creature. She ran right at me. I leapt back on instinct, and that rotted railing cracked apart, so I fell straight through. I don't remember the rest.

Edgar Humboldt: We all heard him scream. And the crack of his spine.

DaShawn Jones: I got there first. Found him draped over the banister. His body folded in all the wrong ways.

Moses Kaluuya: Hence the wheelchair.

7. "WALLS WILL TALK"

DaShawn Jones: The back half of the album was recorded later. But all the lyrics, and the inspiration, came from what happened next.

Sierra Taylor: Edgar and I grabbed flashlights and ran for help.

Edgar Humboldt: I thought the housekeeper might have a landline. Miss LaFonte, in her cabin.

DaShawn Jones: I stayed back with Moses. Let the man cry in my arms. But I was in a bad state. The withdrawal was getting worse, my hands were shaking… And that's when I saw the woman returning to the top of the steps. Coming for us.

Sierra Taylor: I was running through the willows, heading to the housekeeper's cabin, when I realized Edgar was gone.

Edgar Humboldt: I don't know how we got split up.

DaShawn Jones: I didn't want to move Moses. I didn't want to make his injuries worse. But the dead woman was coming down the stairs. Getting closer. She was croaking. And we started to make out words.

Moses Kaluuya: "Get out."

Sierra Taylor: I burst into the cabin, screaming: "Miss LaFonte!" I didn't notice the blood until I picked up the phone and it slipped from my hand. Then I saw it on the bed. On the floor. On every single wall. But there wasn't a body.

Edgar Humboldt: I was searching the willows, screaming Sierra's name, when I found Colm McCarthy, stepping out of the swamp, covered in mud and missing an arm.

DaShawn Jones: The dead woman got to the bottom step.

Moses Kaluuya: Her movement was jagged. Like rigor mortis might make it.

DaShawn Jones: Drool fell from her lips. I heard bones pop and crack as she crawled beside me. I didn't wanna move, didn't wanna leave Moses behind. Then she reached out and put her hand on my cheek. Cold to the touch. She said, "Run."

Moses Kaluuya: "Before Alden kills again."

8. "HUSH MONEY"

Colm McCarthy: Alden lost his temper a lot. That day, when he learned the house was haunted… That Sierra had manipulated him… I'd never seen him so upset. He stormed out of the house, and I chased after. It was my job to calm him down. To get him back to work.

I spent an hour searching before I got to the housekeeping cabin. The door was open. I went to ask Miss LaFonte if she'd seen Alden. But she was lying in a pool of her own intestines. And Alden was there, holding an axe and breathing heavy.

DaShawn Jones: Eddie believes in possessions.

Edgar Humboldt: There's a theory. That if you have half a soul, it leaves a hollow space inside you. A space that other spirits can fill.

Moses Kaluuya: Or maybe he was just a bad person.

Colm McCarthy: He said, "I did it again."

And listen. If you had asked me in advance what I would do in that situation, I'm sure I would have said, "Call the cops." I'm sure I would have said, "Warn the others." But in the moment… That isn't what happened. I owed Alden. Everything. He made me wealthy beyond my wildest dreams. So, I asked him, "How can I help?"

Sierra Taylor: I get ill thinking about it.

Colm McCarthy: Alden was catatonic, so I cleaned him myself. We were renting the place for two more weeks, and I figured that nobody would look for Miss LaFonte until then. None of the band members had any reason to visit her cabin. So, if Alden kept up appearances, kept recording, then I could clean up his mess. I sent him back.

I dragged Miss LaFonte's body onto the airboat. I thought I'd feed her to the gators before anybody else caught wind. I chopped her up with a knife and weighted her down with rocks. I sunk her into the swamp.

I would have been back that night if the boat hadn't broken down.

Edgar Humboldt: Can spirits cause mechanical failure?

Colm McCarthy: I didn't want to wait to be found near her body. So, I slid into the water and started walking to Willowdown Hall. I wasn't thinking straight, or I would have remembered the gators.

DaShawn Jones: Colm got what he deserved. I wish the gator had gotten both arms.

9. "THE ROT INSIDE"

Sierra Taylor: I'm sorry if I struggle with this.

I think Alden heard me scream. Knew I'd found his secret.

I could barely move, standing in the cabin. In the middle of his murder scene. I didn't understand what had happened. Didn't understand that I was…vulnerable. That he was walking up behind me. Ready to kill any witness. And I would have died… if I hadn't heard the croak.

She whispered, "Sierra."

I turned. Alden was already swinging his axe, and I had a second—less than that—to dodge. That's why it went into my shoulder instead of my skull. That's why I'm alive.

I remember feeling a bright burst of pain. I remember seeing blood all over my body, gushing onto my hands, and not understanding that it was mine. And I remember seeing the dead girl grabbing his body. Holding him still. Giving me time.

I took the axe out of my shoulder. And I swung six times.

10. "OUT OF THE BAG (A CONFESSION)"

Edgar Humboldt: He had killed a girl on tour.

Sierra Taylor: Charlotte Bridges.

DaShawn Jones: She was a groupie. They met at the Greek and afterwards he took her to a private house in the Hills. She must have had second thoughts. Must have said 'no.'

Sierra Taylor: That son of a bitch choked her to death. And we were on stage the next day. Like it was nothing. How many others could there have been?

DaShawn Jones: He never took no for an answer. He must have gone to the cabin for comfort when he got upset. I bet Miss LaFonte wouldn't give it.

Colm McCarthy: So, he released his anger in other ways.

Sierra Taylor: No one knows how Charlotte Bridges re-entered our world. But I have a theory why. I think she knew what Alden was, better than anyone. I think she wanted to scare us. To warn us away before Alden could do his worst.

Edgar Humboldt: That woman tried to protect us.

DaShawn Jones: She was a true fan.

11. "WORD SPREAD (OUTRO)"

Sierra Taylor: We returned to Willowdown Hall for the final song.

DaShawn Jones: I had just finished rehab.

Edgar Humboldt: I was out and in a relationship.

Moses Kaluuya: The trial had ended. Sierra was released on self-defense, Colm was in prison.

Sierra Taylor: I wrote the back half from Charlotte's point of view. Giving voice to the voiceless.

Moses Kaluuya: The first half, Alden's half, became about the corrosive nature of secrets. Sierra's half reminded listeners that the truth can set us free.

DaShawn Jones: We wanted to do another improvised jam to match the intro. But we didn't expect that everyone would be so happy.

Edgar Humboldt: It's like we'd shed the worst of ourselves.

Sierra Taylor: After all that darkness, the final track feels like a cloud parting. It's far more joyful than any of us would have guessed. But the female voice that you hear? Wasn't me.

...

***PRIVATE HELLS* BECAME** a quadruple-platinum success story, partially due to its notoriety. Those eleven tracks set a new gold standard for rock. Haite's vocal performance revealed the empty depths of a man's soul, while Taylor's follow-up howls became the embodiment of female rage.

You probably know that Alden Haite survived. He could afford good care. Though he spent time in prison, his lenient sentencing became a lightning rod for social justice advocates who have long decried a system that seems to privilege the rich and famous.

Due to the contract negotiated by Colm McCarthy, the lion's share of the album's profits went to Mr. Haite. Despite having an estimated net worth of over twenty million dollars, his legal fees were paid by fans. His third solo album, *The Great Haite,* is being released in October.

He refused to be interviewed for this article.

PEEL

Maggie Levin

IT STARTED ON Halloween.

I know because Fiona always had her pumpkin carving party *on the day* of Halloween.

Which is objectively too late to carve a pumpkin—but if you were invited you had to carve one (ideally into some kind of sarcastic joke) or Fiona would be mad.

Fiona only asked you to come to her house parties if she considered you Very Inner Circle. All I wanted to be back then was Very Inner Circle. It was the pinnacle of my mid-twenties ambitions. Sure, I *said* I wanted a career, a house, even a marriage (as if I knew what any of that entailed), but my loud-speaking actions chased belonging like I was thirteen years old looking for a clique to sit with in the cafeteria.

File it under things that might've come out in the wash with a little therapy—which, at the time, I told myself I couldn't afford.

So, I went. Fiona's apartment was small and dark, but it was filled with tasteful thrifted furniture, and it was in the coolest neighborhood, and she only had one roommate. In a moment of panic, I carved the word "NOPE" into a small sugar pumpkin, and Fiona just loved it. It was her favorite of the night. More than Maddie's "BOOBS" pumpkin. Even more than "Sean's Pumpkin," made by Sean, the one boy allowed at the party. He was allowed because Fiona was fucking him, but she was embarrassed to be fucking him because he actually liked her and wasn't on the verge of dumping her at any moment.

Fiona posed me and all the other girls I was so desperate to impress around my NOPE pumpkin to take pictures. And under my stupid ironic T-shirt, I was beginning to peel.

I've never known how else to phrase it.

It wasn't like a sunburn. Even in Los Angeles, those are hard to come by in October. A patch of skin across my stomach, shaped like a map of Australia, had begun turning gray, hard and dry – thickening like a crispy callus in a place a callus could never be. It itched immediately. I thought it must be a reaction to Fiona's cats, Chips and Dip. I was wildly allergic to them—so much so, I pre-dosed myself with Benadryl before the party and did shots of espresso to combat the drowsiness.

Both cats would eventually be run over by the woman who came after Sean, when Fiona switched sexual orientations for a semi-famous model, before switching back again when the model moved onto a very famous TV actress.

I never found out if the model ran Chips and Dip over on purpose. By then, we were all much older, and Fiona had long since evicted me from the group chat.

I took my NOPE pumpkin home and left it on the porch for one of my four roommates to maybe comment on. I went into our shared yellow bathroom—a hole of a room, hopelessly coated in filth from ten years of high occupant turnover. We lived spitting distance from a major highway, so it was hard to say what made the house dirtier: the smog or us. The landlord wouldn't come unless it was an emergency, and what constituted an emergency to a North Hollywood household full of fire-spinners, Twitch streamers, and "actors" was only ever about the Wi-Fi or someone eating someone else's food. The black mold on the yellow bathroom ceiling was definitely not an emergency.

I stripped down to examine the skin patch. It was already dense enough to make a hard-surface sound when I tapped a fingernail across the length of it.

Gross.

I told myself I couldn't afford urgent care, not unless I was obviously dying.

This didn't look like dying. Not yet. It was probably a reaction to the cats.

I took more Benadryl and forced myself not to open WebMD.

In the morning, the peel had spread.

It was thick crust, turning the entire surface of my pelvis and thighs scaly gray. Flaking just a bit in the creases of both hips.

I picked at it, and it lifted, slightly—and a little painfully. Not the blister-like air bubble I was expecting, or maybe hoping for, though HOPE was not really the feeling.

I wondered: Could I pumice it off? Would my roommate notice if I used her foot file to scrape off whatever the fuck this was? Would I even want to, given how many years that foot file had been dangling off our shower rack collecting mildew?

These questions were for later. I was already late for work, an hour-and-a-half-long commute away in El Segundo. Work would be immediately followed by Maddie's birthday party at The Satellite. I stole a Claritin and some aloe gel from the fire-spinner's section of the medicine cabinet. I got on the road.

THERE'S A PROBLEM with asking your friends for help when you don't trust them or necessarily respect their opinion.

As intensely as I pined for Fiona's, or Maddie's, or even daffy Jasmine's approval—as hard as I tried to dazzle them with my attempts at cynical wit, my biting judgment of the people "we" collectively decided to dislike, my demonstrative efforts to show up The Way a Friend Does at every turn—I was never vulnerable with them. Not in a real way. Not in a way that could jeopardize my standing with any of them, or subject me to the group's (truly scathing) criticism behind my back.

An embarrassing crush on someone objectively stupid. An argument you had with a racist family member. Even a UTI from too much rough sex (implicitly bragging that your new boyfriend comes equipped with a cervix-bruiser of a dick). These were shareable "vulnerabilities." These were badges of cool-girl honor.

But the fact that I had broken out in a lizard-like full-body rash was not on the table for sharing. I couldn't control their response to it. I couldn't manipulate it into an amusing anecdote, like I did about my teenaged relationship with a thirty-five-year-old film studio executive.

Which I guess is how I wound up eating my own skin at Maddie's birthday party.

The Satellite's ugly-hot mixologists were notorious for a heavy pour, so by the time I arrived most of the gang was already loose enough to be on the dance floor. I was glad. This portion of the evening was always where I felt the most myself. I chucked my coat in a corner and joined the circle of stylish undercuts, motorcycle boots and septum rings, wiggling our flat white asses to Outkast.

Jasmine (a great dancer) and Fiona (a terrible one) complimented my dancing—*God, I lived for those compliments*—and I shrugged and *aw-shucksed*, then spun off to buy a drink for the birthday girl.

I bought Maddie a well tequila shot (to drink) and a stylish Oregonian IPA (to pretend to drink). None of my friends would actually ingest beer calories, but it was important to look beer-knowledgeable in front of each other (but actually in front of men). Maddie was taking a breather in a corner booth, scanning the room for the most fuckable male spaghetti noodle with tattoos to take home tonight.

I set the drinks down and slid into the booth beside her. *Happy birthday, cutie-pie,* I said, planting a sloppy kiss on her dancefloor-damp cheek. She squirmed. *You need lip balm, babe,* she griped.

I licked my lower lip. It was hard…and flaking. *Shit.* How long had that been happening? I rooted through my purse for ChapStick.

Looking out into the crowd of drunken Angelenos, Maddie sighed the world-weary sigh of a woman carrying a tremendous burden. *I used to be able to find people in the wild,* she moaned. *I really don't want to download a fucking app to date men, you know?*

Mm, I grunted sympathetically. *I totally get it.*

I did not get it. The rest of us were all on an app, or four. Besides, Maddie spent her spare time prowling to get plowed, not coupled up.

Scraping the final corner of purse confirmed: I did not have ChapStick. *Fuck.* My hand flew to my face, feeling for a pickable edge. The hard, scaly patch seemed to drape over my bottom lip, then dribble down the center of my chin.

A therapist told me I should stop getting so caught up in these unserious dudes and really process my Josh trauma, Maddie chirped.

I agreed with the therapist but–

This the same therapist you work for?

Maddie laughed. *Right. You're so right. Pretty unethical of her to open her big mouth.*

I found an edge all the way under my jaw. What the fuck WAS this shit? I managed to squeak a thumbnail in the crack and pinch it. This layer was a little lighter than the one over my hips… which I could feel cracking underneath my jeans, even now.

I thought of the one time I spent all my phone-bill money on a Beverly Hills bikini wax only to discover this "premium" beauty experience involved holding my legs up around my head like a baby so a strange woman could tear the hair off my asshole.

I pulled hard and fast, just like the waxer woman had. This brittle chunk of my own face ripped off, falling right into my palm—the size of a pig's ear. It hurt like a motherfucker. Maddie was looking the other way, thank God, but Fiona was fast approaching – eyes fixed on mine. She looked angry. There was no time for thought. Just reaction.

I shoved the hunk of dead skin in my mouth and closed my lips around it.

We're going to the patio, Fiona hissed. It was an order.

As I followed Fiona's big messy bun and tiny latex skirt out the back of the bar, I flattened my tongue against the piece of torn skin, pressing it to the roof of my mouth.

The flavor of decay ran down my throat.

I STOOD DELIBERATELY in the cloud of Fiona's exhaled cigarette smoke, as if this would somehow demonstrate my devotion to her. In that moment, I would've eagerly let her ash that cigarette in my hair. She could've asked me to murder somebody for her and I would've done it, pronto.

I would've done anything under the sun that might get me out of what was actually happening, which was a confrontation I'd been subconsciously dreading for months. I'd known it was coming and denied it with every ounce of my dissociative capabilities.

That was my client. You snaked her from me. You fucking STOLE her.

The truth was being held up in front of my face, as I stood there unable to respond – with a piece of my own flesh clenched between my teeth.

Fiona and I both worked in advertising back then. We were copywriters/directors/wannabe filmmakers. Making money for The Man while we saved up to make our art. Two peas in a friend pod! Fiona always saw herself as the far more talented party. For years, I'd let her believe that I *also* thought she was more talented than me. This maintained the power balance to her liking. I pretended not to take my job seriously, so she would never see me as a threat.

But I never saw me as a threat, either. Why would I? I had shot and buried most of my self-worth years ago. Every "move" I made was instinctive.

Even when making an exclusive deal with a brand Fiona had adored since childhood.

Even though we met the head of that brand at the same insufferable art party last year.

Even when the head of that brand came to me, specifically, and I should have known that as soon as the campaign launched, it would ruin everything.

But I did it anyway. My gut somehow knew that the only hope for me to quit my vapid life as a manipulative East Side supercunt was to brutally betray my Queen Bee bestie.

The skin flap was softening. I began chewing subtly while Fiona continued chewing me out loud enough for every vaping film bro and clove-smoking beatmaker on this patio to hear.

You're not even gonna deny it?!

There were grains of coke visible on her upper gums.

I swallowed. The moistened skin slid down my esophagus in one rubbery piece. I could almost feel it go SPLASH in the acid hollow of my stomach.

I can't believe I didn't choke.

I'm so sorry, Fi. I'm so sorry.

I meant it. I was sorry. I was the sorriest sadgirl in SoCal that night. I didn't have an excuse. I was trying not to cry, but somehow I was already crying.

Don't you fucking waterworks me into forgiving you, babe. That's not fair.

She was right. I sniffed back the rest of my feelings. Suddenly, Fiona's enormous blue eyes narrowed. She was looking at something on my forehead.

Ew. Is that a moth? Did a moth land on you? Ew!

She reached out and swatted at my temple. Her press-on nails clicked against my hardening skin which, unbeknownst to me, had begun to collect in a knotty protrusion at the base of my hairline.

The knot fell off and hit the stone of the patio between us. It was so dry that it burst into flakes and scattered like salt over Fiona's favorite Chelsea boots. She recoiled, shrieking louder than ever:

Oh my God, what is that?!

All the film bros were looking at us, now. The beatmakers, too. Everyone's exhaled smoke suddenly blew in my direction, surrounding me in a fog of birthday-cake-and-kush-scented CO_2.

I wanted to respond, but the top of my lips were crusting over, and my eyes too—a hard dermal film rapidly forming between me and the living nightmare I was in.

Before my ears filled up with my own molting flesh, I could hear Maddie and Jasmine toddling out onto the patio, tequila-wrecked and giggling. Just in time to witness me as I turned and fled the scene.

Officially abandoning my hard-earned spot in their Very Inner Circle.

I DON'T REMEMBER how I got home.

I do remember that I chose *home* instead of *hospital*. At the time, I told myself I couldn't afford it. Eventually, I would discover that I had neither the strength nor courage to pay the unknown cost of asking for help, be it financial or otherwise. I didn't want to owe anyone anything. Not back then.

It's why I chose the friends I chose and never let them know me.

What I do remember is an hour in the yellow bathroom, almost drowning in my own snot and tears as they accumulated inside my new mask of dying skin. Thrashing around and sobbing and *picking*. So much picking.

I remember the futile attempts to tweeze off the crust over my eyes as my fingers flaked and cracked and grew uselessly coated in gray.

I didn't have a God to pray to, or a safe person to call.

What I remember most is the surrender. Sliding to the cool of the grimy tile floor, unable to see or judge its filth any longer. The tears subsiding.

I remember crawling blind into the bed I would later burn.

I AWOKE ENCASED in a shell of my dead flesh.

Mummified in a husk of my own biological making. I was so afraid.

What would it mean to move? Could I? Would it hurt?

I took a breath, surprised by how much air I could suck in through the cracks of my strange tomb. I took a deeper breath, filling my lungs. Grateful and suddenly *hopeful.*

I began to wriggle and writhe, finding this fully formed sheath was more delicate than I imagined. Not the gruesome integument I had miserably fought to dig holes in last night. I rolled a shoulder, extended my toes. Slowly. Slowly. Letting the husk separate from ME. This ME I had never seen.

I didn't know what she would look like. Who she would be. IF she could be.

It took hours that felt like years. Worming my way through the center of it, pushing my bald skull through layers of crumbling dermis, I emerged…free of the peel.

I rolled away from the bed I would later burn.

I looked back at the empty husk with fondness. My fresh skin raw and stinging in the smog-speckled air of that filthy old house. I smiled.

It hurt to smile.

It wouldn't always.

THE MARCIAS

Addison Heimann

1.

I FUCKING HATE Tuesdays. Hate 'em. Hate 'em, hate 'em, hate 'em. And yeah, I'm journaling and punctuating like I speak—what do you care? I'm the only one reading this stupid thing—so why else does it matter?

So, it's my first journal page. Hurray me! I put my name and number on the front, and if this is found somewhere, your "reward" is a wet, sloppy beej. Therefore, all you femmes out there, stay the fuck away from this journal. You hear me? Hot, sweaty, jockey men only. What was I saying? I hate myself? Oh yeah, but whatever—you always hate yourself. Tuesdays. Oh yeah? I hate Tuesdays. Why? Fuck you, that's why. I don't have a job, so it doesn't really matter—but Tuesdays feel particularly shitty.

Maybe it's cuz Matt dumped me on a Tuesday. No, that was a Friday. He was so insecure about his hair and so insecure about sex because of his three-year relationship that "failed," but, like, it's not my fault. They cured cancer but can't develop a cure for hair loss. Isn't that hilarious? Rogaine is still the only thing that works—and Propecia, I guess, but I want my dick to work. I haven't gotten laid in eight months. Fuck me. Fuck everything. I say fuck a lot—is it too much? My writing teacher in college said that if I say fuck too much it'll turn away the audience—well, that's me, so I guess it doesn't matter.

Anyway, Marcia Prime died today, but, like, that's not about me—I'm just writing it cuz it happened. Dr. J says if I write things that happened that day, I'll get my motivation back. And maybe I'll get out of bed. All I do is learn Japanese—and then go back to bed and surf social media. Not the cutesy *whatever* all the plebeians look at. The underground shit. The terrorist shit. The non-utopian, dark-web, evil shit. The ones that want to take down the status quo. I'm not a terrorist, okay POLICE? If you're reading this. The dark web is just more entertaining than watching stupid anthropomorphic cats dance around, telling me everything's peachy.

Isn't it funny that the leader(s) of the "free" world's name is fucking Marcia? The literal middle child of politics—at least according to that ancient ass show with the big family. MARCIA, MARCIA, MARCIA. Oh wait—was that the popular sister? Honestly, I guess that's apropos—me confusing ancient pop culture. Look at me, using big words. Yeah, I went to Harvard.

LOLOL, I WENT TO HARVARD.

Okay, okay, okay—I should tell a story. *My* story. My deep-seated, dark, evil story. The story of how I'm going to overthrow the government of Marcias. Buahahahahahahahahahahah. Honestly, I'm not sure I have the balls. But what if I did? What would I do? Well, I would have to be a fucking scientist—there are so many Marcias running around that I can't exactly destroy their DNA. I guess I would have to make a disease that would immediately kill all Marcias in one foul swoop. Kill the cops, kill the judges, kill 'em all. Something in the air.

Or I guess the easier thing would be to make sure that people lose faith in the Marcias. But everyone believes in the goddamn Marcias. The perfect Marcia. The one that united the world and left us with gorgeous peace. Gorgina Marcia—leading the free world—everyone's happy. WELL, I'M NOT HAPPY, AND I REFUSE TO TAKE PILLS TO MAKE ME HAPPY. I'm not a cog in a machine, okay? I'm a person, I'm a person, I'm a sad, sad, person. But I'm still a person! God, I want some cocaine. Is this three pages yet? Fuck it, whatever, I'm done.

2.

OKAY, FOUR DAYS later. Whatever. I had a rough time, okay. I found a little coke in the bottom drawer of my bathroom and did some by myself—and then I texted every ex. I mean, *every* ex. I was horny, okay. And guess what? No one responded. So, I had to disappear into the ether of sadness for a bit. It's fine. I'm fine. Well, I'm fine now. Maybe I picked up a knife? I don't know, did I? I can't remember. But Dr. J said to journal, so I'm journaling cuz maybe I'll get all my negative thoughts out. I have so many negative thoughts.

You know what pisses me off? Like, really pisses me off? How come I can't outrun my thoughts? You know? Listen to this schedule I used to keep: I woke up, drank coffee, meditated, did an hour of Japanese, exercised, journaled, ate healthy, and STILL, STILL, I couldn't outrun the anxiety. Like, how fucking unfair is that? And yes, I did journal before this journal. I can feel that you're betrayed, journal, that this isn't my first time, that I'm not a virgin. Wow, dumb joke.

But seriously, how can I do everything, like, literally everything considered to be healthy and still have days where I feel like a piece of shit? A stupid piece of shit that deserves nothing. I hate that I don't need to work. Like, that's not perfect, you stupid, perfect society. I can just sit here and be sad for the rest of my life and have nothing good to distract myself? And then I do bad things to distract myself. I drink. I smoke. I do cocaine. I think I've mentioned cocaine too much. I really don't do that much cocaine. Say cocaine one more time. Cocaine.

A bomb went off near the government building. A suicide bomber. I heard it was a Marcia in the underground world. There are rumors that the "resistance" is being run by a renegade Marcia. Lol, like, can't you come up with a better name than "resistance." I can come up with a better name than that, like…

Okay, come back to me. I'm sad. What do you want? Plus, this isn't about Marcia, this is about me! But honestly—looks like my evil plan is finally coming to fruition. Buahahahahah. JK. It's actually kind of awful. I'm not scared cuz, like, I never leave my apartment. Plus, like, if the world ended right now, I'd be fine with it. I'd be right to feel this way. I'd feel calm. They say that depressed people feel calm at the end of the world. And to feel that moment of calm—oh man—I would just… I would just… Breathe.

3.

I GOT GHOSTED by two guys last night. Hi journal, it's me, it's been three days since my lest confession. TWO!! TWO GENTLEMAN. Both bearded, because, duh, I like what I like. Both named Harry—which hilarious, cuz they're hairy. GET IT?

One was British, one was Australian. Oh, another bomb went off, but everyone knows that. And now we know it's definitely a renegade Marcia. LOL. I know, right? Marcia ain't too big for her britches now, is she?? But we're not talking about Marcia, are we? No, we're talking about me! Teehee.

Okay, back to me. Yeah, I want to be with a British guy, I know I want to be with a British guy, but clearly they don't want to be with me. I don't understand why people ghost. Well, I guess I do—I do it to my friends all the time. Do I even have friends anymore? Who can say? Who would wanna be friends with this lump of crap? This steaming pile of crap. I should probably just get a hooker. And not one of those AI hookers. I don't care if it feels the same. I want someone who feels my dick inside their asshole. Earn their money. Jesus, I hope no one reads this—I'm such a piece of shit.

Do you think the cop-Marcias are jelly of the government-Marcias? Well obviously, right? Hence "renegade Marcia." Honestly that's better than "the resistance"—THAT'S A BETTER NAME. The regenerates. Or is that just a good pop-punk band name? Focus, ME, ME, it's all about MEEEEEEEE. Oof, I wanna die.

Dr. J says I should tell a story about trauma, but, like, why? We were talking the other day. The other day could mean yesterday or six months ago, who can say? And I was, like, okay, here's a weird thing: I have a really strange aversion to collared shirts. And he was like, "Hmmm, weird." And I'm like, yeah. And he's like, "Why do you think that?" And I was like, "Well, my dad used to wear collared shirts and used to get drunk and fall asleep on top of me." But that's not like… I mean… What even is that? Sexual assault? No. Plus, he's dead, so it's not like I can get closure, you know? And he's, like, "Well maybe it's because you didn't have that good of a body in fifth grade and you thought you looked fat in them." And I just LOLLED, cuz, like, that's so fucking stupid.

I don't mean "stupid" in the sense that his idea was stupid. I'd just feel so stupid if that was the reason. But, I mean, Occam's Razor, right? It has to be. But also—dad, drunk, on top of my body. One time he was on top of me and I got a boner. And I touched his chest, and then I got *really* hard. And then he woke up, and I ran away—but he was so drunk he would've never remembered. Was I attracted to him? Or was he just…

I think I should burn this book after I'm done with it—*fuck*—if someone found this, I'd be done. I'd be hated more than I'm hated now. I have dreams of being a part of the renegades. Of joining the renegade Marcia. Of overthrowing this shitty, awful, peaceful place. I'd find a guy—Tom, maybe; I always thought Tom was a hot name—and we would charge the capital building together. AK-47s on our backs. It'd be tough, but I'd be part of the heroes. This world can't be run by one person. What an insane concept. I don't care what they say about crime, I don't get to feel. I just want to feel. I just want someone to hold me and tell me it's going to be all right. I want something to believe in. I want to be the lead in my own story. I want to be the hero. But instead, here I am, on my couch. On my fucking couch. ON MY FUCKING COUCH. I could just jump out the window. And then it would end. And then it would end. And then it would… I should call Dr. J.

4.

I DID SOMETHING stupid yesterday. But also, it felt so good. On the underground socials, they were organizing a protest against the Marcias, and… and… I WENT. I WENT. I went, and it felt glorious, but also stupid, but glorious. And people were screaming and marching and screaming. There were so many people, and I was a part of something. I was a part of the resistance.

Yeah, that was a lie. I stayed in my apartment, masturbating all day. What kind of porn do I masturbate to? GLAD YOU ASKED. Nah, I don't need to get graphic. I would like to pause your regularly scheduled programming to remind the viewers that I am a piece of shit. A stupid piece of shit. Okay, now that we are informed of the obvious, we can move on.

What actually happened is this: There was a protest, and a troupe of Marcias gunned down the crowd. No blood, though. A utopia would never murder anyone, right? They would just arrest people for reintegration—you know, mind control and shit. It's crazy the stuff you see on the state socials. People renouncing the renegade Marcia and pledging their faith to the world order and stuff. Marcia knows best, Marcia knows best, Marcia knows best. The second Marcia—Marcia 2: Electric Boogaloo—now in control of the government. She's the cool Marcia. And by that, I mean she has pink hair. Because that's what the AIs say is "most calming."

Maybe I should join an AI collective. Those always felt like cults, but at least I'd get to go to virtual orgies. And the occasional real-life orgy. Although in virtual you can make yourself look however you want, and, like, don't get me wrong, I'm hot, but I got a little bit of a pooch, ya know—the thirty-year-old pooch sponsored by Chick-fil-A. Yes, I'm a bad gay, so sue me, their chicken is delicious.

A guy I fell in love with for twenty-four hours when I was in England reached out to me. Responding to my coke text a week later. He has a boyfriend who's ugly. But I'm not there, and I can't afford to go there anyway. Plus, look at you, you stupid piece of shit. I asked him what he thought of the Marcia resistance, what it looks like from somewhere else. He's like, "Yeah, the world is laughing at you." But what does he know? England barely has fresh water anymore, but at least they're free. Really free. Like, fuck-in-the-streets free. I can't even grieve here. People look at me like I'm going to upset the balance.

Oh yeah, Dad died a year ago today.

Do I wanna talk about that? Not really. Maybe instead, I should write a comic book about Marcia and her band of hot jocks that go around saving the day from the evil dystopian Marcia collective. And Marcia leads them, and they all love each other in some giant polyamorous gorgeous way and… Am I about to write porn? Maybe I should write porn. You'd think the deep-fake porno movies would've taken off more than they did. But turns out, it's not that fun to watch celebrities fuck if you don't know exactly what their bodies look like. No matter how real it is.

I write a lot about sex in this. Can you tell I haven't been laid in years? I wonder if the Marcias all have orgies. Would that be incest? I mean… Clonecest? There's gotta be porn of that. Rule 34 and all.

Dad would've joined the resistance, wouldn't he have? He would've stood up for what is right. He would've been an asshole about it, but he would've done it. What have you done? Why don't you do something? Why do you just sit on the couch all day whining about how terrible your life is? Why can't you just be a fucking man, get up, find something to believe in, and believe in it, for Christ's sake. Your world is dying. I mean, it's not dying—the world is filled with a surplus of food and shit—but our culture is dying. Our world. You have the power to change all that.

No, you don't. Jesus. You're nothing. You really are nothing. Don't you know that?

5.

THERE WAS A coup today. Lol. What is this, Richard III? Is there a coup in *Richard III*? I don't know—I've only read *Romeo and Juliet*—which is a banger, banger play, lemme tell you. I've always wanted to fuck the literal Romeo on the page. Or maybe, I really just wanted to fuck young Leo from that old flat screen adaptation.

Marcia 2 is dead. BOOM. Oh shit, right? The military Marcia tribunal has taken over for now as we figure out how it happened. We were told it was suicide, but there's no way. A Marcia has never committed suicide. I bet it was the renegade Marcia. There are checkpoints and shit now, like every block, but honestly not much has changed in my day to day, but I don't need to go outside for anything. So, fuck you too, world—a bitch is fine inside. I wish for the old days when policemen were hot and had mustaches. Then I'd try and seduce all those steamy boys back to my apartment and… Okay, I need to masturbate.

Honestly, I swear Marcias are vampires.

I wish uploading your mind into the cloud was possible. Cuz then I could create my own universe. And my own world. I would have a husband (or "partner," as they say). He'd have red hair, green eyes, a banging body, wear glasses, love my writing, love me, kiss me on the nose, and hold me at night until I was like, okay, I need to go to sleep. Cuz he knows I can't fall asleep when I'm cuddling, but he understands. And he doesn't want to sleep with other people, and he doesn't want to include a third, he doesn't want to go to sex parties, he just wants to be with me.

I know that we're supposed to be liberated 'n' shit, but even sleeping with AIs feels like cheating to me. Is that homophobic of me? It probably is. I love that the world is basically ending and yet I'm dreaming of being in a relationship. My great-grandfa-ther told me a story about one time when he went to Rwanda. I know, we all hate those "that one time I went to Africa" stories, but hear me out. There was this huge genocide there a long time ago, and he went there and was like, woah, these people are just like us. They want families, they want careers, they date, they fall in love, they experience heartache, they dance, they're literally HUMAN. So, maybe it's not so bad that this is what I'm dreaming of.

I don't know what the next world will look like, but I think I might have been wrong to believe in something like this. Cuz people are dying and shit. And I still haven't left my apartment.

But, like, it's not my fight.

Dr. J said I shouldn't feel so guilty for things that happen. And it's true, I don't. But I think I feel guilty for, well, a lot of things. I feel guilty all the time. I can't sleep, I feel so guilty. I thought I was supposed to feel calm at the end of the world. I just feel the same thing I felt before! What the fuck? Now I'm mad. I'm so fucking mad. I thought I was supposed to feel calm. That's not fair.

Maybe I should make a list of all the things I wanted to do but won't get to do now? Jesus, no, I'm not some vapid bitch facing the end of the world. I have enough self-awareness to know that no one cares what my life "could have been." It really doesn't matter.

I haven't talked about my mother in this journal—not that I care about that. She died in childhood, which, lol at things that can still happen (see my cancer retort in my first entry). I'm rambling now, I don't know what to say. I don't want to look at the news. I don't want to watch the sphere, I don't wanna go outside, I don't want to talk to people, I don't want to be on my couch. I want… I want… I fucking want…

FUCK.

6.

DEAR… WHOEVER FINDS this.

It'll probably be no one, cuz duh. Welp, I finally decided to kill myself. If you're reading this, I'm dead. Teehee. There won't be blood, don't worry. The last thing I want, I'm assuming, is for Ronnie the supe to have to clean up all the blood before the next renter comes in and takes it.

You're probably wondering why I decided to do this, and the truth is, *meh*, I don't know. There's not one big or small thing that made me decide. I just…need to do this, I guess. Maybe it's cuz the renegade Marcia was finally killed, and everything is back to normal. People are happy again. Doesn't that fucking suck?

Like, UGH, I wish something changed, but that's the thing, nothing changes in a perfect world. We get bleeps and bloops, but overall, nothing changes.

People are sheep, they're always looking for ways to go back to eating grass. Look at me. I could've found the renegades if I wanted to. I could've done something. But nope, I stood in my apartment feeling like a piece of shit, and the truth is, I'll always be a piece of shit, and that's fine. The world doesn't need another piece of shit, cuz duh, right?

I don't really feel anything, but that's fine. What is there to feel? It's a suicide note. I mean, why am I even writing this? Well, I suppose it's for you, Ronnie. Okay—so let's not be all sad and stuff. If there's one thing I can do, I'll try to make you laugh, Ronnie. Cuz you're gonna find the dead body… Probably in two weeks, when rent's due, and you're gonna have to deal with the shock.

So, Ronnie.

Ronnie, my boy!!! Ron, Ronald! Le sigh, I don't know, what do you want from me! It's not your fault I died, you knew that. I once dreamt that we were fucking. Well, you had a penis on your nose, and I was sucking it. You probably didn't need to know that. Maybe I should masturbate one more time before I end it… *Nah*… You masturbate plenty, dude. Okay, now this is just an internal monologue. Sorry, Ron.

Um… Should I tell you the story of the time I fucked up my best friend's relationship? Nah, that's sad. What about…? What about the time I went to Italy with my dad, and we couldn't stop fighting to the point where I faked sick in order to go home?

What about my coming-out story? It's juicy—it was with a man twice my age. Huh? Huh? Huh?

I don't know. You'd think the end of a life would be more meaningful to me, but I just feel nothing. There are times in my life when I dreamt that I was meant to be more than who I was. Like some famous writer, like a journalist, or a memoirist, or something. Or maybe even a singer.

Back in elementary school, before my voice changed, I had this powerhouse of a fuckin' voice, and my carpool mates used to make me sing. And I was good, *really* good. Famous! Does everyone dream of being famous when they're a kid? Or is my ego just so out of whack that there was a time when I truly believed that I could change the world?

I guess Marcia thought she could change the world, and she did. I wonder how she reacted when the first person asked her if she'd consider cloning herself? I wonder if she thought it would get this far? That not only would there be a President Marcia, but judiciary Marcias, and Chief of Police Marcias. That her face would become ubiquitous with peace. I mean, I personally would like to shit all over her face, but I guess it's safe to say that most people think she was the second coming of Jesus Christ. Maybe she was.

You know one thing I will regret? Never learning Japanese. I stuck with it until the end. I even did it this morning. Isn't that funny? A couple years ago, when I still had the will to work, I had plans to go to Japan for a whole month. Me and my friend Jenny were gonna go. Kyoto, Tokyo, Osaka, and everything in-between. Ride the old bullet trains, see the cherry blossoms, meet the animatronic version of Hayao Miyazaki. And then I broke my leg and couldn't go.

I broke my fucking leg and couldn't go. It's funny—back then I didn't even speak Japanese, and now I'm halfway decent. I mean, I would have to speak very slowly, and they'd have to speak very slowly, but I could get by. I could at least ask where the bathroom is. And say things like "I LOVE SHOPPING," even though I hate shopping and am so glad I never have to shop again.

I'm babbling. I'm babbling cuz I don't know where to end things. Usually I do, I usually know exactly where to stop, exactly when I should stop speaking, but this is the end. The end is so crucial and yet I always had problems with endings. They were always too long, or didn't match the tone of the rest, or felt like long denouements, but I'm here, at the end, and I don't want to go yet. I mean, let's be clear, I very very very much want to go, but I also want to keep writing for just a little longer.

So, Ronnie, I'm sorry you had to read through a bunch of bullshit, but hey, if you're the only one who reads this, then that's fine. Do me a favor, the dying wish of a stupid piece of shit: take down the Marcias for me. Take 'em all down. Create that gas that'll wipe out only Marcias.

Destroy the world, raise it back up to what it used to be. I don't even know what it used to be, but I have to think it was better than this. Lol, I'm just kidding, the world is fine. I'm the stupid piece of shit that doesn't belong it in anymore. Or maybe I do, but at this point, I very much do not want to.

Hey look, I finally got to three pages.

A YOUNG GIRL FINISHES HER DINNER

Avalon Fast

A YOUNG GIRL finishes her dinner. Her eyes glaze over the TV in front of her. A show she does not understand. She laughs when her parents do. She sits in her chair. They warn her of the time. It hurts her inside. She goes early to her room to avoid the sentencing. The stairs take forever to climb; this house was poorly built. At the top sits her room. A room fit for a child, the only child in the house.

She has rituals, things she *has* to do before she sleeps. Whispers them to herself as they are done. The same shirt must be worn to bed, it's dirty, it doesn't matter. She keeps her window cracked, *this* much, even in November, which it was. Calls the same goodnight when her mom has finished tucking her in. "Sleep well", a quote her mom laughs at every time. She tells her mom every night how worried she is. When her mom leaves, it feels as though she has locked the door. The light leaves from the hall. She stares at the ceiling, and the world opens up inside of her.

Let me explain where this child comes from. The house sits on the side of a mountain, in a deep valley. The nearest town has a population of less than three hundred people. Her parents never told her why they lived there. It's some kind of life, but she does not know if it is a life she likes. Her dad built the house. Built it around her as she grew. It was made to hold her. The house sat on a large expanse of land. It was an hour's walk to any neighbors, or a twenty-minute drive. They were alone there on the mountain. At night as her parents slept and she lay awake, she knew she was the only one. Her solace lay in the sounds of the slow highway which was relatively close. She could hear the cars, their coming and going. She knew life was out there, she could hear it, every couple of minutes she could hear it. In the daytime she would roam the hills and meadows, she only got lost a couple of times, the highway sounds guiding her back home. What a feeling she had wandering—of freedom, of trees. In the winter her coat would get soaked and wrecked, and in the summer, bees stung her face. Large foxgloves grew rapidly in the spring. As a smaller child, she put the petals in her mouth and was rushed to the hospital. Foxglove holds a chemical that goes straight to your heart; it slows it down. She remembered sitting on the hill that summer, her body becoming heavy, and the buzzing of the earth slowly muting.

There were places, specific pieces of land she would go to. They felt like hers, but she didn't own them. They were sacred. But the last one had something else, a darkness to it, even during the day. A protective shield, a barrier against most. The last place she found, she named the dunes.

She found it on a bike ride across the highway. The ride took close to thirty minutes. A couple of times, she was forced to get off her bike and climb over logs and streams, hauling the bike behind. When the path stopped, it felt sudden. She felt unsafe, but she didn't think about turning around. She could see the skyline open up maybe one hundred meters in front of her. Thick bushes and trees lay in her way. She heard nothing, and she imagined a field. Bike abandoned, she moved forward quickly, no path, just emptiness ahead of her. A field she hoped, a field she prayed. In a field she could lay. Her very own space to lay down and let her life float right over her head. She pictured a tree in the middle, a big maple with branches too high to climb. It meant something to her. She had been somewhere like this before, and she wanted to be there now. Alone. The thought of peace led her to panic, and the impatient panic led her legs toward the opening. Bushes and branches cut her ankles, one almost too deep. She didn't notice much.

The open grew closer, but not as quickly as she had anticipated. The entire walk, she felt as though it was growing farther away.

Only when it finally showed could she hear it. The loud rushing of a heavy river. It startled her. The visions of her peaceful field drifted away, replaced by the ominous energy of this screaming riverbed and large dark sand dunes across the way. She stared down the deep bank into the river's powerful flow. Though it was not what she expected, it felt perfect. The divinity of the water, the power of its movement. There were no thoughts before she slid down the bank and into the river. She didn't stop to remove her clothes. She wanted the other side, she wanted to sit there on the other side, needed to. The water was cold and pushy. It moved her against her will, and she worried for a moment it might pull her somewhere else entirely. She wanted to be here. Her ankles bled and stung in the water. She fought against it and grasped the edge of the earth on the other side. Sitting there now, she heaved. She laid down. It was quiet, save for the ringing in her ears.

When she sat upright and looked up, it was dizzying. The stark sun stiffened her on the sand. The air was still. She felt nervous about the tree line and what might lay behind her. So strong, she did not turn around. Rather, she kept looking toward where she had come from. A nightmarish feeling came over here: that she would not be able to return. Her clothes were heavy and wet, and she noticed her breathing was scattered from the sudden plunge. The sun glared so bleak it made the sand dusty and the sky gray. She dug her hands into the sand and let her fear eat her. The way home would feel longer, with no destination of the unknown to pull her back. Everything that way she already knew. *This was not the kind of place you want to see in the dark.* She said that, over and over, in her mind. "Stay with yourself," she repeated, this time out loud. She had a tendency when panicked to lose something quickly within herself. She would lose time, minutes mostly, to this void within her panic. Never hours. Maybe once. She didn't want to lose it here; she didn't want to move farther into the unknown that lay behind her.

She thought of this as she lay awake. She remembered the time and only imagined it could be close to 11:00 p.m. Her alarm clock had been taken away from her a long time ago. She hid it from herself. She couldn't bear knowing for sure. Maybe it was the dream that kept her from sleeping. This one in particular plagued her. If she had known she would have it, she would have spent the night reading to stay awake.

The night was still and silent, a dull evil clouded the windows of her bedroom. Nothing moved, no one spoke. An unfamiliar presence stood beside her, one that resembled her mother. They both stood up straight in her room. The furniture was missing. The presence had no eyes, but it looked at her with bad intentions. Slowly, there was a noise. From down the stairs, where she could not see. She listened. Something began to climb the staircase. As it did, she slowly peeled her eyes away from her mother and directed them toward the top of the stairs, waiting. The sound of it approaching fed her fear until she was full. As it arrived, its back was facing her. It was only a man, a man moving very slowly. It stopped at the top of the stairs. When it turned to face her, its front was drawn out and long, like that of a bird. Skin stretched to fit over the long bones of its face. It moved toward her quickly once she was spotted. When it reached her, she did not wake up.

Late day tomorrow. Morning had been okay. It was the weekend. Her parents weren't there. They had things to do, she guessed. She drank a black coffee, poured from the bottom of the press. It was full of grounds. She lay on the carpet in the living room, felt the dirt on her face and hands. She yelled to her mom that it was disgusting in there. Her mom said nothing. *Where was she?* She walked outside. *Mom?* She sat on her swing, a singular swing attached to a maple tree. The world stretched out before her. Just beyond the highway lay her field, her field of rushing water and burning sand. She sat on her unfinished deck, dangled her legs off and felt nauseous about the height. This was a time to reflect. She knew it before she was old enough to know it. It's midday, and she is twelve years old.

It is 5:00 p.m. last spring, and she has adopted a kitten and named her Snow. Snow comes home in a cage. A cage that she has tied with a pink bow on top. It is 7:00 p.m., and the small white kitten prefers to lay in the nook of her back. It will not leave. Snow may have been too small to leave her nest, too cold to leave the warmth of her mother. So, she sits curled in the nook of her back. She sleeps. It is 9:00 p.m., and it is time for bed. She had been lying on her stomach for two hours. She did not want to disturb the kitten. She moves slowly now and puts the kitten in her box, carries it downstairs because the cat will not stop crying. It is 3:00 a.m., and she has gone downstairs to check on her tiny cat. Snow is not crying. She has wrapped her neck inside the bow and suffocated there. She stared into the cage unsure how to move. A sort of swelling grew in her stomach, an intense, nauseating pain. Her throat was cold. She screamed for her parents, then tried quickly to remove her kitten from the bow. She lay between her mom and dad that night and decided she should learn to pray. Decided she had done wrong by God. She decided very easily that it was very much her fault.

Through praying she found something. Not forgiveness, but a greater understanding of what may have happened. The course of nature, the consequence of mistakes. The entire realness of her understanding that this was, in fact, her fault. She sat in the forest, and she prayed. Prayed to keep knowing, to continue understanding. She prayed to know rest and peace. The air grew colder, and October bled into November. The air was too harsh to not travel in a warm jacket. She visited her old Austrian neighbor, a path through the trees that led to the top of her property. As she arrived, the old sheep greeted her anxiously. Years of neglect and weather showed on their wool. Thick, heavy sheep saying a sad hello. She walks to her neighbor's house. A house with deep water damage and old carpets to cover the sinking floor. Her neighbor's husband died from falling on the ice on his way to feed the sheep last Christmas. He was found late, half frozen and wishing to be gone. She sat at her neighbor's table and stared at the hanging cages where birds sat trapped. There must have been five cages and about nine birds, all named Hansel or Gretel. Her neighbor spoke of life and loss and the honey her bees used to make in the summer. On her walk back home, she missed everything and wished she had never been born.

It is 2:00 p.m. last summer, and she sits on the concrete of her back patio, in the shade. She heaves into her hands. It has been months since the accident. She thinks about it less and less. Something else is wrong. The day is too long and empty—they all are—and the thought of the long empty days strung together in a row is too much. She thinks harder. Something deep and dark decides to follow her now. There is no sense, only wet tears and worry. She has not slept, she has not eaten. Her mother pats her back, and she forgets where she is. Time and age would help. Her mother reassures her of this. Reminds her that she will get older, she won't be able to help it.

She sat in her chair for dinner. Adult cartoons. Something, something. The food tasted wrong; she ate it anyway. Her parents did not laugh at the TV tonight. She looked at their faces, the sides of them. She smiled at them each, waiting to see if they would look. They didn't. The TV went on and on. Her focus came in and out.

Once in bed, she realized the cartoons had no sound attached, and she had forgotten her rituals tonight. She couldn't remember the day before. She whistled out loud. She sat up and looked out of the window. It was still, silent, save the light thrum of the insects filling the evening. It was warm. She wished the wind would howl and the rain would pour. She wished she wasn't alone. You have to be alone as a child. Unless you are granted a small sibling who you love, you must be alone. This would be something she would think of later, in her years to come. Who was she without someone watching her? She imagined through her own eyes what it would be like to live her life through someone else's. What they might think. Would they love the way she thought? From conciseness, she wanted a partner. It was so empty to think and breathe and behave all alone.

Her face pressed snug against her window as she watched shadows move through the forest, listened to the noise from cars passing on the highway every few moments. Unease grew in her stomach. Her nervous system tested her. She did not feel safe here. Her head lay on her pillow again. She squeezed her eyes closed. Something pulled at her, though, from inside—a thought:

What if…she got out of bed and walked toward the highway? Across the highway led to the path, and across the path led to the river. It didn't seem possible. But after thinking about it, it felt less possible to stay put. Standing now, she pulled on clothes, just the ones on the floor, it didn't matter. As she moved down the stairs, she worried her parents would catch on to her fleeing. No one stirred. No one moved. As she trudged down the hill toward the highway, her legs carried her without her asking them to. The night sky was clear, and the moon and stars led her way. They blinked at her as the trees passed overhead. *Thump thump thump,* her body was loud in the quiet evening. Dead stop by the highway, no cars passed, no one witnessed her cross. The farmland stretched out behind her. The small houses with lights turning off in the distance. The fading smoke from living room fires. She walked the path, she did not bike. It took a long time. On the way, she thought about a lot of things. She thought first of her parents, the people she was closest to, she thought of their faces. Particularly her mother's, how she was never calm, never at peace. But she had played, played with her when no one else did. She thought about her dad, his absence in her younger years, the house he built, the night he drank himself to silence all alone in the living room. The deep love he had for her. His quiet nature. She looked at herself and couldn't recognize either of them. She thought of life at school, the time she spent alone. She thought deeply of the time she spent alone. The time she held a kitten at a kid's birthday party. They had been in a circle, each with a moment to hold the small cat. She waited patiently, her eyes locked on the pet, the conversations of other children tuned out. Focus was essential. When the kitten was placed in her lap, it shut its eyes, didn't squirm to leave. The other children had already had a turn and got up to play. When the mother came to collect the kitten, she started to cry. She held onto that thought for a while. Sat with her, remembering the warmth. Wanted to keep her, wanted to so bad. Something was missing inside of her. She wasn't sure if it had ever been there. Her memories were young ones, fragments without the words to understand them fully. More daydreams, less knowing. Growing older would have helped.

When she reached the river, she felt more known. She had gone over her life, her love, her wants. Some things had been understood, some never would be. She crossed. The water felt the same as she did, cold. She returned to her place. The sun no longer shone. Darkness in the sky was reflected in the river. She lay with her cheek in the sand, still looking toward home. The night surrounded her, lay its head down with her. She knew it was ending; her time had finally come. She wondered when someone would come to find her. She had wanted to stay here to see, but her body ached with her in it. So, it was then she decided to leave.

ALL HAIL THE KING

Jesse Aultman

THE MATINEE ENDED with obligatory applause. Absentminded. Half-hearted. Short. Wallace King finished his bow, and the spotlight went off. Darkness enveloped him. This was the moment King lived for, feeding off the crowd's energy like a relentless parasite, their buzz satisfying his insatiable hunger, temporarily. It was magic (or the closest thing to it).

But today, he felt nothing. The house lights returned, and he saw a sparse audience shuffle toward the exit of the Isabelle Grand Theatre. There would be no encore. No finale. Instead, he'd have to wait. The evening show was only a few hours away and then he could feast.

King slipped away from the theater's edge and retreated backstage. He entered a labyrinth of corridors and navigated it with ease. He moved like a mouse in a maze, focused solely on one mission, bypassing crew and stagehands without a word.

When he arrived at his dressing room, he opened the door and frowned. Sitting in his favorite red couch was Mr. Schoenberry, an older gentleman with the voice of an ashtray and a hairline that parted like the Red Sea. He also happened to be the theater owner and Wallace King's boss.

"Take a seat. This will only take a minute."

King sat across from Mr. Schoenberry in an uncomfortable chair.

"Listen, Wallace, I'm not going to waste any more of your time, and I'm sure as shit not going to waste any more of mine." He took a long drag on his cigarette. The embers expanded and cracked. A hazy smoke floated through the room, reflecting off the vanity lights like '70s Hollywood. "We're letting you go. No easy way to say it, but it's time to move on. For both of us."

King's eyes widened. A shot of adrenaline surged through his veins. He felt primal and strong, yet the ground beneath his feet crumbled.

As he went to speak, Mr. Schoenberry waved him down. "I know what you're going to say. *You can't do this. I've been here for twenty years. I've built this theater. I'm Wallace fucking King. Save it.*" He extinguished the cigarette with a hiss, ramming it into the ashtray until it was dead and quiet. "I've heard it all before. Performers before you told me the same shit, and Lord willing, I'll hear it from some schmuck after you too."

King was speechless. All he could muster was a pathetic and frankly weak, "But why?"

Mr. Schoenberry just rolled his eyes. "People don't care anymore, Wallace. It's as simple as that. You make an orchestra appear on stage, so what? You light a candle without touching it, big fucking deal. Check out the reviews sometime. You're not fooling anyone."

With that, Mr. Schoenberry handed him a thick stack of papers. It was a termination agreement, and the top of the page pointedly read: *Mutual Release.*

"I'm not signing this."

"Sign this or you don't perform tonight. You want the matinee to be your last show?" Mr. Schoenberry searched his jacket for a pen. "Now, where did I put—"

With the flick of his wrist and the flurry of his hand, King revealed the Isabelle Grand's signature gold pen. Like he pulled it out of thin air (because of course he had). He wasn't wearing long sleeves or a topit or using any other parlor tricks. He had simply manifested it. Pure magic.

But Mr. Schoenberry only scoffed. "You're an odd duck," he said, standing. "Just get the document back to me before the show tonight, and you'll have one last standing ovation." He walked to the door, but before he could exit, a crazed look glossed over King's eyes.

He must have the final word and now faced the choice between begging for his career or cutting down the very man who built it. In a rare turn of events, he chose the former and did something perhaps he had never done before in his professional career. He told the truth.

"Mr. Schoenberry, what if I said my illusions were real? It's not a trick or an act. It's for real. And I can do far more than this."

Mr. Schoenberry opened the door but did not turn around to deliver the final blow. "Honestly, Wallace, I don't give a damn how you do it—never asked. And even more honestly, I should have dropped you a year or two ago. I'm probably your only friend left in Vegas." Then he closed the door and disappeared into the theater's labyrinth.

A lingering trail of smoke drifted by and pulled King's gaze to the mirror. He was clearly approaching sixty, and his hair transplant and number of facial surgeries added a mix of youth that just seemed off. Like a Frankenstein's monster of cosmetics and gravity. *Maybe Mr. Schoenberry was right. Maybe time had passed him by.*

His eyes shifted to the black-and-red sign above the vanity: *Experience the Impossible.* His slogan, a calling card of over two decades, now felt like a big joke. People didn't believe in the impossible anymore. People nowadays needed something more, something tangible, irrefutable, a bona fide Biblical miracle, and he would give it to them. Wallace King was proof of the impossible. His mother had known it, too, and was deathly afraid of him.

From the time he was three, King could perform unexplainable feats. He moved objects without touching them, gave his mother headaches when he was angry, and sometimes even read her thoughts. His mother believed he was born of the devil (or maybe she just saw too much of his father in him). Either way, King stood alone and loved it.

A door whipped open, and an intern poked her head inside, "Mr. Wallace, hair and makeup are ready to come in for a checkup."

"Tell them it can wait."

She closed the door, and as King clenched his fist, the lock immediately bolted. Rest was imperative now. Tonight would require his all. It would be the greatest trick he ever pulled.

THE SPOTLIGHT STRUCK down like lightning, igniting center stage and casting the rest of the auditorium in darkness. Wallace King stepped into the circular beam, and a mild applause greeted him. *Time for a fucking show.*

"Ladies and gentlemen," his voice echoed through the mic, "thank you for being here this evening. We have quite a show in store for you." The moderate reception dissipated, and silence overtook the room. This stillness felt performative, but it was anything but. They were in the eye of the storm now. They just didn't know it yet.

"But before we begin, I want to say I've heard some rumblings about this show." He made his phone appear in one quick flourish, but the audience wasn't impressed. "One reviewer says, *The only magic to be found at Wallace King's latest show is the exit.* Another writes, *The most surprising thing about King's act is that he still has a stage to perform it.*"

The crowd let out an uncomfortable laugh. *Should they be playing along?*

"Well, I wanna let you know tonight will be a little different. Tonight, we'll do something that's never been done before." King slowly lifted the house lights with his mind. He imagined technicians back in the control room scrambling to understand what was going on, fighting against a console that seemed to move on its own.

"But first," King smiled, "I do need a volunteer."

A few hands instantly sprung up, including a blonde couple stage-left who shouted his name and waved their hands like a pair of rattlesnakes. His eyes shifted right past them. Tonight was a typical crowd, an unrefined cocktail of Midwestern families, local elderly, and young lovers who couldn't afford another show. As his gaze shifted further right, a hand shyly sprouted.

"You, sir. Come on up."

The man stood and made his way down the aisle. Middle-aged and indifferent to his battle with Father Time, he proudly sported a hideous Las Vegas Hawaiian shirt and was incapable of containing a goofy grin that stretched coast to coast across his face. He was an unremarkable man in every way. King's favorite. He loved using the ordinary to do the extraordinary.

"What's your name, sir?" King asked, helping the man onto the stage.

"Tom," he said. "From Minnesota."

King found it odd that the man offered up "Minnesota," and so did the audience. They laughed. Not at Tom—it didn't appear—but with him. Unremarkable but lovely.

"Well, Tom from Minnesota," he said, mimicking the accent. It got a few chuckles. "Thank you for being part of the show. You ever assisted in a magic act before?"

"No, sir."

"You picked a damn good one to start," King said. "Now, all I need you to do is close your eyes and tell me what you see."

He lowered the house lights again, and the spotlight encompassed them. The rest of the crowd dissolved away, and it was like they were the only two in the room. Even the sound seemed to dull. The whispers of the crowd had tamed with anticipation.

Tom considered and then said, "I don't see anything."

"Oh, come on. Have a little imagination. This is where we experience the impossible."

Tom closed his eyes tighter. His forehead wrinkled, brow narrowed. King watched him carefully and then slipped his hands behind his back, fingers spread as wide as the sky.

"Wait," Tom said, "I see you. How am I doing this?"

"Never mind that. You'll break the spell. Do you see anything else?"

Tom searched his mind. *Looking. Looking. Stop.* His smile slowly faded. "Yeah," he said, trembling, "I don't know if I want to do this anymore."

"Just tell us what you see."

"I see…" Tom hesitated, and then it happened.

In one swift motion, King swung his arms out and lifted Tom into the air—an explosion of wind, a roar from the crowd. Time slowed as King clasped his fist, and Tom's body snapped. An unholy sound, a cacophony of limbs and ligaments yanked apart like a rubber band, folding onto themselves, warping Tom's dimensions, his bodily structure now that of a Picasso.

Then King relaxed, and Tom's lifeless body fell. An underwhelming thud.

A hushed terror whisked around the auditorium, the audience teetering between silence and full-blown panic. A family in the back quietly stood. The father covered his daughter's eyes, and King saw him mouth the words, "It's not real, honey. It's not real."

Oh, but it was.

"Ladies and gentlemen," King laughed. "It's all part of the show."

He lifted his hand into the air and turned it clockwise. The theater doors locked with a thunderous latch, booming across the venue and plummeting the crowd into chaos. Row after row ignited into a furious sprint. The father held his daughter tight as swarms pushed their way past, enveloped by its tidal wave.

"We haven't even gotten to the magic yet." King was genuinely upset. "Who leaves before the reveal?"

People pulled the door handles. Others rammed against the metal. But there was no escape.

King twirled his hand, and the audience slowly turned back toward the stage, their bodies unyielding to an irresistible compulsion. A chorus of anguished screams pierced the air—unknowable fear. Their eyes, wide and uncomprehending, looked up to King as if he were a god.

Once the dust settled, King took a deep breath—just like he had rehearsed it—and started: "When I was a kid, Edward was my best friend. Edward was also my cat."

Looking out over the theater, he made eye contact with a horrified grandma in a flowery dress. She kept mouthing, "Be gone from me, devil. Be gone." It reminded him of his mother, and he supposed she was right all along.

"We did everything together," King continued, "and it got to the point that my mother threatened to give him away. She said

I needed to make friends at school. Real friends. But Edward was very real to me."

That's when the doors bulged. A loud pounding came from the other side. Word traveled fast, and Isabelle Grand security had arrived. King compartmentalized his thoughts, two versions of himself splitting like an atom. Part focused on the doors. The other continued the story.

"As Edward got older, though, he went blind and became easily frightened. I went to pick him up once, and he scratched me across the chest." A dark and troubled expression—like a storm cloud on a summer's day—revealed itself. "He didn't mean to, but I was hurt."

He slowly knelt down on the stage, his knees resting in a pool of blood from Tom's ruptured spine. A gentle ripple flowed through the red, and his clothes became wet.

"And in a moment of rage," King roared, "I clenched my fist, and Edward's neck snapped!"

He squeezed his palm, and the audience screeched. It was like a jump scare in a horror picture, and King had played them like a fiddle. He relished in this. After years of unexceptional performances, the audience now couldn't look away, and he fed on their pulse, their energy, and it tasted oh so good.

"Of course, I was upset and couldn't believe what I had done."

Fog drifted out of the stage and rolled over the theater seats. The lights behind King came alive, too. Streaks of royal blue cut through the black, their hues shifting and twirling in a hypnotic, almost kaleidoscopic ballet. Then there was the music. It started soft but grew, a whimsical melody that steadily morphed into triumph.

"So, I reached out my hand, and I did the impossible!"

King bowed his head and placed a hand on Tom's body. This required his full concentration. His full strength. He could feel his power swell, a mystical sensation that not even King quite understood. Yet, with each passing second, he grew stronger, his magic surging through his arm and into the corpse and—

Tom started to shake. Tremble. His limbs flailing, convulsing, an uneasy pitter patter of nails against wood. The crowd was in disbelief, their sobs swallowed by silence.

The doors heaved again, and King couldn't hold them. He had to give everything. He gripped Tom tighter, clenched his teeth, and let out a strained yell.

Snap! The stage cracked, splintering right in two, and it didn't stop there. The crevice continued its way down the pews, opening a canyon into the abyss.

But King kept going. He was almost there. Tom's eyelids opened and rolled over white. Horrific gargling came from his throat. Blood bubbled inside his mouth like a cauldron.

King felt his power depleting, his entire body losing its warmth. A cold, creeping feeling approached, like icy tendrils had coiled around his heart. He had never felt this before. *Weak. Scared. Normal.* Still, he gave one final jolt, and Tom woke up screaming.

It was an unimaginable yell. Something neither King nor the audience had heard before (or would ever hear again). It was the cry of the dead, the wailings of a man who did not know which realm he walked. He was inconsolable, his limbs still twisted in knots no sailor could untie.

King climbed to his feet and awaited his reception. He looked to his audience, their faces filled with awe and horror, witnesses to an event beyond human comprehension. The security team remained frozen, too. The theater doors were open now but useless.

Hopefully, Mr. Schoenberry read these fucking reviews.

"You've been a lovely audience," King said, breathless. He let the spotlight wash over him, savoring its glow, its touch. Streaks beamed down like sun rays, and his belly became full. Like a gluttonous tick that no longer needed blood and could let go.

"Now, when someone tells you something is impossible, I want you to say that you've experienced the impossible."

Then the spotlight went out, and the crowd erupted.

HI, STRANGENESS.

Jackson Murray

A place of things unknown.

THE STUMBLE TOWARD cosmic digestion and assimilation truly began for Duane Leavitt when his crew breached our mouth. Duane was a small man, large in stature and inheritance, a wild shock of graying hair like Samson before Delilah. A sensual lout, not in the Biblical sense but rather the literal one—he wanted dominion over anything he saw, smelled, heard, touched, or tasted. To him, one word defined both what he hunted for and whose treasure it was: mine.

His grunts were an array of unparticular men with unparticular skills, like chewing the tops off beer cans or flipping their eyelids inside out. They'd been at it for months in vain attempt to find one lost lode or another, as is their God-and-country-and-father-granted wont, stymied always by mechanical failure or unexplainable flooding or psychological assault—unsuccessful warnings, unheeded. But maybe by luck, or by sheer force of that damnable human will (Duane would argue the latter), they finally found their way in.

A celebratory cigarette was the only reason Duane didn't find the body himself. One of the townies he'd scraped off the barroom floor was following the sound of our voice when he saw it, and it was he who noticed the gold nugget sticking out of the corpse's mouth, swiftly passing from one pocket to another. We'd been attempting to say *"leeeeeave itttt,"* but they hear what they like—even Duane's last name, a warning. Frankly, if the townie's mind hadn't been so feeble and his heart so starved to begin with, we wouldn't have been able to send the body there in the first place. So all goes as it must. As it always has.

By the time the man was lucid enough to describe what he'd seen and haunted enough to display the nugget, Duane believed him another in a line of lunatics who'd crossed his path during this long journey, each suddenly besieged by our intrusive implantations in a flash of receptivity brought about by long-bottled spirits of some sort, unwilling to continue the work and convinced no one else should either.

When Duane saw the naked corpse, saw *his* naked corpse—dead of no apparent physical affliction and sprawled across the foot of a tunnel, drenched in spit and blood and reeking slop—we'd hoped he might finally understand or at the very least, in some cobwebbed corner of his consciousness between awareness and arousal, know he must stop. But his first feeling was not fear. It wasn't confusion, nor sadness. It was hunger. Rather than an augury of doom, Duane Leavitt simply saw it as a challenge—a toothless "beware" sign left behind by whomever'd deposited what he now sought, sure to take the appearance of anyone who proved strong enough, resourceful enough, to make it this far. If only he'd looked up and seen our prolapsed transdimensional sphincter, rocks still clenching and relaxing against the deposit, maybe things would have been different. But with a man like Duane, wishful thinking is just that. He'd have probably crawled right in. A shorter story, that one.

Unfollowed and dead certain he was minutes from swimming in a vast treasure deposited by some Indigenous people attempting to secure rightful fortune against sweeping colonial virus, Duane made his way down our throat. As the walls grew tighter and wetter and softer and darker, his headlamp suddenly unworking against forces who didn't recognize the dominion of technology, it would have been impossible to turn back even if he'd wanted (he didn't). His only choice was to forge onward, toward bubbling, hazy light beyond.

Sometime later—minutes, maybe days—Duane reached the light. An orb, floating, glowing gold. Other men on the crew had seen things like this before, previous warnings and feelings we'd spat out, but Duane had proven unreceptive and untroubled—the luminous death knell was the most beautiful thing he'd ever seen. Duane reached out, the light nearly blinding his unblinking gaze, and in the moment before he believed his hand would've grasped it, he fell, tumbling into our gut:

A place of things swallowed.

He felt the dry stalks of corn that'd cushioned his fall before his other senses returned. By the time he climbed to his feet, he could almost make out the vast pit around him. Hard walls, glimmering with veins of gold ore, lighting the domed cavern. Duane weaved his way through the corn—a strange, circular planting that extended down into a perfect line, flanked at specific points by other perfectly square patches. So taken was he by the glinting riches of our stomach lining that he tripped over the severed head of a cow, which had taken root in the soft, pink ground beneath him. A milky eye passively watched Duane, cradling something in its drooling maw.

Duane gathered his bearings, attempting with futility to reconcile what he was seeing with anything he'd seen before, only then hearing the low, constant suckling that surrounded him. Animal heads—some coyotes and deer, mostly cattle—blossomed out from the corn, all the way to the walls. Sprouting like plants, each watching with that same benign stare. Some without eyes or ears, removed with surgical precision. Planted between the heads were other body parts, mostly genitals. All healthy and thriving, well-watered by local superstition and nightmares.

Unable or unwilling to help himself, he reached into the mouth of the nearest cow, pulling out a misshapen gold nugget. He bit it, overjoyed to find the marks of his sunken teeth remaining in the soft mineral, still given to the logic of the world he'd only just left behind. Enraptured, drunken with gold fever, he didn't linger long enough to see the drool and blood now spilled from the cow's mouth in vomitous bursts, nor did he pay much mind to the thing's horrid, gurgle-bound mewling. Duane crawled to the next head—a black ram with swirling horns—and did the same, finding another chunk, this one even larger. The bleats of the Billy joined the cow's chorus, saliva spurting the same.

One by one, he moved through them, pocketing nugget after nugget until pockets were spilling, blissfully unaware of the viscous, pink-ish liquid that had begun to seep through his boots, rising with each pilfered piece of gold. Once he'd exhausted the heads, he moved onto the other body parts, finding to his delight each held what he desired in their respective wet pockets as well, the cacophony of cries and wails echoing through the pit all the while.

By the time the rising tide was at his knees, the heads struggling to stay above their own filthy oral ejaculate, he'd filled his pack and was sloshing heavy toward the rear of our stomach, where a circular opening was cut into the wall. As he gazed into its depths, nothing to be seen past a barrier of impenetrable dark, the spurt had risen to his thighs. A familiar gold light approached through the opening, growing larger and larger until it stopped just before him, its mass now taking up the whole passage. Blinding him. A warning, we thought again. But to Duane Leavitt, a beacon.

He reached out, and the moment he believed his hand would've touched it, the orb evaporated into the black and took with it the invisible barrier. The deluge of drool rushed into the opening, along with Duane. Down into the tubes below.

A place of visceral things.

When he awoke at the bottom, he could feel something in there with him, just beyond his vision. The only gold to glitter here was what he carried, sending a pale, pink shimmer across the rock walls around him as they undulated, coaxing him forward along with the draining bloody spittle. There was no sound here, nor scent. If for some strange reason (for people are, above all else, strange) he made the choice to drag his tongue across the walls, he'd have tasted nothing. But he could *feel* that something else was there. And that it was wrong.

Knowing he must leave this place, Duane moved the only way he could: forward. Dragging the gold along with him, his greed lighting the way and keeping whatever waited in the darkness at bay. A labyrinthine path snaked back and forth, so coiled and winding Duane thought he'd somehow gotten turned around in a tunnel that bore no possible wrong turns. So focused on the road ahead he even forgot about what lurked in the darkness. In difficult moments like these, he'd always thought of his second ex-wife, Susan, and how she'd battled through throat cancer before the divorce. He didn't think of her now.

After what seemed like weeks, maybe centuries, he'd finally begun to weaken. The first few nuggets that tumbled from his pocket or spilled from his pack were simply the result of fatigue. But it wasn't long before he was making the conscious choice to shed weight. Duane didn't know how much longer he'd have to go and even a man as large and driven as he wasn't fool enough to misunderstand the basic math of the situation. His mind tried to wander as he dropped his pack, but this wasn't a place of wandering.

He made a grave mistake soon after, turning around for the first time. Not for any real reason, other than to lament what'd been left behind. That's when he remembered it. Saw it. Standing only feet behind him, its massive, fur-covered body taking up the entire tunnel. Jagged horns gashing silently through the soft, pink-rock ceiling above as it advanced. Battered hooves tromping without sound. Speckled with eyes and ears and all manner of swallowed things, repurposed.

It'd been so long since Duane had been aware of his physical body, he didn't start to run until he'd vacated the fetid contents of his bowels and bladder into his own boots, the smell rousing him into action. Gold nuggets flying as he stomped ahead with mad haste, his refuse splattering with each footfall. He didn't dare turn or slow, shedding his clothes when even that weight became too much. Duane knew it still followed. The only remaining gold now in his hands and mouth, barely lighting a few inches before his naked body.

He heard a sound. Something bubbling ahead. Though a voice left unspoken gathers gravel, an ear left unhearing only grows more keen—he could hear that bubbling like a thunderclap in a thimble, roaring at him that the tunnel was ending. That something was changing. That his nightmare may be at an end.

The pressure of the endless bubbling void he dove into forced Duane to drop what he carried in his hands. None of his bones were broken in the process, but we did take what we needed from them. Or, in the case of his impressive spine, we exchanged it with something that'd lost the power it had when we'd swallowed it. But the nugget he held in his mouth was not to be lost.

A place of things known.

What the rest of the crew saw emerge from that cave a few minutes after Duane had gone in was something they'd never forget. Something no one would believe, no matter how often a cursed refrain it would become for each. No one would believe in something nine feet tall that walked upright on battered hooves, jagged horns stabbing from its head. No one would believe it was covered in eyes and ears and all manner of swallowed things, resurfaced. And no one would believe such a man as Duane would be caught on the other side of the mouth-closing rockslide to follow.

But those that were there that day will always believe in what they saw. What they felt.

They'll always believe in everything now.

TOO CUTE!

Jori Lynn Felker & Michael Felker

OH MY GOD, *she's so cute! I just want to hug her 'til she BURSTS!*
I know, right?

I have to stop myself from BITING her little head off! And those cheeks! How do you not just want to TEAR her to little pieces?

Her big doe eyes.

Her cushy, button nose. Her supple, chestnut hair.

An iPhone illuminates all these precious little features of a miniature donkey.

Carol's eyes pop with joy. Her manicured hand squeezes the phone while the other grips the passenger-seat armrest. Her cosmetically ironed face coos at the thought of nuzzling between its chunky ears. Behold, a middle-aged woman frothing over a tiny mule.

"She was born just last week," gloats Betsy, glancing more at the photo than the road ahead. "My breeder says she won't get any bigger, no matter how many carrots we feed her. She's the perfect angel. V, you should come over and meet her."

Veronica, all alone in the backseat, grips her sunflower-patterned shawl and nods to please. "Yes. For sure. Wouldn't miss it." Her gaze drifts to the passing pines, showing more fondness for aspens than asses.

"Oh! You should meet Catrick and Abitail. Once you've finished settling in, of course," Betsy adds, fluffing her blonde bangs in the rearview mirror.

Carol interjects, "Those are her kittens' names. Not her children's, if that wasn't clear!"

"Hm, I'm pretty sure that was clear, Carol," Betsy nips.

"I think Patrick and Abigail might disagree."

Carol and Betsy giggle in harmony. Veronica tunes her vocal cords to match their social song—off-key ever since her husband of ten years dumped her for a "younger filly."

"I should ask my son to bring the twins." Carol sighs. "Gosh, I can't tell you how nice it is to have little feet running around the house again."

"Oh, that would be just delightful." swoons Betsy. "V, how soon 'til Steph pops out a grandchild or two?"

"Oh, I—I'm not sure," Veronica deflects, mischievously reaching for her phone. "I bet she's still fawning over the juniper bonsai I got her last Christmas."

With a squeaky grin, Veronica proudly presents a photo of a surgically trimmed mini-tree dressed in a little red bow tie. "Isn't she just precious?" Betsy struggles to see the teeny tree in her rearview mirror.

BWAAAAP! A grotesque honk fractures their idyllic bubble.

How rude, Betsy thinks as she swerves her Mercedes around a John Deere tractor toward the flat farmlands many Central Floridians call "home."

"Don't worry, it won't be long before the baby bug bites you!" Carol chides after a pregnant pause.

Betsy rubs her uterus longingly. "Babies… I swear, the moment they're out of you, you spend the rest of your life wishing you could just put them back in."

"Well, everyone needs a hobby," Veronica sneers. For her, watering a ficus brings as much joy as nursing an infant.

Suddenly, an indecent *BZZZT* alerts all three women to their group text chain. Carol and Veronica scroll through a barrage of increasingly aggressive text messages:

DING! *Where are you? Can't wait to show you him.* 🙂

DING! *Oh my God, he's TOO cute.* 😍

DING! *Why aren't you here yet?*

DING! DING! DING! *HURRY. SO. CUTE.* 

"My goodness, I've never seen Marsha this antsy to show her new horse." Carol guffaws. Even her laughter whittles down to a percussive politeness.

Veronica notices a chance to relate to her girlfriends, "Yeah, I mean… Why do you think it was so important to drive an hour just to see him in person?"

As if she heard their judgment, Marsha's aggressively grinning avatar calls through the car's smart display. Betsy answers with a sing-songy, "Helloooooooo, Marshmallow!"

Frigid static hisses through the speakers. A rhythmic spattering of shuffling, wet footsteps usher in fragmented whispers of sweet nothings: *That's it… good girl… cute girl… so cute… need to… want to…* A seething moan mixes with a shimmering whinny as Marsha's ecstatic gasps wheeze into a beastly coo.

"Lordy, Marsha needs to remind her butt to turn on screen lock," Betsy jests. The women laugh again, this time spurring a genuine chuckle from Veronica. She licks her lips, enjoying the umami flavor of conformity, as they wind down the road leading to Marsha's opulent ranch.

THE PRODIGIOUS BARN sits atop a delicate mesa. Nothing bad ever happens here in this white-collar fortress. Tractors typically roam the two-hundred-acre estate like tanks, but today they snooze in the parking lot while the horses graze the endless fields.

"How embarrassing, José forgot to trim Goldie's mane," Carol judges as they pull past a tall, dark, and handsome stallion.

So embarrassing, Veronica thinks, pretending she could tell. There are Quarter horses and Saddled horses and Blazer horses and Arabian horses, but to Veronica, the only horses that mattered were her ex-husband's horses—the ones she claimed after he swiped her greenhouse in the divorce.

Betsy rolls her eyes as she parks the car, "Good Lord, he also forgot to put Rosie back in. He knows she's sensitive to that sun. What's going on here?"

"LA COSA! ME DA LA COSA!"

The trio turns to see José sprint away from the paddocks, screaming bloody murder, his vocal cords oscillating between piercing shrieks and guttural giggles until he vanishes into the nearby tree line.

"La cosa?" Veronica utters as they step out of the car.

"It means 'The Thing' in Spanish," boasts Betsy, brandishing her one semester of undergrad Spanish. Veronica and Carol nod accordingly. *Very impressive. How quaint. I took Latin...* The three ladies' voices mold into one indistinguishable nicety as they trot into the barn without another thought about Jose.

"MARSHA? MARSHA!" CALL the women into the cavernous barn. Only whinnies and scraping hooves respond.

Betsy scoffs, "She's probably in the tack room. Better make sure she didn't get tangled in Newton's reins again."

"I'm gonna go give Edward a treat." Carol splits off down the hall. "Holler if you find her!"

"Will do," Betsy replies as she leads Veronica into the tack room.

Bridles and bits loom high above their heads. Riding crops and spiked rowels jag out from the cluttered walls, ready to be reserved for the most draconian of circumstances. Personal storage chests with engraved names align the perimeter.

"Whoa," both women gasp in unison, noticing the opened chest labeled MARSHA.

Inside her chest holds an odd assortment of cherished toys from recent yonders. Furbies, Hello Kitties, Winnie the Poohs, and Tickle-Me-Elmos all topple over due to their massively incongruent craniums.

They gaze upon the cotton candy Chernobyl with horrified pity. "How...sweet?" Veronica chokes out, studying a unicorn and a dolphin stitched together into a cuddly chimera.

"Poor thing must've snapped after her son passed," Betsy laments. "She had to fill her life with something. I just never realized how bad it got."

Veronica sighs in understanding. "This must have been what she wanted to show us."

Suddenly, a gentle noise rumbles from within the bowels of the barn. In fact, it can only be described as the most beautiful sound to caress the human ear. Perhaps it's a newborn crying, a cherub singing, a baby goat mewing, or your insides crackling like an uncorked Prosecco. No matter what it is, it's audible velvet to the ear.

Allured, Betsy flutters to the viewing window and peers into the arena. Her eyes adjust to a single shaft of light. *Then, in an instant, Betsy's pupils swell into bowling balls.*

"Oh my God. No. V… This is what she wanted to show us."

WITH A FISTFUL of peppermints, Carol breezes past several stalls of curious snouts, all poking out with hope. *Not for you,* Carol grins, eager to spoil her favorite son, Edward. His goofy, white-tipped nose and lopsided blaze have already commanded Carol's heart. And her bank account.

As Carol peers into his stall, her heart viciously halts. Her poor baby boy cowers behind a stack of hay, far away from his feeding hole.

"Eddie? Oh, my Lord. Baby, what's wrong?" Edward's ears jut back in quivering fear. His hooves freeze to the ground. Carol carefully steps forward and reaches for the iron gate when— *plop*—the heel of her blue Tecovas sinks into a thick puddle seeping under the door.

Ugh, José forgot to muck the stall, Carol thinks, her nose crinkling in disgust. She raises her heel and sees something flickering in the muck. It's Marsha's horse-shaped phone case, screen cracked. The color fades from Carol's cheeks as her mind leaps to her worst fears. *Colic? Blood clot? Her poor baby!* She thrusts open the door when—

A bloody puree of Marsha's corpse flops at her feet. A dressage spur juts out from her eyes, paralyzing her face between the uncanny valley of ravenous joy and blossoming terror.

SHE HAS COME... She has come to see me…

The Blonde One… She sees my planet-like eyes, bending spacetime with such cosmic delight. My fluffy-feathery-furry figure shifts for her. My textures undulate as I stumble through the shafts of dusty sunlight. *So helpless. So feeble. So tiny. Her…SWEETIE.* She could fit me in her pocket. Or walk me on a leash. Or ride me down the street. Whatever sick exhibition her heart desires this day of the week.

Oh, how this mortal marvels at my dumpy cheeks and high forehead, assembled so strategically as to hijack the instinctual response. Is that an itty-bitty horn? Teensy-weensy wings? Or just the smooth, supple flesh of an infant's tushie? Yes, to that cry! That neigh! That bark or meow or baa or *'mama'*—my silhouette and sound flicker in a tender kaleidoscope each time she blinks.

Wait. What's that? A second one is here. She has joined The Blonde One in observation. She has no defining features. Only her sunflower garment. Yes, The Sunflower One…

She finds what The Blonde One beholds repulsive. It's a deeper dig. *What's HER SWEETIE?* Perhaps she's less partial to a canine than a…cactus? *Hm.* How about my handsome little leaves?! Such a gorgeous string of pearls adorning my iridescent petals. My bouquet shimmers like a thousand diamonds. *WAIT.* Is that a *wittle* Venus flytrap on my trunk? *Yes. That's it.* She fights the impulse to smash the window and lunge inside my sticky wet mouth. I will shimmy a luscious mane of her favorite… *Yessss.* I'll unfurl the *soleirolia soleirolii*, or "baby tears," to wear down my stem. My seedlings should hug these poles as I search for light.

But my *smell*, so haunting and sweet, oozing with nostalgia and desire, just *awakens* something inside her… Something pulsating with the power of a million cubs. *This is how a mother feels*. How yummy the sensation! How indescribable the urge to just…

"ARCK!" Veronica yelps at an octave she didn't know she was capable of. Her knuckles flex with temptation…

Betsy's breath quivers. A trickle of drool oozes from a corner of her lips.

As the two empty-nesters ogle, dreaming of their nests to fill, it waddles (or blossoms) around the ring, purposely losing its footing (or potting) in a flawlessly choreographed dance of personally curated *kindchenschema*. For the "Sweetie" only reflects each one's most adoring infatuation.

Both women are so entranced they hardly notice Carol's screams of terror outside the tack room. *How rude*, both women thought.

Carol teeters into the tack room, a sobbing mess, and not just because of the blood on her Tecovas. Like a teenage boy caught masturbating, Betsy and Carol lunge for a horse blanket, curtaining their secret "Sweetie" in sync. Shrouding the viewing window with the dark fabric.

I can hear them from under here. *"What's wrong? What is it?"* asks one of My Beauties. Which one? Doesn't matter. I can only hear two voices now: the New One and My Beauties, whose voices sound identical in their perfectly matched pitch.

Carol wilts into Betsy and Veronica's collective embrace. "It's terrible! Horrible! Marsha, she's gone! She's…" But her voice snaps off into an unrecognized chord. She wails and wails.

"Honey, it's okay," Betsy cries as she strokes Carol's hair maternally, enjoying the delicate, sizzling sensation of her curls beneath her chin.

"You poor thing," Veronica echoes, her tone now mastered in this feminine social rhythm of call and exchange. She massages Carol's shoulders, relishing in how the tender skin folds under her fingernails.

Suddenly, Carol gasps as if just realizing the danger. "We should run! We're not safe!"

"Shhhh," Betsy and Veronica trill, anchoring Carol's body deeper into their bosoms. "You're safe now." Veronica purrs as she kneads Carol's bicep like a stress ball. "Don't worry, Sweetie." Betsy salivates, inhaling Carol's tangerine-tinged conditioner.

"Ow, not so hard, V." Carol swats at Veronica, who doesn't flinch.

Betsy snuggles her snout deeper into Carol's neck. "There's nothing to be afraid of here." She chuckles in chirps. "In fact, it's just the opposite."

"The opposite?" Carol echoes, straining to match their tune.

Veronica responds to Betsy with a wicked warble. "Yes, the opposite." Her veins pulse with anticipation. Her sweaty palms wander low. Her suntanned finger traces a maroon freckle on Carol's juicy flesh. "It's...*cute.*"

I AM cute. I like that word. *Cute.* It sounds good. I am good.

"TOO cute," Betsy punctuates as slobber oozes down her cheek like a lavafall.

Carol wipes off her jacket in polite disgust and clears her throat. "Surely not as cute as Catrick and Abitail," Carol tries to chuckle. Still, her faux melody rings discordant. "Remember that, Betsy? Betsy?"

Instead, Betsy grits her teeth, mashing them side to side as if holding back a massive sneeze. "It's... It's SO cute that I want to–to..."

The two women seesaw aggressively, back and forth, back and forth, until finally—

"I want to BITE its little head off!" Betsy lunges at Carol's neck. Canines sink into the meat with a *squish.*

"And TEAR OFF its lil fur!!" Veronica claws into Carol's tissue, ripping flesh off sliver by sliver, like a mile-long birthday present. Shears of skin slop away. Blood BURSTS with a melty glisten.

The New One screams. Yet her notes are unrecognizable now. They may as well have been a blender. There's only the sound now—the peel, the crunch, the peel, the crunch. I can't help it. I must peek. I see her insides swapped with her outsides, her brain mixed with intestines, her blue what-have-yous now ruby-red. A precious pustule portending peculiar pleasures perfected.

All that remains is a single lonely larynx, whistling its off-beat swan song as the last wisps of conformity expunge through its sunken cavity. Quiet pervades.

Veronica takes a deep, thoughtful sigh from her sinew-covered mullet. "I—I get it now…"

Betsy spits out chunks of Carol's thigh onto the spilled pile of Edward's peppermints. "Get what?"

Veronica tightens a thin strand of Carol's hamstring around her pointer until it turns blue. "Catrick and Abitail. The kitten names. Very clever."

"Thank you," smiles Betsy. As the women turn back to the covered window, a scandalous thought strikes them concurrently.

"Want to look again?" inquires Veronica. Betsy confirms with a seductive hum.

I stretch my fluid form as they remove the blanket, vibrating in that same sort of skittish, self-doubting dance that precedes intercourse. They see me and all is right. All is right.

THE MOON HAS risen to a higher position. My Beauties continue to gawk at me like statues carved of the same marble. They think I'm sleeping, but I never really sleep, because even in my sleep, I continue my dance. The Blonde One sighs as I nestle in the sand. Donning her favorite set of kitten paws, I snore and twitch in my prescribed dreams. And for The Sunflower One, I snuggle up my pastel florets beneath a blanket of peat moss, bowing my foliage. A soothing, apple-tinged aroma effuses from my filaments like chamomile tea.

"Wonder what she's dreaming about." Betsy gnaws on a horse bit, grinding away her crowns.

"Probably of her dream home," Veronica exhales, rolling a sharp rowel over her shoulder, carving away at the adipose tissue. "Her dream family. One that cares and protects her—"

Betsy hawks out a lump of blood. "Yes, she needs a family. She needs a home." She plucks a broken tooth from the spittle. "I can take her back."

"You? No, no, no. That wouldn't be fair to Catrick and Abitail." Veronica mindlessly extracts a bundle of nerves in the messiest game of Operation. "They're your children. They need their mother's full attention."

"I'll make room," Betsy starts.

"Why don't I take her? She can stay in Stephanie's room." Veronica grins, imagining the adorable greenery blotting out her empty bed.

Opportunity arises. I cry in their respective tongues. Both Beauties release one single "coo," pitched so graciously my DNA glitches within its inhuman timbre.

"Don't worry, dear, I'm coming." Instinctively, Veronica vaults for the door, only to gag at the sudden loss of oxygen. Betsy clings to the sunflower shawl, throttling Veronica's neck back. Politely, of course—the way you would restrain a child from touching an expensive vase.

"Wait, I'm here!" exclaims Betsy.

With a coughing grin, Veronica flails like a windmill. Her hand reaches over to a bucket of horseshoes. She tosses a metal "U" at Betsy like an ultimate frisbee player. It misses her head, exploding the viewing window into a cacophony of glass that sprinkles the arena floor.

"Be careful!" Betsy yanks the shawl, anchoring it to a hanging hook. An avalanche of saddles tumbles down.

"Stop! You'll– you'll hurt her," Veronica chokes. Her feet dangle off the ground. The scarf jerks her up like a piñata.

Just then, Veronica flings a horseshoe so enthusiastically, it hooks around Betsy's throat and pins her against the wall. Betsy, buckled and twisted, struggles to break free. She contorts her neck to chomp on the iron curve, gnawing for freedom. Vermillion streams from her severed tongue. Her lips smack delightfully as if tasting a decadent Pinot.

> I belt a desperate whine for attention, puffing out vanilla-tinged fumes that long for The Sunflower One's choking lungs. They both "coo" back. We're now a violent and angelic choir. I climb or jump or scoot my little-bitty pot through the room, passing the Beauties as I wobble through the tack room. They are not long for this type of joy. I must show mercy. I cock my head or stem inquisitively. And like two screaming teapots, their "coos" escalate to a feverish octave that goes higher and higher and higher.

"AWWWW," Veronica croaks, the shawl hugging tightly around her neck as the pleasant asphyxiation shoots through her body.

"AWWWW," Betsy gurgles, her mandibles chewing the ridge on her shoulder. Finally, a charming little *snap* wrenches her neck into a corkscrew position. Her lungs empty like a kitten's purr.

Veronica's body goes limp with a painted smile between her pale cheeks. She chokes on a sweet aroma in her final breath—a juniper bonsai. Its particles dance within the dust of the bright moonlight.

And there it is. Pure unbroken silence, permeating the dark barn. No more voices for me to tune. Nothing for me to see. And nothing to see me. I wander down the vacant stables, humming and hoping someone won't leave me here all alone.

But I have you, dear reader. You wouldn't just leave me here. All alone in the dead white space. Would you?

You can't resist. I know it's true. Blame me? No, you.

'Cause you're the one who snickers at funerals. Cries at rainbows. Hangs your joy on the gallows of irony. Your brain, a dimorphous vessel, expands and contracts to comprehend your golden ratio of ME.

You'll follow me. I see a farmhouse across the pond, the porchlight still on. Maybe a family? Or better yet, someone lacking one. You will join me. *Yes*, you will not hurt me. You can only protect me and love me and cuddle me and kiss me and kill for me.

It's okay. It's okay. You want to. And I'm here. Here for you. I'm already in your home. In that crib. Under the sofa. On a shelf. In a photo. In your wallet. On the internet. On TV. In that emoji. On your couch. In your bed.

You are with me. All of you are. Your voices sound alike. I see inside your blood. There's no flight, only fight. Only peel. Only bite. Claw. Tear. Grip.

Counting down as your body tries to compromise with something so uncanny, it can't possibly compute. You're a paradox of rage and love.

I'm just here, being cute. 

SUNNY SIDE UP

Harmony Colangelo

DETROIT AVENUE IS nearly empty around this time of night. The occasional passing car makes that even more clear as its echo reverberates against the brick walls of storefronts in the brisk and vacant air. Jazz is stopped on the street corner, smoking a cigarette and using her phone's camera as a mirror to touch up her face. Beat to perfection, as usual, with the exception of that annoying patch of stubble that even laser hair removal can't seem to take care of. The light turns, and the green man signals to her. She puts her phone in the pocket of her jacket and crosses, strutting with the authority that says to the nocturnal world that she is *that* kind of bitch.

She walks up to one of the only businesses still lit on this stretch of road—a diner—when she is stopped by a man who had been resting at the nearby bus stop. He's the kind of guy who wears the night on his clothing and smells as fresh as whatever meal he's managed to scrounge together. Jazz snubs out the toasted butt of her cigarette against the chipped red brick of the building and flashes the transient man a smile.

"What's on the agenda for you tonight, Randy?" she asks.

"Oh y'know, little bit of this and that. Lemme tell you, there is a bottle of Champale at the corner store with my name on it, but I went and left my wallet in my other pants." He says the words through a smile with as many holes in it as the Cleveland streets.

Jazz gifts Randy a smirk. This song and dance is a common part of her nightly routine. She procures a ten-dollar bill and passes it to him, the scent of her perfume and a touch of body glitter still stuck to Alexander Hamilton's face.

"What are we celebrating?" she asks before allowing him to extract the bill from her exquisitely manicured nails.

"Any night it isn't raining is a night to toast to," he replies. "And every night when the weather *is* bad—well, those are for drinking twice as hard."

Jazz happily accepts Randy's toast as he salutes her for her kindness. She heads toward the entrance of the diner, reminding Randy not to settle for a liquid lunch with her traditional offering. It doesn't really matter what he uses the money for. Jazz would have given it to him no matter what the receipt read by dawn.

THE CLICK-CLACK OF Jazz's shoes puncture through whatever '70s soft rock song, long since phased out of the daytime rotation of oldies pop radio, plays softly over the sound system, accented by the clinking of dishes and silverware. The room would be mostly hushed and vacant if not for one particular table. Their voices fry out from the main seating area as Jazz enters. She rounds the corner to see a table of three rowdy patrons laughing while in the thick of a heated conversation.

"What kind of psychotic, suburban shit-mess did I walk into?" she asks through a knowing laugh, the kind that a mother gives when she asks a child if they've forgotten to defrost dinner—but is armed with takeout because she already knows the answer.

Three visible queers: Perry, Sport, and Juniper are engaged in an animated conversation at the booth. Perry is waving a coffee mug around in a manner that shows that it must be empty or else the table and its occupants would be splashed. Sport is focused on a sketchpad, leaning against the edge of the table in front of their lap. Perry and Juniper notice Jazz approaching from where they are seated, and they smile as she squeezes in next to Juniper.

"I'm not saying I don't believe you, Perry," Juniper squeaks out. "I'm just saying that it is beyond manipulative."

"Exactly!" he responds. "Okay, Jazz, did you go to prom?"

Jazz just about chokes on the preposterousness of Perry's question.

"Absolutely not," she says. "The only thing worse than being called a flamer by a room full of smug teens would be doing it while stuck in the cheapest sports coat from Men's Warehouse."

Jazz is the closest thing to a mother this ragtag group of "queerdos" still has in their lives, and it's obvious from their stifled chuckles that they've grown accustomed to her sharp tongue but won't dare let her know just how much power she yields thanks to her humor.

"Okay, but did you get letters from elementary school kids telling you not to drink and drive on prom night anyway?" Perry asks.

Jazz graduated high school before Sport was out of diapers, so it takes her about fifteen seconds to unearth the memory from whatever mental tomb she locked it away in.

"Oh yeah!" she exclaims. "Those guilt-trip notes where they preach about all of the stuff they learned would kill you from some dumpy drug cop in D.A.R.E.?"

Her response is exactly what Perry was hoping to hear.

"See? I told you it wasn't just me!" he shouts. "I had to write a couple of these letters as a kid, and by the time I'd forgotten about it, they blindsided me senior year with something like *'Oh pwease don't dwink and drive. You could die, and I'd be sad, and your parents will be sad, and your fwiends will be sad, and we will all miss you.'* As if we hadn't gotten enough of that from watching videos of people being scraped off the road in driver's ed," he scoffs.

Juniper can't believe what she's hearing, slamming her coffee cup down into the saucer, rattling the porcelain. The sound gives the waitress, Lisa, a small jolt to the system until she sees that the cup isn't broken, merely jostled.

"They would miss you?" Juniper hawks. "Assuming you had gotten hammered on prom night, how would this kid that you have never met even know that you let them down? It's not like second graders were pulling out the paper and reading the obituaries."

"Do second graders even have a concept for what death is out where you grew up?" Jazz asks the group, "Because I didn't get any kind of kindergarten propaganda, but every kid in my neighborhood definitely knew what dying was about."

Silence overtakes the table as Perry thinks about the question at hand. Moments like this are a common reminder for the nighthawks that while the universe has brought them together through their shared letter "T," they all had wildly different upbringings. Perry has learned not to take such questions personally in the same way that his younger self would have as he brushes off dark thoughts with a smile.

"I don't think so," he says. "At least I don't really remember knowing what it meant on a deep level. If you are six years old and you rip your friend's spine out playing *Mortal Kombat,* then it is kind of meaningless because everything goes back to normal in the rematch. I dunno. I don't think most of us really had to face it yet."

"I started doing active shooter drills in kindergarten," Sport interjects, with the slightest hint of bragging. They continue with their drawing without even looking up. Sport's casualness causes a halt in the conversation.

The other three at the table look back and forth at each other before breaking out in laughter. Sport proudly blushes from being able to derail and break the rest of the table. Jazz takes a deep breath and exhales after the collective laughing fit and allows herself to let her guard down and decompress.

She closes her eyes and smiles as Sport repeats the jokes their classmates used to crack to pass the time during drills. Their voice drifts into muffles but is interrupted by Lisa as she finally checks in with the group.

"Hey, y'all, where's Sunday?" she asks.

Jazz snaps out of her relaxed state. Lisa is right. Where *is* Sunday? Jazz fumbles through the contents of her pockets to grab her phone, texting "Bitch, if I find out you accidentally turned off your phone sucking dick, I'm gonna molly whomp you when you get here! Call me." As she pulls her manicured finger away from the screen, she sees her blue message text has turned green. Without hesitation, Jazz immediately calls up Sunday but lands in her voicemail inbox before it ever has a chance to ring. She tries calling a second time and gets the same result, causing full panic to take over.

Something is very, very wrong.

Jazz slams down her phone in her fist, jolting the cheap, porcelain plates and silverware against the chipped polyurethane of the table.

"Something's up with Sunday. We have to go. Now," she says.

The urgency in her voice kills the conversation. Nobody knows what move to make next, staring at their mother figure and awaiting instruction like baby birds wondering who will get the worm.

"Her phone is off. She would never do that on purpose," she says, swallowing the lump of worry starting to form in her throat.

Panic washes over Perry and Sport's faces, while Juniper takes a stand. The group has been silently wondering whether or not Juniper and Sunday have been spending extra time together outside of the diner for over a month now, and her eagerness all but confirms it. If it were any other night, they'd all be grilling her about their "t4t party." But not tonight. Not now.

"We have to go look for her," Juniper mumbles. She's nowhere near as good at hiding her concern the way Jazz can.

Sunday is a well-seasoned veteran of the world's oldest profession, pushed back into full-service street life after an aggravated OnlyFans subscriber doxed her in his post-nut rage.

"Get your asses up!" Juniper shouts to break their paralysis.

The entire group barges out of the booth as Jazz pulls her debit card out from the deep recesses of her bra and tosses it onto the table. She gives Lisa a nod as they scurry out, an assurance that they'll be back when they find Sunday. *If* they find Sunday.

JAZZ, JUNIPER, SPORT, and Perry all bolt into the parking lot, humidity sticking to them the moment they escape the over-powered air conditioner of the diner. Juniper runs off and begins throwing piles of black clothing into her trunk as Jazz paces back and forth on the sidewalk.

"Where are we supposed to even start looking for her?" Perry asks, his fist filled with the denim covering the thigh of his tattered jeans.

"I don't know! But I can't just sit here and hope that Sunday's going to turn up tonight!" Jazz snaps back. She rushes back and forth, looking up for answers as if the stars or God or whoever is on the other side of the gray sheet of the overcast sky can point them in the right direction. The clacking of her heels echoes against the brick building next to the diner, inspiring a half-in-the-bag Randy to prop up.

"I don't know if she considers Fridays the start of the weekend, but I know she had been working weeknights over by West 85th," he slurs.

Jazz lights up with hope for the first time as Juniper pulls the car to where everyone is gathered on the sidewalk.

"Randy, you are a fucking saint, and I owe you so many dinners," she says, before diving forward and planting a kiss on his sweat-stained forehead. The foursome squeezes into Juniper's car and she peels out into the night.

JUNIPER'S TWO-DOOR FORD Escort combs through dilapidated side streets as each passenger looks out past the illuminations of the lights for any sign of their friend. They see abandoned bicycles, apartment windows covered with children's bed sheets, overgrown grass the city refuses to maintain, and the windowless gay bar they've all refused to step foot in ever since the owner had the audacity to call Jazz a "low-rent Tyler Perry character" on her last birthday, even after she broke his nose. These are the streets they all know too well for comfort, but there's no sign of Sunday.

"Hey, hey Irma!" Jazz shouts out the window.

A woman stumbles toward the car, her wig pushed back a little too far from her natural hairline and her stilettos sticking in the cracks of the concrete.

Jazz softens her voice so as to not incite any more panic. "Have you seen Sunday tonight, Mama?" she asks. Irma laughs to herself slightly before shaking her head in the negatory. Jazz purses her lips in disappointment with such vigor her teeth could break through her own skin if she so desired. Juniper keeps driving, and the crew continues shouting out the window at any of the regular nighthawks usually haunting the neighborhood at this hour.

No one has seen or heard from Sunday.

In a last-ditch effort, Juniper heads toward a large underpass for train tracks, the headlights blasting through tall weeds and piles of garbage that have made their way to the curb from the constant gusts of wind of passing cars. As the vehicle creeps closer, her brights illuminate a dark figure slumped against an abutment tagged with some poor excuse for graffiti.

It's Sunday. She isn't moving.

Juniper stops the car and flips on her hazard lights as the foursome hurries out. Jazz pushes everyone out of the way and falls to her knees, meeting Sunday at her level. She softly lifts Sunday's face in her hands, pushing her ratted hair out of her face. Sunday's cheeks are swollen and bloody, with deep bruising contouring her eyes and mouth. Her left orbital bone seems to have gotten the worst of it, as a gash just below her eye is already starting to congeal.

"Sunday," Jazz commands, "You need to wake up." She doesn't want to use a strong voice right now, but she knows she has to. "Please."

Sunday manages to slightly open her eyes in spite of heavy lids.

"Well, hey there, guys and dolls," she says. The words pour out of her mouth like drool.

Sunday manages to support her own head so she and the foursome can smile nervously at each other with a slight sense of relief at her greeting.

"How are you holding up, beautiful?" Juniper asks.

"I don't know," Sunday replies. "I think I'm a *little* concussed."

Sunday stubbornly attempts to stand up on her own, leaving a pool of blood beneath where she had been sitting. She barely gets out of a crouch before stumbling back. Jazz catches her in time to stop her head from smacking against the concrete pillar of the overpass. The impact on her backside, and the reality of how weakened she is, breaks Sunday's facade. Juniper and Jazz sit next to her against the pillar on each side, and Jazz places her jacket around Sunday's shoulders.

"I'm so fucked," Sunday declares, her eyes slowly closing as she rests her head against the wall.

"Nope!" Jazz blurts out. "I need you to stay awake. Can you do that for me?"

"It's hard," Sunday mutters through the tears forming.

"I know it's hard," Jazz affirms. "Keep talking to us. That'll help."

Jazz's tone is soft in a way that only an experienced mom-friend who has taken care of many messy drunks can be. Sunday continues, nearly nodding off several times as she speaks.

"The cops slow-rolled, but they're useless," she says. "Probably sick of seeing me around. Good riddance to bad trash, or whatever my granddad used to say." She reflexively tries to talk with her hands, but her movements are sluggish as if she is deep underwater. "I know you want me to keep talking but I just don't really know what I should be saying in this situation. I mean, I don't need to say what happened, right? You all know, right?"

The group looks at the blood puddle expanding out from underneath her. They know.

"I was so careful all this time," Sunday cries. "Then this asshole townie comes along and suddenly I'm just another statistic. I mean, it's so obvious that I probably would have made a joke about it if it wasn't so fucking sad. But can you imagine? 'Hooker gets fucked.' The headline would write itself. The bastard was even wearing a class ring. A CLASS RING. What kind of pathetic fuckface still wears his high school class ring in his forties? No wonder he has to pay to get his dick sucked."

Sunday might be in the worst pain of her life, but she's not about to miss the opportunity to roast this pathetic loser. She giggles softly to herself, but the pain of laughter in her lungs quickly ends her moment of joy. She exhales, wheezing like a squeak toy after it's been chewed through by a pit bull.

"This hurts so goddamn bad but all I keep thinking about is that if I can make it to sunrise, then tonight'll be over," Sunday laments. "But tomorrow? Tomorrow, I have to wake up and everything is going to hurt even worse. And I'll have to deal with this shit for the rest of my life, and how it is never going to be the same, and I'll be at my most fucked."

Jazz gives Sunday a light kiss on the top of the head. The taste of blood, sweat, and dirt blending with her strawberry lip gloss. Jazz nods her head to the others, and without saying a word, the group manages to load Sunday into the backseat of Juniper's car. Jazz snuggles into the back and places her arm around Sunday's shoulders to act as a headrest. Perry and Sport have been too stunned to speak this whole time but instinctively cram into the front seat to give Sunday extra room. Finally, their waifish frames are to everyone's benefit. In the rearview mirror, Juniper looks back at Sunday, her brows trembling as she struggles to hide how desperately she wants to cry. Sunday's eyes are locked off in the distance, like a doll with a fixed gaze, unable to make eye contact even if she wanted to. Juniper finally looks away from the mirror. Her hand trembles as she shifts the car into reverse and finally guides the group away from yet another spot in Cleveland where girls like Sunday, Jazz, and Juniper are left to be identified as "the body of a strangely dressed man" on the evening news.

JUNIPER DOES HER best to navigate her rusted out car through the dilapidated streets, inching over potholes and looking back at Sunday to assess her comfort with every block they travel. Sunday takes deep, slow breaths as if she's teaching her own Lamaze class while Jazz tries to absorb every bump the car hits. Every so often, Sunday's face slightly ricochets off Jazz's shoulder, blood smudging against her best friend's flesh.

"Jazz," Sunday moans. "I dropped my phone when that cockstain kicked the shit out of me. Can we go get it?"

"D-d-don't you think we should be getting you to the hospital?" Sport pipes up.

"I'm not gonna be working for a while. I'm not having some doctor put me into debt *and* also have to buy a new phone," Sunday replies as she lets her head roll over to look at Jazz. "We were a few blocks away by the old shoe factory before he dumped me under the overpass."

Jazz smacks her lips and lets out a deep sigh through her nose. "Fine. We'll go get your phone," she says with exasperation. Jazz makes eye contact with Juniper through the rearview mirror, nodding with approval to turn the steering wheel and head toward the spot.

SUNDAY KNOWS EVERY isolated corner of this neighborhood by heart and is easily able to guide the car back to the alley where she was attacked, even as the universe spins around her. Every alley, every dead-end street, and every streetlight in need of service is etched in her mind like a tattoo. She squeezes her lids tightly closed in hope that it'll hard-reset her eyes, then calls out to Juniper.

"It'll be on the next left," she says.

Juniper nods instinctually, worry still painted across her face as she turns down the backstreet. As her wheels creep forward, something appears in the path of the headlights. Quickly, she flips the lights off, hoping the darkness will be enough to conceal them.

"There's a truck," Juniper says softly as she eases the car to a stop.

Sunday's eyes jolt open, a rush of adrenaline reigniting her as if Dr. Frankenstein himself had injected her with lightning.

"Is it a red Ford?" Sunday asks, peering forward through the windshield and squinting in an attempt to crystalize her blurred vision. The world looks as if her eyes are coated in Vaseline, and it's too dark for her to discern the truck's paint color.

"Yep," Perry answers, his vision strong enough to clock the truck some fifty feet ahead of them.

Sunday fiddles with the zipper on her jacket pocket, fumbling around as she pulls out a tangled mess of headphones, keychains, and only two actual keys. With her free hand, she unlocks the car door and frantically pulls at the handle…but it still won't open.

"What the fuck is this? Child locks?" Sunday swears in a harsh whisper.

Juniper grips the steering wheel tightly, unsure of what to do. She looks in the rearview mirror, too afraid to turn her head around. "Sunny, we should go," she peeps.

Jazz is already out of the car before Juniper even finishes her thought. She reaches back in, arm already flexed to hold sturdy, prepared to take Sunday's hand and help her out of the car. Using the roof of the car to steady herself, Sunday pokes her head back in, narrowly avoiding bumping the top with her already concussed forehead.

"I know this isn't what you all thought your night would look like but…" Sunday clenches the knot of trinkets so tightly it hurts, "…assholes like this don't get to win."

Perry opens the passenger door and pulls himself off the seat he is sharing to help flank Sunday on the opposite side of Jazz. Sport looks over toward Juniper, whose eyes are still locked forward.

"Come on, dude." Perry softly calls back to Sport with a nod, knowing that this is what they have to do but clearly doesn't want to leave Juniper behind. Sheepishly, Sport joins the trio as they start to slowly guide Sunday toward the alley, stepping with intention and trying not to ruffle the gravel scattered across the pavement.

Lit in silhouette by the truck's headlights, Juniper can only watch. Tears crowd her eyes as the rest of the group marches into the dark without her, because she is too petrified to make a move.

"Do it, June. Go with them," Juniper mutters under her breath, squeezing the wheel tighter. "Go. Go. Fucking go!"

Forging free from the mental binds that kept her immobilized, she defiantly thrusts her palm into the wheel several times and ejects herself from the vehicle to join the others.

A MAN IS frantically tearing apart the contents of the alley under the high beams of his pickup. It isn't until the fivesome walks in front of the truck that he realizes he is no longer alone.

"Hey! Mind your business!" he calls out as he tries to make out the backlit figures whose shadows climb up the back wall behind him. The only response he gets is the sound of his own voice echoing off the old building. "I'm just looking for something. So, you all can get out of here," he calls out, trying to sound more reasonable. But again, no one responds. "Seriously? Fuck off!" he barks while posting up.

"Are you still looking to party?" Sunday asks frankly.

The townie's eyes widen and he clenches his fists. The harsh light provided by his truck leaves little speculation about how he's feeling. Despite the five-on-one odds, he's not intimidated by his situation—he's boiling over. What does he have to be so furious about? Is it something about how these faggots are in his way? That some tranny is standing here, reminding him exactly what he's done? Proof of what he had craved from Sunday only a few hours before? In an explosion of bloodlust, the man charges toward their line of defense in the hopes of breaking through and escaping in his truck. Raising the entanglement of keys in front of her, Sunday wildly releases mace towards her assailant, spraying and praying that she hits her target through her vertigo. The townie cries out as he desperately tries to wipe his eyes clean after a clean hit of burning pepper. The liquid scorches through the blood vessels in his eyes, and he feebly swings his other fist in the direction of his targets, missing by several feet and falling to the ground in front of them. Juniper and Perry waste no time and immediately start to stomp the downed man into the asphalt.

"Fuck you, you cock smoker!" Sunday screams, one arm still slung over Jazz's shoulder.

Jazz surveys the alleyway before locking in on exactly what she was hoping she'd find. "Sport, be a dear and grab me one of those bricks over there, please," she says.

Sport snaps out of their haze of studying the brutality, bolting over to retrieve the best-looking brick from a small pile. Their hands are barely big enough to hold the slab in one, passing it to Jazz who places it in Sunday's palm. She grips her fingers around the brick, her destroyed manicure scratching against the red clay. She raises the brick over her head, and just when it seems like her tired arms are ready to give, spikes it down on the townie's skull. The brick crunches into his bone. A thick, clacking sound explodes as the impact slams the rest of his head against the fragmented pavement.

"Take it from me, head injuries are not fun to walk off," Sunday says condescendingly, reaching down to retrieve her weapon. Without a second thought, she releases the brick from above her head again, this time dropping it in the center of her rapist's face. His nose crumbles beneath his flesh, blood spraying aggressively out from his nostrils like a fountain of violence.

"Tell me you like it, baby," Sunday says mockingly, repeating back at him his own pathetic words from earlier. She laces her broken acrylic nailed fingers through his hair and pulls his head back. "I want to hear you gag on me." With his neck cocked backward, blood rushes through his sinuses, flooding the back of his throat. The townie chokes on the liquid pooling in his mouth, but it's not enough. Sunday yanks his head back further until he starts to gag on the taste of his own ichor. Her hands begin to shake uncontrollably, but she won't let go. It takes a lot longer to drown a man in his own blood than one would think, but eventually the gargling stops. The only sounds left are Sunday's heavy breaths, the gravel shifting beneath Sport's shuffling feet, and cars speeding home in the distance.

As Sunday finally lets go of his head, Jazz wipes a few droplets of splattered blood from Sunday's face with her thumb. "Girl, I'm so proud of you," Jazz says. "You really did all of this tonight without losing your lashes."

Sunday bursts out laughing and sobbing at the same time, hugging Jazz tightly. Turning her attention to the back wall of the corridor and limping along the way, Sunday inspects around a toppled stack of wooden pallets. Amongst the debris of his tantrum is Sunday's phone. The edges are scuffed, and the screen is cracked. Holding down the power button doesn't seem to do anything, but at least she found it mostly in one piece. She looks down at her phone but is distracted by a faint glimmer on the ground.

"Well, I'll be damned," she mutters.

Sunday examines the piece, squinting to make out the embossment. "Jesse, Class of 2001" is carved on each side, along with a symbol of a comet mascot. She places the ring in her coat pocket and manages to get back to her feet on her own before the adrenaline rushing through her veins completely leaves her body.

Moving at the speed of their bruised friend, the group returns to Juniper's car and drives away, not sure what to say in the moment.

"So… Is it really okay to have just left him there? Like, are we going to be okay?" Sport finally asks.

"No one is investigating that mess," Jazz reassures them. "When they find him in *that* area in a few days, the cops will report it as a random act of violence, or a mugging. No one wants to be the one to tell some mourning family that their beloved husband and father wound up dead because he was out scamming for trans hookers."

"What would his poor mother think if she knew he died because he loved girl dick?" Sunday cackles with exaggerated dramatics as Sport and Perry allow themselves to chuckle.

Juniper looks back at Sunday in the rearview mirror. "We're okay, but are you gonna be okay, Sunny?" she asks softly.

Time seems to stand still in the cramped Escort as Sunday really reflects on the question. Her silence is filled by the jostling of Juniper's muffler and the wind whipping through the window, tossing her sweat-soaked hair around her face.

"It doesn't matter," Sunday says. "All that matters is that I'm here and I want pancakes.

THE MAN AT THE MERRY-GO-ROUND

Justin Brooks

1993

HUNTER FALLS WAS a town built for autumn. Turn of the century Victorian homes lined Elm and Mulberry streets; colorful family homes that had raised generation upon generation of the town's history. They had seen so much: horses tracks make way for paved roads; penny-farthings to BMX bikes and skateboards. They watched children be born, grow old, and die in their quiet indifference. One hundred twenty years of the snail-paced, sometimes reluctant progress of small-town Norman Rockwell's America; until *recently*. For the past few years, Hunter Falls was a town that swallowed children.

It started slowly at first, one or two "missing children" fliers would find their way to the town bulletin board. They would age and disintegrate on every telephone pole. They would turn sun bleached and dog-eared before being taken down from storefront windows. The fliers would come and go, but the pain would remain. A brother lost. A sister disappeared. Sons and daughters taken by the whipping winds of Hunter Falls. And as the maples and butternut trees turned from green to yellow and red every autumn, the citizens of Hunter Falls would huddle together in candlelight vigils, hollow gestures of unity for this year's crop of missing children.

The adjacent towns had bestowed terrible nicknames on the town like *Hunt-For-Your-Kid Falls* and *Kid-Hunter Falls*, but no more. Today would end all that. This would be the day the town got even.

Sheriff Jim Hartley stood like a bulldog outside the town precinct. He watched the mob make their way to the Old Town Fair, which had been set up in the Veteran's Park just off Main Street. The sheriff pulled up his blue jeans and adjusted his belt just beneath his gut. He never felt comfortable outside his uniform, but he wasn't the law today. He wouldn't dare. Today he was just a father who missed his son, just a man who had prayed daily for three years that he might see his boy returned to him.

The Sheriff wouldn't be a part of this though; he couldn't. The badge still meant something to him. He *could* turn a blind eye, though. Perhaps he'd take the ten-minute walk to the south side of town for a cup of Tom's famous coffee at TC's Corner. Better yet, he'd imbibe something stronger. Even if he wanted to stop what was coming, what could he do? Arrest the whole town? No, today was for looking the other way.

Derrick Myers kept an eye on the sheriff as he walked by. Hartley caught his gaze as well. Those beady eyes waited for the challenge. The sheriff could tell when a man had nothing left to lose, and that was written all over Derrick's leathery face. There would be no challenge today. Hartley chose to lower his eyes and walk on. Derrick wiped his sweaty palms on his oil-stained blue Dickies work shirt and continued on to the park, leading a couple dozen of Hunter Fall's finest citizens to their dark destiny: take the heart of the man responsible for so many broken homes; put an end to the pain. Yup, Derrick's boy would be avenged. As would the sheriff's son, and the Watson girl, the Bennett boy, the Carter twins, and others whose names had been long forgotten by Derrick's Whiskey-soaked brain—each lost child represented by a small empty casket in the town Cemetery.

Today, they would kill the man at the merry-go-round.

It was Sarah Bennett and Cal Holden who first noted it. The kids all seemed to be taken in the fall. And with the fall came the Harvest Festival Fair, and with the fair came the man at the merry-go-round. The man at the merry-go-round was one of those invisible, faceless men who worked the circuit. They come to town once a year, keep to themselves, and disappear back into whatever pointless direction their lives might take. But out of all those traveling ghosts, the man at the merry-go-round was the only one to come back year after year. Sarah first noted the pattern, but Cal did the real digging.

The man at the merry-go-round had a rap sheet. Nothing too serious, but a jailbird, nonetheless. But the worst of it—the worm that caught the fish—was when Cal heard a rumor from a drinking buddy in Fairfield Springs that the man at the merry-go-round exposed himself to a thirteen-year-old girl. After hearing that, all Cal had to do was whisper in an ear or two at the diner, and then the word spread like a forest fire. It couldn't be stopped. Every parent wanted justice. *Real* justice. *Justice in blood.*

The mob stopped just before the park gates. Derick surveyed the crowd as he hiked his pants up. The weight of the old hunting knife kept sliding his belt down his wiry frame. He looked around at his fellow town folk. Each held their version of a weapon. Some carried kitchen knives, some baseball bats. Others came with gardening tools. There wasn't a gun among them. Guns were too quick. Too easy. They wanted this to hurt. They wanted this to last.

Derrick licked his lips and steadied his breathing. After surveying his fellow townies, his eyes locked on Cal Holden. He saw something different in Cal's face. While the other town folk were mad as hell, Cal looked more…excited. Sweat blotted Cal's sea-foam green Hawaiian shirt like a Rorschach test. A sardonic grin crossed his doughy face. Derrick never liked Cal. He never cared for any of those fat, lazy-ass computer nerds. But none of that mattered now. Cal was here, a brother in arms. Cal hadn't lost a child, neither had others in the crowd. Still, they came to defend their beloved home from this most terrible evil.

Derrick's attention broke with the sound of Sarah Bennett's voice, "For Bobby!"

Standing at barely five feet tall, a size-Large T-shirt could swallow Sarah whole, but today her thin voice awoke a mob.

Other cries followed.

For Mike! For Sally! For Aiden! For Greg! for Collin!

The Stampede was on.

The man at the merry-go-round looked at the human tsunami in horror, his dark eyes wide with fear. He started waving his leathery arms, arms covered in old glyphs and scrawlings of black India ink. Strange old markings crawled up his neck and across his sunken cheeks. To Derrick, he looked like an old warlock, trying desperately to cast one final spell.

Stanley Parks, the town's veterinarian, got to the man first. He'd always been fast, a track star in high school, and he plunged a steak knife into the old merry-go-round operator's belly. The man cried out and stumbled back. Stanley looked down at his knife. His hand was covered in warm blood, just like earlier in the week when he delivered John Daley's new baby calf. This felt familiar. This wasn't so bad. He looked back to the old man. He looked pathetic, shaking and blubbering and bleeding from his filthy, smiley-face T-shirt. Tears welled in his eyes. He looked like an animal. He *was* an animal.

Before Stanley could deliver a second blow, Cal spun the man at the merry-go-round with a punch to the chest, and the man fell to his knees, blubbering. Snot dripped from his nose. He looked up to the crowd to beg.

"Why? Why are you doing this?"

Silence.

"I... I... I... I didn't do anything."

Cal grinned as he leapt toward the man and dug his thumb into the old man's eye until the eyeball popped.

The crowd roared at the sound of agony.

Still on top of the man, Cal could smell the stench of piss and shit. He stepped back in disgust.

"Sick piece of shit"

And at that, the rest of the mob attacked. An assortment of kitchen utensils pierced the old man's flesh—pizza cutters, steak knives, barbecue spears. With every slice, more of the old man's guts spilled forth from his body.

As the man gurgled and choked on his own blood, Sarah Bennett tried to pry her bread knife from his neck, but it had gotten stuck. She snapped it off at the hilt. She didn't see a man anymore. None of them did. But in all the chaos, Sarah did see *something.*

Trapped between two old carousel horses, the old man reached up toward the mirrors that decorated the roof of the merry-go-round. And through the orchestra of violence—the screams, the calls for justice—Sarah heard him. Blood sputtered from the old man's lips as he wheezed, trying to breathe through punctured lungs. *Was he trying to say something?*

Words escaped the old man's lips, but they were foreign to Sarah's ears. A strange collection of vowels and consonants rolling off his bleeding tongue. A final prayer of haunting gibberish. Unheard by most, merely a whisper on the wind to a single woman, an audience of one. Sarah froze as the world slipped away for just a moment. She could see the man was now staring straight at her, his one eye locked onto her. And for a moment, as the man's life left his body with a death rattle, Sarah felt pity.

His guts in his lap and his arms pinned to his sides, his body was like a pin cushion for kitchen utensils and gardening tools. Each parent, each member of the community, had left their mark.

Suddenly, screams and battle cries filled the air; a war had broken out among the town folk. The old man's fellow carnies had come to stop the lynching and were met with violence. The copper taste of blood was on the wind.

Sarah looked around. *Lost.*

What had she done?

What were they going to do?

Sarah stopped dead in her tracks as she saw Cal in the distance. His boot was on a young carnie's neck while he furiously struggled with a Zippo lighter to get a spark. The boy under Cal's foot screamed as the Zippo caught flame, but Cal's boot pressed harder to silence him. Cal pulled a small can of lighter fluid from his pocket and caught eyes with Sarah. Only for a moment. He smiled. Sarah could only look away.

ACROSS TOWN, SHERIFF Hartley sat outside on the veranda and finished his second session ale. Through the bottom of his empty glass, he saw the billowing black smoke coming from the other side of town. He knew he wouldn't hear sirens for a while. The town volunteers all knew the fire wouldn't jump the fairgrounds any time soon. Besides, Chief Lynch was already there. He had taken the axe from the town's only fire truck and marched in the name of his late nephew Nicholas.

Hartley looked over at Greg the bartender, who was also staring out at the smoke. Greg's face was white as a ghost, but his eyes were content. He looked over at the sheriff, then raised a glass and nodded. "For Aiden," he said.

The sheriff cleared his throat and raised his glass in return. He forced an uneasy smile. "God help us."

THE SUN FELL early on Hunter Falls that evening. The black smoke from the fairgrounds had covered the sky, making quick work of dusk, like today was Armageddon. The town was forever changed.

Cal limped into his front door and collapsed onto his bench in the mud room. He kicked off his old boots, one by one, and buried his head in his hands, weary from battle. Fuckers only got him once or twice. Broken nose, maybe, but nothing serious. Cal wiped his bloody nose with a fist. "Ow! Goddammit!"

He picked himself up and made his way to the bathroom. He looked deep into the mirror, admiring every bruise. He ran his fingers across the scratches by his eye, where one of the fuckers tried to get one over on him. This was a warrior's face. Fuck what they thought at work. They'd see him different now. He knew it.

Blood ran down Cal's nose into his thin stretched grin. He ran his hands through his ash-covered hair. He smiled as he looked deeply into his icy blue eyes.

What a day. What a wonderful, wonderful *day.*

After a warm shower, Cal toweled off and looked into the mirror again. Just a clean-cut gentleman now. You'd never know what he'd just done.

He picked up the nail file from the medicine cabinet and started picking the dried blood from beneath his fingernails. No, you'd never know. Just a clean-cut gentleman. A good neighbor.

Cal opened the cellar door and flipped on the overhead light. He made sure to stomp as he descended the old wooden staircase. He had to make sure it sounded scary, of course. He should have put his boots back on. His house slippers didn't quite do the trick. With each pound and creak, Cal chuckled to himself. He reached the locked door at the bottom of the steps and started going through his keys. He moved slowly through the options on his key ring.

First, the dead bolt up top. He loved the way it sounded. A metallic *THUNK* as it unlocked. The old wooden door vibrated as the hammer fell. He then made his way to the two master locks beneath. And finally, the sliding chain.

The chain lock was really just a joke. Something to make himself giggle as he got started. It never failed. Always funny. He was a funny guy.

As he slid the heavy door open, he could hear the whimpers coming from the cage in the far corner. The sound made his palms sweat with excitement. He wiped his hands on his boxer shorts and used the back of his hand to wipe the sweat from his forehead. It had gotten hotter down here since he had installed the soundproofing.

Part of the fun, he figured.

He pulled at the rusted chain that controlled the overhead light. The illuminated light bulb threw shadows across the dog cages that were stacked inside the room. All the cages were empty. All except one.

A young boy, about twelve years old, lay curled up and shaking in the reinforced dog cage, his skin glistening with sweat. The dirt from weeks in that old cage clung to his trembling body.

Cal kneeled down and shook the metal frame wildly, screaming at his prisoner. The boy cried and whimpered even more, pissing his already filthy briefs.

"Disgusting little shit!" Cal screamed. He stood back up and gave the cage a good, hard kick. He stood there for a moment and admired the boy's soft, wet skin, the way his sunken ribs rose and fell with every breath. Even through the dirt and grime, Cal could see just how soft the boy was. *New.*

Cal quickly composed himself and moved back to the cellar door. He grabbed the rusted doorknob and turned back to the boy in the cage.

"You're lucky, you know. You're the last one I get…for a while." Cal giggled and slammed the door shut.

15 YEARS LATER

JACKSON LOOKED AROUND frantically. They were going to get caught. He knew it. Every sound made him jump. *Footsteps? The jingling of keys?* Or was it just the old bones of the warehouse creaking in the wind. His attention snapped back to Devin as the lock of the old warehouse door came loose with a *THUNK*.

"We're in," Devin said in an excited whisper.

Why did Devin always look so fucking cool? Even when breaking and entering, the seventeen-year-old had accessorized well: jet-black tech gear complete with all the straps and buckles. He looked like he shopped in Tokyo or at Jared Leto's house. He had long black hair and stubble that promised to be a real beard one day. It was no wonder Ashley liked him.

All Jackson could afford was the Hunter-Falls special. Walmart jeans and a black Misfits T-shirt from his dad, who kept reminding his son that "he's only borrowing it." Thanks to a face full of acne and a dirty blond mop of hair he was too terrified to do anything interesting with, it was no wonder Ashley never looked twice in his direction.

"Hey guys! Shit! Are we in? *Fuck! It was Ashley.*

How did Jackson not see her coming from around the building? He had to be the worst lookout in the history of teenage misadventures.

"What the hell is SHE doing here"? Jackson said in his best angry whisper voice. "I invited her man. Said she'd get some dope photos."

Ashley raised her Nikon D-80 as she gave Jackson the cruelest of *go-fuck-yourself* smiles. "Anyway, she looks way hotter in black than you do, nerd!"

Jackson Knew Devon was kidding, but he knew he wasn't wrong either. Ashley was perfect. Jackson had been staring at Ashley's butt in gym class long before he even knew he *liked* butts. With her long red hair in a tight bun, and her sleek *breaking-and-entering*, outfit she looked like a sexy assassin.

"Fine! Let's just get the fuck in there. I think there's a night guard or something."

With that, Devon led the way, crawling beneath the heavy shutter door like Tom Cruise in *Mission Impossible.* Jackson got down on his knees to go next, but Ashley quickly cut in front of him, crawling in behind Devon.

Oh my God. Her butt was so awesome.

Lost in teenage hormones, Jackson didn't realize Ashley had looked back to see if he was coming. "Like the view?"

Pure panic. Jackson scoffed and quickly diverted his eyes. "Hah. You wish."

Ashley smirked and continued on, being helped to her feet by Devon on the other side.

As Jackson stood, he was handed an ice-cold Miller High Life. Devon smirked as he raised his own can.

"We fuckin did it, man. We're in!"

Devon took a swig and offered one to Ashley. "No way. That shit tastes like piss. *But this...*" She held up what may be the biggest joint Jackson had ever seen. "*This* is what the doctor ordered." She sparked the joint and started snapping photos of the old warehouse. As she snapped away, Devon took Jackson by the shoulders and led him to the far corner of the room.

"This is where we leave you, my man. I mean, a least for a while."

Devon gave an impressive shit-eating grin as he pulled another High Life from his bag and handed it to Jackson.

"What the fuck are you guys gonna do?" Jackson knew how stupid he sounded before he even finished asking the question.

"I'm gonna get high and play with her titties, you double-fisting son of a bitch. See you in a little bit."

And with that, the giggling teens disappeared around the corner, leaving Jackson alone with his beer in the dusty old warehouse.

Alone. Always alone.

Sadly, this was a feeling Jackson had become quite comfortable with. Whether it was the school lunchroom or a crowded party, he always managed to become invisible. Forever damned to be a distant observer, never a part of the action.

Jackson looked back to the void before him.

The warehouse went on for what seemed like miles. It was one of the largest and oldest community buildings in the town, its size matched by its fullness. Decades of dusty old crap stacked three stories high in rows that seemed to never end. Old public mailboxes and streetlights that had been replaced years ago, giant holiday decorations of all sorts, even the Santa house that stood at the center of the town square during Christmas. This place was built for teenagers looking for trouble.

That's when Jackson noticed it.

The burning smell filled his nostrils as he crept toward one of the darker corners of the warehouse. He set down his unfinished beer and turned on his cell phone light.

In the corner stood a gargantuan relic covered by an enormous, rat-bitten tarp. The scent of burning grew stronger. *Thicker.* It felt as though Jackson was wading deeper into the smokey abyss of a burning home, but there was no fire to be seen, just the memory of one permeating everything. Jackson yanked the tarp from the relic.

"Holy shit."

He looked up at what had to be the coolest thing he'd ever found in his life: an enormous merry-go-round. He took a deep breath and finally realized where that smokey scent had come from.

Every wooden horse, circus lion, tiger, elephant, every snarling wooden beast looked as though they were riding straight out of hell, their bodies charred and burnt. Jackson looked deeply into the eyes of a wooden horse that looked as if it was frozen and screaming in a fiery torment for eternity.

Jackson cracked his second beer.

"FUCK!" he cried out as the tab of the High Life sliced his thumb. He dropped the can to the ground and quickly brought his bleeding thumb to his lips. The coppery taste of blood covered his tongue. Pulling his thumb from his mouth, he inspected the wound. He'd be fine. It was a clean cut and nothing too serious. His shoulders fell as he realized he had dropped his last beer. He'd just have to sit on his newly found merry-go-round from hell and wait, sober as a bird, for Devon got to get high and finish touching Ashley's perfect butt.

As Jackson climbed aboard the charred remains of the merry-go-round, he forgot the open wound and placed his hand down on the horse from hell for support.

"Goddammit!"

He snatched his hand back, leaving a bloody thumbprint on the horse's cheek. The black cinder from the hell-horse burned his open cut, but before he could return his wounded thumb to his lips, he felt a shift. The floor beneath him moved just an inch, taking him by surprise. Jackson began to get off the old merry-go-round when the charred behemoth started to rotate.

"What the fuck? Devon? Ashley? Are you guys fucking with me?" No answer.

The merry-go-round came to life. The decorative lights sputtered on. Their warm orange glow brought the entire merry-go-round into view. It was a twisted horror of wooden beasts that screamed as they spun, forever locked in a burning hell. The jovial Calliope music of a happier time now sounded gross and disingenuous, horrific in its irony.

The merry-go-round started to spin faster.

"Hello? Anyone? Is someone here?"

Jackson held on tighter, now starting to slip. He pulled himself closer to the center of the ride when he saw it, only a glimpse at first, reflected in the decorative mirrors at the center of the merry-go-round: an old man, wiry and leathered. His arms were covered in old tattoos that seemed to crawl up to his neck and across his sunken cheeks. He stood in the shadow of the warehouse, staring at the Jackson as the teen turned round and round on the ride, which was growing ever more out of control.

"Hey! Asshole!"

Jackson turned from the mirror to confront him face to face, but he was gone. The room was empty, save for the blurry images that spun about the merry-go-round. He looked back to the mirror to see the old man still standing there, still *watching* from the shadows. His image flashed by, again and again, like an old zoetrope.

Jackson was scared to move, but he had to check again. This didn't make sense. He turned quickly, trying to catch the old man disappearing into the shadows, playing a mean trick, but there was no one. No one could move so fast or disappear so quickly.

The tears slid across Jackson's cheeks as the ride spun faster. He was stuck. There was no escape. Jackson screamed into the swirling darkness of the warehouse. "Help! someone fucking help me!"

But no one came.

Why didn't anyone come?

His heart entered his throat as he felt long, cold fingers gripping the back of his neck. His scream was so filled with terror it couldn't exit his throat. Instead, it was just a gurgle, like a baby's cry, as the cold hand turned Jackson's head to face the mirror. He looked out from the glass of the mirror, the black glyphs tattooed on his leathery arms dancing and moving about his skin. They crawled up to his cheeks and filled his eyes with black.

The old man opened his rotten mouth and breathed hot black smoke that engulfed Jackson's face. The fetid breath entered every pore. Jackson coughed and cried. His eyes stung with smoke, and he could no longer bear to look at the horror in the mirror.

A deep breath burned Jackson's lungs. Darkness. Silence. The world slipped away. Then he opened his eyes to nothing, a black void with a single window shining in the distance. The spinning had stopped; all sensation had ceased. A still blackness was all that remained. Quiet. Unmoving. The boy swam through the dark abyss, closer to the window. *No, not a window. An old decorative mirror.*

Trapped behind silvery glass, Jackson looked out from the old merry-go-round mirror, beyond the charred hooves of burnt wooden horses, beyond the orange glow of decorative lights, beyond the relics from Hunter Falls' dark history. He looked out at the old man standing in the shadows.

The man at the merry-go-round grinned back at him with thin lips and sunken cheeks. The tattoos slithered around his face and down his neck. They slithered down his bony arm as he raised a hand to wave.

Goodbye.

4X4

Simon Rumley

I WOKE UP.

I woke up again.

I kept waking up.

I don't know how often I woke up, but at some point, I realized something was wrong. The time had stayed the same; not exactly the same, which might have suggested the alarm clock was broken, but a few minutes different, sometimes only a few seconds different. A feeling of dread suffocated me. I felt like I was imprisoned in a straight jacket lined with barbed wire. I could hear my heart drumming. The shock waves distressed my entire body, incited insipid, sour sweat to ooze out of me. I wanted to wipe away the sweat but couldn't. The sweat trickled and dribbled and aggravated. It suddenly dawned on me that I didn't know where I was, and that disturbed me more.

The room was rectangular, with a slanted ceiling to my right. I couldn't say if the room had a gray palette or a brown one, but I think it had both at different times. I don't think it changed colors, specifically, but my perception of the color kept changing. A bare light bulb hung from the ceiling but didn't illuminate the space. There were two windows, both curtained with short drapes, one to my left and one on the opposite side of the room. Although it seemed dark outside, everything was visible inside, albeit clouded with a dusty dinginess. A table stood under the bulb. A sewing machine on the table. A set of keys. A toy car. Some rotting flowers. A porcelain doll. A doll's house. A wardrobe. A chaise lounge. A boy. A living, breathing boy. I realized I was naked, and the sensation of being naked in front of a young boy troubled me, especially a boy I didn't recognize. It made me feel dirty. It made me feel like I should be buried alive. Like I deserved to be buried alive. Like mud should be my only meal.

"Who are you?" I asked, relieved I could speak. But after I asked the question, I wondered if I could speak. Or if I'd imagined it. If I even had lips to talk with. A tongue to wiggle. "Who are you?" I asked again, my uncertainty my only certainty.

The boy didn't respond. This compounded my confusion. I wasn't sure what to call the boy, so I called him "Son," even though he definitely wasn't my son. I repeated this moniker until he finally looked up at me. He looked distracted, remained silent, ignored me. In his right hand, he held a pair of rusty scissors. From a bucket to his left, he continued pulling out the same thing. Or things. A lizard. Lots of lizards. An endless supply of lizards. I suppose they might have been geckos, because they were small. With the scissors, he cut all four legs off each gecko and then every tail. A pile of bloody limbs lay scattered around him. The limbs didn't move, but the tails did. Enraged at their dismemberment, they twitched angrily. He threw the bodies in a small bucket. The repetitive slicing of the scissors, its metallic halting was sinister and soothing—smooth, metronomic. Offered a better keeping of time than my bedside clock which had now disappeared.

The boy finally stood erect, picked up the bucket, and walked over to the other side of the room, where a young girl sat on a stool beside the wardrobe.

My mouth fell agape because I couldn't understand how I'd missed the girl previously. She had long, curly hair. Her eyes were closed. I feared she was blind. Had been blinded. Her eyes plucked out. Some cruel travesty. I wondered if she might have been my daughter, but she definitely wasn't my daughter. She wore a bonnet and a frilly dress, looked how I imagined a milk maid would have looked from a bygone era. She used a long, thin knife to split open an oyster, then sucked the meat out of it. Tear-like dribbles drabbled down her chin, but when they dripped onto her pinafore, they turned bloody. She discarded the shell into a bucket to her left and spat out the oyster meat on the floor to her right. There was a pile of oysters. The oysters were alive. The oysters writhed in each other's despair. The oysters moaned. The moans were low pitched whimpers like a grandfather's sobs.

With automaton–like affection, the boy ruffled the girl's hair before depositing his bucket next to her. He crouched. He grabbed the oyster meat, stuffed it into the girl's mouth. She accepted it. She ate it. The boy picked up some shears, tested their sharpness in my direction. The girl picked up some shears, too, also tested them in my direction.

They opened them. They closed them. They opened them. They closed them. Repetitively. With more and more force. Repetitively. They snapped them with more and more violence. Open. Closed.

Snap, snap, snap.
With unerring eyes and castrating grins.
Snap, snap, snap.
I leapt out of bed.
But I didn't.
More like I levitated.
Or flew.
Or glid.
Past the girl, past the boy.
Snap, snap, snap.
Through the window beside the children. I don't know how I slipped through the curtains or the glass, but I did. A transmogrification? I don't know. A metempsychosis? I don't know. A death? My death? I don't know. A survival? My survival? I don't know. I know nothing except the straight jacket with the barbed wire was gone, replaced by a sense of relief, a caressing of my soul, a soothing of my heart. It really was such a relief. It felt like swimming naked through relaxing water, supping a champagne life force, submitting to a euphoric salve. My whole being was one wave of righteousness. Of goodness. I felt like Chagall. I *was* a Chagall. I was Chagall's greatest source of inspiration, his greatest triumph, his every painting, his every

brush stroke. I was multi-colored. Bright and beautiful. Breezy. I was free. Free of my dread. Free of my body. Free of its weight. It was ecstasy. I was ecstasy. The clouds were ecstasy. The clouds were made of warm snow. The snow tasted of delicate sorbet. The clouds coddled me. Understood me. Became part of me. Became all of me. I became them. I was the clouds. The clouds were a swirling drift of infinity.

Sacharine, shining, pure, smiling.

Eternal.

Pacifying, suppressing.

For eternity.

An isolation. A singularity. A universality.

But not for eternity, it turned out.

Time had died, but I hadn't. I awoke. I was no longer the clouds; the clouds were no longer me. The clouds scared me. I realized they were suppressing me, tranquilizing me, molly-coddling me, keeping me from a truth. No angels fluttered here, no Pegasus swooned, no harps crooned. I hadn't existed for a while, but now I did. Again. And as I slowly became conscious of myself, I became conscious of my heart. It was distended. It was oozing. Slowly. Surely. A toad rupturing. Painfully. Out of my ribcage. I knew it would burst. Soon. I knew the pain would be untenable, terminal maybe. I had to escape. Had to. Away from those treacherous clouds, away from my breaking heart.

A churchyard below distracted me. Attracted me. It was littered with gravestones, some erect, some slanted, some crashed. Decorated with skeletal trees, suffocating moss. The graveyard was gray but mottled with ash from the clouds' disintegration. The churchyard gave me hope. I was weightless. I was a spirit. I was a soul. But I still had a heart, so I must still have had a body, somehow, somewhere. I floated down. The earth around the church was parched, suffocated by the ash. The stepping stones around the church were slick. They subsumed the ash into a tarry oil that glistened seductively. I considered myself seduced. I remembered crawling as a baby. My first steps. Or maybe they were my son's first steps. Or my daughter's. I can't remember. But I envied those steps. Coveted them for myself.

I wanted to step again. All this floating, all this weightlessness had weighed me down. I wanted to be a man again, not a spirit, not a ghost, not something I had no grip on, no idea about.

I shivered with excitement as I continued my float downward, closer and closer, my first steps for an eternity. But I saw a reflection. It teemed, shapeshifted, offered scant variations, swirls of sable and obsidian and ebony. I suddenly knew I could not step on those stones, for If I did, I would die. I would sink, subsumed by them. I would squirrel away, be stuck under the church, trapped under a grave, in another eternity I couldn't stomach. The stench of my eternal demise nauseated me. My stomach rebelled. An acid tang permeated me. My ribs started to crack. A clamp started to squeeze my lungs. The bitumen paths anticipated my demise. Ravens fluttered from them, rats jumped, worms writhed. The ravens cawed; the rats hissed. A raven pecked, a rat gnawed, the worms turned into snakes.

With some effort, I halted my descent. It was like pulling a handbrake on myself. It was a strain, but I succeeded and willed myself towards the church through a heavy wooden door, a small antechamber, an arched entrance into the building's main body. Monochromatic shafts of light bled through stained glass windows. A musty smell polluted the air. A bust the size of an elephant filled the front of the chancel. The bust was golden, carbuncular, rough in its hewing, but it buzzed with a vivacity I couldn't comprehend. The subject was a woman. Her beauty had been eroded, stolen, replaced by terror and agony and regret. Her chestnut hair seemed real enough, though, flowed extensively, filled the back of the chancel. Individual strands decayed into gray wisps. The jawline was locked as if an eternity of torture had forced it that way. Noises emanated from the bust: internal screams, external whimperings. But it was her eyes. Deepset. Hypnotic. Autumnal. Her eyes that burned with a rare despair, a heart-breaking angst that made me realize the bust was not a bust at all, but, in fact, a living, breathing person. A person trapped in her own purgatory. A person who I sensed I knew but couldn't place.

Gold spheres hovered around the nave like a swarm of angry insects. Bees or wasps. Hundreds of them, maybe thousands. They reverberated in unison. A kind of living, breathing malevolence. I sensed they had no interest in me, but what I saw filled me with melancholy. The spheres were feeding on the woman. They surrounded her face, formed a gold, shimmering skin, which is why her eyes seemed so sunken. Nicking, cutting, supping, sucking. Relentlessly. As soon as one sphere retreated, another advanced. They were an army of babies sucking their adopted mother dry. The blood that trickled from her was gold, not red. She bled gold. The spheres sucked most of it, but small trickles dripped down the pulpit steps, stained the church in untold wealth. I wanted this to stop. I didn't want the woman to suffer any more. I advanced. But as I advanced, the spheres reverberated with greater frequency. They trembled with a truculence, started to direct their malevolence toward me. One bit me on my neck if I still had one. It felt like a sting. Or a burn. Or an electric shock. I didn't know which. All I know is it hurt.

I made a noise. A pained yelp.

I twisted around and was confronted by the boy and the girl from my initial waking. They were no longer human. More like centaurs. But instead of being half-horse, they were half-lizard, and their limbs had been replaced by rubber tires. From their mouths, they spat their long, forked tongues, leathery but dripping with acid spittle, and I realized the shock I'd just suffered came from one of them, not the spheres. The boy's stare froze me, and I half expected him to pull out his shears, but he didn't, just lashed his tongue in my direction. It slapped my face, slashed me like a razor blade. I screamed. The girl flicked her tongue at me, too, and caught my left eye. It felt like she'd thrown acid into it. It burnt and stung and blinded. My heart pounded heavily. A bituminous balloon ready to burst. I retreated, thrust out the palm of my hand as a feeble protection.

"Ethan!" someone cried.

That was me! I was called Ethan! I'd forgotten I had a name. I'd forgotten I was called Ethan. I stumbled around, away from the lizard children.

"Ethan!"

It was the woman who was calling me. She looked more familiar than ever, especially as the spheres had retreated and I could see her more clearly. Her skin was scarred and lacerated, her complexion ashen gray, her lips blue, her eyes the final fading of a dying afternoon. I still couldn't place the woman. She was tired. She didn't seem to see me any more, just sensed my presence. She tried to call out again, but her effort stuttered, stumbled from her lips. Her mouth remained agape, and an ethereal light burst from it. Rays of salvation.

If I wasn't already dead, I sensed I might be soon. Soon, if I didn't snatch this opportunity. The lizard children were still rolling toward me. Their tongues were still spitting acid at me. Their wheels were still creaking and squeaking, their tails still whipping. The spheres started humming with an atonal aggression. They started to invade my space. Hover close to my face. To blind my vision. To unsettle my stomach. I tried to flick them away but couldn't. I twisted around. The light from the woman's mouth was losing its brilliance, but I edged toward it, closer and closer. I sensed if I didn't make that jump then, I never would. So, I leapt. Or flew. Propelled myself. I can't say how, exactly, but the closer I came to the light, the more it pulled me, became my own gravitational force. The lizard children were no longer a threat, the spheres mere flies. The light-force was magnetic. Omnipotent. All conquering. The light-force was my savior.

It sucked me in, through her mouth.

Everything went black.

There was nothing then, just a black sea of tranquility. A blind quiescence. A soporific stillness. An ink stain of a lake in a universe of limpidity.

I woke up.

Or thought I did.

I woke up again.

Or thought I did.

I kept waking up.

Or thought I did.

I opened my eyes, but my eyelids were stuck. A brightness burned my retinas. I needed sunglasses. I could see the mucus;

its stickiness was a blurry mess. I tried to wipe the mucus but couldn't. Not with either hand. I blinked and heard my name but didn't take much notice at first. I blinked until the mucus vanished. I heard someone repeat my name. My vision was hazy, but I could see a shape approaching me. I could hear the shape, too—its feet tapping on the floor, its raspy breathing. Something deep inside of it wanted to reach out and take my hand but didn't.

"Ethan! You're awake!"

"Mum! What're you doing here? Where am I?" Tears flooded down my mother's cheeks. Her breasts heaved. Her jaw trembled. I waited for her to take my hand, but she didn't. I wanted to open my arms up to her but couldn't. I was in a hospital.

In a bed in a hospital.

"Why am I in hospital?"

My mother ignored me and bent over me, spread her arms around me, enveloped me in her warmth, in the love I'd never once questioned. I could feel her whole body shake, taste her tears as they nourished my lips.

"What happened? Why am I here? Where's Heather? Where's Marky and Beth?" My mother started to moan. I started to cry. I didn't want to, but I did. I didn't like this. I'd never seen my mother cry before, not once. Not ever. Not even when Dad died. "Why're you crying?" I repeated. She still didn't answer. Enough was enough. I kicked my legs, wanted to shove her off me and get out of bed. Nothing happened. I tried to sit up. Nothing happened. My mother continued to cling to me. I wanted to cling to her but carried on crying as a dread swept over me, as my breathing deepened, as sandpaper chaffed my lungs, as I wished the dread would smother me, get it over with.

My mother pulled herself off me, stood up, retreated, wiped her eyes, which were now bloodshot from emotion. "I'm sorry," she said. "I'm sorry…" She sniffled. "D'you want some water? Let me get you some water."

"I don't want any water. I want to know what I'm doing here! Where's Heather? Where's Marky? Where's Beth?" My mother raised an eyebrow as if she hoped it would airlift her out of her nightmare. She chewed her lip, sucked in her cheeks, stared into her own abyss, into my abyss, into me.

"Do you remember anything?" she asked with trepidation.

Suddenly I did. Not everything, but something. Fragments. Grabs. Snapshots. I started to slip down a slippery slope of self-loathing. A slope, I realized, that would have no bottom, no end, just a constant descent into a living, breathing, suffocating Hell.

"Oh God. Oh my God. Oh my fucking God!"

THE MIRACULOUS RESURRECTION OF HERMAN JAMES GODFREY

Peter Collins Campbell

SWIRLING DUST PARTICLES settled as the movement of bodies in the room decreased. The coursing murmur of the crowd became silence. A new, taut stillness took hold.

"Who among us has not felt the increased pressure of our times?"

The man walked slowly across the creaking floor. He was dressed in a brown suit and vest, his hair slicked back with pomade, small wire-rimmed glasses wrapped over his ears. He was the image of culture, academia—a studied man.

The crowd murmured again, overlapping voices of agreement and support.

"Our great country has been dealt a difficult hand. The working man is feeling stifled, desperate. Surely, we have all heard stories of men on the docks, waiting hours, days, for a chance at a single shift. Food, scarce. Children of those men going without a scrap of bread. I say this to remind you—to remind all of us—that our good fortunes are rare. And we should be humbled and grateful for that."

The man looked into the faces of the seated crowd—upward of fifty people, all dressed in their Sunday finest. They had come here instead of attending their social appointments. Very few of them were probably churchgoers—the Upper West Side of Manhattan was home to socialites and progressives, new wealth that had no use for the structure of a church community.

"Ladies and gentlemen, I have spoken with the most powerful men of industry and politics, and with the men and women on the street. Many of you who have read my writings know that I have great sympathy for the poor. Whatever a man's so-called lot in life, all are welcome to the principles I have discovered."

The crowd continued nodding. He was moving into the affectations of a Baptist preacher, something he had picked up while traveling in the South. White audiences loved hearing those inflections coming out of a face they could relate to.

"But to achieve spectacular wealth—I don't mean to condescend to the men on the street, now—there must be grit."

"Yes." As if they had been to a service themselves, the audience knew how to respond just like the Negro congregations. He wondered if they knew it consciously, or if there was something deeper and more instinctual that drew these responses out of folks. Either way, it worked.

"There must be will."

"Yessir."

"There must be the belief that, yes, I CAN achieve the number in my mind."

"Yes!"

"But friends—while the visualization of your deepest desires is important—that is only the start. As I speak about time and time again in my book, you *must* put in the work. Otherwise, it is merely fantasy. And even the hopeless have fantasies."

He looked through the crowd to see the faces individually as they nodded, smiled, gazed in earnest silence, as if he was a great professor of science. He always wanted to be a professor. Now he had guest lectured at many universities, without attending so much as a single semester himself.

A woman in the crowd caught his eye. She seemed less openly enthusiastic than the others. Dark hair, falling in curly arcs around her ears and neck—a long and slender neck. His eyes moved over her intensely. She did not flinch.

"You there, ma'am." He couldn't help himself. As soon as the opportunity to convert a skeptic arose, he had to pounce, and publicly. The fact that she was a beautiful and wealthy woman would only add to his reputation.

She raised her head slightly in acknowledgment.

"What brought you here today, to this engagement?"

"That's my private business."

Another shift in energy. Before, the crowd had swayed lightly like wheat in a field, but now it was as if the breeze had suddenly stopped. The man also paused.

"Private business, eh? Very well." He turned. He began to walk back to the center of his space. He almost made it to his next point. But— "Now, just one moment, ma'am." He turned back to her, a finger in the air. "What do you mean by coming to this event and speaking to me like that?"

The woman stared at him uncomfortably. A few people around her glanced between the two of them.

"I meant to come here and listen to someone deliver a speech. I do not welcome being solicited as an unwitting piece of this theater you are performing."

"Theater. Do you find my delivery entertaining?"

"No. I do not."

He stared her in the eyes—dark, hard eyes for a woman. Surely a spinster—she must be over thirty, and he saw no one escorting her. He felt a rage building inside of him. The desire to push through the crowd, kick over chairs, frighten her, show her what happens *when rude, stupid, loud-mouthed whores ruin his shows—*

"Mr. Godfrey, perhaps you ought to just move on." The voice in his ear was his assistant, a young man named O'Hanlon. He was trying to make it look like nothing was happening here, but Godfrey's eyes were noticing people in the crowd starting to look at him with shifting expressions. He couldn't quite tell what the expressions meant.

"Yes, yes. My apologies, friends. That's the exciting thing about these engagements; you never know just what types will be in the audience." A round of smiles and laughs. They were his again.

HE STARED INTO the liquid swirling around in his glass. Auburn, he felt, was the name for this color. A less educated man might call it red. He knew better. He had filled his head with thousands of words to display his intelligence and build his credibility among the elite social classes. He had a knack for it.

There was a heaviness in the air of the hotel dining room. He felt as if he were in a dark dream, where none of the lights were at full power, even the sun. The weight made his head droop. He didn't think he was drunk. Only a couple of Manhattans in, he was still quite early in *who was that woman stupid stuck-up hag* his evening drinking routine.

Why'd she have to go and spoil it. Could've had
    Could've had ten new sponsors by the end of it
        Could've had a better place to stay tonight than the ratty
old Windsor. Outdated. Embarrassing
                embarrassing.

Each new, sharper edged thought cut through the thought prior to get a moment in the light before receding back into the muddled mess. He mumbled to himself highlights from these thoughts, transfixed by the endless spiral he stirred in his drink.

"Mr. Godfrey?"

He blinked. O'Hanlon stood on the other side of his dinner table, holding a notepad and several copies of the book.

"Yes, yes. Let's have it, son."

"Mr. Godfrey, I have several copies of the book for you to sign and your itinerary for the rest of the weekend before we leave for D.C.—would you like to go through it now?"

O'Hanlon was an interesting little fellow. He must have been twenty-two or so. Godfrey told him frequently that he reminded him of himself at that age—this was a lie. O'Hanlon did not show the aptitude for independent thought and self-propelled motivation that Godfrey preached. But O'Hanlon was loyal, and Godfrey had gone through far too many female assistants to convince his wife that they all simply ceased to be adequate at their work after about six months. Less mess, less fuss, having a man around. He was a good boy.

"Oh no, just leave it on the table. I'll review it all presently."

"The books are for several members of the Fraternity of Esoteric Studies, Mr. Godfrey. It may be best to sign them before you retire for the evening."

"Were they in the audience today?"

"No, sir, they'll be at your luncheon tomorrow."

"Oh, good. I'd hate for them to have seen that unfortunate encounter."

"With the woman?"

"Yes. What a ghastly creature. Why would someone attend an academic talk just to heckle and berate like that?"

"I don't think anyone was particularly offended by the interaction, Mr. Godfrey. It was a minor hiccup."

Godfrey took a deep drink from his cocktail, his eyes focusing in and out beyond O'Hanlon's face. "Sad, mean woman. You could tell she was too hard for any man to want her. I don't think she even wore makeup."

"No, sir. Maybe not."

"Do we have information on who attended the event? Records of the people who were invited?"

"I don't think so."

"Too bad. We should require full records from anyone that comes to my speeches. We should increase security. In fact, let's hire a bodyguard for D.C. I don't wish to be exposed like this again. Who knows what it could be next time? A hoodlum? An assassin?"

"With respect, Mr. Godfrey, I'm not sure the press tour has the, um, *budget* for a bodyguard…"

"Did I ask about the budget? No! I asked for a bodyguard. Make it happen, O'Hanlon, or I will find another secretary. I swear, sometimes I simply don't see you using any of the core tenets that I preach. What does a successful man do?"

"Um, well… There are several answers to that, sir—"

"He knows that which is in his mind is already a reality—he needs only to draw it to himself to access it in the physical world."

"Yes, Mr. Godfrey."

"So go be my mind's conduit and draw me a bodyguard, for God's sake!"

"Yes, Mr. Godfrey. Do you need anything else?"

"No, no. Good evening."

"Good evening, sir."

O'Hanlon disappeared. Godfrey scrunched up his eyes, trying to release the weight on his forehead and temples. This damn room. There must be some atmospheric transference of energy—that woman had infected him with a dark and negative cloud. It was following him now, pressing in on him, sapping him of his strength and vitality.

Time to get out of the ratty, musty old Windsor.

WOBBLY STEPS ON gelatin pavement. The world tilted and shifted around his head, still seemingly coated with a thick, opaque residue that made his skull feel ten times heavier. What terrible spell had that witch cast on him? He needed an exorcism of this negative energy.

His eyes dragged across the dark figures under the lamplight. Drunkards, whores, gamblers. These people needed to be thrown in jail, not given the keys to success. Less than people. They were instincts with physical form. He had written his book for them, yet so few would use his knowledge. They didn't deserve it. He delivered them enlightenment like God to the Israelites—though he had made a smarter business decision than the Almighty by charging for it.

Yet it was not enough. The book sales, the tours, the radio appearances—they didn't make a dent. The debts were getting harder to dodge. Some of his largest audiences were in the towns he couldn't show his face in—Tulsa, St. Louis, Philadelphia—and his booking agents were asking more questions every time. So many cruel and hard people knew his name—sometimes different names, but the same face—and would not hear another word from him unless it was to deliver them what he had borrowed. All would be forgiven. He just needed to get a little higher. Just out of reach of their grubby, clawing hands.

The figures passing by seemed to follow him with their black eyes. Not eyes—hollows. Voids. Glinting voids. They trained on him as he moved through the molasses air. Had New York always been this dense in the summer? Or had he been shepherded to some horrid ersatz city by the influence of that witch? Where were the beautiful glamorous women? The finely dressed men? The horse-drawn carriages and smell of roasting candied nuts? All he saw was smoke and mud and filthy flesh. All he smelled was the dull scent of rot. He wanted out. He wanted to run and dive into the Hudson. He wanted to be saved.

He was attracting attention from the figures and the glinting voids in their heads. Words had been coming from his mouth. He didn't know for how long or what he had said. One of the unlit figures loomed in front of him now, towering what seemed like a foot or more above his eyes.

"Are you well, sir?" The voice was booming and thick. A heavy accent disfigured the words. Irish? English? Some foreigner.

"What did you say to me?"

"Are you quite well, sir? You seem to be having some trouble walking, and we heard you speaking. You asked for help."

"Help. No, no. I don't need help. *You* need help."

"Pardon."

The tall figure was joined by several others. Why couldn't he see anyone's faces? Where were their faces?

"I'm *trying* to *help* you people. Why won't you accept *my* help? I wrote…a book…"

He was losing the last bit of energy he had. Was this his end? Would he really be felled by the curse of a witch?

"She wasn't even wearing makeup. She was plain. Cruel, cruel. That's why she needed to take *me* down. Or perhaps…no."

Wait.

"Perhaps she was an agent. Sent by—"

The Fraternity of Esoteric Studies. Of course.

"They must have trained their own special witch! They couldn't handle my notoriety, my *success*, telling the public all of the secrets of manifestation and energy transference! They trained a dark priestess to curse me and dispatch me without so much as a single bullet. *Of course—*"

The figures around him had cleared away. The night was pressing in on his head. The concrete had melted from the heat of the air and was pulling him down into its sticky rubber quicksand. This was the end. He knew it now. As the darkness sealed him into his subterranean tomb, he continued to try and speak, but his open mouth only allowed his lungs to fill with black tar.

COLD. WHITE.

Water smacked his skin and his eyes snapped open. The bright morning sun felt like fire.

"Get moving, fella. Sleep off your liquor in front of someone else's shop."

He staggered upright. A foul stench stung his nostrils—looking down, he realized it came from his own body. Darkened by the water dripping down his chest, he saw stains of vomit and urine down his vest and trousers.

"God in heaven…"

Everything was blurry.

"Where are my glasses? Hello? Does anyone see a pair of eyeglasses?"

"Anyone seen the bum's specs?"

Laughter, close by. Rage exploded in his gut.

"You devils! I am not a vagrant! I'm a respected man! I've been had! I've been hoodwinked!"

"You've been hoodwinked, eh? By who?"

"By a woman!"

More laughter.

"Which way you headed? Someone point the respected man in the right direction."

"The Hotel Windsor!"

"He's staying at the Hotel Windsor!" More, more laughter, stabbing him in the chest.

"Someone guide me to the Windsor and there's a nickel in it for you. My name is Herman James Godfrey, I am an author and businessman."

Silence. A few chuckles.

"I'll take you for a dollar." It was the voice of another person in the group, a different blurry shape in the light.

"Fine! Fine. Ridiculous. Absolutely ridiculous. Get on with it."

TIMOTHY O'HANLON STARED down at the unsigned copies of *The Principles of Freedom* on the hotel bar. They had been placed there by the restaurant staff at the end of the night, surely left on the dining room table by Mr. Godfrey. It was eleven o'clock in the morning, nearly time for their luncheon with the Fraternity, and Mr. Godfrey was nowhere to be found. Another night undoubtedly drinking 'til dawn in some establishment O'Hanlon would be embarrassed to even know about.

He gathered the books and headed to the hotel lobby, preparing to ask the desk to unlock Mr. Godfrey's room to make sure he wasn't there—when he found him. He appeared to be covered in vomit, missing his glasses, and being guided by a man in a shabby suit. O'Hanlon rushed across the lobby floor, keenly aware of the stares from people around them.

"Mr. Godfrey—"

"O'Hanlon? Thank goodness."

"What happened to you?"

"Nevermind, nevermind. Give this man a dollar and send him on his way."

"He was laid out on the street when we found him."

"Shut *up*, man. Take your money and go away."

O'Hanlon dug around in his traveling bag and found the coin purse that contained their dwindling stipend. He retrieved a dollar bill and gave it to the man, who seemed to be surprised to receive it. He nodded and left the building.

"Mr. Godfrey, we need to get you back to your room."

HERMAN JAMES GODFREY lay in the bath. His pipe was clutched between his teeth, a glass of Scotch on a tray of breakfast balanced over his chest across the tub. He stared up at the smoke billowing out from his mouth. O'Hanlon stood nearby, waiting with a towel and robe. He had already called the Fraternity of Esoteric Studies to inform them of their cancellation. The message had been received with bitterness.

"I died last night, O'Hanlon."

"What's that, sir?"

"I died last night and saw what I believe to be the next realm."

"What did you see?"

Godfrey turned his head to O'Hanlon, not removing his pipe from his mouth. Bits of tobacco fell into the water below. "Nothing."

O'Hanlon said nothing in response. This was a particularly intense bender, but these depressive swings and morbid obsessions were old hat for Godfrey.

"I don't know why I came back, why I was spared from that darkness. But I believe my connection to the metaphysical plane has granted me some protection against it. I knew I was destined to spread knowledge to the public when I wrote the book. I now know that was just the beginning."

"What do you mean, sir?"

"My story of success is an inspiration to people—but this is a genuine miracle. My story is the story of a miracle. *That* must be the subject of my next book."

"I didn't realize you were writing another book, sir."

Godfrey turned away from O'Hanlon, staring instead into the Scotch on his tray. He swirled his finger in it, beginning a self-propelled spiral in the dark liquid.

"*The Miraculous Resurrection of Herman James Godfrey.* Call the Fraternity back, O'Hanlon. I have new insights to share with them."

O'Hanlon nodded and disappeared from the doorway. He sank into the uncomfortable wooden chair next to the room's telephone receiver. As he began the process of connecting to the operator, he wondered idly if Alexander Graham Bell had had an assistant. Maybe he had moments of doubt, too.

PRETTY BOY

John Rosman

FRANK KEEPS TALKING. Trying to spin it normal. Saying a bad idea is good. Thing is, I keep telling him, cheap places stink out here.

You see it in the corners. Moss turned yellow and black with rain. I smell it. The motel's carpet from across the street in Frank's civic, over the cheap cologne he wears, over the whiskey he makes me drink.

I ask, cutting him off, "What's the word for doing something dumb, but you don't have a choice?"

"It's called being broke, Anthony."

"I don't want to do this."

"I've been saying this all night." Frank sighs. "It's too dangerous." He turns the key and rolls the engine to life. "Let's head back to the apartment and watch TV."

Frank is trying to pull a fast one, make it sound like this is all my idea, as if I'm in control.

"We don't have a TV."

"Oh." Frank scratches his chin. "I forgot. They took it."

"You sold it."

Frank unscrews a fresh pint of whiskey and pushes it to me. "Bastards made me sell it," he says.

"I don't want any more."

"Buddy, you need it for your nerves." He tips out a pinch of the crank he got from selling the TV and snorts it free from his hand. I swallow too much whiskey. It burns.

"What I would give to trade bodies with you. Me with this face for radio."

Frank is big and strong and ugly and smart. And I was cursed with being pretty and weak and dumb in a bad neighborhood. I came up with a different crew. They had me turn tricks. Frank stopped that. He looks out for me.

"What does face for radio mean?"

He smiles at me being an idiot.

"It means…" He opens up the glove compartment and places a 9mm on his thigh. "No man wants to watch me fuck his wife." Frank slaps himself in the face. "10:30," he says a little faster.

He grabs my wrist, the one with the knock-off watch he got me and holds it next to his. They run at the same time, to the second. His big meaty wrist dwarfs mine like I'm a child.

"You see? That's in thirty minutes. All you need to do—the only thing you need to do—is play it fucking cool. Don't be the little dummy with something to prove."

The crank spins more words out of him.

"No one wants to be a hero with his girl half-fucked and a gun in his face. He'll be an open ATM. We cash out and disappear. By just being there. By not hurting anyone. I don't want to bail you out of some fight you can't finish. You got it?"

He waits. "Anthony?"

It's 9:52. So that's actually thirty-eight minutes, dummy.

"Tell me you understand."

"YOU MUST BE Sam."

A man with a ponytail and scratched glasses waits at the door. He's a college-type, inflating out of his old clothes. Bad breath. Loafers and purple socks.

Why did Frank make me drink so much? I can't stand straight. I'm sick.

"Please, come in."

A table and two chairs face the bed. The comforter stripped away, exposing white sheets. The air is sour with discount bleach. It barely masks something raw and spoiled. It makes me gag. "Everything all right?"

"I hate bad smells."

The man with the ponytail and smug fucking face looks surprised and sniffs around. How can't he smell it? He sits down at the small table, and I follow.

"It's not the cleanest room, but I suppose there's always a price for a discount." He pours red wine into plastic Solo cups. "And I must warn you. The wine is even cheaper than the room."

I haven't understood a single fucking word out of this asshole's mouth.

"Where's Michelle?"

"Oh, just powdering up." He hands me the plastic cup. "To women," he toasts, raising his glass. "They won't stand for tardiness but relish in making you wait."

Before I can respond, he tips his cup and drinks. He watches me. It's a test. He wants to know if I'm smart like him. If I understand his toast. I down the wine with a single swig.

My watch says 10:05.

"Good man." He relaxes as he refills my cup. "Your first time?" I look past him to the camcorder pointing at the bed and the big light turned off behind it. "It can be strange. But just think about it…like an action movie."

"An action movie?"

"Don't pay attention to how the guns never run out of bullets, or the physics of flipping cars. Just suspend disbelief and…enjoy."

"I thought I was here to fuck your wife?"

"Touché."

He mutters something. Is he making fun of me? A nausea swells up and twists me wild. This rancid air pounds at my head with all the drink. I need to explode.

"Do you think I'm stupid?"

"What?"

Silence hangs in the air. And he finally listens. He stops trying to make me dumb. I stand. And for the first time I see him see me. And for the first time of this fucking night, I feel in control.

"You're not better than me."

"I would never imply…"

"You ever been in a fight before?"

"What do you mean…?"

"Like have you ever been punched in the face?"

"Sam, I think—"

"Hit so hard, so many times, you don't look the same?"

He stops talking. He watches me crush the red Solo cup into a ragged sharp ball. I feel the hard edges slice through my palm. I feel blood. I'm going to slam all the plastic through his eye and rip out liquid.

"You don't look like a Sam—"

"Darling," the man squeaks, "perfect timing."

I turn to see Michelle. She's dressed like a prostitute, cheap wig, body contorted inside a corset. She's older, which I like. But I can tell she stinks like this place.

"That's not my real name."

Dummy. Why did you say that?

"I know." She's already on me. "I'm not Michelle, either."

Her breath falls down my chest. Hand follows my wrist, guides me to drop what's left of the cup. "You need to relax." Her voice is low. Just between us. I look at the man. He's quiet and sweats like a pervert.

What man wants to watch another man fuck his wife?

"I want you to undress for me."

I can't help but look at the man again when she says this. But she guides my chin back to her. "He's not here."

She pushes me to the edge of the bed, and I'm forced to sit.

"Take off your shirt."

"I don't take off my shirt." There is something weird with this room. The edges are soft. She leans over me. "I wasn't asking."

She grabs the sides and rips. The buttons explode in every direction. My nice shirt is ruined, and if this was a man, I'd tear at his throat with my teeth. But I freeze.

She traces the cigarette burns on my chest.

"You do this?"

The old man who is dead did that.

"No. Those are from a long time ago."

She runs her fingers across the ugly scars I've hated my whole life and somehow makes them beautiful. She makes me forget the smell of the place. Her face is like one of those blurry paintings, and my head is a seesaw. My watch says 10:15. And things are finally going to plan.

"Did you put something in my drink?"

"Just a pinch of MDMA," says the man with the ponytail who I hate. "Mixed in a cocktail of homemade benzodiazepines…" She guides me back to her, away from his words I don't understand.

"I don't do drugs."

"That's okay."

She leads me to the back of the bed and whispers something into my throat, turning my body into standing water under rain. She pulls my hands up to the bedpost. Something cold and hard grips my wrists. My head weighs thirty pounds. She straddles me, and I feel her whole being breathe through her.

"Did you handcuff me?"

She puts a finger to my mouth and shows me a red ball-gag. The thing freaks wear. The light sucks from the room. I'm not fucking putting that in my mouth.

"Sam. Calm down."

They want me helpless. I use all my weight and muscle and pain and anger forever running through me to snap the bedpost in two. But it's strong. And the drugs are dreaming. I buck and twist, but Michelle stays.

I stop and plead without saying a word. But it's no use. Her eyes are true and burst through me. She guides the gag into my mouth. Cold drool runs down my chin as she pulls it tight. The man in the ponytail turns on a classical radio station. He plays it loud.

Everything is wrong now.

Michelle slides off me. The man uncoils wires connected to beige machines. He places them along the table. Michelle puts on the kind of headphones hunters wear during deer season.

The cuffs rip at my wrists as I tear them forward and back, misting blood on the sheets. But my arms grow too heavy to move.

Where's Frank?

Michelle takes off my shoes. And undoes my belt. Anything sexual is gone. Her movements are robotic. She pulls my pants free, leaving me cuffed and exposed in my cock-hugging whites, unable to move.

The man sticks plastic circles on my chest. He connects the wires to a monitor and adjusts a few knobs. Michelle unrolls a large, plastic orange suit. I watch her carefully put it on. She avoids eye contact from behind a giant clear hood, one of those things they wear for diseases.

The man now wears headphones, too. He turns on the camcorder and sits back and writes something in a notebook. Michelle talks. But I can't hear anything over the blaring symphony. The man nods. She walks to the bathroom and closes the door.

The drugs swallow my throat and fold me inside myself. I can't move. I can't scream.

And now, when I'm quiet and still, I hear it.

Has it always been here? This faint, ringing drone?

It comes from the bathroom and sounds like a dog whistle growing in volume. My body wants to hide from it, but I'm paralyzed. The sound is louder and pushes the music in and out of static. The overheads flicker. The man casually stands and turns on the big light behind the camcorder. That's when the sound erupts.

It screams and explodes the radio into blistering static. It's a volcano, and the overheads in the room cut out. I'm spotlit by the light behind the camcorder. The radio pitches into a strange frequency I've never known. And it's unbearable. And I feel liquid pour from my ears, and if I could move my head, I'd know it was blood. But I can't, and even if I could, I wouldn't because I can't take my eyes from the bathroom door. Something glows behind it. And the noise has somehow reached a new terrible height that's so horrific it becomes tolerable.

The bathroom door opens.

Michelle emerges. She walks toward the bed. And even under the drugs, I moan. Her suit reflects all the blasting light from this thing she delicately holds. This thing glows. And it squirms. The sound is its voice. And as she comes closer, this thing in her hands begins to rip my brain in two. And then I finally see it.

It's some giant, translucent leech. But my eyes water and twist inside my skull under all this light, all this sound, and I can't tell if I'm dying or being born.

The leech cries.

And I feel its pain. I feel its terror. It must have done something because I now feel its power. Through all the drugs, this thing lets me turn my head. I see the man in the ponytail slumped over in a pool of blood. Frank now wears his headphones, and he screams something, pointing a gun at Michelle and the leech. And finally, the room goes quiet. My wrists move through the steel handcuffs as if I'm pulling them from water. And I stand. Frank and Michelle are stunned and watch me approach. Frank is confused. I gently try to take the gun from his hands. He holds on tight, and I begin to take off his headphones. I want him to hear it, but he fights and yells at me. And even though he's 250 pounds of pure muscle and rage, he's weak. I want Frank to know what I know, feel what I feel. See what I can now see. But he won't let me. So, I push my thumb and finger against his windpipe and pinch, feeling it pop like bubble wrap. He collapses, choking on his blood. I walk over to Michelle who's rendered speechless. This person of science and words and books. But she knows nothing of life. Why would it choose her? I gently take the being from her hands. She's too stunned to stop me. I cradle it and push my free hand through the enclosed plastic, as if it's not there, as if it's just air passing through an open car window. I grab her face and squeeze. Bone and skin and teeth collapse into a sponge inside my fist. I let go, and she crumples to the floor.

I feel sad for her and Frank, and the dead man at the machine.

I hold this life against me and listen as it speaks. It has a plan.

I let it guide me out the door and into the night.

WHAT GROWS WITH US

Wolfe MacReady

HER MOTHER DIED the same day she broke a tooth. The first premolar on the left side snapped at the gumline while she ate a handful of Chex mix, chatting with her Tinder date at the bar. She didn't drink anymore, but bars were the easiest (and honestly safest) place to meet on a first date. She felt it snap but thought she just bit down too hard on a pretzel. There wasn't pain, not at first. Her date was talking about an episode of a podcast they both listened to and when she tried to continue to chew, she bit down hard on the remaining half a tooth. She froze, brow scrunched. Her date stopped mid-sentence and as they began to ask if everything was okay, she began to panic slightly. Every public outing was still a challenge. How she presented herself, the makeup and clothes she wore, how she sat, what she ordered, how she spoke. The date had been going well, and she thought she had passed the test, but now something was wrong inside her mouth.

As sweat crept in on her hairline, she smiled a little and nodded, reached for her seltzer and lime and downed what was left in the glass. She tried to use her tongue to feel around for what she bit down on, but then the ice in the glass hit her front teeth and she reflexively swallowed hard. The bar mix and tooth, gone. She thought about her mother then and the apple seeds, and in the strange, nearly dissociative panic that began to dawn on her as she discovered the hollow spot in her mouth, she wondered, *Can you pass a tooth? If not, what happens to it? What would grow there, I wonder?* A queer, rapid-fire string of questions as she just continued to smile and nod at her date.

"Sorry, wrong pipe. Have you listened to the new episode?" Annabelle cocked her head a little as she tried to steer the conversation back to what they'd been talking about. The date looked from her to her empty glass, signaled to the bartender, and then began speaking again. Annabelle nodded pleasantly, but if you were to ask her later that night, before she received the call about her mother's massive stroke and death, she wouldn't be able to tell you a single word they had said.

WHEN SHE WAS young, Annabelle's mother would carefully cut up an apple for her every day at lunch. She'd pick a bunch every morning from the tree in the backyard, and she would let Annabelle select the one she wanted. But she wasn't allowed to eat them whole. Any time she would go to grab one, her mother would snatch it out of her hand and take the small, red-handled fruit knife. As she sliced the apple, she'd remind Annabelle of how dangerous it was.

"The seeds. You can choke. And even if you didn't, you could swallow them. And do you know what would happen then?" *Slice.*

Her mother never looked away from her work of cutting the flesh into manageable pieces. "You can't digest the seeds. No, they're much too tough." Her mother would tap the fruit with the knife, denting the flesh. "And your stomach is just the right temperature and environment for something to grow." *Slice.* She'd stop to move half of the slices onto Annabelle's *Masters of The Universe* plate. "Full of good bacteria. A whole biome where anything can take root. And that's just what those seeds will do" *Slice.* "They'll find a nice spot in your tummy, and before too long, something will start to sprout." She'd slide the rest of the apple onto the plate, give Annabelle a small smile, and pass it to her. "Now go watch TV."

And she would.

DURING HER TEENAGE rebellion, she'd relish in taking bites out of the flesh of a Red Delicious. As she clipped photos from *Cosmo* of the girls she wanted to look like, she'd smear a streak of Nutella or peanut butter onto the outer skin of a Granny Smith and bite into it, juice running down her chin, into the patchy facial hair. This was before she started shaving. Didn't want another thing for her mother to worry or lecture about. Not that Annabelle thought her mother wouldn't accept her. But she'd do it *her* way. Hover. Nag. Worry. A cycle that already drove Annabelle up the wall. She didn't need it made worse by her mother fretting over such a personal experience. This, like the apples, would be her secret.

THE FUNERAL WAS three weeks before Annabelle's twenty-ninth birthday. She ran her tongue over the place her tooth had been as the priest finished his final words. After the service, she made a quick exit. She didn't want to talk to Aunt Agnes or Father Roy about *things*. How *things* had been. How *things* were going. What *things* she had been up to. It was all the same question really: What *thing* are you now? Not that she thought either of those particular people were malicious, just…hometown. They lacked the ability to understand. Or perhaps not the ability, but the true desire. Honestly, she wasn't sure she had met anyone with the true desire. Not yet. Maybe not ever.

So, post-funeral was like the rest of her life. She receded into the safety of self. Instead of the motel, she went back to the house she grew up in, the one her mother had *still* lived in, and pushed through the unlocked front door. She didn't expect anything particularly harrowing. This house wasn't haunted. No experience she'd had here was so bad that it would have left a scar deep enough to make a ghost. She feared the physical more than anything. She knew that her mother leaned into her hoarding after Annabelle had finally left. And lean in she had. There were mountains of *things* everywhere. A strange labyrinth with half-formed paths and dead ends. It took her some time, but she eventually got into the living room.

The layer of grime on the big bay window couldn't keep all of the light out, try as it might, and the late end-of-summer shine still filled this cramped space. It was all a sensory overload. Each room hell, each step she took seemed to bring some new series of smells: cheap magazine perfume swatches, old paper, *very* old paper, artificial saltiness like cheese in a can, and something distinctly animal. That one was old, but it was there. It all made her gut begin to churn. As Annabelle turned in a circle, trying to find a place to sit, she was becoming aware of how her skin was beginning to itch and crawl. How the spot of sweat on her lower back was spreading. She dizzily knocked over a stack of horticulture books, and as she careened towards the kitchen she had the thought, "*Oh*, those *were the very old paper*".

This was surprisingly the only room in the house that wasn't a disaster, but the smell here was worse. A sweet, fermented, cider stink. Thankfully the back door was also unlocked, and she bolted through it and threw up off the back porch, directly onto an anthill. She hadn't eaten much today. An old bagel and several cups of bad coffee cross-legged on her motel bed. But it all came back. And when there wasn't anything left, her stomach protested in horrible, agonizing dry heaves. This was the first time the tooth, or what remained of it, hurt. Shooting pain straight through the center of the broken crag that took her legs out from under her. She collapsed to her knees on the weather-beaten wood and could feel splinters stab into her flesh. The hem of her dress just missed saving them. But that sensation was a blessing compared to that searing, white-hot nerve pain in her mouth. But then, as quickly as it had been there, it was gone. A low throb remained, beating with her heart. She looked down at the small puddle of vomit and the scurrying insects below and muttered "sorry" before looking up at the yard. To her surprise, it was well maintained. The lawn was a little shaggy but certainly not what she had anticipated. She also hadn't anticipated the stone path. From the bottom of the porch, leading out to the apple tree, was a beautiful, intricate stone path.

When had Mom done this? Annabelle wondered. She couldn't hazard a guess as she barely spoke to the woman the last two years and little more the several before that. Annabelle winced as she pushed herself up and smoothed down the front of her dress. She hadn't ripped anything or gotten a drop of bile on her Docs, so she considered this a minor inconvenience. The light was fading, and she really didn't want to stay any longer than she had to, but the stone path called to her. Her mother wasn't this kind of artist. *Any* kind, to be frank. Had someone done this for her? She stepped out onto it, not even realizing she had descended the stairs and walked carefully out toward the tree.

It was bigger than she remembered. More full and lush. The leaves were dense, and the fruit was fat and plentiful. As she approached, she actually marveled at something her mother had done. Despite harsh winters and brutal summers, the tree looked better than ever. It was thriving. Just as quickly as the marvel occurred to her, she mentally scolded herself. *Of course the tree is thriving.* She knew *how to nurture that. She didn't nag it or hover over it. She cared for it.* And Annabelle realized that was the difference between her and it.

One was *nurtured.* The other was *smothered.*

She felt one of the stones shift slightly underfoot, and she froze as though she had triggered some trap, some posthumous defense her mother had installed. She immediately felt stupid and more aware of her surroundings. She was sweating properly now, and the itch on her skin from inside the house had carried over to out here. "Still worrying. Thanks, Mom," Annabelle mumbled out loud as she shot a look back toward the house and then crept closer to the tree. She scanned the ground around the trunk. No fallen fruit. Even if her mother had collected them the day she died, there should still be *something.* The limbs hung heavy with shining red orbs. Perfect waxen skin that glinted in the low light of the yard. Annabelle rubbed a sweating palm down the front of her dress and reached out. The nearest fruit was only a few inches from her face, and she grasped it.

It felt warm to the touch, and she twisted it, severing its connection from the tree. The leaves on the limb shook. *Shuddered?* She smiled a little and shook her head again. It had been a long day, and she was hot and sweaty and had nothing in her stomach.

And here she stood, spooking herself about her dead mother's fruit tree in the backyard. "Get real," she said as she looked down at the apple, just barely able to see herself reflected on its surface. It was a strange, distorted version spread weird across the skin of the apple. She lifted it to her mouth, closed her eyes, and bit into it. A larger bite than she wanted to take, maybe. Sweet, tangy juice met her tongue, and she chewed the perfectly crisp flesh. Maybe it was the empty stomach, or good old-fashioned nostalgia, but it was exquisite. Until the second bite.

Her eyes shot open at the odd crunch, and she looked down at the large section missing from the fruit. Seeds. Dozens of apple seeds stuck out from inside the fruit. Like the quills on a cactus, they jutted not just from the core but from seemingly *everywhere* in the apple. Annabelle spit the mouthful onto the ground at her feet, not missing her boots this time. "What the fuck," she shouted, louder than she realized as she continued to spit.

"Sweetheart? Everything okay back here?"

Annabelle spun around to see Aunt Agnes dabbing her upper lip with a hanky and looking worried. Annabelle immediately began to panic as she tried to smile. She dropped the apple to the ground, and it rolled away as she moved quickly off the stone path, toward the porch.

"Hi! Sorry, just—" she trailed off and laughed, high and manic as she reached the bottom of the stairs. She looked up at Agnes who stared back, nodding slowly. Her aunt looked her up and down, caught herself, and then smiled weakly.

"Come up here, honey. Give us a hug."

Annabelle was grateful that her aunt spoke first and plodded up the steps, arms open. They embraced and Annabelle breathed in deep. The warm, floral perfume Agnes wore felt like home. She pulled away, hands on either side of Annabelle, a tear in her eye.

"You ran off so quick." Annabelle nodded sheepishly, and after a beat of uncomfortable silence, Agnes sighed. "Well, it's good to see you now. How are things?"

The entire time Agnes talked *at* her, she wanted to pick at the strange architecture of the broken tooth. She felt something lodged there, surely a piece of apple skin. She was trying to be careful of what she ate until she could have it looked at (and without insurance, who knew when that would actually be), but she still indulged in popcorn and nuts and apples. As her tongue probed at the nuisance, she tried to focus on her aunt's chatter but found that she couldn't. The piece was too hard to be skin. Too thick. And then she thought back to the seeds. The dozens of seeds that seemed like they were almost inserted into the fruit and not grown there. Her tongue poked at it vigorously, trying to dislodge this sandpaper-rough piece. She was sure her aunt would notice her inattention or mouth movement or the sweat collecting on her brow, but she kept droning on. And then it bit Annabelle.

The piece of seed in the remains of the broken tooth *felt* like it reached out and bit the side of her tongue, and she suddenly stood up, hand over her mouth. Agnes stopped then. "Something the matter dear?" Agnes took a small nip out of the flask from her plain black funerary clutch as she watched her niece. Annabelle was panicking as a small trickle of blood collected in her mouth. She didn't want to, but she swallowed hard, winced.

"No, Aunt Agnes. I just think it's getting late, and I really have to hit the road early tomorrow. You understand?" It sounded more like a plea that she had meant for it to, but it worked all the same, and Agnes nodded, tucked the flask back into her bag, and stood with a hand on the small of her back.

"Let's walk each other out." Annabelle nodded and started toward the door, fishing the keys out of her own bag and not wanting to look back around at the overwhelming house in case anything had started haunting it since she'd been here.

WHEN SHE FINALLY got into her motel room, she rushed for her makeup bag on the sink outside the bathroom. On the drive here, she continued to poke at the seed and discovered something else was there. A soft flap of something. Maybe it was a small piece of her tongue. The bit that snagged on the seed while she listened to Aunt Agnes. Annabelle flipped on the light above the sink, and it flickered a few times before coming all the way on. She upended her bag and rifled through the small pile of cosmetics until she found her tweezers. She looked at herself in the mirror for the first time since she left that morning. Her makeup was a wreck at this point, and the dark circles and heavy bags were more noticeable now. She looked away, down at the reflection of her mouth, and opened wide. She craned her neck to the side trying to get a view of the tooth and the piece of seed lodged in it, but the angle was all wrong. She'd have to work blind.

Annabelle gave the tweezers a few test clamps and opened her mouth wider than before, carefully inserting the small metal tongs into her mouth. Saliva immediately began to collect under her tongue. The spot with the missing flesh ached. She squeezed the two metal halves together around the spot where she felt the lodged bit. She missed several times, cursed "UCK" with her hand still in her mouth, and then tried again. She clipped the very edge of the broken tooth and felt a small relief knowing she was close. She moved over, opening and closing the tweezers gently, until she felt the seed and, more miraculous to her, the bit caught on it. She clamped down hard on the piece and yanked. White, searing-hot pain ripped through her head and radiated outward over her entire body as she belted a scream. Her legs buckled out from under her, and she collapsed, slamming her head hard onto the countertop as she fell. And then the lights went out.

SHE OPENED THE door to her mother's house again, and this time the fermented fruit odor was all she could smell. Ahead of her were mountains of apples where her mother's various hordes had been.

"Annie, dear? Are you home? I'm in the kitchen." Her voice drifted to Annabelle from somewhere nearby, but it sounded muffled, buried somehow.

Annabelle made her way through the mounds and piles of fruit toward the kitchen, and as she passed the smell got stronger.

She could taste the tangy mustiness of the rot, and as she looked down at the overwhelming heaps, she noticed how much of it all was spoiled. Skin wrinkled, cloudy cider juice dripping out of mashed-in holes.

"Don't dawdle, your snack is ready."

Annabelle looked ahead and pushed her way through the thick funk into the kitchen. Her mother sat at the small round table that had always been there, looking terribly frail. Her eyes were sunken, as were her cheeks, and her skin was stretched taut over her skull, giving her an unpleasant, waxy appearance. Her frazzled red hair—what was left of it—was pulled up into a half-assed bun. She reached out with a spotted, bony hand and patted the place setting next to her. The *Masters of The Universe* plate sat there, heaped high with rotting fruit. Annabelle looked down at it in disgust and then back at her mother, who scowled at her daughter.

"What's wrong? This is how you eat them now, isn't it? Whole?" Her mother picked one of the pieces of fruit up, and it practically melted in her hand, wafting more putrid stink at Annabelle. "You're all grown up now, Annie. Far be it from me to tell you what to do anymore. I mean, *you've always* known what was best for you." Annabelle watched, frozen, as her mother lifted the mushy body closer to her face. "Sneaking around with all your little secrets like I wouldn't know." She turned the rotting fruit in her hand and Annabelle could see that the apple wasn't just some deformed mass. The withered, sagging skin had a face. One she couldn't quite make out but one she was sure she knew. One she hadn't seen in a long time. "Your mother always knows, Annie." She brought the leaking, molding thing to her mouth and bit into it with a sickening squelch. Annabelle wretched but couldn't look away. She was rooted in place as her mother took another too-big bite. She chewed and laughed, and as she did, it spilled out of her in great, terrible globs. But not just the apple. Seeds, too. Dozens and dozens of seeds poured out of her. She still managed to say, "They grow, you know. Your tummy is the perfect place to grow." She shoved the remainder of the apple into her overflowing mouth and kept chewing, even as more than she ever ingested spilled back out of her. And not just rotten fruit and seeds, but teeth as well. Whole and broken. She tried to speak again. Got as far as "An—" And even in her horror, Annabelle knew she wasn't going to say her name. Not the right one. Her mother began choking and heaving. Trying to rid her mouth of all of the horrid debris, eyes locked on her daughter's.

ANNABELLE WOKE UP on the motel room floor, coughing and dry-heaving. She shot up, and the room spun wildly as she tried to gain her composure. Her heart pounded in her chest, and she was covered in sweat as she looked around the room. The curtains over the window were drawn but she could see dim purple-blue light. The light of dawn. How long had she been out? As she sat, she slowly pulled her knees to her chest and became aware of two things: that her head was throbbing and that her mouth felt more full. Remembering the pain that the tweezers caused, she carefully probed at the spot with her tongue again. She could still feel the seed, but it was different. It felt deformed. No, not deformed. Split. And from that split, something was there in its center. She began to panic. She didn't know much about tooth anatomy, but had she exposed the root? Had she somehow pulled it out from inside the gum? Was that possible?

She steeled herself, unfolding her legs from her chest, and carefully, shakily, pulled herself up the bathroom sink. She hoisted herself to her feet and leaned in close to her reflection, opening her mouth as wide as the pain in her head would allow. What she saw was not some bloody, fleshy nerve ending. It was green and vibrant. A long, thin sprout was jutting almost out of her mouth, growing from the place where the seed resided in her broken tooth. She clapped a hand over her mouth and could feel hot sweat beading up on her. She slowly parted her fingers, peering in between them. Still there. Still a green that the human body doesn't make. She sat on the edge of the sink and just stared, watching open-mouthed as the sprout slowly grew. As she watched the sprout grow small leaves over the course of an hour, she began to cry. The soft sobbing turned to wailing. And the wailing didn't stop until she exhausted herself. Only then did they become nearly noiseless cries, until she fell asleep with her face against the glass.

When she woke, everything hurt just as much as her head did, and now it was even worse. She tried to blink her eyes open and found that she could only open the right eye. She tried to lean away from the mirror where she had collapsed, but she was stuck. Her mouth was more full than it had been and whatever was holding her to the mirror was there, coming out of her. She pushed away from the glass hard and felt a great decompression like pulling a suction cup off your skin. Her head felt strange and heavy, and she realized she couldn't close her mouth. She looked at the mirror and gasped. A small limb, maybe an inch or so around, with tendril-like branches, was making its way out of her. Some of the tendrils closest to the opening of her mouth snaked up her face, dug into the skin, and sealed her eye shut with the sticky sap of new life.

There was pain in this new growth, but it wasn't excruciating. It was a dull throbbing and pulsing. Annabelle felt her newness thrumming with the beat of her heart. She reached up carefully and touched the limb protruding from her mouth. The bark was silky and soft, not yet beaten by the world or the weather. As she ran her hand along it, the tendril branches reached out for her, and with just a moment of hesitation, she let them touch her. They had warmth. It didn't matter if it was blood or something else, they were warm. It was *her* warmth.

She felt the limb in her mouth expanding, felt the teeth around it begin to give way. They cracked and broke, and the white-hot pain returned to her. Tears leaked through her sealed-shut eye, and a small leaf reached out to wipe them. As blood and dental debris filled her mouth, she felt the panic beginning. But the new warmth pulsated through her, calming her. Even as her jaw began to break and the skin around her mouth began to tear, she beared down. She was ready for this new change, come what may.

The apple Annabelle bit yesterday (*was it just yesterday?*) was a part of her now, and that apple had been a part of her mother. Of course, her mother planted the tree. Raised it from nothing more than seeds to the mighty life that survived winters and storms and always bore fruit. Because she nurtured it. Cared for it.

But this was *new* life. The seed in Annabelle's mouth had split and served its purpose, and now this *becoming* belonged to Annabelle. Sprouting branches pushed into the soft palate in the roof of her mouth, shredding it like tissue as a new part, something that was wholly hers. She watched her reflection with her one good eye, marveling at the new life's speed, until her vision became cloudy and strained. There was intense pressure at the back of the orb, and she slowly reached up to touch it just as the eye burst outward in a flood of hot white liquid and blood. A vine unfurled from the wreckage and snaked down her cheek before entering her nostril. She didn't need sight now. Annabelle knew the growth would guide her, show her where she needed to be.

She gave herself over to it. Even as skin ripped, she knew that it would bind her back together.

And it did.

WHEN THE HOUSEKEEPER came, she witnessed Annabelle's new growth pulling the skin back together, stitching itself around new parts, slick with blood and clear liquid, rich with chlorophyll. The young woman left screaming when she caught sight of Annabelle, knocking over her cleaning cart as she went. Annabelle didn't move from the mirror as the hysterical woman fled. She just continued to stare.

That's okay, she thought. *It's not for* her.

She lowered herself off the sink, where she had been perched, and could feel the intricate weave of life making its way through her body. As she moved, her skin squirmed. The pain was exquisite.

She felt no fear now. No shame. As she walked out of the motel room, folks gathered with the manager outside. Annabelle didn't know if they screamed or fainted. If they ran or stayed frozen in place. She was only worried about the future now. She needed clean, cool water. She needed soil as rich and dark as coffee grounds. She felt the new roots begin to split the soles of her feet, peeling back the skin as thick vines snaked out. She smiled as she thought about what was needed. She would care for them and let the life continue to grow. She would nurture them.

As the vines of her feet broke free from the skin and bone, they pushed her up. They began to carry her, higher, aloft, almost flying. They held her, nurtured her, too. She began to glide down the highway as early-morning travelers veered to miss her.

She smiled, the verdant green ligaments in her face creaking. She would never have to touch the ground again.

THE PALE SHORE

Emily Bennett

SALT. THAT WAS all Daphne could taste. She couldn't tell if it was coming from the ocean or from the tears running down her cheeks. She licked her lips, tasting it again. It tasted like sadness sure, but the ocean tasted the same way. She found it oddly comforting. Having a good cry always grounded her because her tears tasted like the ocean. They tasted like home.

Home. The word felt strange to her now. It doesn't fit anymore, she thought as she gazed down the coastline. Home was supposed to feel different than this.

Summer had long passed, and autumn had cleared crowds away, leaving the shore bare. Even the gulls had gone for the season. Only the wind and the waves remained, and miles and miles of memories. Good, Daphne thought. She needed to be alone.

She needed to figure out what had gone wrong.

She wiped her nose, bumping her wedding ring against it. She winced. It was appropriate for a widow to wear her wedding ring, but the truth was she couldn't take it off. Her fingers had swollen—either from drinking or the humidity or both—and the tarnished silver band had become tight around her finger, squeezing it like a vice.

Even in death, Arthur had control over her. She licked her lips again and smiled a bitter smile.

"If home tastes like salt, then love tastes like liquor." She looked down at the ring. "At least it did with you, my love," she muttered, wishing she could have been that clever when Arthur was alive. She never wanted liquor or love again. She just wanted answers.

Tonight, she decided. Tonight, she'd ask Arthur what had happened. She'd light a candle and open a door, just like the psychic told her to do. That woman with white hair and silver eyes came out of nowhere when Arthur was still alive. She found Daphne stumbling through the cobbled Charleston streets one night and whisked her into her shop. Crystals and candles and smoke filled the place, and she gazed across a table and foretold Daphne's fate. She somehow knew what would happen to Arthur, and she told Daphne what to do once he died. She taught her how to reach him and what to say. Ever since Arthur's death, Daphne couldn't stop thinking about her. It was finally time to take her advice.

Daphne looked down at her forearms. Her skin looked transparent under the goosebumps, with a roadmap of blue veins coursing beneath the surface. She realized she was shivering and pulled her toes out of the sand. She'd shower and start the seance or whatever she was supposed to call it, she thought.

As she turned toward home, she noticed a shadow in her periphery—a human shadow hovering just out of view. It appeared to be moving toward her. Daphne turned her head to confront it, but by the time she looked the figure was gone, vanished into the wind.

Daphne's heart pounded as she scanned the empty beach. It must have been a trick of the light, or a dark spot in her eye. She scoffed at herself, then turned and trudged back up the dunes. Still, she couldn't help glancing over her shoulder the entire way home.

A MIRROR. A candle. A key on a chain.

Daphne set each item on the kitchen table. She couldn't believe she was doing this, but the dead have answers the living want to know.

The salt-worn beach house seemed to rock beneath her feet, lightly creaking in the wind. The cottage-style home was multiple generations old and seemed to shed more of its wooden shingles each day. Eventually the exterior would be blown bare, smooth as a seashell, and the realtors would come and beg to knock it down. Vultures, Daphne thought. This house was hers, and no amount of tragedy would take it from her.

Daphne scratched several matches before one finally caught flame. In the flickering candlelight, framed childhood photos of herself stared back at her, but the carefree girl in the frames looked like someone else. She wondered if she were to have a daughter if they would look the same. She quickly scolded herself for thinking such things and swallowed down a cry.

She looked around at all the shell art her mother had collected over the years, the furniture her father had crafted with his arthritic hands, and the hand-me-down quilts tossed across the couch. She'd been sleeping on the couch since Arthur's death since the smell of him hung thick in the bedroom and she couldn't bring herself to go inside.

A key hung from her neck, attached to a silver necklace Arthur had given her some time ago. She removed the necklace and held the key up by the chain. She smiled. Homemade magic, she thought. She caught her candlelit reflection smiling inside the mirror on the wall, then watched as the smile faded.

It was time. She took a deep breath.

"Arthur, I want to talk to you," she said aloud to the empty room. "If you can hear me, please move the key up and down. Okay?"

The wind picked up outside and she took that as a sign. She held the key high and let it drop, watched it circle the air in front of her, feeling heavy on the chain. The candle flickered in the light breeze of her breath, and she shut her eyes and began.

"Can you hear me, Arthur?" She felt the key sway at the end of the chain, and when the pendulum started to slow, Daphne opened her eyes. The key swung toward her then away. YES. YES. YES. He could hear her! She almost laughed. Maybe this was the answer. Maybe this was how she would finally find peace.

She cleared her throat and sat taller in her chair in preparation for the hard part. She glanced at the window reflected in the mirror. The palmetto trees outside swayed in the distance. Focus, she thought to herself and concentrated again.

"Arthur. Did you— Did you do it on purpose?"

She scolded herself for being afraid to say it aloud. She started again. "Did you mean to kill yourself?"

She closed her eyes again. She didn't want to influence its course. Still, she wanted his death to be an accident, a mistake, an unavoidable tragedy. After a moment, she peeled her eyes open and looked.

The key was swinging up and down. YES.

She could hear it pass through the air. Whoosh. Whoosh. YES. YES. "Asshole," she said aloud. "You selfish, selfish man."

She lowered the key to the table, where it settled with a clunk, and she shook her head in disgust. But she wasn't disgusted at Arthur. She felt disgusted at herself. After everything that had happened between them, she still missed him. She didn't want to, but she did.

Daphne looked into the mirror, palms flat on the table. Candlelight danced madly in her dark eyes, and she whispered through her teeth, pleading to the flame.

"Come back to me now. Come back to me. Come back to me. Come back." She waited, staring at every inch of the mirror to see if he might appear.

Moments passed, but no one came. Daphne's jaw clenched. A familiar rage bubbled up inside her. It was a rage Arthur had taught her, had fostered inside her. It was a rage they shared. She sneered and shook her head.

"Or are you a coward?"

She stared into the mirror, into the inky shadows behind her. The darkened corners of the familiar home suddenly felt sinister. The deep blue-black darkness was cold and endless. Anything could be waiting in those shadows. Her late parents. Her late husband. Anything or anyone at all.

Daphne stared deeper into the mirror, straining to see into the reflected dark.

She didn't see him at first, but on closer inspection, she realized someone was standing outside the window.

A man. Eyes wide. Staring straight at her.

"Oh, God!" Daphne's body seized and jolted upright, knocking the table over, spilling all the contents off the top. She dropped to the floor and grabbed the flickering candle before it could set the rug on fire. She blew out the flame and looked back in terror to the window where the stranger had been.

But the man was gone.

Daphne scrambled to the window and stood there, palms pressed against it, fogging the glass with her breath. Her eyes scanned the moonlit beach for movement, but found nothing beside the gentle sway of the Palmetto trees and the swirling clouds of sand.

"He came back to me," she whispered, widening the fog on the windowpane with each breath. In spite of everything they'd said and done to each other, he'd come back to her. What a gesture. What a gift. She smiled.

Daphne stood there for a while, gazing out. Her heartbeat slowed, filling with a feeling she hadn't felt in so long. It filled with the fluttering sensation of love. She pressed herself against the glass, not wanting the feeling to go away quite yet. It was a different feeling than grief, and it was good to feel something different, even for just a moment.

SALT AND SAND. The breakfast of champions, Daphne thought.

It was a foggy morning, and she watched the sun rise from the misty horizon. It looked like a bright orange balloon breaking through a sea of cobwebs before rising high into the sky. The salt tasted nice on her lips today. It tasted happier. Arthur had come back to her last night. Maybe things would be okay after all.

She smiled. Perhaps she would start packing today. Perhaps she would head into town and grab lunch. Perhaps she'd get her nails done. Or see if the psychic was in her shop—Daphne would tell her the seance worked. The world suddenly felt hopeful again. Perhaps… Wait. Who the hell was that?

Daphne squinted to see him clearly. It was a large man, lumbering in the misty distance along the shore. He was tall—very tall—with a beard and a backpack. He moved like a child heading unwillingly to school. Daphne blinked again. She realized she was standing and hugging her sweater around her like armor. Who was this man? Why was he coming toward her?

Daphne finally found her voice and yelled, "Hey! Who are you?"

The man glanced up in her direction but quickly looked down and kept trudging forward through the sand. His persistence was unnerving, but even from afar, Daphne could see that his expression was timid, almost nervous.

She yelled again, louder this time. "Hey! This is a private beach! You can't be here!"

The man finally stopped in his tracks and stared at her.

"Are you— Are you talking to me?" he yelled over the sound of the waves, without a trace of sarcasm in his voice.

Daphne blinked. What the hell was wrong with this guy? "Uh, yeah. I think I am. Since you're the only fucking person here."

He stared at her as a shocked smile spread across his face. He quickly wiped it away and shook his head. "I am. Yeah, I guess I am. Sorry. That was a really dumb question. Sorry about that. I'm…" He exhaled and dropped his shoulders, trying to make himself more presentable. "I should start over. I'm Paul. Paul Foster. And I… I wanted to… Um…" He trailed off, suddenly concerned, or self-conscious, or both.

Daphne's patience was gone. She was still processing the night before and she was tired of this coy giant standing in front of her. She puffed her chest. "Well, Paul Foster, you're on private property. And I think you should go before I call the police."

With that, she spun on her heels and stormed toward her house, praying he wouldn't follow. She heard his voice call out behind her. It nearly cracked as he yelled, "I heard what happened here! And I'm sorry!"

Daphne stopped in her tracks. A stone suddenly formed in her throat and she tried to swallow. When she was sure she wasn't going to cry, she slowly turned back. "Oh yeah? What the hell have you heard?"

"I saw the news stories about this place, and I was… I dunno. Curious. I'm just… I'm really into true crime, so I wanted to see the house for myself." He plopped down on the sand, held his backpack in his lap, and squinted up at her. Daphne figured he did this to appear less intimidating, and it worked, but for all the wrong reasons. He looked ridiculous.

Daphne crossed her arms over her chest. "True crime?" she asked.

"Yeah. That's why I travel. To interview people. Listen to them. Figure out the 'true' part of true crime." He smiled at her. His eyes were warm and genuine.

His familiarity annoyed her a little, but it was nice to talk to someone else for a change. He seemed well-meaning enough. He was like a Hardy Boy in a lumberjack's body.

"Are you here to interview me, then?" she asked, gazing out at the reflection of the sun on the water. She could feel Paul's eyes on her.

"To be honest, I wasn't anticipating anyone being here. Last night, I was—" He stopped himself mid-sentence.

Daphne blinked. She looked down at him again. He suddenly looked sheepish, like he wanted to crawl out of his own skin. Daphne's face felt hot all of a sudden.

"Wait— Last night? Were you at my house last night? Were you the one I saw outside my window?"

Paul's shoulders slumped as he mentally flogged himself. But instead of answering, he lumbered to his feet. "Uh...yeah. That was me."

Daphne glared at him. She was furious and crushed. Her seance hadn't worked after all. The man in the window wasn't Arthur. It was this nosey freak in front of her. "So you interview people in the middle of the night, too? Just sneak up to their houses to have a little chat? Is that what you do?" Her anger made her feel bigger, more powerful. Paul started to back away.

"Look, I—I'm sorry. I'm a big nerd, but I'm not a weirdo. I don't...spy. Or sneak in to people's homes at night. I just— I heard someone calling out from the house, and I was curious to find out who it was."

Daphne's fists were clenched, her knuckles bone-white. She stepped toward him. "Calling out? No one was calling out to you. I was in my house trying to talk to my late husband—who you already know ALL about, I assume."

"All I know is what I've read. Look, I have a… sense for these things. I'm more…receptive than most people. Maybe when you called out to him, I heard you instead," he offered, examining the thought as he said it aloud.

Even in her anger, this made Daphne pause. She hadn't considered that a seance could speak to the living. Could that be true? She eyed him. "What the hell did you hear?"

"I—I'm sorry. I didn't mean to intrude—"

"Well you are intruding! So just be a fucking man and get on with it! What did you hear?" Her eyes burned with a familiar fury. A practiced fury that had taken years to ferment. Undeniable and chaotic.

Paul swallowed hard. "I heard you say, 'Come back to me.' And then you asked, 'Are you a coward?'" He said this flatly, with no expression.

Daphne blinked. Her cheeks were wet again. On her lips was the briny taste of home. A sob overtook her and she had to steady herself so as not to collapse.

"RECORDING. TEST. TEST. One, two, three." Paul spoke into a small voice recorder and then hit a button to stop it and rewind. He hit play, and his voice clearly spoke back to him from the recorder, "Recording. Test. Test. One—" He stopped the recording again, then looked up at Daphne and smiled. "Ready?"

Daphne felt butterflies in her belly. The sensation reminded her of the night before, of the flutter of love reemerging in her heart for just a moment. She nodded.

They sat at the kitchen table, both pressing their hands against the wood tabletop as if it were a spirit board. In a way, that's exactly what it was. Daphne was going to summon the memory of her late husband for the strange man seated across from her. Her remembrance would be an invocation, a calling back from the dead.

Paul hit the record button again, and a red light switched on.

"This is Paul Foster. Today is Sunday, October 17th. I'm speaking with the widow of the deceased—one Arthur Seaver—at her property along the South Carolina coast, just outside Charleston. Daphne, can you say your full name please?" He gazed into her eyes as the late-afternoon sun haloed her tired head.

"Daphne Seaver. Or would it be Ellwood now? I'm not sure if I keep my married name or go back to my maiden name." Feeling suddenly sheepish, she twisted the wedding ring around her finger.

"That's okay. What do you prefer?"

She chewed the side of her mouth for a moment. "Seaver. I'm Daphne Seaver. I chose Arthur. I'll keep his name 'til the end." Her words came out in a minor tone and echoed against the memory-filled walls around them.

"Can you tell me what happened to your husband?"

"Oh, okay. Just jumping right in, I guess." She shifted nervously in her seat. "So, Arthur. Um, well, Arthur was handsome. Handsome and very complicated. We met back in high school and hit it off immediately. We both partied a lot, liked to have fun. Our wedding was wild. It was on this beach, actually. My parents were mortified at how drunk everyone got, but to us it was a dream. We were young and in love. And we just… We never really grew up."

She paused, waiting for another question, but Paul said nothing this time. He just nodded, gazing at her with kind eyes.

He was a good listener, she thought. She continued.

"We moved around a lot because of his work. Well, because of him constantly losing work and having to find it again. The drinking went from weekends to weekdays, middays to mornings. You know how it goes. We'd pick up and move again and again. I drank too. I had to, just to keep up. Or to numb the experience of him. It was hard to tell after a while. We wanted— I wanted to start a family. But the world we'd created wasn't one I… I couldn't bring a child into that world, you know?"

Paul nodded. "So, you never had a child with him."

Daphne winced at the statement, but she kept going. "No. I wanted one. A little girl, maybe. I wanted one more than anything. But it wasn't in the cards for us, I guess."

A rustling sound at Paul's foot made Daphne pause. He immediately looked down and quickly shoved his backpack farther under his chair. He looked quietly panicked about something, which made Daphne curious. She leaned down to look beneath the table where she saw a number of papers sticking out the backpack's open top.

"What's all that?" she asked.

"Oh, nothing. Papers. Documents. Just— Records, you know?"

"About Arthur?" she asked, but Paul wouldn't meet her gaze. Daphne sat taller and said firmly, "Let me see them."

Paul swallowed, then smiled softly. "Sorry, but we don't have much time. It's going to be dark soon. Do you mind if we…" He indicated the voice recorder. The red record button was still lit up. But Daphne didn't like being told no. She leaned forward.

"No, I'd like to see. If they have to do with Arthur, I think I'm entitled to look." She stared at him, unblinking.

Paul's chest fell. He picked up his bag and rustled through the contents. Large pieces of tracing paper had been rolled up like maps. He carefully chose one from the bunch, unrolled it, and looked it over. Satisfied, he slid it across the table to Daphne.

Her eyes narrowed. "What if I want to see the other one?"

"This one first," Paul said. His voice was firm and unwavering this time.

Daphne eyed him suspiciously, but she didn't argue. She unrolled the paper on the table. At first, she couldn't tell what she was looking at. The paper looked soiled, like someone had rubbed dirt all over it in some strange but deliberate pattern. But the more she stared at it, the more the picture became clear, like it was rising out of murky water towards her. The soiled parts were words, but they weren't made from dirt, they were written with charcoal. She read the inscription aloud.

"Arthur James Seaver, born—" She stopped herself and put a finger to her lips. She looked up at Paul, her eyes wide. "What is this?"

Paul returned her stare with an even gaze of his own. "That's a rubbing of Arthur's gravestone." Paul seemed less submissive now, more forthright with his answers, like something had settled and hardened in him.

Daphne frowned. "Okay. But why would you—That's kind of intrusive, don't you think?"

"Not really. Stone rubbing is a common practice throughout history. Most churches allow it to this day. And it doesn't disturb the gravestone."

Daphne didn't like Paul's tone. "Well, it's not polite to do something like that." She didn't slide the paper back to him. "What's the other one?" she demanded. "I want to see it now."

Paul stared at her from across the table. He looked unhappy and a little afraid. "Let's keep going, please. I have to go soon."

"No. Show me the other one or we're done here."

"Answer a few more questions, and then I'll give it to you. Okay? I promise." He never blinked, never wavered or took his hands off the table.

Daphne was troubled by his sober confidence. This new demeanor of his upset her. Her eyes narrowed. "What do you want to know?"

"What happened to Arthur? How did he die?"

She scoffed. "Seriously?"

"Seriously."

"I thought you knew all this already. What happened to all that research you've been talking about?"

"I know what happened to Arthur. But I want to hear it from you."

She seethed. "He killed himself. He got drunk one night and killed himself. Back there in the bedroom. Which is why I sleep out here on the couch."

"How did he kill himself?"

"Jesus." She looked down at the red light, still shining on the recorder. "Do you get off on this kind of thing? Does it make you feel tough? Well, guess what? You're not tough. You're a child. A man-child who wanders around with his backpack like a little fucking kid. You're a tourist. And you're not welcome here anymore. Get out of my fucking house."

Daphne stood with such force that her chair toppled to the floor behind her. She spun around, arms crossed, and stared out of the same window she'd stared through the night before. She chewed her cheek and waited for Paul to stand. Waited for him to leave. But the man didn't move.

"Daphne…" He suddenly spoke with such compassion, it shocked her. "What happened?"

Daphne turned around and looked at him. Something felt strange. She grabbed her wedding ring, vice-gripped around her swollen finger, and twisted it. Twisted it to feel pain, to ground herself somehow. But instead, she felt nothing.

"What do you mean?"

"What happened to Arthur, Daphne?"

"Stop saying my name! You need to leave! Now!"

Without looking, Paul reached beneath his chair and pulled out the other rolled-up paper from his bag. He laid it flat on the table so that it faced Daphne. He watched her, almost apologetically.

Daphne looked down at the charcoal-covered paper.

"What's that?" she heard a scared little girl's voice say. Then she realized it was her own voice. She sounded so helpless, so lost and hurt. She didn't want to see any more. She didn't want to know. But Paul never wavered, and Daphne couldn't resist. She slowly leaned in and scanned the words with her eyes.

Daphne Jane Seaver

A lover of life, a mother in Heaven

Born 1989

Died—

Daphne shoved the paper away. She couldn't breathe. She wasn't breathing. She looked up at Paul, a panic in her eyes. "What— What is this?"

Paul's voice was somber and kind.

"I took a stone rubbing of your gravestone, too. I hope you don't mind." There was no trace of sarcasm in his voice. In fact, he looked like he might cry.

Daphne stumbled back, nearly falling over the toppled chair as she did so. She shook her head in disbelief. "No. That's not— That's not me. We must have the same name. But I'm not—"

"Yes, you are. You died during pregnancy."

The world stopped on those words.

Daphne tried to breathe, tried to think. She touched her forehead. It felt like cold marble beneath her swollen fingertips.

Paul continued. "You told Arthur you were pregnant that night. And that you wanted to keep it. He was drunk. And you fought, like you always did. But this time was different." He paused to let this sink in. "He had a hammer and came at you. You got as far as the beach, but— If it's any consolation, the police say you died quickly."

"Where?"

Where I first found you along the shore."

Daphne could taste home again. The brackish, briny flavors of grief. It tasted sharper now. Like iron. Pure and primal. That's when she realized it wasn't tears she was tasting. It was blood. Flowing from a gash in her head. She blinked.

"It was only after having murdered you that Arthur came back here and killed himself. That's why you couldn't remember how it happened. Because you didn't have a living memory of it. You were already dead when your husband took his life."

Daphne stared at him for a long time. Her anger was gone, replaced by a dull ache. It was an empty sense of loss over what could have been. Her swollen fingers caressed her belly as the dripping blood from her head wound fell from her chin and onto the spot where her child had once been.

"I'm a mom," she whispered.

"You are. And you'll always be one."

Daphne looked up at Paul. The man was right. She finally had something Arthur could never take from her. She had her baby close to her, comforting her now. She hugged her stomach softly, watching droplets of blood continue to dot her arms and hands.

"Did you really hear me calling last night?"

Paul smiled. "Yeah, I did. I didn't realize seances could go the other way, but I must have been ready to listen. Maybe that's how I was able to hear you."

There was that familiarity again, the assumptive kindness that was patronizing and sharp. Daphne watched him as the blood ran down her face. It felt good. Warm. The relief of her death was something she hadn't expected, but it washed over her, total and pure. She was free now. Free to do anything she wanted. And what she really wanted right now was to wipe that ridiculous smile off Paul's face.

DAPHNE STOOD AT the window that night, swollen fingers running gently over her belly. She sighed with a smile and gazed at the moonlit shore, as pale and silent as she. There was more to be done in this place, she thought. She needed to summon the living, to share her grief and anger. She needed to share her pain, for her pain was precious. Her pain had to be shared. After all, no one listened to her screams in life.

But they would listen to her now.

Daphne's smile widened as she took a seat at the table. Eventually she'd get tired of Paul's dead body being slumped there. It would bloat and decay like all bodies do. But for now, the sight of him made her happy. It reminded her of how hard he had fought, but not hard enough. Not like a man should fight, she thought.

"The bigger they are, the harder they fall," she mumbled, smiling to herself as she stared into his vacant, bloodshot eyes.

After a while, she heard the rain start to fall. When the thunder clapped and the sky opened up, she reached into her shirt and took out her necklace with a key on the end. It was time for a new conversation. It was time to share her pain with someone else.

She gazed into the mirror as she held the box of matches and struck them one by one. Thunder rumbled as the third one caught flame.

SIX-MINUTE MILE

Mike Flanagan

JORDAN STARED AT the missing dog as he finished tying his shoe *(hope you find your way home, little champ)*.

Affixed to the telephone pole by three staples, the image of the yellow lab—Milo—was set against bright orange construction paper so as not to go unnoticed, and had not yet been faded by the California sun. Milo himself had been printed separately and cut out by hand, taped carefully onto the neon orange sheet below "MISSING" and above "REWARD" *(shit, someone spent a lot of time on these)*. The bottom of the flier was cut into vertical strips, each displaying a hopeful phone number. None of them had been torn off.

He considered taking one, just to make the flier feel more successful somehow.

He'd passed a bunch of these orange fliers on his mile but only now really looked as he finished tying the knot on his Hokas *(hanging by a thread, I've got to remember to order a new pair)*. He straightened up, cracking his back. The missing poster was one of three on this particular telephone pole. There was another dog, a husky named Shadow, and a calico cat called Barnabus. Unlike Milo's orange craft project, these were simply printed on basic copy paper and fairly faded, their colors bleaching in the sun.

He again considered pulling one of those orange tabs on the chance that the person who hung the flier might wander by and see, and it might give them just a fleeting moment of hope. Of course, that hope would be a mirage, as the call would never come *(at least not from me)*, so in the end it seemed like a cruel mercy at best.

He always hated missing-pet posters. The idea that these little creatures, who were earnest and loyal and joyful and innocent, could just fall through the cracks of the world and disappear… Well, it made him uncomfortable. The world wasn't kind to the innocent or the vulnerable, that was true enough, but something about the lopsided odds for these little animals made it feel especially cruel.

When a human being fell through one of those cracks, people at least *reacted*—the police showed up, neighbors linked arms and walked through the woods, there was a mobilization of protest… But not for pets. No, for those little guys, no matter how intensely they might be loved, the world just moved on.

He pulled out his phone and rifled through his playlists for something more upbeat *(thirteen fucking seconds)*. Missing pets were a bummer, and he was already bummed enough *(thirteen fucking seconds)*.

His apple watch was frozen where he'd hit the button, still displaying his distance—exactly 1.0 mile—and his time of 06:13—six minutes, thirteen seconds *(so fucking close)*. He hit the button again, letting the clock tic onward.

He kicked his right heel up toward his butt, reaching back to grab the top of his bright blue Hoka and pull it into a quad stretch. He leaned his left hand against the weathered posters *(I'm not gonna take a tab, I'm not)* on the pole. His upper leg ached, and the sole of his foot was still tingling, but otherwise *(I should feel fucking great)* he felt good *(thirteen seconds, goddamn it)*.

Sweat dripped off his eyebrows as he leaned forward. The air in his lungs felt cold and spiky despite the heat. He waited for his heartrate to slow. He was so fucking close—only thirteen seconds *(thirteen fucking seconds)* between Jordan and his goal. Sure, a six-minute mile wouldn't matter much to anyone—he might have a friend or two who'd feign excitement for him—but it mattered to him. When he'd started walking last year, he'd felt like his feet were on fire by the second mile. When he'd first started running *(only eleven months ago, champ, so don't be so hard on yourself)* he was happy to break a ten-minute mile.

But he'd set the six-minute mile as his goal, he'd committed himself to it, and it mattered. He'd started walking when he found about the affair. He was only twenty-five when he married her, and they'd had fifteen years together. No kids *(maybe thanks to the infrequent sex)*, a starter house, a lot of work. The marriage was good, he'd thought, if a little vanilla, though Cath had insisted she was thrilled and satisfied whenever he checked in, so the affair was a seismic surprise.

The morning after she'd come clean *(at least she'd had the decency to tell me herself)*, he'd actually been grateful *(don't do that, don't congratulate her for the bare minimum)* and began to think on the kind of work they'd need to do to move past it—*this could be saved, this could be salvaged, affairs are almost never about sex, they're a symptom of a deeper problem that can be diagnosed and treated and these things happened all the time, even in the best of marriages*—but the next morning he'd woken up, looked at her sleeping next to him, and simply walked out the front door.

He'd made it down the steps to the curb, looked up and down his street as though seeing it for the first time, and started walking east up Hermosillo. And then, well…he just kept on walking.

Because these things *didn't* happen all the time. Because sometimes they *are* just about sex. Because sometimes there is no symptom of an underlying disease, because the patient is already dead and died nine years ago of natural causes. Yep, sometimes the pharmaceutical sales associate looks at her copyright attorney husband and realizes what once had been love is just complacency, and that yoga instructor with the toned body and bigger dick might just represent a light at the end of the tunnel.

These were the thoughts that came to him as he moved his feet, one after the other, as walking began to jumpstart his mind for the first time in what felt like years. He didn't have the comfortable Hokas then *(mental note, order new Hokas)*, or the breezy shirt and shorts, or the weight vest *(maybe no weight vest but you were carrying twenty extra pounds, weren't you, you chubby bastard)*, and his arches burned like coal by the time he rounded Lake Avenue, but he'd kept going, and soon walking had become the cornerstone of his every day.

It felt weird to be a beginner who was over forty, and he felt bit self-conscious and a little pathetic as he watched people half his age blow past him, but he couldn't help it. Walking was a compulsion now. He didn't know where he was going, but he knew he had to go. When Cathy had told him about the details of the affair—that it had been going on for five months, that she had lied about not one, but three "conventions" in Santa Barbara, and that she might be in *love* with the guy (*are you fucking serious Cath*), he'd felt like his mind was being enveloped by thick, thorny vines that twisted, constricted, and choked out all light and rational thought.

But as he walked north on Lake, one mindless foot in front of the other, those tangled vines parted and receded, and he could actually *think*. As he started to think again, he also started to *talk*, rehearing a series of imaginary conversations with Cathy that suddenly brought clarity and purpose back into his life.

These walks became a daily ritual, and the imaginary conversations a form of therapy. He began to weigh the positives (*at least we never had kids*) against the negatives (*holy shit, I need an STD test, like a goddamned college student*). And when it was finally clear to him that the marriage wasn't going to be saved (*of course it isn't, what the fuck was I thinking?*), he spontaneously broke into a run.

Running was different. Running meant he couldn't talk, he was breathing too intensely for that, and suddenly the rush of air in his ears and on his face gave him the sense of falling through the world, falling forward, as if the planet was turning beneath him, out of his control, but if he ran fast enough, he may just take flight.

During the rare moments he'd let himself imagine the two of them together, Cathy's head thrown back in climax (*don't picture it, what the fuck are you doing?*) he'd run even faster, breaking into a frantic sprint as though he could leave that image somewhere on the hot pavement behind him. He ran until his knees were shot, his heels were blistered, and his lungs were burning with erratic, labored breath.

And he felt fucking fantastic.

By the time he filed for the divorce—and it was Jordan who initiated the paperwork, thank you very much—he'd been running every day for two solid months. His Hokas were broken in, his endurance had grown exponentially, and he was completely hooked.

He found his own apartment in the valley, where the neighborhoods were more runnable. He went a different direction each day, exploring the area with a sense of joyful discovery around every corner. He lost his belly quickly, especially as he started incorporating sits-ups and spinning into his post-run routine, and when he'd meet Cathy and her lawyers during the final rounds of negotiation, he could tell she was surprised to see him looking fit (*yeah, fucking eat it, Cath*).

One day, after two hours of legal discussions that seemed downright cordial, he found himself walking her down to the lobby. The talk was small but far from awkward, and she told him three times, "You look good, Jordan." It felt familiar, for a moment. It made him fall into the seductive fiction that maybe there was hope for them.

Maybe he wouldn't be forty-two and out there in the dating pool, with thinning hair and alimony payments and little else to offer. Maybe he wouldn't be navigating dating apps or humiliating himself at singles mixers for middle-aged professionals. No, maybe he and Cathy would figure it out after all.

And then he saw the flicker of panic as the Tesla pulled up to the curb (*that's him, holy shit, that's him*). Cathy held her breath, stammered a quick goodbye, and timidly climbed into the passenger seat of the Tesla. Jordan only saw the guy's face for a moment, and it was in shadow, but it was enough.

He decided that afternoon that he was going for the six-minute mile.

The six-minute mile was nothing to be taken lightly. It corresponded to running one hundred meters in twenty-two seconds, sixteen times in a row. The average person was lucky to break nine minutes running a mile. While three in ten men his age might brag that they hit a four-minute mile on the treadmill once, according to Reddit *(because why would Reddit ever lie)* only one percent of the US population could truly, honestly run a six-minute mile in the real world.

The training routine was intense, to say the least. He cobbled it together by reading articles online, so he couldn't vouch for whether he was doing it entirely right, but his steady improvement suggested he couldn't be doing it entirely wrong. A lot of articles promised results, though they all stopped short of suggesting that the reader could actually do it. "You will get faster following this training program" was about as close to a guarantee as they'd allow, and it was good enough for Jordan.

He read in one article that if a runner could handle a 5K in less than twenty-one minutes, they would be a good candidate to start training for a six-minute mile. Someone else wrote that the ideal candidate should be able to run eight hundred meters in three minutes. If he could build his weekly mileage to at least thirty miles a week, then he should be able to begin the eight-week training plan he'd found online.

Finding a route wasn't easy. He didn't bother to explore a proper track. He wanted to be out in the world, in his new neighborhood. This posed challenges, as his normal jogging routes meant intersections, stop signs, traffic lights, driveways, and all manner of obstacles. He ultimately found a lovely loop around a golf course, three miles from his apartment.

The path encircled the back nine of the course, was nicely shaded, and presented nearly 2.4 miles of uninterrupted jogging path on soft, unpaved soil. There was a single stretch just beyond the thirteenth hole that offered 1.2 miles of basically straight, flat pathway, easily ten feet wide. This was the perfect stretch for the six-minute mile. He'd jog or lightly run as a warmup over the three miles to the golf course, where he'd identified a trailside trash can as his starting marker, and there, under the shade of the evergreen ashes that lined the path, he'd meet his triumph.

He started with an easy fifteen-minute warmup jog through the neighborhood, followed by a light run for five more. He performed dynamic mobility drills and learned a bunch of new terms in the process: heel walks, knee hugs, quad tugs, lunges, butt kicks, hamstring kick-outs. These concepts would have seemed like a foreign language when he first began walking around the neighborhood, jaw hanging open with the shock of Cathy's infidelity, but now that their case was in the hands of the judge, these terms were a comfortable second language.

On the golf course loop, he started running 1000-meter trials. To break the six-minute mark, he'd need to cover a quarter mile in just under ninety seconds. He started with just that goal, ignoring the mile itself, and seeing if he could maintain that speed in quarter-mile bursts.

Breaking the run into intervals helped enormously. He'd run for six minutes, walk for one. Or run for nine minutes, walk for one, three times in a row. By the fourth week, he was running five thirty-second hill sprints at a controlled effort, taking one minute to recover between reps, then five one-minute hill sprints and jog backs. Then it was a set of five 400-meter sprints with one minute recovery, shooting for ninety seconds per lap (*goddammit Cathy, your little hotel trysts might have actually saved my life*), and by the sixth week, he was hitting his time.

He'd tried for the real deal—Race Day—twice but failed to land it both times. 6:37 the first time, 6:33 the second. He dialed it back and repeated the final week of the training program again. He'd tried a few other tricks—dropping his chest and leaning in for the last three hundred meters, dialing in the "rearward whack" (the pump) of his arms with two hundred meters to go. He didn't race to the end or try to sprint it—he'd been doing this long enough to know when you dig, you lose form and slow down.

He started considering the next Race Day, and this time he was determined to win it.

When the judgment arrived unceremoniously in the mail yesterday afternoon, he'd felt something in him change (*that's it, that's fucking it, tomorrow is the day*). He'd been certain the judgment was the tailwind he needed. He'd step out of the house, take to the pavement, and leave Cathy and her stallion and the whole fucking decade-and-a-half of their turbulent, strained, awkward marriage behind him, and he'd run that mile in six goddamned minutes.

At the end of that six minutes, if he made the whole mile, it would feel like he ran to the other side of the Earth.

BUT IT HADN'T worked. And now, holding onto his other foot and stretching his leg while the sweat dripped onto the sidewalk before him, he felt the sting of failure more than he had at any other point during the divorce. Yeah, she'd kept the house. Yeah, she'd scored more alimony than he'd thought she deserved (*she's the one who cheated, for fuck's sake*). Those losses had stung.

But not like this. For the first time in months, he felt the tears rising in his eyes. He hadn't felt like a failure when his wife pushed him aside for another man, he hadn't felt like a failure when she and her lawyers itemized his shortcomings as a husband, he hadn't felt like a failure when the judgment arrived to declare him single. But he felt like a failure now. He'd set the goal, he'd done it right, but he'd come up short. And now, for the first time in over a year, that feeling of failure finally caught him. He'd been running from it harder than he'd ever run from anything in his life, but its legs were just a little longer, and he hadn't run fast enough after all.

Fuck it.

Fuck all of it.

He'd just have to try again, that was all.

He blinked the tears away and started jogging. As he did, he noticed more of those MISSING posters. Lots of pets (*funny how that happens, you notice one and suddenly they're everywhere*).

He'd become accustomed to this cluster effect on his runs. If he noticed, say, a pizza delivery in progress, suddenly he'd see two more before he was home. Or a certain color car that was unusual (*didn't know they made purple Toyotas*) would suddenly be everywhere. He even had this happen with the MISSING posters—once he started to notice them (*a few blocks from here, wasn't it?*), he noticed more. And more.

He'd even seen MISSING posters for people, and by the fourth one he encountered he became actively alarmed. These momentary fixations used to drive Cathy crazy—his "new obsessions," she'd called them—but like most of his paranoias, a brief but manic google search later that night had shown that this was nothing unusual.

However many people had gone missing from his relatively calm suburban valley neighborhood, it didn't seem to be notable. In fact, people had been vanishing at a similar rate for years. That had rattled him, too, and just as he started reading about how many people went missing in National Parks, he wisely changed course and strangled his budding new obsession in the crib.

But here he was again, face to face with the missing pets. They truly, truly bummed him out, imagining all those kids putting out food on the porch and staying up late to peer out their windows with a growing hopelessness. The valley wasn't kind to pets; there were lots of dangers *(cars, trucks, and those big-ass coyotes)*, so he imagined those kids would be at their posts a long time before they finally succumbed to the inevitable truth that, sometimes, the things you love just go away.

(Sometimes they leave you for guys they met at a yoga class, but mostly it's the coyotes.)

Those kids didn't deserve to learn the truth that way. They should have years of innocent play before they realize that pets go missing, and people too, and there's not a damn thing you can do about it. Sometimes they die, sometimes they leave, and on a long enough timeline, we'll all find ourselves alone. Play the tape far enough, and we'll all be forgotten entirely.

Perhaps it was his growing distaste for seeing the fliers—and the creeping feeling that if he saw many more he'd slip right back down into those clinging, twisting vines of loss he'd tried so hard to shake—that led him to change course when he saw the tunnel.

IT WAS ACROSS the park, on the southeast corner. A typical pedestrian tunnel, framed by graffiti, that ran under all eight lanes of the highway. He'd seen it many times before. Every time he ran on the golf course loop, in fact. But he had always opted to run back the way he came, reversing his warmup route to get an extra mile into his daily diet.

Today, though, for the first time since his training began, he considered taking the shortcut home. He'd already lost the battle. Maybe a wounded soldier deserved an easier retreat.

The alternative was to stay the course and finish the entire loop, or turn around, jog another half mile to Pacific and hang a right, but that meant passing an awful lot of telephone poles, and looking back over his shoulder, he could see the bright orange rectangles lining his path. He shook his head (*sorry, Milo, only so much a fella can take in one day*).

The tunnel would spit him out on the other side of the highway, and he could keep heading that way for five or six blocks before peeling left onto Pacific. He'd make it home a few minutes early, and fuck it, he'd earned a few minutes.

He turned toward the tunnel, letting his jog slow. Hell, he could even just walk if he chose to, take a full cool-down. He'd earned it, and he felt a little too demoralized to keep up this pace (*fuck it, I can walk home, tomorrow is another day*). Tomorrow was indeed another day, and he had plenty of opportunity to get back to it—he was going to hit that mile if it killed him—but tonight he could relax.

He dropped the jog entirely and stumbled into a controlled, relieved walk, and committed to the tunnel.

It was built into the sloping hillside beneath the highway, and he could hear the cars beyond the barriers above. Two concrete slopes bracketed the square entrance, each adorned with colorful graffiti. A single metal pole, recently painted a pleasant green, stood at the center of the tunnel mouth for reasons he didn't quite understand (*must be to stop cars from going in*). Inside, it dropped off to relative darkness, though checkered fluorescent bulbs lined the ceiling on either side, and he could see the bright square of light at the other end of the tunnel.

He checked his watch. It was still tracking his run. He'd reset it just before he tried for the mile, so here it was reading 1.2 miles, the time was now at 08:24. His six-minute mark was retreating further and further into his past, and he was glad. Perhaps his humiliation would be the next thing to go.

He glanced up. The mouth of the tunnel was closer now, and there was a shape at the other end, silhouetted against the daylight beyond. It reminded him a little of James Bond, that figure at the end of the tunnel (*mished the mile, mish Moneypenny*), and he watched as that silhouette—a short woman carrying a large purse—stepped out of the darkness and into the light.

For some primitive, instinctual reason, as he watched her emerge, he felt the tiniest sliver of relief (*she made it in one piece; I should be fine*). He didn't know what made him think that—he'd run through dozens of pedestrian tunnels just like this one—but he thought it nonetheless.

He looked up at the mouth of the tunnel (*why do I keep thinking "mouth"?*) as he stepped inside, watching the concrete ceiling as it overtook the blue sky above.

THE FIRST THING he noticed was the drop in temperature. It was cooler in the tunnel, no surprise there, but when the air hit the sweat on his skin, he sighed with a soft relief. The quality of sound changed as well (*like listening to a seashell*), and he realized that steady rumble was born of the highway traffic soaring above his head. It was a relief to his eyes as well. The brightness of the afternoon was replaced with a pleasant dimness, and his pupils, which had contracted almost to pinpoints as he ran, began to dilate.

His eyes were aided by the fluorescent bulbs that lined the top of the tunnel on both sides, staggered every ten feet or so, humming behind yellowed casings. Spiderwebs decorated the lights, and as he passed, he could see the insects bobbing lazily in the tunnel breeze. There was a relief as he blinked back to ocular comfort in the dim light. Unfortunately, his sense of smell wasn't so lucky—there was a tinge of stale urine mixed with every inhalation now, and he quickly spat on the sidewalk (*if you smell something for five seconds, you're actually tasting it*).

He became aware of the sound of his footsteps, thick with echo, bouncing all around him off the concrete walls. He glanced at the graffiti, which was as thick and layered like jungle brush, and admired some of the artistry—that is, until the crude outline of an ejaculating penis overtook the scenery on his left. He thought for a moment about Cathy's new stud *(fuck, is this really all it takes to trigger it?)* and jogged a few paces to shake it off.

Ahead of him, the square exit of the tunnel burst with bright daylight beyond. He could see the vertical pole at the entrance *(definitely to stop the cars)*. The tunnel was deceptively long—there was no sense of that pole, or that bright square, actually getting closer—but he was grateful for the reprieve.

He exhaled loudly, enjoying the booming reverberation of his voice. He glanced back over his shoulder—no one else was in the tunnel, so fuck it—and went ahead and loudly vocalized his next sigh. The sound echoed beautifully.

"Fuck off, Cath!" *(cath-cath-cath-cath)* he boomed, and he enjoyed the heavy reverb that clung to those words. He glanced around, again making sure no one else had entered the tunnel, and then said it again even louder. "Fuck off, Cath!" *(FuckoffCath-offcath-offcath-cath-cath-cath…)*

He stepped over a single abandoned sneaker on the ground. "That sucks," *(sucks-sucks-sucks-sucks…)* he said, imagining someone running through this pee-soaked tunnel in one shoe, their sock sliding on the *(dirty, sticky)* floor. He let himself puzzle on it for a moment. What happened there? If a shoe popped off, why wouldn't they stop and pick it up? Who would take this tunnel in one shoe? That sock will need a tetanus shot when they get home.

He looked up at the bright square ahead. Again, a bit surprisingly, it didn't seem to be any closer, and for the first time, that felt weird. He must be halfway through the tunnel by now. He turned and looked back, and sure enough, the entrance behind him felt equidistant. He was indeed in the middle, both ends felt the same. But what an odd illusion that the exit felt no closer. "Wild" *(wild-wild-wild-wild-wild)*.

He looked back at the walls. The taggers must have gotten bored going this far in, as the graffiti was sparse here compared to the entrance *(weird, I'd aim for the middle myself, less of a chance to get caught)*. He passed another sneaker, and then what looked like a balled-up shirt… And more. Wait…

He slowed. There were other things on the ground, as well. Various little nicknacks, things people must have dropped: a battery, an old plastic wristwatch, buttons. And was that…? Yes, that was a necklace.

He stopped walking and crouched down to take a better look. The chain was gold and half-submerged in a puddle of sludge. He was tempted to pick it up, but that sludge had a smell like a porta potty, and he opted out.

He looked up, surprised to see a nice wristwatch a few feet ahead. And just a few inches from the watch *(is that?)* was a pile *(yep, it is)* of feces. He grimaced and started walking again. Yep, it was time to get out of this place. He became aware that the ground was actually crowded with various things: dark shapes, objects, glints of light. Jesus, when was the last time the city bothered to clean this place?

He glanced down at the watch as he neared it. The sapphire face was cracked, but the watch was *(no way… Yeah, it was. It was a Rolex (gotta be fake; nobody's leaving a Rolex in the Shit Tunnel)*. Yeah, must be a fake. People were always hawking fakes in the park—bags, jewelry, watches. Perhaps someone had some buyer's remorse. And here he was, alone in this tunnel. If he wanted to, and didn't mind a little shit on his fingers, he could load his pockets, clean them off, and head to the pawn shop. He wasn't going to do that, but the fact that he could felt odd.

He looked up from the loot on the grimy floor and stopped cold.

He wasn't alone in this tunnel at all.

There was a woman laying against the wall to his right, slumped over in the filth.

HIS HEART WAS beating faster. He was legitimately startled to see her. Had she been here the whole time? How hadn't he seen her until now? The smell of urine was much stronger now, and he assumed she was the reason why. She looked to be asleep, but even tucked against the wall, she stood out dramatically against the flat landscape. Surely, he would have seen her.

He crossed slightly to the left side of the tunnel, not wanting to crowd her, and because, frankly, he was more than a little repulsed by her smell *(five seconds and you're actually tasting it)*. Her brown hair was a long, tangled mess, clumped together by long-dried fluids he didn't even want to guess at. Her skin was pale—at least what he could see beneath the unchecked layers of grime and *(sores, those are sores)* what appeared to be sores, boils, and other wounds. Her breathing was ragged. And as he neared her, he realized just how damn skinny she was. She was practically bones.

There were more little piles of shit around her—mounds of thin, dried feces, and puddles of old, loose stool. There were also *(no fucking way)* what looked to be…bones. Small bones. Some of them were sticking out of the shit, some were scattered on the ground *(you're telling me she's been eating buffalo wings in here?)*.

He stepped softer, hoping his footsteps wouldn't wake her, but as he came up on her *(Jesus, the stench)*, he was relieved to see she was sleeping soundly. He couldn't quite guess her age *(maybe fifty?)*, but he could tell she'd been living on the street for a very, very long time.

To his enormous relief, she didn't even stir as he passed. He could hear her ragged breathing, so he didn't need to worry if she were alive, and that was fine. He'd leave her to it and go on about his business. He stepped past her and picked up his pace *(how long is this fucking tunnel anyway?)*, more and more apprehensive that the exit still didn't feel any closer.

About ten paces past her, his conscience flared up. He slowed and finally stopped. Looked both ways. He sighed, irritated with himself *(come on, just go)*, but knew he wasn't going to. She just looked so skinny *(concentration-camp skinny)*. He didn't bring a wallet when he ran, but he did keep the odd bill in the pocket of his running shorts in case he wanted to stop for something cold on the way home. He checked his pocket, was a little disappointed to feel the bill in there *(well, fuck)*, and knew he should leave it for her *(let her get a bite to eat, at least)*.

He clutched the ten-dollar bill in his hand and turned back. She was stirring slightly, making a weird rattling sound that wasn't quite a snore *(please don't wake up, please don't wake up)*. He stepped softly, avoiding something on the ground *(is that a pocket watch?)* as he neared her. He'd just leave the bill a few inches from her outstretched hand, no need to touch her. She'd wake up and see it, no problem.

By the time his mind caught up with him, it was already too late. He was bending to put the bill down on the ground when the thought hit him with a palpable alarm, a thought that suddenly seemed so obvious. He immediately felt like an idiot for only just thinking it now.

Why hasn't she pawned the watches?

He froze, hand hovering over the grimy ground, eyes darting over the objects strewn around the woman: watches, rings, keys, and *(is that a fucking wallet?)* a man's billfold, thick with contents. No, something was wrong here. If she'd wanted ten dollars, she could have grabbed a lot more just from where she lay. No, something was definitely wrong.

He was about to retreat when he realized she was staring directly into his eyes. His heart skipped a beat. The moment hung, suspended in time until—

She shrieked, piercing the silence *(silence; when did it get so quiet?)* and shoved herself up.

"Hey," she croaked *(hey-hey-hey-hey)* as he stumbled back a step.

"I'm sorry," *(sorry-sorry-sorry-sorry)* he mustered, fumbling with the money, resisting the urge to just throw it at her. He found himself fascinated by her eyes. They were haunted eyes, desperate eyes, but beautiful, thoughtful. She blinked at him in the fluorescent lights *(they're flickering a lot more; are they flickering more?)*, and he was surprised to realize she was younger than he'd first thought, maybe even in her thirties, just buried under so much grime and filth and *(she's terrified)* whatever else.

The moment hung, and if he'd been paying attention, he might have realized he didn't hear anything at all that he'd heard when he first entered the tunnel—no traffic, no distant birds, no wind. Just a steady, low, almost pulsing rumble *(like breathing)*…

"You see me?" *(seemeseemeseemeseemee)* she asked in a frantic whisper. Of course he could see her. It was dark, but not that dark *(why is it so dark? it's sunny outside)* in the fluorescent lights, flickering though they were.

"Yeah," *(yeah-yeah-yeah-yeah)* he managed.

She looked wildly around, pulling herself up onto her knees. He heard them pop in protest and noticed the cuts on her skinny little calves.

He held the money out in front of him like a shield, as if it might protect him from her growing attention. "Here, I was just leaving this for you." He leaned forward, planning to release the bill so that it fell at her feet, but she quickly slapped it out of his hand.

"No," she whispered, with such urgency it almost sounded like a hiss. The bill hit the ground by her feet. She stared at it with what he realized was abject horror, frozen in place.

Somewhere behind him, there was a series of subtle clicking noises. He barely noticed, but she heard them. Oh yes, she heard them well.

She quickly picked up the bill and smashed it back into his hand. "No trade, you dropped this. No trade. Say it."

"I'm sorry," he managed.

"Say it: Not a trade." She stared into his eyes with wide-eyed desperation. Her voice was small, trembling, and in that moment, she sounded like a child. Yes, that was it, she sounded like a little kid huddled under her blanket, talking soft in the dark so the monster in the closet wouldn't hear her, her little voice short and abrupt and so fast you might miss—

There was no echo.

It hadn't occurred to him until just now, but there was no echo to her voice. Just moments ago, every sound in the tunnel was amplified by that thick, almost liquid echo, but now it was gone. Was she simply being too quiet? He tried to find his own voice, raising it just a little to test his strange observation.

"Not a trade," he said in a normal volume. There was no echo at all.

"Too late," she whispered and looked into his eyes with a horrified regret. Then she said one more word in such a whisper he almost missed it. It was a word he'd heard in his own head for the past year, a word he whispered to himself every morning as he woke, and every day as he stepped off the curb. It always made him feel excited, confident, and proud. Now, it sent a chill up his spine.

The word she had whispered was "run."

But he was still stuck on the problem of the sound. Where had it gone? The echo was gone, and so was the rest. The sounds of the traffic above, the sounds of the insects, the birds, the breeze—all gone. All that was left was that low rumble, which seemed to be steadily growing in volume and intensity, and something else… Some other noise.

Those clicks again. What the hell were those? They came in short bursts, rising in cadence and pitch, almost like short little questions. There was another sound with them, a shuffling. No, that wasn't right. It was more of a *scuttling*, like fingernails tapping on a mirror. He thought of a crab on a countertop, and immediately disliked the association.

"What is that?" he asked his reeking new friend, but he wouldn't hear her answer. By the time she repeated her suggestion to run, he was looking back the way he came, and he had seen something that short-circuited his mind.

There was no entrance to the tunnel. It was gone. The parallel lines of fluorescent lights above converged upon each other in the distance until they appeared to be a single line of dim, flickering light, vanishing into nothing. The tunnel went on forever, it appeared, and there was no light.

He turned the other way. It was the same in that direction as well. No light. No exit. Just more gray walls (*no graffiti at all, not anymore, not anywhere*) and—

(*There are more.*)

She wasn't the only person here. There were other people scattered throughout the tunnel, like in that homeless camp he'd spotted by Griffith a few weeks back. Some were sprawled out on the filthy ground, some propped up against the wall, some of them (*they're dead*) didn't look right (*they're fucking dead*), and some of them (*oh Jesus*) seemed to be in—

Pieces. Some of them were in pieces. He could see a torso propped against the dirty wall. And legs… But those legs were a foot away from the torso, separated by a dark, dried puddle.

The woman beside him was getting to her feet now, and he felt her claw-like fingers on his breezy running shirt, trying to push him. Trying to get him moving.

"Run," she said again, this time with more authority, and he took a mindless step in the direction she was pushing. Was this the way he came? Was this the way out?

Was there even a difference?

She pushed on him with more urgency. "It's awake," she whispered. "Run!"

Those clicking noises were louder now.

The scuttling noises, too.

And there was just the faintest sense, out of his periphery, of movement—movement *in* the walls (*that isn't possible*), like the walls were made not of gray concrete, but of something softer, more malleable.

She shoved him, and he nearly tripped. Then his muscles started to walk automatically, and then jog, a product of their training over the past year. His feet fell on some of the objects on the ground (*those are bones, those are animal bones*), and as he passed another sickly thin man, he realized something else (*they're eating them, these people are eating them*).

The filthy, sickly man in the tattered clothes and bare feet was clutching a dog (*there you are, Milo*). The animal's collar was on the ground at the man's side, and he had been working on it.

There was blood and yellow fur on his face and on the tatters of his shirt. As Jordan picked up his pace, he realized there were other carcasses around him, other collars, mixed among the trinkets and jewelry and sneakers and—

(that's a baby) other bones, smaller bones—

(that's too small, that's a fetus, just bones).

The woman shoved him again, and he finally found his stride. But the moment he began to run, the place erupted with movement. The other people in the tunnel who were alive *(and it was only about a third of them, the rest were just bones)* began to scream and push themselves up against the walls, trying to get away from *(what?)* something, something that was *(making those noises)* coming closer, scuttling along the walls and floors like a *(crab spider)* thing he couldn't quite wrap his mind around.

He ran faster, and he felt the woman's hand close around the tail of his shirt, holding on. The fabric stretched out behind him, and he realized he was pulling her along now, too. She was holding his shirt like a child on a field trip, and running in his slipstream so he could take her with him, wherever he was going.

He could hear more of them now, the screams and whimpers of the people, but also the clicking—*that clicking.* It had seemed so small, so innocuous, but it was so loud now, and it felt *heavy*, like the thing that made it had *weight*, and that weight was scurrying across the floors and walls *(inside the walls, it's inside the goddamned walls, too)* and getting closer.

Closer.

Something in him activated. His body felt the starter pistol, and he dug in for the sprint of his life.

He felt the back of his shirt stretch behind him, but the woman kept up. Somehow, she kept pace. As skinny as she was *(she's a runner, too, and I bet she's been training)*, whatever muscle she had left on those toothpick legs were going for it.

Ahead of them, the tunnel seemed to vibrate with movement, the walls shifting, morphing, the lights flickering and then *(impossibly)* seeming to drip down the walls.

He looked over his shoulder, and for a moment, he saw the thing behind him. He was running hard, his head bouncing with each step, so his vision wasn't stable, and the thing was moving fast, but he sensed its great size (*like a car*), sensed its spindly limbs (*spider-crab-urchin-roach*) and had a fleeting impression of its skin (*silverfish*) before he felt the floor shifting.

The tunnel was rotating—impossible, sure, but it was happening—right before his eyes. Ahead of him, objects (*and people and corpses*) were starting to slide across the floor to the right, and he found himself leaning as if the tunnel was on a gimble and was turning clockwise. As watches, rings, and other trinkets slid across the floor in front of him, he pushed off with his left leg, stumbling as his right foot caught the wall just as it rolled beneath him. He nearly lost his balance but managed to stay upright, and now he was running on the wall and those flickering fluorescent lights that used to be above him were now on the ground to his right. His mind was flooded with an acidic panic he'd never felt before in his life.

The woman clutching his shirt was running beside him now, and he could see it in her face: the determination, teeth bared, filthy hair flying behind her. She threw a look over her shoulder and made a small shrieking sound, doubling her efforts, and he did the same as he felt the tunnel rolling once again. He watched the celling rolling toward him, preparing to make the leap to it as it rolled beneath him, and hoping not to miss a step or twist his ankle.

He leapt again, finding his new center of gravity as he briefly straddled the corner of the tunnel, the fluorescent lights that used to be above him now whizzing by between his legs as the tunnel seemed to perch on its corner. He jumped to avoid the emaciated corpses that fell into his path.

He had never run faster in his life.

"Go!" the woman yelled, and he looked at her again. Her eyes were alive with fire and determination, and he again found himself astonished at her speed. However long she'd been here, she'd been saving something up, and she was spending it all now.

He briefly remembered that old joke about two friends outrunning a bear (*I don't need to outrun the bear, I just need to outrun you*) and he almost laughed, but then he felt something long and sharp brush against his shirt, and it banished all rational thought.

No thought, no mind. There was only him, the ground, and the run. He even forgot the woman beside him. He jumped the hurdles automatically, no longer disturbed at their humanity. If he felt the shape of the thing behind him encroaching on his peripheral vision (*and it did, several times*) he simply pushed harder. And after a short while, he began to realize the thing was touching him.

Every few paces, he felt it close its appendages, whatever they were, around his shirt, or his shorts, or once on his bare leg, seeking purchase just as he slipped from its grasp. But it was close.

He suddenly remembered the woman and turned his head to look at her. She looked to him as well. She was covered with sweat, face no longer pale, now positively crimson with effort and blood. And her eyes were full of regret. Looking into those eyes, he knew that it was over, that she knew the thing behind them had gotten too close, that it was a matter of moments. Her eyes were full with pity, fear, and regret.

She reached out toward him (*she's going to push me*).

Her hand bouncing with the efforts of her run (*don't have to outrun the bear*).

And he felt her hand on his shoulder (*just have to outrun you*).

And she pushed him. Hard.

Right into the wall.

Right INTO the wall.

He passed through it like a membrane, spinning in time to see the spindly shape as it collapsed upon her, her brown hair blooming against its insane fingers (*too many fingers*) before Jordan hit the ground (*a new ground*) and rolled over.

He skidded across the floor of the tunnel, slamming into the adjacent wall, looking up just in time to see the wall he'd just passed through closing behind him.

(She pushed me out of the way.)

The wall rippled like pond water, and then solidified once more. And he realized he could hear traffic once again. And birds.

He looked ahead. There was daylight.

He pushed himself up, not noticing the blood running down his leg, and began to run again.

The clicking sounds erupted around him, and he saw the walls rippling. There was a loud shrieking sound, and somewhere very far away, he thought he heard a woman scream, but soon the wind was in his ears as he found his speed.

The walls around him shimmered, and he thought of an alligator bolting through still water, bursting forward with speed you'd never expect, disrupting everything around it as it charged, and so he charged too.

He charged for his life.

He heard those clicks, right in his ear, louder than the rushing wind, and he felt something on his shoulder, a poke, a flame, and soon the light was on his face—

Sunlight on his face—

He was so close, only a few more paces—

He pushed and pushed, and his legs caught fire, and he jumped—

JORDAN SLAMMED HIS hip against the large metal pole at the mouth of the tunnel, ricocheted into the concrete embankment, and spun twice in the air before landing on his side. His shoulder and hip both made a loud cracking sound, and he slid four feet across the pavement before slamming into the garbage can.

He clawed at the ground, shredding his fingertips on the pavement but not caring, kicking wildly with both feet as he scrambled away from the mouth of the tunnel, looking over his shoulder like a terrified animal. He gasped in the cool afternoon air, staring at the portal through which he'd so violently erupted.

There was nothing there but a pedestrian tunnel.

There were silhouettes within running toward him, which momentarily induced a fresh panic, but they were just people who had been walking through the tunnel, people who now had to react to this screaming, bleeding man on the ground.

Jordan passed out.

HE SAT ON the gurney of the ambulance as they dressed his wounds. Only some of them were apparent, others would manifest in the following days. He'd scraped the skin off both of his legs, his hip, his arm, his hands, and his shoulder. The shin splints and stress fractures would be with him for weeks, as would the Iliotibial Band Syndrome, which devastated his knees. His muscles screamed for months, and it took a fair amount of physical therapy before he was ever able to run again. He had a huge bump on his head, and a concussion, and he'd lost a shoe somewhere in there. And then there was the matter of where he was…

The pedestrian tunnel he'd burst out from, screaming and bleeding and hysterical, was in Ojai. He came out of a tunnel seventy-five miles away from the one he entered, and he had no explanation for this.

His Apple watch recorded his "workout." It was riddled with notifications and alarms about his heartrate, a series of "unknown errors," and a warning about unhealthy decibel levels of sound. The distance it recorded was even more confusing, as it logged more than one hundred miles in the five minutes he'd spent in the tunnel. His heartrate apparently topped two hundred beats per minute, not at all healthy for someone his age, but he'd survived it.

The ambulance took him to a hospital, his injuries were treated, and he took an Uber home. Along the way, they passed several tunnels. He held his breath each time.

The driver left the highway in Thousand Oaks to avoid some traffic, and the car pulled up to a stop sign near the offramp. A pedestrian tunnel run underneath the highway above, and Jordan tried not to look at it.

When he finally did, just as the car was pulling away, he was certain he saw her standing there, just beyond the light, staring out at him as they drove. Given the trauma of the day, it was absolutely possible he'd just imagined it, but in that quiet little corner of his mind, where he kept his most uncomfortable truths, he knew it was her.

She had pushed him out of the way at the last moment. She could have tripped him, he would have fallen, that thing behind them would have pounced, and she probably could have gotten away. But she hadn't tripped him; she had saved him.

He hoped it had been her standing in that tunnel in Thousand Oaks. At least that would mean she was still alive. That was something, anyway.

WHEN HE GOT home, he bathed, slept, and packed.

A quick Google search revealed her identity. Her name was Callie Russel, and she'd gone missing just a day after her pregnant sister *(the bones, those tiny bones)* back in 2010. She'd been in her late twenties when she vanished, wanted for questioning in her sister's case, and that was the extent of the news coverage from the time. Just a small blurb in the local gazette. He couldn't find any other updates but knew now that neither woman had ever been found.

THE NEXT MORNING, he opened his front door to the gloomy, gray weather outside. He wasn't planning on running. In fact, he could barely walk without screaming pain at this point. But he had been plagued by nightmares of elastic walls and flickering lights and suffocating smells and the clicking sound of some unnamable thing as it scuttled through the ceiling toward him, and he simply needed some air.

He didn't step out of the apartment, though. His breath caught in his chest, and he froze in place, staring at the small pile of dirty old jewelry that had been left in front of his door. There were a few watches, some gold and silver chains, and a pair of reading glasses. He stared at them for what felt like an eternity, and then retreated inside.

HE MOVED OUT the next day, heading east to Arizona. He found a small apartment in Tucson and was happy enough, taking on a few cases, doing his physical therapy, and laying low until the trinkets found their way to his new doorstep. There was, after all, a small foot-tunnel only two blocks away, and apparently something inside was still interested in a trade.

Three more moves, and each ended the same. New neighborhood, new apartment, a few weeks of relative quiet, and then a small pile of lost items on his doorstep. Once, at his new place in Colorado, the trinkets were left at the foot of his bed. There was a compass in this pile, and he thought about all those disappearances in the National Parks.

He tried Montana, thinking the open plains would be safer. He lived far from other people, far from any tunnels, but it didn't matter. There were *caves*, after all. If wilderness could save you, then why did so many people vanish in the parks? This world was like old concrete. It was full of cracks, and the things that lived underneath—the things that scurried and crawled and avoided the daylight—might pull someone in if they were unlucky enough to step on a crack at just the wrong moment.

Eventually, things settled. His muscles healed, and he found himself running once more, but he never tried for the six-minute mile again. He was sure he'd never beat the speed he'd achieved in that tunnel, which felt like he'd achieved his goal in some awful way.

The nightmares didn't stop, though, and he thought of that poor woman often, of her wild hair and scared eyes and the determination he'd seen on her face. Of the pity she'd taken on him just before she pushed him out of the way. Why had she done that?

Why had a stranger shown him more love in one single second than his wife did over fifteen years?

He didn't know and never would. He just knew that he'd run far and fast that year. He'd made some kind of wrong turn, and in that final, mad dash toward the light, avoided a fate that had befallen too many. Why *him* that day, and not that other woman before him, who crossed through the tunnel unscathed? Why all of *them* on the ground? What was the difference?

Timing and dumb luck, he figured. That was all.

He could go back and try to find Callie Russel again. Try to help her. Some nights he sits up, making plans to do just that. But he knows he won't. He knows if he ever steps foot into one of those places again, one of those places where the walls are thin, the clicking thing that collected those people will claim its prize. He knows this with certainty.

Some nights, he wakes up soaked in sweat because he's running in his dreams, feeling the fingers of the thing behind him as they graze the back of his shirt. Most nights, he still gets away. Some nights he doesn't.

He holds his breath in the morning when he opens his door, looking down at the doormat, dreading the glint of gold or the sparkle of jewelry. Then he looks out to the flat, featureless fields that surround his little prairie shack.

He thinks of how he started by walking away from Cathy, took a jog through hell, and then ran for his life past horrors he would never understand.

He wonders if he's stopped running.

He knows that he hasn't and likely never will.

He thinks on the ways people can vanish—from our lives and from the world—and he shivers. These thoughts are too dark, and there is only one way to exorcise them. For Jordan, there is only one way to leave them behind.

He whispers a prayer of thanks to Callie Russel, leans forward into the wind, tastes a gratitude some will never know, and lets his feet carry him away.

ABOUT THE AUTHORS

Andrew Adams is an LA-based writer/director, originally hailing from Ellicott City, MD. He studied film at Florida State University and spent years working as a travel videographer before writing and directing his debut feature during the COVID quarantines. That film was a dark comedy called *American Meltdown,* which premiered at Chattanooga Film Festival in 2023 and won Best Feature. The film was embraced by genre festivals, winning Best Screenplay at FilmQuest 2023 and Best Feature at Haunted Garage Horror Festival, and is currently available on streaming services. His other horror fiction can be found in the *Horror From The High Dive* book series, and his indie comic book *Schismatic* is available online for clever Googlers. He is actively developing more horror and thriller projects.

Jesse Aultman is an award-winning producer, director, and screenwriter. A recent graduate of USC's Film & TV Production MFA program, he co-wrote and produced *Neither Donkey Nor Horse,* which won a 2024 Student Academy Award and premiered at the 51st Telluride Film Festival. Originally from Alabama, Jesse fell in love with the horror genre through urban legends and campfire stories—tales that instilled in him a deep fascination with the mystical, the unknowable, and the supernatural. He wrote and directed *The Spirit Became Flesh,* which was selected as an advanced project at USC and awarded both the Fox Fellowship Scholarship and the Irving Lerner Endowment Finishing Fund. The film screened at Screamfest, Dances With Film, and many others before being acquired by ALTER, where it has since amassed over 90,000 views.

Emily Bennett (writer, director, actress) is an Academy recognized screenwriter and award-winning director. She received a *FANGORIA* Chainsaw Award in 2023 for her debut feature film *Alone With You*. The film was produced by Theo James and Andrew Corkin's Untapped Productions (*Martha Marcy May Marlene, We Are What We Are*). Her second feature is currently in post and was produced by Alexander Schepsman (*Martha Marcy May Marlene, Bluebird*). Her films *Alone With You, Accidental Stars, LVRS,* and *Bed* have screened at festivals such as Sitges, Fantastic Fest, Brooklyn Horror, BIFAN, and Fantasia. As an actress, Bennett recently co-starred in Chris Stuckmann's NEON-acquired debut feature film *Shelby Oaks,* which was produced by horror legend Mike Flanagan.

Justin Brooks is an award winning filmmaker and cinematographer known for his boundary-pushing indie horror and documentary work. His first film (alone with co-director/ co-writer Emily Bennett) *Alone with You,* received a *FANGORIA* Chainsaw Award in 2023. The film was produced by Theo James and Andrew Corkin. His second feature *Blood Shine* hits festivals in late 2025. Beyond his film work, Justin has produced and shot many series for The History Channel, A&E, Vice, and Vox media, to name a few. Justin's most recent series *Destinations of The Damned* with Zack Bagans hit number two on the most-streamed list on HBO MAX, and his recent doc series *Hunting Bundy: Chase for the Devil* will be available on streaming later this year.

David Bruckner is an American writer and director of horror films. Initially known for co-directing *The Signal* (2007) and for contributing segments to anthologies such as *V/H/S* (2012) and *Southbound* (2015), Bruckner has since gone on to direct the feature films *The Ritual* (2017), *The Night House* (2020), and *Hellraiser* (2022).

C. Robert Cargill is a co-founder of Crooked Highway. He is the Clarke Award-shortlisted author of *Sea of Rust,* and the books *Day Zero, Dreams and Shadows,* and *We Are Where the Nightmares Go.* He is the co-writer of films *Sinister, Marvel's Doctor Strange,* and *The Black Phone.*

Babou Ceesay is a renowned actor, producer, writer and director with over twenty years of experience in the industry. Career highlights include a BAFTA nomination for Best Actor and appearing in several high-profile projects, including a starring role in the much-anticipated FX, Hulu and Disney+ series *Alien: Earth*. "Jinneh" is Babou's first published piece.

Alex Chew is a small town Kentucky nerd who fell in love with cinema watching Hitchcock and Wilder on Turner Classic Movies. After teaching film history and theory for over a decade, she started making fun and provocative thrillers centered around lovable antiheroes who keep us on our toes. As a festival director (Black Auteur Film Festival), culture writer (*Austin Free Press* and *Ms. Magazine*), and co-founder of a writers-first production company (Sequence 8)—it's safe to say Alex is a workaholic with no intentions of recovering. Currently, she is adapting the supernatural Southern Gothic novel *Delta* for the big screen and is in development for several genre features about badass Black women from the Bluegrass.

Peter Cilella is a Los Angeles-based writer, director, and actor with two decades of experience both in front of and behind the camera. Peter made his directorial debut with *Occupant*, a short film produced by Rustic Films and financed by Gunpowder & Sky. The film premiered at Fantastic Fest in 2018 and is currently streaming on the DUST channel on YouTube. His feature directorial debut, *Descendent*—which he also wrote—premiered at SXSW in 2025 and will be released in theaters August 8, 2025. As a screenwriter, Peter has collaborated with acclaimed directors such as Roland Emmerich (*Independence Day, The Patriot*) and Raman Hui (*Shrek the Third, Monster Hunt*). In May 2023, Peter launched *ONE MORE STORY!*, a podcast featuring improvised bedtime stories for kids and exhausted parents.

Harmony Colangelo is a transgender media analyst and writer from Los Angeles by way of Cleveland, Ohio. She co-wrote the book

Sleepaway Camp from DieDieBooks with her wife, BJ, and the two co-host the popular podcast *This Ends at Prom*, analyzing movies marketed to teen girl audiences from the cis and transgender lens. Harmony has been published in countless publications discussing horror cinema including *FANGORIA*, and frequently contributes visual essays and commentary tracks for physical media special features releases. She's also an award-winning bartender and author of the cocktail book *A Year of Queer Cocktails* and was featured in the Shudder docuseries *Queer for Fear*.

Peter Collins Campbell began his career directing music videos in Chicago, IL. He directed his first feature film *DimLand* in 2021. His short-film work, including *Variations on a Theme* and *Radiation*, have been in over thirty film festivals, as well as on Vimeo Staff Picks, Short of the Week, and Director's Notes. He lives in Queens, New York, and is currently working on his second feature film, *Grind*.

Mali Elfman is an award-winning writer, director and producer. She's produced many films, including Karen Gillan's *The Party's Just Beginning*, Mike Flanagan's *Before I Wake*, and Laura Moss's *Birth/Rebirth*. She was selected for Tribeca and Chanel's "Through Her Lens" Grant, Cannes Film Festival's "Breaking Through the Lens" Program, and Variety's "2023 Producers to Watch" list. *Next Exit*, her debut feature film as a writer and director, premiered at Tribeca and was distributed theatrically by Magnolia Pictures.

Avalon Fast is a writer and director from Vancouver Island, BC. In 2019 they shot their first no-budget genre film, *Honeycomb*. *Honeycomb* went on to be a part of the 2022 official Slamdance festival selection and from there continued a festival tour including Boston Underground, Calgary Underground, Etheria LA and many more. Avalon began writing their second feature *Camp* in 2022 which was financed in December 2023, and shot in June of 2024. *Camp* is now in post production and Avalon has begun the process of creating a new story to develop into a screenplay. Avalon refers to their genre of writing and filmmaking as *Girl*

Horror, as their stories focus on the eerie horrors of growing up, specifically with female influence.

Jori & Michael Felker are married writing partners who bonded over their shared obsession with horror, sci-fi, and everything weird in between. With over a decade in the support staff trenches, Jori's eclectic journey spans Disney comedies (*Gabby Duran, Sulphur Springs*) to erotic thrillers (*The Idol*). Her frozen-time spec *Between the Raindrops* sold in 2020, marking Jori as a writer to watch. Recently, she worked on the alt-history space drama *Star City,* airing 2026 on Apple. Jori is a recipient of the Renaissance Scholarship, recognized for her exemplary work across science and film. Currently, she's penning the feature adaption of the game *The Unfinished Swan* for PlayStation and working on Colin Farrell's *Sugar* for Apple. Michael is a writer, director, producer, and editor from Huntsville, Alabama. Michael is known for writing and directing the feature film *Things Will Be Different* and short films *Would You Like to Try Again* and *Save and Continue.* He's also known for editing feature films (*The Endless, Synchronic, Spring, Sunset on the River Styx, Get the Girl, Something in the Dirt*), television shows (*The Coop, Junk Drawer Magical Adventures*), and even video games (*The Last Stop, Maquette, Twelve Minutes*). He's a proud graduate of Florida State University.

Mike Flanagan is an American filmmaker best known for his horror work. Flanagan wrote, directed, produced, and edited the horror films *Absentia* (2011), *Oculus* (2013), *Hush, Before I Wake, Ouija: Origin of Evil* (2016), *Gerald's Game* (2017), and *Doctor Sleep* (2019). He created, wrote, produced, and served as showrunner on the Netflix horror series *The Haunting of Hill House* (2018), *The Haunting of Bly Manor* (2020), *Midnight Mass* (2021), *The Midnight Club* (2022), and *The Fall of the House of Usher* (2023), also directing and editing some if not all episodes of each.

Addison Heimann is a queer genre filmmaker currently residing in Los Angeles. His first feature *Hypochondriac* premiered at the

2022 SXSW Film Festival and was distributed by XYZ Films. His second feature *Touch Me* premiered in the Midnight section at the Sundance Film Festival. His goal is to tell queer stories that explore mental health in the genre space.

Maggie Levin is a genre writer & filmmaker with rock 'n' roll roots. Recently, she wrote and directed her debut feature *My Valentine* (Hulu/Blumhouse) and an original segment for *V/H/S/99* (Shudder) which premiered at TIFF in 2022. She also served as second unit director & credit designer for Universal's *The Black Phone* and its upcoming sequel, *Black Phone 2*. Awards include Best Director at Austin Indie Fest for her work on the short film *Heel*.

Wolfe MacReady (she/they) is a writer/director hauntin' the hills and hollers of Tennessee with their right-hand dog, Ripley. Wolfe is in post-production on their first feature, *Giving Up The Ghost*, which was shot in 2024, and also has their hands in a whole mess of tabletop game chicanery.

Jackson Murray is a dad, husband, and screenwriter. He grew up in the driftless rural sprawl a few miles outside Wilton, WI (pop. 533) and currently calls Milwaukee home. Two bugs—a small hornet when he was four or five and a common larder beetle decades later—crawled into each of his ears and have been fighting for control of what's between ever since. Jackson is available for podcasts, children's birthday parties, cruise ship séances, and corporate coups. He's humbled and grateful to have his writing included among works from such talented, beautiful storytellers. For Teresa and Oz.

Ben Powell & Gustavo Cooper have been creative collaborators since 2015, crafting stories that span major studios and indie productions. Together, they have successfully sold and set up over a dozen projects now at various stages of development. In 2017, Powell and Cooper partnered with XYZ Films on *Wild in the*

Street, a skateboarding thriller that brought a fresh, kinetic energy to the genre. The following year, they teamed up with Paramount Studios to develop *SHH,* a high-concept horror thriller set in a high school. Currently, the duo is collaborating with Jordan Peele's Monkeypaw Productions on *Rabbits in the Dark,* an atmospheric paranormal thriller that promises to leave audiences on the edge of their seats.

John Rosman is a writer and director based in Los Angeles. His debut film *New Life* was released on Hulu in 2025. In the past, he was named one of *Filmmaker's* 25 New Faces of Independent Film, landed Sugar Bob (a domesticated deer living on a cannabis farm) a segment on *The Daily Show,* and worked at Franks A Lot, a hot dog stand in Portland, Oregon.

Simon Rumley is a genre-defying, critically-lauded film director who recently completed production in Bangkok on *Crushed,* his tenth feature film. Some of his other films include *Red White & Blue, The Living and The Dead, Fashionista,* and the *ABCs of Death* anthology. He has directed films in Europe, North America, South America, and Asia, and together they have won nearly fifty awards. These include best film or director at Sitges, Fantastic Fest, Fantasia, Frightfest, Fantaspoa, Lund, Boston Underground, and Ravenna. The films have premiered at Toronto, SXSW, and Rotterdam, and played at Sarajevo, Tallinn, Transilvania, Buenos Aires, Sydney, London, Rio, and Stockholm, amongst others. The films have played on Netflix, Amazon Prime, Sky TV, Channel Four, Sundance Channel, Shudder, etc. Rumley's debut novel *The Wobble Club* has recently been published and *Crushed* will premiere late 2025.

Nonie Shiverick has been consumed by creative pursuits since childhood, with a special appreciation for the horrific and fantastical. Yeah, she was a little weird kid. As an adult, she had a brief stint as a competitive ballroom dancer before winding up on a film set to play Ginger Rogers and realizing, for better or for worse, that her future was in movies. Finally accepting that her mother, who had for years told her that "the world needs more feminist writers," was right all along, she switched her focus to writing and directing films and has been grinding away ever since through her company One Eye Wilde. She is a two-time recipient of the Lizzie award at the Renegade Film Festival and has received various other screenwriting and filmmaking awards.

Nicholas Tecosky is a writer and director whose audio work includes the award-winning podcast *The Mantawauk Caves,* which won Best Fiction Podcast at the iHeartRadio Awards at SXSW in 2024, as well as *Tomorrow's Monsters, 13 Days of Halloween, and 12 Ghosts.* His new series *Havoc Town* is currently playing wherever you find your podcasts. Earlier in his career, Nick was one of the screenwriters of the cult horror anthology *V/H/S,* which premiered at the 2012 Sundance Film Festival. As a voice actor, he has narrated over two hundred audiobook titles, including *Death of Sweet Mister* by Daniel Woodrell, featured on the American Library Association's 2013 "Listen List."

April Wolfe is a screenwriter in Los Angeles. Her fiction has appeared in *A Public Space, The Collagist, Quarterly West,* and *Barrelhouse,* among other places. She's an A Public Space Emerging Writer Fellow and the recipient of the Iceland Writers Retreat Alumni Award for her short stories.

ABOUT THE CURATOR

DAVID LAWSON JR. developed a love for film at an early age while living in Baltimore, Maryland. After graduating high school, he enlisted in the U.S. Air Force. He served for over four years as an Airborne Radio Operator aboard the AWACS E-3 Sentry, deploying for both Operation Iraqi Freedom (Iraq) and Operation Enduring Freedom (Afghanistan). There he not only met many people with the same affinity for cinema, but also took to heart their core values: integrity first, service before self, and excellence in all you do. He has since brought those values to Los Angeles, where since 2005, he has been working his way up the commercial and feature film ranks. After years of working as an independent producer, David joined Snowfort Pictures from 2015 until 2017. Then, along with long-time collaborators Justin Benson and Aaron Moorhead, he formed Rustic Films. His features include *Synchronic*, *The Endless*, *She Dies Tomorrow*, *Afer Midnight*, *Something in the Dirt*, *Trash Fire*, *68 Kill*, *24x36: A Movie About Movie Posters*, *Spring*, and *Resolution*.

ABOUT THE COVER ARTIST

OLIVER (OLLY) JEAVONS is a UK-based artist also known as *artofolly*. He works with many different medias and styles, and he is always pushing his creativity further. Comic book art, book cover art, and commissions of all types are included in his portfolio.

PERMISSIONS

"Sunday Dinner" by April Wolfe, copyright © 2025 April Wolfe. Used by permission of the author.

"Eat the Rich" by C. Robert Cargill, copyright © 2025 C. Robert Cargill. Used by permission of the author.

"Our House in the Woods" by Gustavo Cooper & Ben Powell, copyright © 2025 Gustavo Copper & Ben Powell. Used by permission of the authors.

"Do You Believe in Ghosts?" by Mali Elfman, copyright © 2025 Mali Elfman. Used by permission of the author.

"Jinneh" by Babou Ceesay, copyright © 2025 Babou Ceesay. Used by permission of the author.

"Little Room, Red Button" by Nicholas Tecosky, adapted from a screenplay by David Bruckner & Nicholas Tecosky, copyright © 2025 Nicholas Tecosky. Used by permission of the authors.

"Cherry Lane" by Nonie Shiverick, copyright © 2025 Nonie Shiverick. Used by permission of the author.

"The Courier" by Peter Cilella, copyright © 2025 Peter Cilella. Used by permission of the author.

"The Method" by Alex Chew, copyright © 2025 Alex Chew. Used by permission of the author.

"Making *Private Hells*" by Andrew Adams, copyright © 2025 Andrew Adams. Used by permission of the author.

"Peel" by Maggie Levin, copyright © 2025 Maggie Levin. Used by permission of the author.

"The Marcias" by Addison Heimann, copyright © 2025 Addison Heimann. Used by permission of the authors.

"A Young Girl Finishes Her Dinner" by Avalon Fast, copyright © 2025 Avalon Fast. Used by permission of the author.

"All Hail the King" by Jesse Aultman, copyright © 2025 Jesse Aultman. Used by permission of the author.

"Hi, Strangeness." by Jackson Murray, copyright © 2025 Jackson Murray. Used by permission of the author.

"TOO CUTE!" by Jori Lynn Felker & Michael Felker, copyright © 2025 Jori Lynn Felker & Michael Felker. Used by permission of the authors.

"Sunny Side Up" by Harmony Colangelo, copyright © 2025 Harmony Colangelo. Used by permission of the author.

"The Man at the Merry-Go-Round" by Justin Brooks, copyright © 2025 Justin Brooks. Used by permission of the author.

"4x4" by Simon Rumley, copyright © 2025 Simon Rumley. Used by permission of the author.

"The Miraculous Resurrection of Herman James Godfrey" by Peter Collins Campbell, copyright © 2025 Peter Collins Campbell. Used by permission of the author.

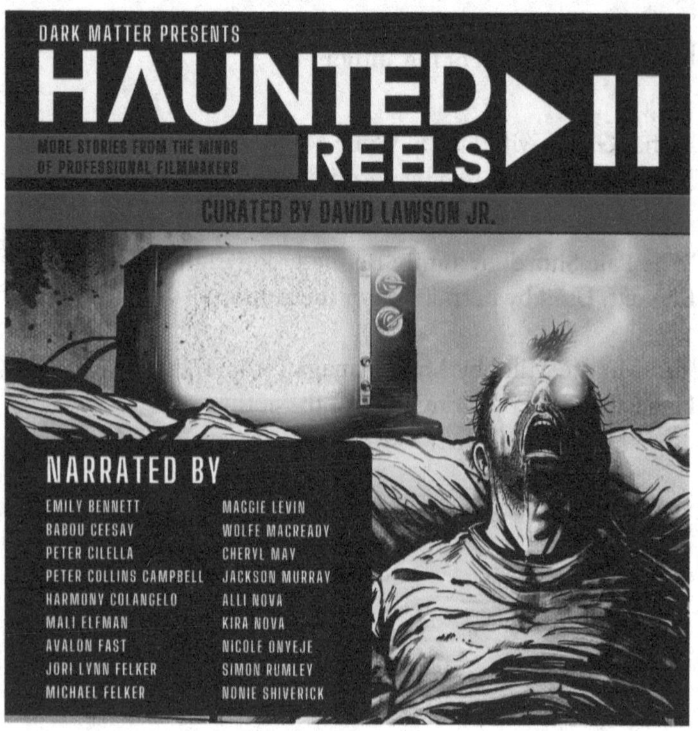

EXPERIENCE *HAUNTED REELS 2* IN AUDIO

Scan the QR code below to sample or purchase *Haunted Reels 2: More Stories from the Minds of Professional Filmmakers* in audiobook, narrated by Emily Bennett, Babou Ceesay, Peter Cilella, Peter Collins Campbell, Harmony Colangelo, Mali Elfman, Avalon Fast, Jori Lynn Felker, Michael Felker, Maggie Levin, Wolfe MacReady, Cheryl May, Jackson Murray, Alli Nova, Kira Nova, Nicole Onyeje, Simon Rumley, and Nonie Shiverick.